DEVIL WITHIN

DEVIL WITHIN

BY
CATHERINE GEORGE

MILLS & BOON LIMITED
Eton House, 18-24 Paradise Road
Richmond, Surrey TW9 1SR

First published in Great Britain in 1984
by Mills & Boon Limited

© Catherine George 1984

Australian copyright 1984
Philippine copyright 1984
Reprinted 1984
This edition 1992

ISBN 0 263 77775 8

Set in Monophoto Times 10 on 10 pt.
19-9206-63732

Made and printed in Great Britain

CHAPTER ONE

IT was a toss-up as to which one was in the worse condition, her car or her passenger. Claudia drove on doggedly through the rain, giving an occasional anxious glance at her friend Liz from time to time as the other girl shivered uncontrollably, her coat collar tightly clutched against her flushed face. Claudia was relieved when they finally left the crowded outskirts of rush-hour Coventry behind and were on the way to the quieter town of Kenilworth. While the little sports car was in fourth gear all was reasonably well, but Claudia had grave misgivings as she changed down at the approach to traffic lights outside the town. Grinding and shuddering, the car lurched to a halt, but at least consented to go on idling.

'It sounds worse than I feel,' said Liz hoarsely. She coughed dryly. 'I'm truly sorry about this, Claudia. This 'flu bug must have been a present from one of our dear little pupils.'

'Don't worry, it can't be helped.' Claudia smiled comfortingly, her eyes on the lights as they turned green. 'Say a prayer, Liz, this clutch needs all the encouragement it can get!'

There was a snort from Liz as Claudia eventually managed to get the car into gear with much jerking and bouncing and they were on their way again, though at hardly more than a crawl.

'I feel so rotten, spoiling our trip to the Lakes like this,' said Liz miserably. 'I suppose you won't go on your own?'

Claudia hooted.

'How? Even if you were fit we'd have no transport, love. It'll be a miracle if I get this car home, let alone up to Kendal!'

'You'd better take it to a garage in Kenilworth,' advised Liz. 'No point in chancing the extra few miles.'

Claudia shook her head.

'I'd rather my own little man had a look at it. He knows the car.' She peered through the steamed-up windscreen. 'I think the rain's eased a little. I hate to suggest it, Liz, but could you manage if I dropped you at the bottom of your road? If I try anything ambitious like a three-point turn I fancy the car might die.'

'Yes, of course. Give me a ring when you get home— *if* you get home!'

'Thanks for the vote of confidence!' Claudia brought the car carefully to a halt and said goodbye to Liz with strict instructions on aspirin, hot drinks and immediate bed as she eased the car on its way again.

From then on the journey was nerve-racking. The car shuddered and ground its way along until five miles and almost an hour later Claudia finally reached the garage where she normally took the car for servicing, lucky to find her usual mechanic before he left. Obligingly he pushed the car into the workshop and gave it a cursory examination, then shook his head apologetically as he wiped his hands on an oily rag.

'Sorry, Miss March. I'll need to strip it down, of course, but it looks to me like a clutch job, and late on a Friday like this—well, it's just not on.'

Claudia shrugged philosophically.

'When could you have it ready?'

'Not before Tuesday evening, I'm afraid.'

She nodded, and stooped to remove her umbrella and bulging briefcase from the car.

'Can't be helped. I'll give you a ring on Tuesday afternoon to make sure. Goodnight.'

The man watched with pleasure as the tall, slim figure in the belted trenchcoat weaved its way through the echoing cavern of the garage workshop, her tawny hair streaming in a sudden gust of wind as she paused in the doorway to put up the umbrella before plunging out into the miserable evening.

The chill, driving rain of late October met Claudia in full force, and she hunched her shoulders against it as she walked quickly across the Market Square past the small museum, the ground treacherous with the slick wet pulp of fallen leaves. The clock in the square tower of St. Margaret's Church struck the half hour as Claudia hurried through the small town, battling her way down the narrow street of small shops, all closed now except for the pizza parlour and the King's Head at the bottom as she turned the corner to reach the relative shelter of the neatly-tended gardens of the block of flats where she lived. It fronted on to the busy main road, but Claudia had been lucky enough to get one of the smaller apartments on the top floor at the back, its view of the town's rambling green park amply compensating for a decided lack of space. Keeping to her habit of ignoring the lift, she mounted the four flights of stairs quickly with the ease of long practice, letting herself into her small domain with a sigh of relief.

While the kettle boiled Claudia rang Liz as instructed, then hung her raincoat on a hanger in the claustrophobic little bathroom, towelling her hair while she looked at her post, the expected electricity bill accompanied by a thick white envelope addressed to her in a familiar hand. Claudia tore it open to find a wedding invitation from Richard Freer. She sat down, staring at it. She and Richard had met when she was a freshman at Cambridge, and from the very first all their free time had been spent together, the bond between them strong and unshakeable, more like a friendship between two members of the same sex than an affair of the heart. After graduation their jobs had taken them to different parts of the country, and gradually the ties between them had loosened over the years, nevertheless it gave Claudia a sharp pang to read the copperplate evidence of Richard's marriage to someone else. Scrawled across the back was a message. 'Thought you'd like to be the first to know'. Did he indeed!

Claudia tossed the card on her battered second-hand desk and made her coffee, flopping in front of the television news to drink it, the usual dose of depression hard to take after a day designed to test anyone's strength of character. On the last day before half term her lively Upper Fourths had been more concerned with a week's freedom than any nuances in the boring old relationship between Antonio and Bassanio in *The Merchant of Venice*. More like hooligans than the privileged young ladies who attended Highdean School for Girls, they had been exuberantly impossible, and only rigid self-control had kept Claudia from screaming at them like a fishwife. After a trying day it had been a blow to find that Liz Arnold, who taught Latin at the same establishment, was obviously feeling rotten with the first stages of 'flu, which meant goodbye to their planned half-term holiday touring the Lake District together.

Dispiritedly Claudia went into the cupboard-like kitchen and began to cook bacon and egg, her culinary enthusiasm at low ebb. The car had been the final straw. Crawling back from Coventry in the rush hour with a rapidly expiring clutch had been no joke, and the garage mechanic had only confirmed her own diagnosis. Liz had an irritating tendency to preach about the little car, which was admittedly elderly, but Claudia's priorities had been firmly apportioned when she was first appointed as Junior English Mistress at Highdean after graduating. She wanted her own home. Any economies would have to be made in other directions, mainly transport. For years she had travelled by bus, but a short time ago had bought her dashing little green car, which had proved only as unreliable as its age would lead one to expect. Without it the week of the half-term holiday yawned in front of her as arid and empty as the Sahara—but a lot colder and a lot wetter by the sound of the rain beating against the window.

After her meal Claudia felt better, and settled down to read the daily paper while she drank more coffee. As she turned the pages idly a small boxed advertisement in the Situations Vacant section took her eye.

GOVERNESS REQUIRED for girl of five in British family home, Minas Gerais, Brazil. Mature, highly qualified applicants only. Athletic accomplishments an advantage.

Claudia's interest was caught, her imagination instantly fired by thoughts of hot yellow sunshine

pouring down on a lush, verdant landscape from a
burning blue sky, in vivid contrast with the wet greyness
outside. She searched her memory for facts from
schooldays' geography, dredging up something to the
effect that Minas Gerais was a Brazilian state where
gold, iron ore, precious and semi-precious stones were
found in abundance. It had a wild and romantic sound.
She bit the tip of one finger, gazing absently at the quiz
game on the television screen, wondering just how
mature was mature in this particular instance. She was
twenty-seven, hardly young and foolish, her qualifications were impeccable, slightly overpowering for
teaching five-year-olds perhaps, but for the rest she
played tennis, squash, swam and did twenty minutes'
exercise every day.

Impulses were a luxury Claudia never normally
allowed herself, but suddenly she felt reckless and
sprang to her feet, dialling the London telephone
number given in the advertisement. She found it
belonged to the Park Lane Hotel in Piccadilly, and after
referring to the advertisement she was put through to a
pleasant, feminine voice which said 'Good evening'
briefly.

'I saw your advertisement for a governess,' began
Claudia.

'I'm sorry, but I already have a full quota of
applicants. The advertisement has been in for several
days.'

'Oh, I see. I've only just seen it.' Claudia's
disappointment was keen, to her surprise.

'However, since you've troubled to ring,' went on the
voice, 'you may as well give me a brief outline of your
qualifications.'

'Nine A-grade O-levels, three A-grade A-levels, and a
first from Trinity, Cambridge. I teach English.'

There was a distinct pause.

'With those credentials you certainly merit an
interview, but the only time I have free is at two
tomorrow afternoon. Could you come here to the hotel
to see me at that time?'

Claudia's long grey eyes widened.

'Why, yes. Yes, I can.'

'May I have your name?'

'Claudia March.'

'Let them know at reception when you arrive, Miss March. My name is Treharne—Miss Beatrice Treharne. Goodbye.'

Claudia sat down on the corner of her desk, staring at the telephone in surprise. She had never really believed for a moment that her phone call would result in anything as concrete as an interview, and her spirits rose considerably as she thought of the next day. Miss Treharne had sounded pleasant, and if nothing else, the trip to London would at least enliven the weekend a little.

Claudia was up early next morning, giving herself plenty of time to achieve an efficient, well-groomed appearance. She decided on a plain white shirt to go with the grey flannel suit kept for parent's evenings and speech days, and coiled her waving, shoulder-length hair firmly on top of her head. Make-up was left to a minimum. She never used much on her clear pale skin, but liked a touch of charcoal shadow to emphasise the pure, clear grey of her heavily-lashed eyes, added a hint of colour to her high cheekbones and her full, generous mouth and felt ready to face Miss Treharne with confidence.

The weather was worse, if anything, than the day before, and Claudia put on her trenchcoat over the suit and added the checked wool scarf that matched her umbrella. In the cold, clear light of day she felt almost embarrassed at doing something so uncharacteristic as chasing off to an impulsive interview for a post she had no intention of taking even if it were offered to her. Liz would have a fit at the mere thought of Claudia taking off for some isolated mountain fastness in a country she knew little about except its coffee, carnival and fantastic football. The train journey to Paddington went by at unusual speed as she stared unseeingly at the sodden passing landscape, slightly aghast at her own temerity in even contemplating giving up a steady, remunerative job for such a pie-in-the-sky alternative. She knew very well that if she and Liz had been off to the Lakes as planned, or if the car had behaved itself and there had been no unsettling invitation from Richard—or even if the weather had been less atrocious, she might never have noticed the advertisement. Nevertheless she had, so she might as well enjoy her trip to London and treat the interview as just an item on a programme of things to do on her day out.

Once in London Claudia made her way to Bond Street by tube, emerging to indulge in an orgy of window-gazing for an hour, then eating a quick snack at a sandwich bar before wending her way through the crowds to Piccadilly and her appointment. Icy rain was sheeting down once more, in gusting showers that spattered like hail on her umbrella before she reached the warm haven of the hotel lobby.

Claudia gave her name at reception and was given the number of Miss Treharne's room. She took off her raincoat in the lift and had a quick look in the small mirror in her handbag, combing back a few errant strands of hair smoothly. Outside the appropriate door she took a deep breath and knocked, opening it as she heard a voice ask her to go in.

She found herself in a small sitting room. A slim, erect woman with elegantly dressed grey hair rose from a brocade sofa at her approach, her dark eyes examining Claudia with frank interest. The woman smiled warmly, the eyes kind above the frankly Roman nose, and immediately Claudia felt at ease.

'Miss March? How do you do. I'm Beatrice Treharne.'

'How do you do, Miss Treharne.' Claudia's eyes lit with an answering smile as she sat in the easy chair the other woman indicated, settling herself comfortably while Miss Treharne resumed her place on the sofa, notebook in hand.

'I'll just get the necessary details down, full name, age, address, etc.,' said Miss Treharne briskly. 'Then we'll have a little talk.'

Claudia duly supplied the information, covertly studying the other woman while she made notes. Her age was difficult to guess, late fifties possibly, her figure trim in the expensively simple cashmere suit in mist-blue, real pearls in her ears and at her throat. She removed a pair of gold-framed spectacles and smiled at Claudia, her manner casual and friendly.

'Now, Miss March, have you any experience in this type of work?'

'Not with this age-group. I teach English to the junior and middle-school girls at Highdean, an independent girls' school near Coventry. But I do have some experience in dealing with five-year-olds, even though I've never actually taught children of that age.'

'I see.' Miss Treharne was thoughtful. 'Your qualifications are impressive, even top-heavy for the task, though, of course, there is the possibility that you could be required to prepare my great-niece right up to Common Entrance, should you stay the course—and should her father's work keep him abroad that length of time.'

'I understand.' Eight years, thought Claudia. A long, long time.

'Where did you come by your experience of small children?'

'I was brought up almost from birth in a children's home. As I grew older I lent a hand with the younger ones.'

Miss Treharne frowned slightly and consulted her notes.

'Where did you go to school, Miss March?'

'From five to eighteen I went to one of the Girls' Public Day School Trust, from which I won an Exhibition to Trinity Cambridge. My present post has been my only job since then.'

Miss Treharne hesitated delicately.

'You had an expensive education, Miss March, for a child from an orphanage.'

Claudia looked at the other woman candidly.

'I was lucky, Miss Treharne. One of the governors of the orphanage was a very rich old gentleman willing to pay the necessary fees for a student likely to prove worthy of his support.'

'And you won his sponsorship.' Miss Treharne smiled, a twinkle in her dark eyes.

'By means of slogging,' said Claudia ruefully. 'I rarely had time for anything else—I worked myself into the ground all the way through school, then even harder at Cambridge, where I survived with the aid of a very sparing diet, Oxfam as my couturier and working as a waitress through the holidays.'

'Why a waitress?'

'Free food!' Claudia's eyes danced involuntarily.

Miss Treharne chuckled.

'Of course. Slow of me. Now, Miss March, tell me something of your interests and spare-time activities.'

Miss Treharne was obviously genuinely interested, and Claudia found it easy to talk about the rather quiet life she had led, and her enjoyment of tennis, squash, swimming, walking, reading, the cinema and, very occasionally, the rare treat of a visit to the theatre or dining out.

After scribbling a few more notes Beatrice Treharne settled herself more comfortably against the soft cushions.

'You've told me about yourself, my dear, so I'm sure you'd like to have some idea of the kind of post offered. My nephew, Saul Treharne, is employed as Engineering Superintendent of a privately-owned goldmine in a town by the name of Campo d'Ouro in the state of Minas Gerais, Brazil. His little daughter, Rebecca, has only lived there with him for the past few months. Since her mother was killed, in fact.' She paused, as if choosing her words with care. 'I feel bound to furnish some information that may strike you as personal, but is nevertheless necessary to illustrate some of the problems involved.'

Claudia's interest quickened, and she inclined her head in polite agreement.

'Saul and Elaine—Rebecca's mother—were divorced when the child was very small and Elaine proved very awkward about 'reasonable access' to the child by her father. Consequently Saul is virtually a stranger to his daughter, which has not made Becky's adaptation to her new way of life very easy.' Miss Treharne's aquiline

features wore a troubled expression. 'There are excellent
schools in Brazil, of course, but as Becky flatly refuses
to admit any knowledge of Portuguese, or to try to
learn, Saul has no alternative but to employ a British
governess. I myself had no hesitation in making my
home in Campo d'Ouro with Saul when Elaine died, as
I'd spent many holidays there and always loved the
place. Not only that, I knew the child would need some
feminine influence in her life, though unfortunately I'm
not qualified to teach her.'

'I see.' Claudia was intrigued, and listened intently as
the other woman went on.

'I must stress that whoever is selected for the post
must be very sure of what the life entails. Campo
d'Ouro is sixty miles from Boa Vista, the nearest town,
and often in the wet season the only road becomes
impassable. There is no cinema or theatre, and little in
the way of entertainment, few young people with whom
to associate. There's a club where you could play your
tennis and squash, and if you play bridge you will be
welcomed with open arms, but beyond that very little in
the way of diversion.' With a sudden change of subject
she asked, 'Are you fond of children, Miss March?'

Claudia was on firm ground here.

'Yes,' she said with conviction. 'Otherwise I would
never have chosen to teach. I feel strongly that teaching
should be a vocation fully as much as a job, after all I
spend far more time in the company of the young than
with adults.'

Miss Treharne nodded in approval, then looked at
Claudia in speculation.

'At the risk of being personal, my dear, may I ask if
you have any ties in this country?'

'If you mean emotional ones, no,' said Claudia
serenely. 'I have women friends, of course.'

'Surely an attractive young woman like you must
have some interest in the opposite sex!'

Claudia smiled, shrugging.

'Well, yes, naturally. I knew a lot of men in college,
and had a fairly close relationship with one of them. At
the moment my acquaintance is restricted to two

schoolmasters, both of them from Coventry. I go out to a meal or to the theatre with one or the other of them occasionally, but the conversation inevitably turns to education rather than anything more romantic.'

'Extraordinary!' Miss Treharne shook her head, then sat just looking at Claudia for a minute or two, studying the overtly intelligent attraction of the girl's clear-cut face as though memorising it, before nodding with a smile, as if satisfied with her conclusions.

'Thank you, my dear. Should you be offered the post would your headmistress accept a half-term's notice?'

Claudia's eyes narrowed.

'I couldn't say,' she said guardedly. 'A full term is the usual period.'

'I would need the lady's name and telephone number for reference purposes, of course,' went on Miss Treharne. Claudia supplied them, her mind working overtime as the other woman continued. 'I will be open with you, Miss March. You are a great deal younger than the age my nephew had in mind, not perhaps as— well, motherly as he would have wished. However, I shall now ring him in Campo d'Ouro and give him an account of all the candidates I've interviewed and leave the choice to him. I shall let you know whether or not you were successful as soon as I can. My time is very limited as I leave for Brazil in two days and must utilise Monday for Christmas shopping—an exhausting prospect!' She rose to her feet, holding out her hand, a pleasant smile on her handsome face. 'Goodbye, my dear, it's been a pleasure to meet you. Thank you for coming at such short notice.'

Claudia went down in the lift with her mind buzzing. It was too early to think of catching the train home, so she decided to treat herself to a cream tea in the Art-Deco opulence of the hotel's Palm Court Lounge. After her brief, but highly interesting time with Miss Treharne she needed breathing space to think before the return journey home. Home. That was the real key-word, of course. Her mind not really on her elegant surroundings, Claudia enjoyed a cream-laden mille-feuille pastry and drank three cups of Earl Grey, her

mind very much preoccupied with the interview. It had
been the word 'home' in the advertisement that acted
like a spur to her impulse in answering it. There had
also been the romantic, Jane Eyre connotations of the
term 'governess', of course. But, discounting the
glamorous temptation of Brazil, or possibly the idea of
it given by all those old Hollywood musicals, what
really drew Claudia like a magnet was the thought of
being part of a family, actually living in a private home.

To date all Claudia's life had been spent in institutions
or lodgings, and apart from odd nights spent at Liz's
house she had never actually lived as part of a household.
Her own small flat was a home of sorts, of course, but a
quiet, solitary place—a retreat. A contrast from the
orphanage, to be sure, but a bit lonely at times.

Once on the train Claudia sat in a window seat,
oblivious to her surroundings as the train rattled on
through the darkness, wondering how she would
respond if, by some quirk of fate, the unknown Mr
Treharne should pick her name from the hat. The salary
offered was adequate, particularly as no living expenses
would come out of it, and Claudia did endless sums in
her head, weighing the pros and cons of taking on the
job. Her answer to the advertisement had been almost a
joke, a reaction to an unpleasant day, but somehow at
this stage the whole idea had begun to assume very real
possibilities. No reference had been made to any social
standing, but surely the days were gone when a
governess occupied a nebulous position in a household,
neither family nor servant, but relegated to some
indeterminate niche somewhere between the two.
Claudia smiled at a sudden vision of lonely meals on
trays in some large foreign house where she was neither
fish, flesh, fowl, nor good herring. Miss Treharne had
seemed much too warm and kind a person to condemn
anyone to that type of existence.

But what of Mr Rochester himself—Saul Treharne,
the unknown quantity? At least it had been made clear
from the outset that there was no prospect of a mad
wife in the attic, but Claudia was frankly curious as to
what kind of man he was—the kind of man his wife felt

necessary to leave, presumably, which weighed rather heavily against him. On the other hand, the fact that he was prepared to go to the expense of a governess for his child awarded him high marks in Claudia's book. She speculated idly on whether he was young, middle-aged, tall, short, charming, brusque, the list of possibilities grew so absorbing Claudia almost missed getting off the train at Leamington Spa.

Once back in her warm little flat, however, some of the appeal of the job began to fade as she cooked herself a simple meal and ate it in comfort in front of a film on television. Afterwards she curled up with a new paperback novel bought at the station bookstall earlier, pleasantly tired after her hectic day, her mind wandering from the book, more inclined to linger on the events of the afternoon.

Gradually it was borne in on her that, adventurous and tempting though the job sounded, if she *were* offered it she would have to refuse. Sighing regretfully, Claudia faced facts. As things were at the moment she had a good job, security, a pleasant little retreat she could call her own—well, almost—friends of both sexes, a secure life many women, and perhaps even a few men, might envy. There was very little chance she'd get the job anyway, but if she did it could result in disaster. She might not fit into the Treharne household, Mr Treharne might take an instant dislike to her, and vice versa, and the child might prove utterly impossible to teach. And then Claudia March might find herself back in the U.K. post-haste without a job or a home, and with no relatives to turn to.

Claudia roused herself eventually and jumped up to wash her dinner things. No point in counting chickens before they were hatched. It was hardly likely that Miss Treharne had recommended her, for a start; after all, she *had* made rather a point of saying Claudia's age was against her. And there was no guarantee that Mr Treharne would have agreed even if she had. Sensible Claudia put the matter out of her mind and went to bed early with her book, falling asleep before getting past the first chapter.

Sunday was the one morning of the week when Claudia allowed herself a lie in, and it was almost ten next day when the telephone woke her. She stumbled out of bed yawning, wrapped her dressing gown round her and went into the other room to pick up the receiver.

'Hello,' she said sleepily, then came to life as she recognised her caller.

'Miss March? Good morning, Beatrice Treharne here. I hope I didn't wake you.'

'No, of course not,' said Claudia, fingers crossed. 'Good morning.'

'Forgive my early call, but I felt I should contact you as soon as possible.'

With a sinking feeling in her stomach Claudia kept silent, knowing in her bones what Miss Treharne was about to say.

'I spoke with Saul, my nephew, last night and discussed the applicants in general, and although I must be honest and admit he had reservations about your youth, he has agreed to offer you the post on my recommendation.'

Claudia perched on the edge of the desk, feeling wretched.

'Why, that's—that's very kind of you,' she said slowly at last. 'I never thought for a moment I'd be suitable, Miss Treharne. I thought it over very carefully last night on the offchance, but came to the conclusion that I don't feel it's possible for me to accept your offer.'

There was a pause.

'I see,' said Miss Treharne thoughtfully. Claudia could have sworn she sounded disappointed. 'Do I gather you don't care for the idea of the job itself, or is there some other reason?'

'It's not the job,' said Claudia quickly. 'The idea of teaching one child from scratch is attractive, a challenge, and the opportunity to visit Brazil a great temptation.'

'Then what is the stumbling block, my dear?'

'To reduce it to the basic—security, Miss Treharne.'

Claudia rubbed her eyes wearily. 'I own a flat on which I pay a mortgage so that I have a home to call my own. It cuts mercilessly into my salary, but I have a secure job, and my life-style, if not exactly exhilarating, is pleasant, and the money I earn is sufficient to save a little for my future—or to put it another way, my old age.'

'Miss March, that's a very staid outlook for a girl like you!' Miss Treharne sounded shocked.

'I don't have much alternative—I have only myself to depend on. If I come out to you in Brazil things might not work out well, and after a year, or even less, I might find myself back in this country out of a job, and with nowhere to live.'

'I appreciate your point of view, my dear, but there must be some way of getting round this particular obstacle.' There was a pause, then Miss Treharne went on matter-of-factly, 'Don't dismiss the whole idea out of hand, Miss March. Give me a little time to ponder, then I'll ring you back, so keep an open mind in the meantime. Is that convenient?'

'Yes, of course. Goodbye.' Claudia put the phone down, sighing, and went off to have a bath, wondering what Miss Treharne would come up with when she rang back. Perhaps she intended to consult her nephew again in the meantime to ask for advice. Claudia remained convinced that her only course of action was to opt for the status quo, with its assurance of safety and security.

The telephone rang an hour later and Miss Treharne got down to business straight away.

'I wish you were nearer, Miss March, then we could discuss this in a civilised way over a meal, but as my time is so short we shall have to make do with this disembodied form of exchange.'

Claudia sat down at her desk, listening with attention as the other woman went on.

'I've given the matter careful thought over the past hour or so, Miss March, and I shall lay my cards on the table. Being single myself I'm in a better position to appreciate your views on security than a man could, especially a man like my nephew, who is singularly self-sufficient in all ways; too much so.'

Claudia was interested.

'Please go on, Miss Treharne.'

'Unlike you I do possess relations, some of whom in fact are the Fonsecas, the owners of the goldmine in Campo d'Ouro, but above all I have Saul, who is more a son to me than a nephew since his parents died. Nevertheless I can readily appreciate how very different life would be if I were alone in the world. In short, Miss March, if you will take the job I am prepared to pay you a lump sum out of my own pocket, over and above the salary Saul is offering.'

Claudia's eyes opened as Miss Treharne named the sum.

'Oh, but I couldn't. . . .' she began.

'I haven't finished yet. You would have to undertake to stay with Becky for a minimum of two years. You could sublet your flat, then you could return when the time was up if you wished, and your home would be still there. In addition you would have the security of a nest egg to live on while job-hunting.'

Claudia was glad she was sitting down. She tried wildly to think of something to say.

'I'm at a loss, Miss Treharne,' she said eventually. 'Your offer is very generous. But why are you making it? There must have been several other candidates equally suitable for the job.'

'There were indeed. Highly eligible, sensible, middle-aged ladies all of them. I'll be honest and admit that I just liked you more than any of the others. Remember, this isn't just a job. You would be living in our house as part of the family, and I, in particular, would be in your company more than anyone else. I feel you and I would get on well together, despite the age difference, and even on such short acquaintance. Do you agree?'

'On that count I do, sincerely, but——'

'Don't say any more, my dear. Turn it over in your mind and let me know some time later today. Before seven if you can.'

Promising to be in touch as soon as possible, Claudia put the phone down and decided some food would help her brain to function clearly. She grilled a steak for her Sunday lunch, then afterwards she pulled on her old sheepskin jacket and went out to do her thinking in the park. The rain held off, but there were few people about as Claudia walked at a brisk rate through green parkland and clusters of trees, leafless already after the hail and strong winds of the previous week. The wind was still high, and Claudia turned up her fur-lined collar against its cold attack, thrusting her hands deep in her pockets as she moved swiftly with her usual long-striding pace, her mind occupied with how she should answer Miss Treharne.

There was no point in consulting Liz, even if her friend was well enough, as Claudia knew in advance how she would react. Liz would make no bones about thinking the whole idea idiotic and out of the question, so there would be no help from that quarter. Claudia looked up sharply as the first heavy drops began to fall from the leaden clouds now darkening the sky, annoyed to find herself at the farthest point possible from home. She broke into a run as the drops merged in a driving, drenching downpour, and arrived back sodden and shivering as she let herself into the little flat, gasping and depressed suddenly by its solitude. Dozens of other people lived in the building, yet Claudia felt at that moment she was the only person in the world as she stood at the window, her dripping hair forgotten as she stared down a long, mental vista of speech days and sports days, parents' evenings and school bazaars. Was the life of Miss Jean Brodie really the life Claudia March wanted for herself?

Her mind made up, she switched on all the lights and picked up the phone, dialling the number of the Park Lane Hotel.

'Miss Treharne?' she said, after she was put through. 'Claudia March here. I've come to my decision.'

CHAPTER TWO

LESS than two months later Claudia was finally airborne in a Varig jet bound for Rio de Janeiro. 'Flying down to Rio', she thought with a little smile as the plane soared above the lights of London. She was glad it was dark. This way it was impossible to see England's green and pleasant land recede from view to reinforce any last-minute pangs of uncertainty. Not that she had many. Her bridges had been left intact, not burned, behind her. One of Liz's many cousins had taken over Claudia's flat for the time being while he did a post-graduate course at Warwick University, so if life in Campo d'Ouro proved too hard to take after two years, all she need do would be to cut her losses and retreat in good order. She relaxed as the plane reached its cruising speed and the seatbelt warning light flashed off. Soon she was able to enjoy the meal served en route to the refuelling stop at Lisbon, the elderly lady in the next seat being more inclined to sleep than talk afterwards, to Claudia's relief.

The past few weeks had flown by at unbelievable speed. Miss Todhunter, the Principal of Highdean, had been very kind and understanding about accepting a mere half-term's notice, and otherwise the only problem had been the fairly frivolous one of finding warm-weather clothes in mid-winter Britain. The search for these had been in the company of Liz, who was openly upset at Claudia's departure, and full of gloomy prognostications on the madness of accepting the new job. Even so she had been an enormous help, and it was sad and difficult to leave everything loved and familiar just before Christmas, though Claudia consoled herself with the thought that it would probably be easier to make friends with her new charge over the festive season than during a less exciting time of the year. Mr Treharne had given her carte blanche with regard to

Rebecca's education, and anything she needed in the way of books and educational aids, all of which had already been shipped to Campo d'Ouro. Any time left over Claudia had occupied with a crash course in Portuguese, which she hoped would help start her off on the right foot.

She slept fitfully during the flight, and was awake well before the plane was due to land in Rio. She ate a little of the continental-style breakfast served to her, the butterflies in her stomach preventing any real enjoyment of the meal, then freshened herself up, ready to greet the day. The Rio agent of the Fonseca goldmine would be meeting her at the airport, according to the terse, formal missive most recently received from her new employer, and in reply Claudia had given a brief description of the almond green dress and jacket she intended to wear for travelling so that Senhor Helio Braga would be able to identify her without trouble. As the plane began to lose height Claudia gazed from the window in tense fascination as the beautiful, island-studded Bay of Guanabara came into view in the first gilding rays of the rising sun. As they flew lower the glittering light illumined the summit of Corcovado, the mountain peak where the great white statue of Christ the Redemptor stood, its great arms outstretched in eternal blessing over the city of Rio de Janeiro.

When she was finally in possession of her luggage and had emerged unscathed from her encounter with Customs, she was approached by a portly, middle-aged gentleman with olive skin and greying dark hair, his white suit and shining black shoes immaculate. He bowed and introduced himself as Helio Braga, his English strongly accented and formal. Claudia was deeply thankful to see him, glad to dispense with her jacket now that Senhor Braga had identified her, and within minutes the polite, efficient Brazilian took charge of Claudia's cases and carried them to his waiting car while she brought up the rear with her hand-luggage. He explained regretfully that his instructions were to escort the Senhora to Santos Dumont, the internal airport, where almost immediately she would

board another plane for the hour-long flight to Boa
Vista in Minas Gerais.

They reached Santos Dumont with only minutes to
spare, and before Claudia had time to do more than
express hurried, sincere thanks to him, Senhor Braga
had bidden her farewell, and she was airborne once
again, this time in a much smaller plane which took off
above the same beautiful bay but headed inland above
the mountains behind the city. The flight, over endless
vistas of mountain peaks, was brief, but bumpy, and
Claudia began to regret the sketchiness of her breakfast,
her stomach distinctly queasy long before the plane
landed in Boa Vista. The airport was picturesque, small
compared with those in Rio, the small terminal building
reminiscent of a conservatory, with its expanse of glass
and banks of potted plants and greenery everywhere, all
of them exotic and unfamiliar. By this time Claudia had
begun to feel that travelling was a way of life, and
wondered wearily how long it would take to reach
Campo d'Ouro. As she followed the test of the voluble
passengers into the airport terminal she felt an odd
tightening of her stomach muscles, an abrupt realisation
that she was on alien soil, among strangers in a foreign
land. The feeling intensified as no one appeared to take
charge of her. Wondering whether to go off in search of
her luggage, or to stay put for the time being in the
hope that someone would turn up to collect her,
Claudia opted for the latter and chose a central
arrangement of flowering plants where she had a fairly
good view of the small terminal in general. She stood,
outwardly composed, watching the passing crowd, her
interest genuine enough, but scarcely strong enough to
dispel the curl of disquiet deep inside her. If I knew the
Portuguese for 'lost property', she thought dryly, I
could deposit myself there until someone remembers
I'm supposed to arrive today!

Claudia's composure was beginning to wear thin.
Inwardly she battled with a feeling of misgiving, not
daring to admit to herself for an instant how lost and
alone she was beginning to feel, concentrating instead

on making bets with herself as to which of the men within sight was Saul Treharne. Her concentration was so effective she almost jumped out of her skin when a voice, male and British, spoke almost in her ear. She turned sharply, her eyes, accustomed to meeting most people at their own level, obliged to travel upwards, a considerable way upwards, to meet expressionless dark blue eyes in an even darker face that might have been described as handsome, but was marred by a broken nose and the rigid compression of the mouth above a cleft chin, too masculine to merit the word dimple. Devil within, no doubt, thought Claudia, her spirits sinking a little as she ventured a polite smile in response to the man's query of 'Miss March?'

'I'm Claudia March,' she said, dampened a little as she received no smile in response to her own.

'Treharne,' said the man, and stooped to pick up her grip. 'Saul Treharne.'

Mr Rochester in person. Claudia held out her hand, inclining her head.

'How do you do, Mr Treharne.'

Saul Treharne touched her outstretched hand with the hard, calloused palm of his own for the briefest of contacts, then gestured to the far side of the terminal.

'I'm pressed for time, Miss March,' he said shortly, 'so let's collect your luggage and get back to the jeep— unless you feel like a very swift cup of coffee before we start?'

Claudia was well aware he expected her to refuse, but some wayward urge of defiance prompted the saccharine-sweet smile she turned on him.

'How thoughtful! Thank you, that would be lovely. I drank only tea and fruit juice on the flight, so this will be my very first experience of Brazilian coffee.'

Without a word he turned and headed for the snack-bar, leaving her to hurry in his wake, the two tiny cups of coffee already steaming on the bar by the time she caught up. The *cafezinho* he pushed towards her was a demitasse of liquid intended to be drunk in true Brazilian style, very hot, very strong and, in Claudia's case, very sweet, though she noted that her taciturn

companion took his undoctored. It took less than a
minute to dispose of the drinks before Saul Treharne
hustled her on her way again to collect the three large
suitcases brought with her. Despite Claudia's protests he
took charge of all four pieces of luggage as he ushered her
from the air-conditioned terminal into the heat outside,
his long strides testing even her unusually long legs as he
forced her to hurry to keep up as they approached the
vehicle Saul had referred to as 'the jeep'. To Claudia's
relief it was far removed from her idea of an army jeep,
more like a British Range Rover, standing high up off the
ground and necessitating a greater show of leg than she
would have preferred as Saul heaved her up into the
passenger seat with scant ceremony.

While he was stowing her luggage in the back
Claudia took firm control of the hot resentment that
was threatening to gain the upper hand, compressing
her own lips together every bit as tightly as those of this
oversized, bad-tempered man who was making no effort
to conceal his disapproval of his aunt's choice of
governess. He could at least have expressed some sort
of welcome, however lukewarm, asked her about the
flight, or even her opinion of her first taste of Brazilian
coffee. She kept her eyes straight ahead as Saul
Treharne leapt up into the driving seat and started the
jeep, reversing in a wide sweep before driving out on to
a highway that, to her disappointment, led away from
the town of Boa Vista that was just discernible in the
heat-hazed distance as a frieze of tall buildings, chalk-
white against the cobalt blue of the sky.

'We don't pass through the town?' she asked,
disappointed.

'No. This road is called the BR3, which would
eventually take you back to Rio, but don't be misled.
We branch off it a few kilometres away.' Something in
his tone made her glance at him sharply, but his face
was blank, concentrated on the road ahead.

Claudia sat in rapt silence as the road wound
smoothly between undulating hills, pierced at intervals
by sharper, more jagged mountain peaks. The vegetation
was green but sparse, broken sporadically by clusters of

palms and shrubs, the earth a rich rust red with a scent entirely its own, nutty and distinctive as it pervaded the jeep's interior. To her surprise Saul told her to wind up her window, doing the same with his own.

'Is it really necessary?' she asked. 'I enjoy driving with an open window.'

'You won't in a minute.' He gave her a brief, sidelong look. 'Just along here we turn off the BR3 and take the road to Campo d'Ouro.'

Claudia soon realised the difference, obliged to hang on to the door handle as the jeep swerved off on a road very different from the highway. The metalling was non-existent in places, the road deteriorating at times to little more than a track, winding through mountainous terrain which abruptly became wilder, harsher, the road swooping in serpentine curves, occasionally doubling back on itself, at other times running straight along a mountain ridge, with vertiginous views on either side into rock-filled ravines far below. Fine red dust seeped into the jeep, infiltrating the finely-knitted fabric of Claudia's dress and coating her face with a fine red film. Her stomach heaved as Saul drove at what seemed like manic pace along the tortuous road, but she ignored it, breathing deeply, determined to hide any physical weakness from this cold, indifferent man.

The lack of cordiality in the atmosphere began to play on Claudia's nerves at last, and she decided it was time to put things on a slightly more normal footing, at least make some reference to the main reason for her very presence in Brazil.

'How does Rebecca feel about my advent, Mr Treharne?' As she looked up at his irregular profile he frowned, taking out a cheroot and lighting it with one hand dexterously.

'I don't think she quite understands why you're coming,' he said distantly. 'I've tried to explain the function of a governess, but either she refuses to understand, or she genuinely has no idea about lessons.'

Claudia bit her lip, the scent of the cheroot escalating her feeling of nausea alarmingly.

'In fact, she loathes the whole idea,' she said wryly. 'I hope I can alter her outlook.'

'My aunt obviously has great faith in your ability to do so.' Again the assessing sidelong look. 'Otherwise, Miss March, we would never have invested so heavily in engaging you.' He turned away to negotiate a particularly blind bend and set the jeep at a sharply rising incline on the other side.

There was an odd edge to his words that intensified another lurch of her stomach as it protested against the last manoeuvre. Claudia could feel sweat breaking out in the palms of her hands and dampening the line of her hair where it was brushed back from her face. To her relief Saul wound down a window and threw out the offending cheroot, closing the window again quickly against the insidious dust as they hurtled down a steep, rutted incline, only to climb up immediately to one of those straight sections of road that seemed to stretch between the peaks like a tightrope. Claudia closed her eyes tightly against the dizzying drop to the ravine-bed far below, wondering how much longer this interminable journey was likely to go on, unaware that Saul was frowning at her pale face.

'Would it, in your opinion, impair your authority if we were all to be on first-name terms?' he said surprisingly. 'Rebecca included, I mean. It might be better if she never thought of you as "Miss March", but someone who's more a friend than a teacher.'

'I have no objection, of course.' Claudia looked at him speculatively. 'I think I'd like to get things clear. Does that mean that you will use *my* first name, and vice versa?'

'When necessary. You can call Aunt Bea "Miss Treharne" if you prefer.'

Saul lost interest in the subject as he glanced at his watch and cursed under his breath, accelerating until Claudia felt as though every bone in her body was grinding against its neighbour. After a few minutes of this treatment her ill-used stomach finally rose up in revolt.

'Mr Treharne,' she gasped, forgetting any instruction about first names. 'Please stop. Now!'

A sharp glance at her greenish-white face obviously convinced Saul it was necessary, and with a squeal of brakes the jeep came to a halt and Claudia was out of the vehicle before it stopped, parting violently with the contents of her stomach in a convenient ditch at the roadside. When she finally considered it safe to stand straight a clean khaki handkerchief was thrust into her hand and, still gasping and sniffing, she mopped her face, unaware that her ministrations were adding rusty streaks to her appearance. Her temper was scarcely improved when she looked up to find Saul doing his obvious best to hide the first sign of a smile she'd been privileged to witness on his face, the corners of his mouth definitely twitching instead of shut like a steel trap.

'Are you better?' he enquired gravely.

'Only relatively,' she said ungraciously. 'Is it much farther?'

'About ten kilometres.'

'Then would it be possible to proceed at a slightly less bruising pace? My stomach is more accustomed to gentler roads—not to mention slightly more sedate driving!' Claudia was unable to resist the last bit, but a shrug was her only answer as Saul hoisted her back into the jeep and got in to resume the journey at about half the previous speed, which made the silent journey interminable, but at least physically viable as far as Claudia was concerned.

A final bend brought them into sight of Campo d'Ouro, which was built mainly on two hills, the red-roofed white houses clinging to steeply sloping streets among patches of verdant plant life, interspersed here and there with tall palm trees. A twin-towered church stood at the crown of each hill looking down on the town, themselves dominated by the great cross at the summit of Morro d'Ouro. Claudia looked in silence, her discomfort forgotten as she stared in fascination at the scene, unreal as a picture postcard, very different from her preconceived idea. Saul steered the jeep sharply to the right and began to climb a steep road which curved well away from the town, past large houses screened from view by shaded gardens, finally driving in through open green-painted gates to come to rest in the drive of the house at the highest point of the hill.

He helped Claudia down to the flagged patio running around the base of the house, and while he unloaded her luggage she stood still, just looking at the house that was to be her home for the next two years. At first glance it appeared to consist of two floors, but as Claudia looked more closely she could see that the ground floor was merely a basement, with green-painted trellis softening its walls and continuing upwards to shade a portion of the verandah of the house from the sun. Her eyes were dazzled by light and colour as yellow-gold sunlight poured down from a brilliant blue sky on the blindingly white walls and red roof, even the dull green of the trellis embellished by a profusion of crimson and purple blossoms where bougainvillaea entwined lovingly with its lattice.

Saul motioned her to precede him up the flight of stone steps leading to the verandah, which proved to be virtually an extra room of generous proportions, enclosed on three sides by the house, only its fourth side open to the sun, and even this was partially screened by the flower-laden trellis. As Claudia reached the verandah the blessedly familiar figure of Beatrice Treharne was waiting to greet her, erect and immaculate as remembered, a smile on the features Claudia now realised bore a strong resemblance to those of her less friendly nephew.

'Welcome to Campo d'Ouro, my dear,' she said with warmth, taking Claudia's hand. 'You must be exhausted after that mammoth journey. How was your flight?'

Claudia returned the smile with infinite gratitude, a slight lump in her throat at the kindness of Miss Treharne's greeting, so markedly different from the reception accorded her by Saul Treharne.

'The flights were just fine,' said Claudia cheerfully, 'though the last one from Rio was a trifle bumpy. It was the journey by road that proved the true endurance test.'

Miss Treharne cast a look of reproach at her nephew

who had just mounted the steps with the last of Claudia's luggage.

'I really don't quite see why you felt it necessary to fetch Claudia in the jeep, Saul,' she said severely. 'After all, Luc had put the Mercedes at your disposal.'

'I'm happier in the jeep,' he said impenitently. 'Unfortunately Miss March is a poor traveller—the road proved to be her undoing.' He stood looking at Claudia with a trace of amusement on his dark features, an improvement admittedly on the almost hostile indifference of earlier on, but it nevertheless acted on her bruised spirit like salt rubbed into a wound.

'I wouldn't say the road was entirely to blame,' she said evenly, but her comment fell on stony ground as Saul ignored it, obviously impatient to be away.

'I must be off—I've been too long away from the job as it is. No lunch for me, Aunt Bea, I'll be home in time for dinner.' He ran down the steps with a tread surprisingly light for so tall a man, and seconds later the revving of the jeep's engine disturbed the still morning air as he reversed it out of the drive into the red, dusty road.

Saul's departure left Claudia feeling limp and suddenly very conscious of her dishevelled appearance, though better able to appreciate her surroundings. The verandah was a welcoming place, with comfortable wicker furniture cushioned in cream and russet and a large glass-topped table holding a work-basket and a writing-case. Beatrice Treharne smiled.

'This is where we eat most of our meals and where I spend most of my time; a combination of living, dining and playroom.' Her eyes twinkled. 'But I'm sure that a bath is of much more interest than décor at the moment, isn't that right? Come with me, and I'll show you your room.'

Claudia followed the trim figure in the crisp blue cotton dress through glass doors into a square, cool hall, its floor polished to a diamond brightness. A number of doors led off it, one of them giving on to a dim corridor where Miss Treharne threw open three doors in quick succession.

'Becky's room, the bathroom you share, then your room, my dear. I hope you find it comfortable.'

After the microscopic dimensions of her strictly functional little flat in the Midlands the rooms looked large and spacious to Claudia, with their high ceilings and gleaming floors, bare except for a rug or two. The two bedrooms were very similar, though Becky's furniture was of light wood and there were teddies and a rag doll on a large chest, while Claudia's room had furniture in what she later learned was Portuguese Colonial style; dark wood intricately carved, with wrought-iron hinges and handles. Flower-printed curtains and bedcovers added to the impression of freshness in both rooms, the finishing touch in Claudia's a white pottery bowl containing pink roses on the dressing table.

'It's charming,' she said with sincerity, touched by the thoughtful flowers, then yawned, suddenly and violently. 'Oh dear, do forgive me! The aftermath of my journey, I'm afraid.'

'Have a nice leisurely soak in the bath,' advised the other woman kindly. 'Join me on the verandah when you're ready. Lunch is cold today, you won't be holding anything up.'

One thing was puzzling Claudia.

'I've seen no sign of Rebecca, Miss Treharne.'

'I sent her to play with the Fonseca children earlier on. She's having her lunch with them and you can make her acquaintance later when you feel better equipped to face the world.' An understanding smile lit Miss Treharne's eyes. 'I felt you might prefer to meet us in instalments, so to speak.'

Grateful for Miss Treharne's forethought, Claudia lay in the big white tub in the bathroom, admiring the austerity of the marble-floored room as she lay supine in the warm water, her body utterly relaxed. Her thoughts, however, were busy, a mélange of new impressions dominated by the brooding figure of Saul Treharne. She had previously visualised him as older; kind and ineffectual, a man incapable of holding his wife. Claudia breathed in deeply, a frown drawing her

slanting brows together. Ineffectual was the last word
applicable to Mr Treharne! Forceful, irritating, overpowering even, ineffectual never. She roused herself and
washed her hair vigorously, conditioning it for dear life,
wondering whether it would ever be rid of all the dust
gathered on the journey. When it was dry and shining
again the effect on her spirits of merely feeling clean
was immediate, and dressed in sleeveless yellow cotton,
her bare feet in mules of plaited white kid, Claudia left
her room and retraced her way back to the verandah,
pausing in the square hall to speculate where the other
doors led. She found Beatrice Treharne sitting at the
verandah table, which was now set for lunch. She
looked up from the letter she was writing, an approving
smile on her handsome face.

'A veritable transformation, Claudia—you look a
different person. Come and sit down.' She rang a little
pottery bell. 'Would you care for a drink before we
eat?'

'No, thank you.' Claudia sat gazing past the
blossom-laden trellis at the view beyond. 'How
wonderful to have a verandah like this!'

'We tend to live on it in hot weather, but at night we
eat in the dining-room.' Miss Treharne indicated
another pair of glass doors. 'The insects are a bit
annoying in the dark if one has much of a light. Ah,
here comes Maria.'

A tall, strapping black girl, a wide smile on her genial
face, brought in a tray and set down an avacado half
stuffed with prawns at each place. Miss Treharne waved
a hand towards Claudia and said something in
Portuguese to the girl, presumably telling her that
Claudia was Becky's new governess. The girl nodded
her head and beamed.

'*Muito prazer,*' ventured Claudia, and was rewarded
with an even wider smile from the girl.

'*Igualmente, senhora, muito prazer.*' She bustled out,
her spotless blue print dress and white apron fairly
crackling with starch.

'What a very pleasant-looking girl,' commented
Claudia, then turned to her plate with anticipation.

'Vinaigrette sauce or garlic mayonnaise?' offered her hostess.

Claudia hesitated, eyes narrowed, then shook her head regretfully.

'I adore both, but until my stomach forgives me for my journey I'll use discretion and leave my prawns au naturel.'

'It's that road. It's a killer, and I've no doubt Saul drove like a charioteer, as usual.' Miss Treharne shook her head and began to eat, pausing a little with a glance at Claudia before going on. 'I trust you won't find my remarks unduly personal, my dear, but I think it's necessary to say that although my nephew may appear—well, somewhat dour on times, his bark is generally worse than his bite. I mention this because you will find that Rebecca is still somewhat in awe of him, and I devoutly hope you may be able to change her attitude.'

Claudia smiled in agreement, and forbore to mention that in her opinion Saul's attitude had room for improvement too, though it was possible he was more human where his small daughter was concerned.

'That reminds me,' went on Miss Treharne. 'Has Saul mentioned what Becky is to call you? I don't want to start her off on the wrong foot.'

'Mr Treharne suggested we all use first names.' Claudia avoided the other woman's eye. 'I find it rather—well, difficult to regard him as Saul, but as far as Becky is concerned I think it's a good idea. Perhaps she might accept me more easily that way. Naturally I wouldn't presume as far as you're concerned, Miss Treharne.'

'Then it rather cancels out the whole thing, doesn't it? You could call me "Aunt Bea" like the other two; pretend I'm another of your aunts.'

Claudia kept her eyes on her plate as she occupied herself with the last of her prawns.

'What have I said?' asked Bea gently. 'Have I touched on a sore spot?'

'Not really.' Claudia gave an odd little smile. 'It's just that I'm totally lacking in the relative department—absolutely no aunts at all.'

'How tactless of me,' said Bea, vexed. 'I'd forgotten.'

'Normally it's a case of not missing something I've never had. But just occasionally I feel I'd like to have known my mother.'

'You should have a fellow feeling for Becky, then,' said Bea, sighing. 'She still cries for her mother now and then, even after several months. Though why I'll never know. Elaine was more concerned with having a gay time with that new husband of hers . . .' She stopped, looking annoyed with herself. 'Do forgive me, I tend to get carried away on the subject of Becky's mother.'

'Did—did Mrs Treharne not care for it here?' Claudia felt a pang of shame at being so curious.

'She never lived here. Do have some cold chicken and potato salad, my dear, by the way. Saul is related to Luc Fonseca, who owns the mine, and when the previous Engineering Superintendent retired Luc asked Saul if he cared to take on the job. Saul jumped at the chance, but in the meantime Elaine had become pregnant and he had to leave her behind. The idea was for her to join him as soon as the baby was born. But she never would. A man she'd known before re-entered her life and, to cut a long story short, eventually Saul agreed to a divorce, only to find Elaine very awkward about letting him see Becky.' Bea frowned, sighing. 'This is why Saul was virtually a stranger to Becky when Elaine was killed, and to the child he's someone who took her away from everything familiar and brought her to live among more strangers. She's improving, but now and then we get scenes.'

'Scenes?'

'When she can't get her own way. Elaine's method of upbringing seems to have been to ignore the child half the time and to spoil her unmercifully at others, which sometimes results in demands for attention, naturally.'

'Poor child!' Claudia touched her napkin thoughtfully to her lips, beginning to wonder just what she'd let herself in for.

'Now,' said Bea briskly, 'have you finished? Would you care for trifle, or cheese and biscuits?' She rang her little bell.

'I think it might be wisest to rest on my laurels,' said Claudia regretfully. 'Would it be possible to have some tea?'

'Of course. I generally have tea out here after Saul returns to the mine. Time hangs heavy sometimes.'

Maria appeared with a daintily set tea-tray and removed the used plates and serving dishes with swift, quiet efficiency.

'Does Mr Treharne normally come home to lunch?' asked Claudia, wondering if her arrival was the reason for his absence today.

'Sometimes. But he's out all day quite a lot, too. That's part of the problem with Becky. She just doesn't see enough of Saul to get accustomed to him.' Bea shook her head, sighing. 'Perhaps you will be able to improve things, Claudia.'

'I shall certainly try—what's that?' Claudia looked up sharply at the commotion outside, a tearful voice raised in voluble protest as its owner was shepherded up the side of the house to the kitchen entrance.

'Becky.' Bea sounded resigned.

'Not over-enthusiastic about meeting me,' suggested Claudia with a smile.

Bea rose to her feet in determination. 'I'll just go and sort her out.'

'Oh no—please!' Claudia looked at her in appeal. 'Could we let her come in her own time? If she's hauled in front of me like a criminal she's bound to resent me from the start.'

Bea subsided reluctantly, and began to pour out tea. 'Have you discussed your timetable with Saul, my dear? When and where as regards the lessons?'

Claudia shook her head. 'Mr Treharne was not over-talkative, I'm afraid.'

Bea looked apologetic.

'I must explain that the very fact he came to meet you at all was unfortunate. I was coming to Boa Vista in the Fonsecas' car with a chauffeur. Becky, however, took it into her head to hide this morning and in minutes the whole household was in uproar, the maids thinking she was lost, or worse, judging from their hysterics. My command of Portuguese doesn't cover disasters yet, so I was forced to ask Saul to come home to deal with things, and needless to say he was in the middle of some knotty problem down at the Reduction plant, and one way and another the entire situation became too fraught for words.'

'What had happened to Becky?'

'She was crouched down behind a whole stalk of ripening bananas in one of the empty outhouses, where Saul eventually located her. When she realised her father had been fetched home to look for her she became hysterical and clung to me like a limpet, so I had to stay.' Bea sighed, shaking her head. 'Saul was deeply upset by her fear, beneath that wooden mask of his, and then, of course, he had to come and fetch you from Boa Vista when he was needed back here, so you can see why——'

'He wasn't——exactly at his best when he finally arrived at the airport,' Claudia finished for her.

'Precisely. The disturbing fact about the whole incident is that Saul wasn't in the least stern with Becky, yet when she saw him she screamed as though he was likely to beat the living daylights out of her.'

'Why is she afraid of him?'

Bea shrugged, her face troubled.

'He tries very hard to be gentle and friendly with her, but she sees comparatively little of him except at weekends, and then of course he's so big and—well, forbidding-looking most of the time. I'm sure it's not anything more deep-rooted than that.'

Privately Claudia felt a great deal of sympathy with the child. She found Saul Treharne more than a little daunting herself, and she was a big grown-up girl, not given much to trepidation about people at all, at least not until now. The fictional Mr Rochester in *Jane Eyre* was a pussycat compared with the dour, unfriendly man who had met her today without a word of welcome. Not that she was any Jane Eyre, either, decided Claudia—it would take more than a bit of boorish behaviour to put her off life in this idyllic spot at this stage!

CHAPTER THREE

AFTER lunch Claudia went back to her room and began to unpack, laying her underwear neatly in the carved black chest of drawers and hanging up her dresses and skirts in the wardrobe. The door stood ajar, and from time to time she glanced over her shoulder towards it, fairly sure she was being watched. She hummed softly to herself as she put out her make-up and perfume on the dressing table, pausing to sniff the roses, only to find them scentless, to her disappointment. When she came to her final suitcase she positioned it carefully so that its contents were invisible from the door, drew a large parcel from it and put it on the bed, relocking the suitcase and putting the keys in her handbag. As Claudia stood at the dressing table mirror to brush her hair she could see the reflected door open a little wider and a small face peer round it cautiously. Very slowly she laid down her hairbrush and turned to look at the little girl staring at her from the doorway.

'Hello,' Claudia smiled, her face friendly, but made no move towards the child. 'Would you like to come in?'

Becky shook her head and stayed where she was, her face suspicious.

'O.K.,' said Claudia carelessly, and turned back to the mirror, spraying on a little perfume. Reflected in the glass she could see the little girl's eyes riveted on the parcel on the bed. The wrapping paper had a pattern of black and red golliwogs, the whole thing finished off with a big red ribbon bow. Very slowly Claudia turned to look at the little figure hovering in the doorway, halfpoised for flight, even though obviously ensnared by the lure of the tempting parcel on the bed. Pale gold curling hair tied in bunches framed an oval face with sunflushed peach-textured skin, the dark Prussian-blue eyes the only reminder of her father. Her over-elaborate white eyelet cotton dress was crumpled and soiled, and there were tearstains on the hectically flushed cheeks. Becky eyed Claudia with suspicion, then spun round and ran down the corridor, presumably to the kitchen, judging by the voices upraised above the clatter of dishes.

Claudia shrugged and made a little face, then closed her door and returned to the verandah. Bea looked up from her letter-writing with a smile.

'Finished your unpacking? One of the girls could have helped you.'

'I'm so used to looking after myself I find the thought of maids a little hard to get used to as yet. At least this way I shall know where everything is.'

From the sundial standing near the house the garden descended the slope in front of her in gentle tiers, each level bright with flowering shrubs and beds of tall, brilliantly-coloured roses accenting the manicured sweep of lawn. The bottom tier of grass levelled out gradually, merging into a belt of tall trees.

Claudia's eyes shone as she gazed at the panorama of colour spread out before her, drinking in the atmosphere of this new, exotic location that was to be her home for quite some time—barring accident. In spite of Becky's resentment, and the forbidding personality of the child's father, Claudia felt optimistic. She was drawn to the entire place irresistibly. She liked it here, and decided that if she couldn't manage to teach one small girl, however rebellious and difficult, after the numbers coped with at Highdean, she would willingly eat the white cricket hat brought in anticipation of this new, blazing sun.

'That's rather a fierce little smile,' remarked Bea with amusement.

'I've just arrived at the conclusion that this is a very picturesque place, and I know I'm going to like it here.' Claudia flung out a hand to include the whole of Campo d'Ouro as she turned to Bea with a sigh of pleasure, then remembered Becky. 'By the way, I've met my little charge. She kept me under surveillance at a discreet distance from the doorway of my bedroom.'

'I expect she wanted a good look at you.'

'Wondering what the ogre was like, no doubt! Though I rather suspect her main interest was in a parcel on the bed, gift-wrapped in golliwog paper with a lot of eye-catching red ribbon.'

'Did you hand it over?' asked Bea curiously.

'No. She turned tail and ran before I could make any real overtures. Don't worry—sheer curiosity will probably win in the end. Best to let her come round in her own time—the last thing any of us wants is a relationship founded on unwilling obedience.'

'I do hope you're right.' Bea sighed anxiously. 'I've had very little experience of children at all, myself, and at my age it's difficult to start learning to cope. I love Becky dearly, but at times I admit she exhausts me!'

Claudia's smile was warmly sympathetic.

'No doubt I'll feel the same on times.' Suddenly the light of battle shone in her eyes. 'But it will work both ways, I promise you. I'm used to children, girls and boys—little ones at the Home, then older girls at Highdean. I intend to earn every penny of my salary.'

'Well, there's no need to make a start at this very minute,' said Bea, her eyes twinkling. 'Let me show you round the house.'

She led the way through the glass doors at the right of the verandah into a long dining-room, its three windows protected with venetian blinds against the afternoon sun. It was furnished with modern jacaranda furniture, the effect uncluttered, the only ornaments plaques in beaten copper on the walls.

'Most of the furniture in the house is fairly old-fashioned,' said Bea, 'bought from the previous occupant, as in your room, but in here it's new. Saul bought it when he was expecting Elaine to join him.'

Claudia was silent, admiring her employer's taste, surprised to feel a pang of sympathy for him as she followed Bea through a pantry lined with china cupboards into a large, marble-floored kitchen where, though the appliances were fairly modern, the white cupboards had obviously come with the house.

Maria was standing at one end of a scrubbed wooden

table chopping vegetables while another younger girl was vigorously polishing cutlery at the other. A third girl sat on the doorstep with the hunched little figure of Becky alongside her pointedly ignoring the newcomers, boredom and hostility in every line of the small body.

'You've already met Maria,' said Bea, ignoring the little girl blandly as Becky gave a furtive peep over her shoulder. 'The girl polishing is Maria de Lourdes, but is referred to merely as "Lourdes", a very popular name in this country. The young one on the step is Afra.'

The girls were both dark-hued, slender young things with long braids, dressed in blue print and white aprons like Maria, the cook. They smiled diffidently at Claudia, who smiled back and ventured *"Como vai?"* to them, hoping it meant more or less "How are you?" As Bea ushered her back into the main central corridor there was a buzz of excitement the moment the door shut behind them.

'I think that went very well.' Bea chuckled softly. 'Did you see the look of indignation on Becky's face!'

Claudia nodded ruefully.

'I think she was all geared up to refuse to have anything to do with me, then we took the wind out of her sails. Poor little mite!'

'Don't weaken. I really believe you're on the right tack, to keep to the nautical. Now; the bedrooms you've already seen, but here on the left is Saul's study.' Bea opened a door and Claudia peered into a room lined with bookshelves holding rows of heavy technical books and periodicals and numbers of paperbacks. The furniture was basic and functional, a large, battered desk with a goose-neck lamp and a telephone, a scuffed leather armchair and sofa, a worn rug on the floor. The entire room had a strong, men-only atmosphere.

'The doors from this room to the verandah are kept closed,' explained Bea. 'Saul does rather consider his retreat off limits, apart from a little necessary dusting and polishing.'

Claudia nodded, Bea's tactful little message received and understood instantly.

Bea threw open the next door and motioned her

inside. To her surprise it was quite small, virtually empty except for the packing case of books shipped from England for Becky's education. 'I fancy Saul has this in mind for your schoolroom.'

Claudia viewed it without enthusiasm. The only light came from the French doors leading to the verandah, and there was an air of gloom and disuse about the room she disliked instantly. 'I see,' she said noncommittally, and followed Bea into the hall.

'There are three rooms left—well, five, if you include bathrooms.' Bea opened the door ahead of her to show a room furnished in similar style to Claudia's. 'This is mine, and the door on the far side leads to what was once a dressing-room and is now a bathroom—Saul had it done for me before I came.'

As Claudia followed Bea into the next room she experienced an immediate sense of intrusion. This was the master bedroom, aptly named to house the autocratic Mr Treharne, she thought. The furniture was in jacaranda, like the dining-room, a woven cane headboard backing the huge double bed with its spartan brown linen cover. Curtains of the same material hung at the two mesh-screened windows, which looked out on a terraced section of the garden at the side of the house. One wall consisted of matching jacaranda built-in wardrobes and dressing-table, with an extra door leading to a bathroom.

Bea withdrew.

'Originally the room had a silk spread and curtains and vicuña rugs, in readiness for Elaine, but as I said, she never arrived.'

Claudia felt as though she were trespassing in some private, vulnerable corner of Saul Treharne's life, and was relieved to follow Bea into the final room, the drawing room. Light and airy, it was the only one fitted with a carpet, in a warm shade of rust-red as a glowing contrast for the comfortable couch and chairs with their covers of oatmeal cotton tweed. There was even a fireplace with a carved ironwood mantel, and jacaranda tables bore big alabaster lamps with rust silk shades, while cream and russet printed curtains moved gently in the slight breeze coming through the open windows.

'This is lovely,' said Claudia without reservation. 'To which category does it belong?'

'The B. Treharne style of furnishing,' said Bea with a smile. 'Saul never used this room until I came. He took the furniture and carpet with the house, but I had new covers and curtains made, bought a table or two, added the lamps and the result is as you see. And now I think we deserve some tea, after which we'll explore outside.'

As they sat chatting over the tea-tray delicious smells floated out from the kitchen as Maria began preparations for dinner.

'Do your maids live in?' asked Claudia.

'Maria and Lourdes, but Afra and José the gardener come in daily.'

'Where do the girls sleep?'

'They have their own quarters behind the house, with a bedroom and shower. It means they can retire in there for a couple of hours in the afternoon after lunch, and Maria does the ironing in there, too.' Bea laughed. 'On Mondays we have a general reshuffle. Maria does the laundry and I do the cooking. She's a superb laundress—I'm sure you've noticed the whiteness of the aprons.'

Claudia nodded, a wry smile on her face.

'Crackling with starch—I noticed too. I wouldn't know what to do with a packet of starch if you gave it to me. To be honest I'm not all that domesticated. I keep my flat tidy due to rigid early training at the Home, but I'm not all that marvellous in the kitchen. I confess it freely—I'm a true convenience-food freak!'

'You'll find life here very different. When do you intend to introduce yourself to Becky officially, my dear?'

'Tomorrow, some time, when the occasion presents itself spontaneously. Perhaps you could arrange for her to stay close to the house so that I can choose my moment.'

'Yes, of course, let's go outside now it's cooler.'

Claudia wandered round the garden with Bea as the

sun was about to set, admiring the flowering shrubs in the cooler atmosphere just before the sun slid below the horizon and the day was gone. In an instant, without the intermediary of twilight, darkness was upon them; a warm, blue-velvet darkness ablaze with stars.

'Glory!' Claudia stared in fascinated awe at the sky. 'I never really believed it happened like that. "At one stride comes the dark", well and truly. And just a couple of days or so ago I was fighting my way through the rain and wind, not to mention the odd snow shower!' She pushed her hair away from her neck and yawned suddenly.

Bea laughed.

'Come along—I think jet-lag is beginning to catch up with you. Have a rest before dinner. Saul will be home shortly and we eat about seven. Then you can go to bed early to prepare yourself for getting to grips with Becky.'

Claudia was grateful to obey, and retired to her cool bedroom to lie down on the bed with a sigh. It seemed only seconds before she woke to discreet knocking on the door.

'Come in,' she mumbled hazily, to find Bea bending over the bed ready for the evening in a navy silk dress, pearl studs in her ears.

'Nearly dinner-time, Claudia.'

Claudia shot up, blinking, and thrust a hand through her hair. She swung her legs guiltily to the ground.

'I'm sorry, you should have chased me up earlier. I'll be five minutes. Where's Becky?'

'In bed and asleep, worn out by the varying emotions of her day, I think.' Bea smiled encouragingly. 'Drinks on the verandah in ten minutes, then.'

Claudia stripped off her crumpled dress and slid into her kimono to dash to the bathroom to brush her teeth and splash her face with cold water. Within minutes her face was made up, hair neatly brushed, and she was zipping herself into a dress of maize-coloured linen piped in white. She left her room as quietly as possible to avoid disturbing Becky and went noiselessly through

the hall to the verandah, dismayed to find Saul
Treharne there alone at the rail, staring out at the night
in moody abstraction, a long, ice-clinking glass in his
hand.

'Good evening,' said Claudia quietly.

He lounged away from the rail and turned at the
sound of her voice.

'Good evening. Do you feel better now?' He stood
surveying her as if she were some miscreant up before
the bench.

'It was only jet-lag. I had a little rest and now I'm
fine.' Claudia felt immediately on the defensive.

'I was referring to your—er—stomach disorder.'

It would obviously be some time before she would be
allowed to forget her unfortunate travel-sickness.
Claudia inclined her head coolly, as unsmiling as her
host.

'What will you drink?' he asked, taking a swallow
from his glass.

'If that's a gin and tonic I'd like the same, please.'

In silence Saul moved to a bottle-laden trolley and
filled a tall glass with gin, tonic water, several ice-cubes
and slices of lime.

'Thank you.' Claudia took a sip, enjoying the icy,
bitter taste, praying that Bea would put in an
appearance as soon as possible.

'Sit down, please.' He gestured to one of the chairs
and Claudia sat obediently, putting her drink down on
a wooden coaster on the table. Saul continued to stand
at the rail, his face invisible in the dim light of the glass-
shaded candle that flickered in a copper holder beside
Claudia. It was just possible to see that his cotton shirt
was white and thin, and his beige cotton trousers had
obviously been made for him, to judge from the way
they fitted his surprisingly slim waist and hips below the
Herculean spread of his shoulders.

'I gather you made no attempt to make friends with
my daughter today,' he observed flatly.

Claudia was deeply grateful for the dim light, which
hid the quick, angry flare of colour that flamed along
her cheekbones.

'On the contrary,' she said with care, striving for calm, 'I feel I've made some progress on that score.'

Even though his face was invisible, the very angle of his head proclaimed his opinion of her answer.

'But you made no attempt to introduce yourself to the child. Becky says you haven't spoken to her.'

Claudia swallowed some of her drink before answering.

'I did say "hello" at one stage, but she ran off like a startled fawn, so I just left it. She was making rather a fuss when she thought she was being dragged home expressly to meet me, so I followed my instinct and left her severely alone.'

'Is this the general method applied to all children these days?' His derisive tone was beginning to get on Claudia's nerves.

'One doesn't apply just one rule to "all" children, Mr Treharne.' Her voice was a little more acid than she would have wished, and she made it deliberately colourless as she went on. 'I believe that each child is an individual, and one must find a separate approach for each one, according to personality.'

'Very high-principled, but hardly practicable for teaching in a large school, surely!'

'Oh, but I'm not,' said Claudia instantly. 'You're paying me very generously to concentrate all my professional skill on just one child.'

Her tiny triumph was shortlived.

'I'm very much aware of the expense, Miss March. Very much,' he drawled, draining his glass. 'The professional skill remains to be proved, of course.'

'Of course.' Claudia was definitely unhappy about his first sentence, but decided to ignore it. 'But don't worry, Mr Treharne, I'm sure Rebecca's natural curiosity will prompt her to make the next move tomorrow.'

Saul moved to mix himself another drink, frowning.

'Aren't you assuming rather too much that she *will* feel any interest in you?'

'I did say curiosity, not interest,' she said gently. 'And I'm not flattering myself that it's directed solely at me, more at the parcel she's already seen on my bed. She has a suspicion it might be for her.'

'So you're relying on bribery?'

'No,' said Claudia with dignity. 'I merely wanted to make Becky well-disposed towards me, and if she is it will halve the difficulties of teaching her, Mr Treharne.'

'I thought we were all going to be on first name terms!' Bea emerged suddenly from the dining-room and sat down near Claudia with a sigh. 'Sherry, thank you, Saul.'

'We obviously need time to accustom ourselves to the idea, Aunt Bea.' Saul looked across challengingly as he poured out a sherry and handed it to his aunt. 'May I top up your glass—Claudia?'

She refused, her colour high, as Bea asked Saul about his day.

'Slight hiccup with the crusher in Reduction, which was my reason for rushing you back this morning.' From his stance at the rail he looked down on Claudia with a sudden glint of white teeth.

'You should have sent someone else to meet me,' said Claudia uncomfortably.

'By the time Becky had finally been located behind the bananas it was too late to organise another willing English-speaking volunteer.' Saul looked at her steadily. 'No doubt you've heard about our little drama this morning. Naughty child, cruel father, etc.'

'That wasn't precisely how I heard it, but yes, I did hear Becky went missing.'

'She wasn't crying for fear of punishment because she was hiding,' put in Bea quickly. 'When she was calmer she confessed to eating several of the bananas, which she obviously considered a far greater crime than the scare she gave us.'

Dim light notwithstanding Saul's scowl was black enough to be plainly visible.

'What the hell do I care for a few bananas?' he said with violence.

'You know that, I know that,' said Bea soothingly, 'but Becky quite plainly regarded her theft as a deadly sin.'

Happily Lourdes came to announce dinner at that moment, and the tension dispelled somewhat as they went in to enjoy the first course of chilled melon and grapefruit balls.

'Maria did something rather special in honour of your first meal with us,' said Bea as the first course was cleared away. 'I hope you'll enjoy Brazilian cooking.'

'If the wonderful smell is anything to go by I can't fail,' said Claudia, her eyes sparkling as Lourdes pushed in the trolley and set down a platter of meat and several dishes of vegetables on the table.

'Does your impressive list of qualifications include cooking?' Saul's eyes were a shade more friendly as he looked in query at Claudia. 'Try your wine, by the way, it's local and very good.'

'I'm a hopeless cook,' said Claudia frankly, and sipped her wine, impressed by its quality. 'I agree, the wine *is* good, and so is this meat, by the look of it. What exactly is the dish?'

'Pork fillet stuffed with apricots and flavoured with garlic,' said Bea.

It melted in the mouth and was utterly delicious, as were the glazed whole carrots, courgettes in a spicy tomato sauce and tiny, deep-fried potato balls, crisp and golden.

'I shall have to watch my weight!' Claudia smiled as she accepted a second helping of meat.

'Your weight's a problem?' asked Saul blandly.

'When I'm doing the cooking, no. But with food like this I might have to resort to self-control!' The laughter in Claudia's eyes died as she met the saturnine gleam in Saul's across the table.

'That's an additional problem?' he enquired sauvely.

Bea interposed hastily, frowning at her nephew. She offered more vegetables, which Claudia refused politely, her enthusiasm for her meal entirely gone.

'I shall have to make sure we have something special for Christmas Day.' Bea plainly considered it time for a change of subject. 'I believe they generally eat pork here, not turkey. What are you in the habit of doing at Christmas, Claudia?'

Claudia laid down her knife and fork.

'It's a time of the year I don't relish too much,' she said quietly. 'It was fun in some ways at the Home when I was young. But when I went to college I always worked in a hotel over the holiday, and lately I stay at hotels instead of working in them.'

Saul looked at her searchingly.

'No friends to invite you to stay?'

'Oh yes. One very good friend in particular.' Claudia's face softened as she thought of Liz. 'But one can't be a perpetual responsibility to someone else. I choose to be independent.'

'Spoken like a true feminist,' he stated dryly.

Claudia's curving mouth compressed, but she resisted the temptation to cut back with a tart answer in deference to Bea.

'I think a hotel at Christmas sounds very dreary,' declared Bea. 'Pass your plate, dear, if you've finished, and I'll stack them on the trolley.'

Claudia jumped up from force of habit.

'Please let me.' She took Saul's plate and put it on the trolley with the rest.

'You needn't act as waitress here,' said Saul flatly. 'God knows there are enough servants for the purpose.'

'Saul!' Bea regarded him with deep disapproval. 'Claudia was just being helpful. Thank you, dear.'

Claudia was annoyed. She returned to her seat with a suspicion of a flounce.

'Forgive me.' Her smile was over-sweet. 'I need time to accustom myself to the idea of being waited on rather than doing the waiting myself.'

Saul's smile was quizzical.

'Are you a Socialist, by any chance?'

Claudia's eyes glittered.

'Now that is against the rules, surely. I was under the impression that politics and religion were never discussed at the dinner-table.'

'And you were right.' Bea paused, looking significantly at Saul. 'Aren't you being just a trifle over-abrasive this evening, Saul?' She turned with relief as Lourdes arrived with a tray bearing a crystal bowl of trifle and a cheeseboard.

The rest of the meal passed fairly amicably, Saul apparently realising that his aunt's remark had been made in earnest. Conscious that Bea was genuinely distressed by the atmosphere of cut and thrust, Claudia turned the conversation to her own first highly favourable impressions of Brazil. They settled themselves in the drawing-room for coffee and Claudia was able to appreciate her second taste of the local coffee at more leisure than the one gulped down at Boa Vista airport. She refused Saul's offer of a liqueur coolly.

'I really was joking when I mentioned dietary problems,' he said surprisingly.

'Were you?' Claudia smiled politely. 'It isn't that. I'm just a little tired.'

'No wonder,' said Bea with sympathy. 'It's something like one in the morning by your own personal clock.'

'I'll be right as rain tomorrow,' said Claudia cheerfully. 'I really do have a constitution like an ox and——' she held up a hand, 'before we hark back to my experience of this morning I must reiterate that it was an isolated occurrence.'

Saul unbent sufficiently to smile slightly at her for the first time.

'We'll take your word for it,' he said. 'Have some more coffee.'

'Thank you.'

'Incidentally, Aunt Bea,' Saul remarked, 'no need to worry about Christmas Day, as it happens. As usual it slipped my mind. Luc had a word with me today, and it seems Emily would like us all to have dinner there.'

Bea was obviously delighted.

'How lovely! We are, of course, related, Claudia.'

Saul handed Claudia her coffee cup and sat beside his aunt, lighting a cigarillo. 'Luc and I are second cousins, and Aunt Bea is old Mrs Fonseca's niece.'

Claudia was little the wiser at this and Bea looked at Saul in affectionate exasperation.

'Really, Saul, I'm sure the poor girl hasn't an idea what you mean. Let me explain.'

Claudia listened, feeling pleasantly comfortable and

relaxed as Bea related how Thurza Treharne had married Jaime Fonseca sixty years before and come to make her home in Casa d'Ouro, where she survived both her husband and her son, and now lived with her grandson Luc, his English wife Emily and their three children, Jamie, Mark and Lucy.'

'Thurza is my aunt, my father's sister,' finished Bea, 'and I've spent several holidays here when I was young. Which is why I needed very little persuasion to come out and live with Saul.' She broke off. 'My poor child, your eyes are beginning to glaze! Off to bed with you, and only get up tomorrow when you feel like it.'

Claudia got wearily to her feet, Saul following suit.

'I trust you'll sleep well in your strange bed, Miss—Claudia,' he said.

'No problem there—I've slept in a lot of different beds in my time,' she said unthinkingly, then could have bitten her tongue out at the expression in the cynical blue eyes looking down into hers.

Bea, fortunately, seemed to read nothing amiss into Claudia's ambiguous statement, and wished her goodnight pleasantly.

'I'll see you to your room,' said Saul unexpectedly, grinding out his cigarillo.

'I can find my way, thank you.' Claudia suddenly wanted to get away from his overbearing presence as fast as she could, and turned away, but he followed her through the hall with that oddly catlike silent tread. She retreated down the corridor at speed, feeling as if she were being stalked by some predator, but to her relief he paused at his daughter's door and wished her goodnight impersonally as he went in, closing it softly behind him.

CHAPTER FOUR

CLAUDIA was pensive as she prepared for bed. Behind that sardonic mask of his Saul Treharne obviously cared for his little daughter deeply, and was prepared to go to great lengths to ensure the best possible for her welfare, including an expensive governess. After going to such expense it was a pity that he disliked his aunt's choice, though. Well, maybe dislike was the wrong word—disapproved was possibly more accurate. She creamed her face absently as she stared unseeingly in the mirror. His disapproval must be a purely personal thing, as surely her qualifications were good enough.

Claudia sighed. She was not naïve enough to expect everyone she met to like her, of course, but the fact remained that most people did. But not Saul Treharne, it seemed, and with father and daughter two to one against Bea life could prove a trifle difficult. Yet even taking dislike or disapproval into account, there was something else in Saul Treharne's attitude that troubled her, like a grain of sand in an oyster shell, grinding away beneath his impassive exterior. Claudia had a nagging feeling she failed to meet with his gold seal of approval in more ways than the mere drawback of relative youth. Maybe it was her rather spectacular lack of pedigree that stuck in his throat. Whatever it was, he had clearly been predisposed against her long before their first encounter today. Her clear grey eyes narrowed as she tissued her face clean with energy. His little dig on the subject of self-control had rankled, too. Was he implying she handed out her favours with indiscriminate enthusiasm? The men she'd known would be surprised to hear it. None of them had ever managed to persuade her to more than a few affectionate kisses which left her senses completely unstirred—the result of channelling all her excess energies into squash and aerobics, as one of them had once commented acidly.

Once in bed Claudia stared out at the starlit sky, unwilling to hide it from view behind the curtains. I *will* make a success of the job, she vowed fiercely. Becky needed love and attention, Bea was patently glad of congenial female company and Saul—well, Saul's battle-cry was value for money, by the look of it, and she would soon show him he had no cause for complaint. This comforting thought was enough to relax her tired mind, and she slept.

When Claudia opened her eyes again the room was bathed in light. Blinking sleepily she glanced at the watch on her wrist to find half the morning was gone. She frowned in dismay and sat up, then stilled, aware that the bedroom door was ajar, and she was being subjected to the scrutiny of a large pair of blue eyes. Claudia watched with interest as Becky, her hair in pigtails this morning, advanced a very small distance into the room, staring at Claudia with rather unnerving intensity.

'Good morning.' Claudia smiled encouragingly, wishing she were less at a disadvantage with her hair in an uncombed tangle. Becky cast a covert glance at the familiar parcel, which now sat, conspicuous and tempting, on the chest of drawers.

' 'Morning,' she muttered ungraciously. She thrust her hands into the gathered pockets of her embroidered pink cotton dress and stared at her white sandals, then out of the window, anywhere but directly into Claudia's face.

'I think I saw you yesterday, didn't I?' said Claudia casually. 'Do you live here?'

The child nodded, her face scornful, disdaining to reply.

'It must be time for me to get up,' said Claudia briskly, and swung her feet out of bed to stand on the fluffy white rug beside it. She thrust her arms into her kimono and searched for her towelling mules, then gathered up her toilet bag. 'Would you excuse me for a moment? I'm off for a shower.'

There was no response.

'Perhaps you'd like to wait here until I get back?'

Claudia left the child and went next door, hurrying
through her morning ritual, protecting her hair from
the shower spray with a plastic cap. When she returned
to her room Becky appeared to be in exactly the same
place, but Claudia's observant eye noted that the parcel
was in a slightly different position.

'Oh good, you're still here,' she said cheerfully. 'Now
what shall I wear?'

With a lack of selfconsciousness due to much
community living she rapidly put on fresh underwear
and took a sleeveless white shirt and thin jade green
cotton trousers from the wardrobe. The little girl
watched in silence as Claudia tied the white rope slotted
through the waistband of the slacks and slid her feet
into white sandals.

'I'll just brush my hair, then perhaps you could show
me where Miss Treharne is so that I can apologise for
being so late.'

Becky frowned, puzzled.

'She's in bed.'

'Is she unwell, then?' Claudia felt concern. She had
banked on a little friendly support on her first actual
day in her new job. Her only reply was a blank stare
from Becky, who stood planted in the middle of the
room, obviously determined not to budge. Her eyes
flicked up at the parcel, then back to Claudia.

'Whose parcel is that?' The question finally burst
from her, her silky brown eyebrows drawn together in a
ferocious frown as she began to shift from one foot to
the other.

Claudia began to make her bed.

'I brought it all the way from England on the plane
to give to a little girl called Rebecca, but she doesn't
seem to be here. At least, she hasn't spoken to me yet.'
Claudia glanced casually over her shoulder at Becky's
face, which was scarlet with suppressed emotion.

'*I'm* Rebecca!'

Claudia solemnly removed one of the small clenched
hands from the frilled pocket and shook it formally.

'Hello, Rebecca. I'm Claudia.'

Some deep-down instinct of good manners prompted

the child to say 'hello', reluctantly to be sure, but deciding the initial hurdle had been taken moderately well Claudia put an end to the child's frustration.

'If you're Rebecca, then this parcel is for you.' She placed the large package carefully in the child's hands. Becky fiercely clutched it to her chest and turned to go, but halted as Claudia said gently,

'What does one say when one receives a present, Rebecca?'

For several moments blue eyes clashed with the steady clear grey of this new presence in Becky's young life. Young as she was, something told the child surrender was inevitable.

'Thank you,' she mumbled sullenly, then whirled in a flurry of pink skirt as a knock came on the half-open door and Lourdes's apologetic face appeared hesitantly round it.

'*Olha,* Lourdes, *ten' presente!*' the child cried, then stopped dead at the girl's smile, her face a picture of guilt.

'*Bom dia,*' said Claudia before the maid could say anything, and Lourdes recollected herself hurriedly.

'*Bom dia, senhora. Cafe de manhã esta pronto na varanda.*'

Claudia's sketchy course in Portuguese had been sufficient for her to understand this perfectly well, but she shrugged regretfully and appealed to Becky.

'What did Lourdes say? I'm afraid I don't know much Portuguese.' Which was only the truth.

If it had been less touching it would have been amusing to watch the struggle taking place in the child's mind, and Claudia exchanged a look of smiling comprehension with Lourdes over Becky's bowed head.

'She said breakfast is ready on the verandah,' said Becky at last, with the air of one admitting to a crime.

'Oh, good—though it seems late for breakfast. Have you had yours?'

Becky shook her head and meekly allowed Claudia to take one hand while the other held on possessively to the red ribbon binding her parcel, even managing an unwilling smile as Lourdes threw up her hands and said,

'*Que presente lindo*. Becky *tem sorte, não e*?'

The child nodded in unselfconscious agreement, and asked Claudia quite politely if she could open her present after breakfast.

Surprised by this unlooked-for forbearance, Claudia praised Becky for her patience and followed the child to the verandah to find Bea, crisp and fresh in white-striped grey cotton shirt and grey linen skirt, enthroned behind an array of china at the table, which was set for three. Becky ran to her, suddenly a normal, noisy five-year-old.

'Aunt Bea! Aunt Bea! Look at my present!'

'Good morning, darling, aren't you the lucky girl!' Bea turned to Claudia with a smile of welcome. 'And good morning to you, Claudia. Fresh as a daisy today, I see.'

'And so I should be.' Claudia smiled guiltily. 'Forgive me for being so late. Good morning anyway, even if it is good afternoon.'

Bea consulted her watch, puzzled.

'It's only just past eight, my dear. I thought you were remarkably early under the circumstances.'

Claudia gave her own watch a shake, frowning, then realisation dawned.

'I'm an idiot! I forgot to put my watch back—I'm still functioning on U.K. time.' She turned to Becky. 'Shall we put your parcel on one of the chairs, Becky, then you can open it the minute you've eaten breakfast.'

Reluctantly the little girl allowed Claudia to relieve her of the box and put it on the chair next to her, beginning to eat a slice of melon-like fruit very rapidly, her eyes returning repeatedly to her fascinating gift.

'Will you try some fruit too, Claudia?' asked Bea. 'In this country the name is *mamão*, but you probably know them as papaya.'

'Only from books!' Claudia savoured the unfamiliar, delicious flavour of the peach-textured flesh and smiled appreciatively. 'Heavenly!'

'There are trees full of them in the upper back section of the garden. We must show you everything properly today.' Bea indicated the two china pots alongside her. 'Tea or coffee?'

'Tea, please.' Claudia exchanged a look with Bea above Becky's head. 'Perhaps Becky will come along too, and tell me the names of all the plants.'

Suspicious blue eyes turned on Claudia.

'Don't know all the names,' said Becky ungraciously.

'Well, you must know more than me.' Claudia helped herself to a boiled egg. 'Are you having an egg, Becky?'

Bea watched in fascination as Becky instinctively began to refuse, then wavered and let Claudia neatly slice the top off an egg set in a yellow pottery chicken. Claudia quickly cut a slice of bread and butter into fingers and popped them on Becky's plate, then left her alone and turned her attention first to her own egg, then to the toast and marmalade that followed it.

Becky drained her beaker of milk and, with the air of one who could endure no more, asked Bea,

'*Now* can I open the present?'

'Yes, darling. Shall I cut the string?'

Becky shook her head.

'My fingers are stiff. Ask Claudia.'

Becky's eyes turned on Claudia with mute appeal and, unable to prolong the child's agony of impatience any longer, Claudia untied the bow and unravelled the knots of ribbon, carefully re-rolling it as Becky tore off the paper and lifted the lid from the box underneath. The pink mouth opened in an O of surprise as she discovered numbers of other boxes and packages inside.

'My goodness,' said Bea, laughing, 'I think you'd best get down on the floor, Becky, then you can undo all the boxes one by one.'

Eagerly the child squatted on the floor, her fingers trembling with excitement as she unwrapped a small box of paints, a painting book, two jigsaw puzzles, a drawing book, a huge packet of felt-tipped pens, a tiny blackboard and chalks, erasers and pencil-sharpeners shaped like fruit, several little jotting pads, a small, furry koala bear, and a wooden pencil-box full of pencils, its sliding lid containing the name 'Rebecca' stencilled on it in large gilt letters.

'That's my name!' squealed the child, her cheeks bright crimson with excitement.

'What a lot of lovely things,' said Bea indulgently. 'Are you pleased?'

Becky nodded absently, busily going over her hoard of loot and smoothing the fur of the little koala with delight.

'Who gave you all these things?' persisted Bea.

'*She* did,' said Becky, waving a careless hand in Claudia's direction.

Claudia hid a smile. Obviously now the present was safely in her grasp Becky felt she could dispense with any soft-soap towards the donor.

Bea frowned, sighing.

'I think you should say thank you, don't you?'

'I already did,' said Becky mutinously, then looked up to meet the unwavering look in Bea's eye, hastily directing a perfunctory 'thank you' at Claudia.

'Thank you what?' said Bea inexorably.

'Thank you very much?' said Becky hopefully.

'Thank you very much, *Claudia*,' amended Bea.

Becky considered this with disfavour, obviously.

'Don't worry, Becky,' said Claudia briskly. 'It's a bit hard for you to say, I expect.'

Bea busied herself in collecting the breakfast things together to hide the smile twitching the corners of her mouth.

'Of course I can say it,' said Becky scornfully, then with an air of weary boredom, 'Thank you Claudia.'

'A pleasure, Becky,' said Claudia gravely. 'I hope you enjoy using all the things.'

To her surprise Becky began to stack all the presents very neatly in the big box.

'Where are you taking them, Becky?' asked Bea. 'To your room?'

'Show Afra and Lourdes and Maria—and José,' panted the child, staggering slightly as she got to her feet with her burden, and bore it off through the dining-room doors.

'You must forgive her lack of grace,' said Bea apologetically. 'Her upbringing was an uncertain, patchy affair, and the few months here with us hasn't been sufficient to give her any real feeling of belonging yet.'

'It's been quite sufficient for one thing, though!' Claudia's eyes twinkled. 'That young lady very definitely speaks a fair bit of Portuguese. I more or less forced her into translating what Lourdes said this morning.'

'I know she does. But for some reason she won't admit she can communicate. Of course you heard just then how accurately she pronounced the servants' names.' Bea looked troubled. 'It's with Saul she's at her worst, unfortunately. He's really very patient and forbearing, but insists on a certain amount of discipline, which I suspect was a commodity totally lacking in Elaine's ménage. When Becky first came here she barely had any manners at all. Another thing Saul insisted on was that presents for her were out for a while. He felt there'd been far too many material things and not enough care and love.'

'Oh dear!' Claudia made a face. 'I've really put my foot in it with my little peace-offering, then. No wonder Mr Treharne was rather acid about it last night.'

Bea shrugged.

'Pay no attention, dear. Saul suffered some very disillusioning treatment at the hands of Elaine. I'm not revealing anything that isn't common knowledge I assure you. She was the most beautiful young woman I ever saw, but unfortunately her soul didn't match. Elaine was selfish, cold. I don't mean physically— naturally I know nothing about that. To be old-fashioned, I think I mean her heart.'

Claudia felt uneasy, disturbed by this unsought glimpse into Saul Treharne's past.

'Do you think he would wish me to know all this?' she ventured.

'You mean I'm a garrulous old woman who shouldn't be telling my nephew's secrets to a complete stranger,' said Bea frankly. 'I've never spoken of it to anyone before, except to Henry, Saul's father. However, you have come to live with us, part of our household with all its problems, and without some idea of Saul's background you might wonder at times why he's—well, somewhat distant.'

'I just assumed he had some personal antipathy towards me,' said Claudia, embarrassed.

'I don't think it's you in particular, Claudia, just women in general.' Bea looked up as Lourdes appeared. '*Obrigada,* Lourdes.'

As the girl cleared away the breakfast things the telephone rang and Claudia got up to stand looking down on the town while Bea went off to answer the shrill summons. The red roofs and white walls of the houses clustering far below were bathed in glittering sunshine, and Claudia marvelled that just a short time before she had been shivering in the British winter. Bea popped her head through the hall door, interrupting her reverie.

'Saul would like a word with you, Claudia.'

Surprised, Claudia hurried to pick up the receiver, Bea retreating discreetly to her bedroom as Claudia said 'hello' cautiously.

'Good morning. I gather you slept well.' Saul sounded positively human, thought Claudia.

'Yes, thank you, I did.'

'You were too tired last night to discuss any details,' he went on. 'But I should have mentioned that any actual lessons won't be necessary until after Christmas. Perhaps you could utilise the time in settling down and getting to know Becky before making a start on the harsh realities of school.'

'As you wish, Mr Treharne.'

There was a pause.

'Perhaps we could persevere with the suggested use of first names,' he said expressionlessly.

'Very well.' Claudia wrinkled her nose at the receiver.

'Good. I'll leave you to get on with the task of thawing Becky, then. Tell Aunt Bea I won't be home for lunch, will you? Goodbye.'

'Goodbye.'

Claudia went off to knock on Bea's door to give her

Saul's message. Bea opened it, smiling at the look on Claudia's face.

'Received your orders for today?'

'Yes. I'm to put off lessons until after Christmas, apparently, so perhaps I can prevail upon you to show me the rest of the garden.' Claudia checked on the time. 'It's still only nine—you start the day early here. What time does Mr Treharne leave the house?'

'Just after six, usually.' Bea looked at her consideringly. 'Are you wondering what on earth you'll do with yourself?'

Claudia shrugged, smiling, as they went along to the kitchen.

'Life was fairly busy when I was teaching. Things seem a lot more peaceful here.'

'You'll soon get used to it.'

The kitchen was entirely disorganised, with the three maids and an older man, presumably the gardener, all exclaiming over Becky's box of treasures. Becky sat in the middle like a little queen bee, and was by no means pleased when Bea suggested she help show Claudia the back garden.

'Perhaps you could let the maids get on with their jobs now,' said Claudia reasonably, 'and after you've toured the garden with me you could come back and sit at the kitchen table to show them how well you can colour one of the pictures in your book with the felt-tip pens.'

It was apparent that Becky badly wanted to refuse, but as the maids guiltily began to resume their interrupted tasks at that moment she gave in with reluctance.

'You go on,' suggested Bea. 'I need a word with Maria about dinner.'

The garden rose steeply behind the house, a grassy slope bordered by tall trees bearing clusters of large, melon-like fruit, a tall privet hedge marking the boundary of the grounds.

Becky waved a hand at the trees.

'*Mamão,*' she said laconically. 'We had some for breakfast.'

Claudia followed her up the rise, her long legs making it difficult not to outdistance her small companion, who toiled on at a great rate until they reached the top of the rise to look down on a series of vegetable beds, which progressed in terraced layers down past the far side of the house containing the bedrooms belonging to Bea and Saul. José was digging in the red earth among rows of rustling corn, the only other vegetables Claudia was able to identify being French beans, lettuce, and what looked like celery, each plant wrapped to blanch it white.

Without a word Becky went doggedly on down the wide concrete path, which descended in broad, shallow steps to the paved patio in front of the house. She led the way to a small gate, which opened into a veritable forest of bananas.

'The *bananeira*,' she announced. 'Mustn't go in. Snakes.'

Claudia looked sharply at Becky's challenging little face and decided to take her word for it, keeping to the lawns that descended the front slopes gently, as she stopped to sniff roses which, although brilliantly coloured, were entirely scentless. One large flowerbed situated directly below the house in the comparative shade was devoted entirely to tall white lilies, stiff and melancholy in their isolation, like mourners waiting for a funeral. Claudia shivered and turned away to peep through the small windows visible through the trellis masking the basement wall.

'The *porão*,' announced Becky. 'Maria hangs the clothes in there to dry when it rains. The jeep's kept there too.'

'Thank you, Becky, you've been a big help.' Claudia felt decidedly hot and sticky. 'Let's go inside and see if you can colour a picture.'

Becky cast her a look of supreme disdain.

'Of course I can!'

She rushed up the verandah steps, almost coming to grief as one of her pockets caught on a protruding nail and tore with a rending sound. She fell on her knees but picked herself up stoically, swallowing hard and brushing at herself angrily.

'Did you hurt yourself?' Claudia examined the knees, but apart from dust there seemed little wrong.

'Stupid pocket,' blurted Becky, scowling. 'Stupid dress! I want shorts like Jamie.'

'Don't you have any?'

Becky shook her head crossly and went on up to the verandah, running through the dining room to the kitchen. Claudia followed more slowly, her eyes dreamy on the view as she lingered on the steps. When she reached the kitchen herself there was a stormy scene in progress. Becky had found Maria making bread on the table, and there was no room for the proposed colouring session.

'*Boba!*' she screamed, tears of rage running down her scarlet cheeks. '*Não deixou lugar para mim. Eu quero pintar!*'

Bea arrived in a hurry to find out what the noise was about and stood aghast at the sight of Becky, her dress torn, screaming abuse at Maria in a language she normally refused to speak.

Claudia decided it was high time for her to start earning her money. She had understood sufficient to know Becky was calling Maria a fool for not leaving enough space for her to paint. Her face was stern as she drew herself up to her full height, looking down calmly on the furious child.

'Please apologise to Maria, Becky.' There was a note in her voice many a young lady at Highdean would have recognised. 'There are other places to do your colouring.'

'Shan't!' The child rubbed dirty knuckles in her eyes. 'Want to do it here.'

'I see.' Claudia took up the box and deliberately replaced the lid. She turned to the distressed Maria and said haltingly,

'*Eu minha culpa,* Maria, *disculpe-me.*'

'*De nada, senhora,*' the gentle black face lit with its usual white smile.

'It certainly is *not* your fault, Claudia.' Bea put a weary hand to her forehead with a helpless little gesture.

'I did say she could come back here to colour, and of

course I should have realised it would be inconvenient,'
said Claudia reasonably. However, there was certainly
no need for all that shouting.'

'What's happened to her dress?' said Bea with
disapproval. 'The dressmaker spent a lot of time on that
embroidery.'

'She caught the pocket on a nail.' Claudia glanced
round at the interested faces of the other maids, who
had both run to see what was happening.

Bea followed her look and said immediately,

'Lourdes, *café, por favor*. Afra, *lava* Becky *e trouça o
vestido d'ela*. Come, Claudia.'

Having sorted out everything and given instructions
for Becky to be fetched to the verandah when she was
clean and her dress was changed, Bea swept out.
Claudia followed, carrying the box.

'My box!' howled Becky, as she was borne away in
Afra's arms.

'I'll keep it safe for you,' promised Claudia, and
hurried through the dining-room—to cannon blindly
into the large, solid figure of Saul Treharne, who
steadied her by the upper arms, frowning blackly into
her startled face.

'What the devil's going on?' he ground out. 'I
thought the idea was to make friends with Becky, not
reduce her to hysteria.'

Bea was behind him, her face creased with distress.

'It's all easily explained, Saul,' she began uneasily.

'Then by all means let Claudia do so,' he said,
releasing Claudia's arms, which were still clutched
around the cause of all the trouble, Becky's box.

'Perhaps I could do so out of earshot of the maids,'
she said quietly.

Saul gave her a frosty look, then waved her in front
of him.

'Very well.'

Claudia marched out to the verandah with her head
held high, and sat down on one of the upright chairs at
the table. Bea followed her and began pouring coffee.
She handed a cup to Saul, who stood leaning against
the verandah rail to drink it, the mere size of him

seeming more daunting than usual as he waited for Claudia's explanation. She related the incident in a few brief words, hoping she appeared relaxed as she drank her coffee. Something in her casual attitude seemed to annoy Saul. He raked a hand through his thick black hair, his mouth compressed.

'It would seem, then, that your present was the root of the trouble—which rather underlines my theory that gifts for no particular reason do more harm than good for small children.'

'Had I been aware of your veto on presents,' answered Claudia, an icy glitter in her eyes, 'I would naturally not have gone against your wishes. I merely thought a few pens and pencils and colouring books might trigger off an interest which would pave the way for lessons.'

Bea intervened in an attempt to lighten the atmosphere.

'What are you doing at home this time of the day, Saul? Claudia said you would be out for lunch.'

'I just called in for some cigars on the way to the Dam.' Saul stood upright, his face grim. 'I'd have done better to go without——'

He broke off as a small figure came hesitantly through the door in a fresh blue dress, her face shining and apprehensive, the silver-gilt hair re-braided.

'Hello, Becky.'

'Hello.' She eyed him warily, then gave him an uncertain smile. 'Want to see my present?'

Claudia felt an ignoble flush of triumph as Becky took her father's hand and led him to the box, showing him each inexpensive item with guileless enthusiasm, all traces of her tantrum disappeared. Saul examined all the bits and pieces with due interest and pronounced the present very thoughtful, asking his daughter if Claudia had been thanked properly.

'I said thank you—didn't I, Claudia?' She gave a swift look over her shoulder in appeal.

'Indeed you did, Becky, very nicely.' Claudia felt a little exaggeration would do no harm under the circumstances.

'Shall I do a picture for you?' Becky asked her father. His face held an unreadable expression as he looked down into the enquiring little face.

'Could you do it by the time I come home this evening? I have to get back to work now.'

'O.K.,' she said airily, and with a brush of his hand over her head Saul stood up.

'Would you walk to the jeep with me, Claudia?' he asked civilly, and bent to kiss his aunt. 'See you this evening, Aunt Bea.'

His aunt watched him with troubled eyes as he descended the verandah steps with Claudia reluctantly following him. She shook her head and turned back to Becky, who was demanding advice as to which picture 'he' would like.

Certain she was in for another lecture, Claudia was surprised when they reached the jeep without Saul saying a word. She stood looking up into his dark, withdrawn face, her hands in the pockets of the green trousers, the sunshine pinpointing fiery glints in her rather untidy hair.

'That was a storm in a teacup,' said Saul finally. He leaned against the dusty bonnet of the jeep, staring morosely down at his even dustier boots. 'I apologise. You were, of course, very kind to buy Becky a present.'

'The entire incident sounded a lot worse than it really was,' said Claudia, in what she hoped was a conciliating tone. 'I promised Becky that she could paint a picture after she'd shown me round the garden and she was, not unnaturally, incensed when she found she couldn't.'

Saul sighed.

'I'm afraid Becky reacts adversely to discipline.' He shot a sudden look at her attentive face. 'I depend on you to accustom her to it gradually. One day she'll have to go to school in the U.K., and life will be pretty hard for her if she can't conform to some extent.'

Claudia nodded.

'I agree.' She hesitated, then looked at him squarely. 'Am I to be given a free hand with how I deal with Becky, or do you have some modus operandi you wish me to follow? It will avoid problems if I know precisely where I am from the start.'

Saul pushed his large frame upright and opened the door of the jeep, his face remote and impersonal.

'Becky's education and behaviour are your department entirely. I shall only intervene if I find myself in total disagreement.' With a curt nod he got in the driver's seat and started the engine, backing the vehicle up the steep drive with the speed of long practice, José appearing instantly to close the gates behind the jeep as it swung out and disappeared rapidly down the hill.

Claudia was thoughtful as she mounted the verandah steps. Saul's answer had been very ambiguous, leaving her none the wiser. She could pursue her own course with the child, apparently, as long as it never ran contrary to Saul Treharne's. Indian giver! she thought crossly, the smiled at the peaceful scene that met her eyes. Bea was sitting in one of the easy chairs knitting, and Becky was installed at the table colouring in her new book with her felt-tip pens, the tip of her tongue between her teeth and a look of furious concentration on the flawless little face. She tore her eyes away from the page for an instant as Claudia appeared, then resumed her labours with painstaking care.

Bea's eyes twinkled over her gold-rimmed spectacles as she laid down her knitting.

'Hauled over the coals?'

Claudia sat down at the table to inspect the artist's progress.

'No. I'm not sure, but I rather think it was more of an apology, really.' She smiled mischievously. 'It was rather difficult to tell.'

'It quite often is.' Bea shook her head regretfully and returned to the small white cardigan she was making for Becky.

It was no surprise to Claudia to see that the picture Becky was patiently colouring was done with accuracy, the various colours kept within the outlines with precision. She was applying herself to an illustration from *Pinocchio* with a great regard for harmony and contrast in her choice of colour, and with a final careful

shading in of blue sky as background she finished the
scene and sat up straight with a look of satisfaction on
her face.

'There!' Her blue eyes blazed with triumph.
'Finished. Look!' She pushed it across the table for
Claudia to see, her face expectant as she waited for
the verdict.

Claudia examined the finished work with due care,
then nodded with approval.

'Very good indeed, Becky. I like your choice of
colours very much. Well done!'

The look of unguarded delight on the child's face was
infinitely rewarding as Becky slid off her chair and ran
to Bea with her work of art.

'Look, Aunt Bea, look at my picture!'

Bea joined in the compliments and gave permission
for the little girl to run off and show her masterpiece to
the maids, smiling fondly as the small figure in the frilly
blue dress dashed off to the kitchen, calling to Maria as
she went.

'She really did well with that, Claudia. I think her
main problem is boredom; she just needs something to
occupy her fully.'

'All children do,' agreed Claudia. 'A case of
channelling their energies, that's all. I think Becky will
be quite happy to start lessons.'

An atmosphere of cordiality prevailed over the lunch
table, with Becky eating everything put in front of her
as she listened to the conversation of the two grown-
ups, Bea naturally being deeply interested in the latest
news from England.

'I miss a great many things, of course,' she admitted.
'Television, friends, and my visits to the local library.
Books are in short supply here.'

'When my trunk arrives you can have your pick of
any of mine,' Claudia offered instantly, glad she had
something of some use to the other woman.

After lunch Afra appeared to take Becky off for a
while, and with her artist's equipment in hand she
skipped off happily with the maid to do another picture
out in the garden in the shade of the trees.

Claudia looked at Bea searchingly when they were alone.

'Are you feeling quite well? You ate very little.'

'To be honest I'm not.' Bea brushed a hand over her forehead, wincing. 'I think I have a migraine coming on—I get them rather often, I'm afraid.'

'Did the rumpus with Becky this morning start it off?'

'Not so much the fuss itself, but Saul walking in on it, I think.'

Claudia felt stricken.

'I'm very sorry—it was all my fault. What can I do for you?'

Bea rose to her feet with care, giving Claudia a wan smile.

'Not very much; no one can. And it certainly wasn't your fault. We've had much worse scenes than that during these past few months.' She patted Claudia's hand. 'I shall take two of my pills, lie down on my bed and sleep it off behind drawn curtains. That usually does the trick.'

Possessing excellent health herself, Claudia felt a little helpless in the face of Bea's obvious distress.

'You get into bed,' she suggested, 'and I'll bring you a cold drink to take with your tablets.'

She saw Bea to her room, then went into the kitchen and asked Maria haltingly for iced orange juice for Dona Bea. She took it along to Bea's room and saw her settled down in the cool gloom of the curtained room, then wandered back to the verandah feeling at a decidedly loose end. Reading seemed the answer, but where to find a book. She went on tiptoe through the hall and approached Saul's study, opening the door hesitantly, remembering only too well that Saul disliked anyone trespassing on his private domain, but with no idea where else to look for something to read. Among the hundreds of volumes on the shelves there was very little fiction, and furtively, like an intruder, Claudia glanced quickly along the titles, most of which were not to her taste. Right at the end of one shelf she found several books by Daphne du Maurier, and chose two, *Rebecca* and *Frenchman's Creek*, first read when she

was a teenager. Claudia hastily left the shadowy room
and went back to her own. She sat down on the bed,
wondering which to read first. As she opened the copy
of *Rebecca* she saw on the flyleaf the inscription 'Elaine,
from Saul, Happy Birthday'. Claudia snapped the book
shut, breathing quickly, conscious of a feeling of
intrusion.

Something fluttered to the floor—a snapshot. Almost
unwillingly Claudia bent to retrieve it. It was the
photograph of a young girl in a brief bathing suit
leaning against rocks on a beach. Golden hair streamed
away from the pure oval of her face and she was
laughing, invitation in every perfect line of the slender
body. So that's Elaine, thought Claudia. Saul had no
need of photographs to recall his wife's face to mind;
Becky was the image of her mother, her face a perfect
facsimile except for its youth and her father's dark blue
eyes. The eyes of the girl in the photograph were half
closed against the sun, their colour impossible to make
out. Very carefully Claudia replaced the snapshot in the
book, then went quietly back to the study and replaced
both books exactly where they were on the shelf.

CHAPTER FIVE

As Claudia left the room Becky came running towards
her with her colouring book. She stopped short as she
saw Claudia, her eyes bright and curious.

'We mustn't go in there—he doesn't like it.'

'I know, Becky. I just wanted to borrow a book, but
your daddy doesn't have any I like.'

Becky lost interest.

'Where's Aunt Bea?' she demanded. 'On the
verandah?'

Claudia shook her head and put a finger to her lips,
taking Becky's hand.

'She's lying down with a headache, so let's go out this
way not to disturb her.'

Claudia and Becky went out to the shady verandah, where Becky looked in her magic box and came up with a carton containing a hundred pieces of jigsaw puzzle that made up a scene from *Snow White and the Seven Dwarfs*. Claudia sent the little girl to beg a tray from Maria, then they both set to with a will to fit the sturdy pieces together once Claudia had established a little of the border. After a while she left Becky and went very quietly to check up on Bea, glad to find her deeply asleep.

When she got back to the verandah Claudia laughed as she saw Becky's progress.

'You've done jigsaws before, young lady, you're too fast for words!'

Becky nodded, her face shadowed.

'But it's no fun doing them on my own.'

'No, Becky, I know.' Claudia was touched. 'Never mind, I'm here now—not that you need much help from me.'

With Claudia to look on and encourage Becky finished the puzzle in record time, a look of such pure glee on her face when she regarded the finished picture Claudia had to resist the impulse to hug her. Softly, softly, catchee monkey, she reminded herself and confined herself to praise on Becky's skill. Soon afterwards Lourdes came to collect Becky for her bath, Claudia promising faithfully to take care of the puzzle for display to Bea and her father later.

As she let herself quietly into the hall Lourdes informed her that Becky had finished her bath and was on the verandah. Claudia went quickly to join her, hesitating a little as a tall, dusty figure rose from one of the long chairs at her approach.

'Good evening, Claudia.' Saul looked tired, the lines pronounced at the corners of his mouth, the cleft in his chin deeply shadowed. 'Please forgive my unprepossessing state. One of the great advantages of a verandah like this is that it allows me to have a drink as soon as I get in, without changing first.'

'Good evening. Where's Becky?'

'Fetching the picture she coloured this afternoon.'

His face relaxed a little. 'I've already admired the puzzle. Have a drink.' He gestured towards the tray on the table.

'Thank you. Gin and tonic, please.' Claudia sat down on an upright chair at the table, accepting the long, frosty glass he handed her and smiled as Becky, looking like a Pre-Raphaelite angel in a white cotton nightgown, ran in with her colouring book open at the picture of Pinocchio.

'See,' she said proudly, as Saul sat down and took the book, 'I did it all by myself! Claudia only watched.'

It was absurd how gratified Claudia felt to hear her name come naturally to the child's lips, though she had as yet to hear Becky refer to Saul in any way but 'he' or 'him'.

Saul inspected the picture with solemn attention before giving his verdict. Becky waited anxiously, studying his face expectantly.

'I should say that's the best painted picture of Pinocchio I've ever seen,' he said gravely, then looked at Becky with a smile, his teeth white in his dark face, transforming it completely from its usual expressionless mask. Instantly an answering smile lit his daughter's more volatile countenance.

'I'll do another one tomorrow—if you like,' she offered, elaborately off-hand.

'I would like—very much,' her father assured her. 'Do one after breakfast and show me at lunch time, but for the moment I rather think it's time for bed, young lady.'

'Aunt Bea always tucks me in,' mumbled Becky, casting a look of appeal in Claudia's direction.

'As she's not well tonight, would I do instead?' said Claudia promptly.

Her only answer was a careless nod, and with another goodnight in Saul's direction Becky went off through the dining room with Claudia following behind.

In the pretty little bedroom Claudia popped the child into bed and tucked the sheet around her, her eyes lingering on the lovely little face in its frame of shining gilt hair.

'Goodnight, God bless, Becky,' she said quietly.

'' 'Night.' Becky's eyes followed Claudia's figure out
of the room. On impulse Claudia popped her head back
round the door and blew a kiss to the surprised child,
then rejoined Saul on the verandah.

'How is my aunt?' he asked, as Claudia sat down.

'Her migraine came on rather badly after lunch, so
she went to lie down, I think she's probably asleep. I'll
check again when I've changed.' Claudia drank the
remaining liquid in her glass and smiled politely at the
long, relaxed figure in the reclining chair. 'Have you
had a hectic day?'

'Very.' His eyes narrowed in amusement. 'How
domesticated we sound!'

Claudia was glad the darkness hid the colour in her
cheeks.

'I was just making conversation.' Her voice was tart.

'You don't have to. After running after Becky all day
long I assure you the evenings are your own. There's no
obligation to entertain me.'

Offended, Claudia said nothing after that, for several
minutes they sat in silence, Saul apparently perfectly
relaxed, while the sounds and perfumes of evening rose
up from the garden below.

'What's that sound I can hear?' asked Claudia after a
while, her curiosity getting the better of her.

'Which? Maria's clattering of pans in the kitchen, or
music coming up from the town below——'

'No, I mean that constant sort of chirruping coming
from the garden. Is it some kind of night bird?'

'You mean the *grilos*—crickets. One gets so used to
the sound it's just part of life in Brazil, like the smell of
the *dama da noite*.' Saul ground out his cigarillo in an
ashtray, his head outlined by the light filtering through
the doors to the dining room.

'At the risk of being tiresome—what is *dama da
noite*?'

'Have you noticed the purple and white flowering
tree not far from the gates? It's scentless by day, but
once darkness falls it gives out the perfume you can
smell—unless the aroma of tobacco is defeating it.' Saul

sounded tired, admittedly, but much less distant than
Claudia had expected after the unfortunate incident of
the morning.

'I quite like the smell of your cheroot. Combined
with the flowers and the earth it typifies Brazil to me
already; exotic, different.' Claudia stood up, Saul
automatically doing the same.

'And do you think you can settle to life here?'

Claudia was almost persuaded her answer was
important to him. No doubt it was after all the money
invested in getting her here, she thought prosaically.

'Yes. Very easily,' she said positively. 'I think Becky
will knuckle down to her lessons very well once we
start, and as for myself, I would have to be very hard to
please if I couldn't enjoy living in a beautiful house like
this.'

'Even though it's so quiet here?'

'Ah, but then there's quiet and quiet.' Claudia cast a
sparkling glance up at the dimly-seen face of her
employer. 'The variety you have here could easily be
addictive, I think.'

Almost sure he smiled involuntarily in response,
Claudia excused herself and went off to bath and change
for dinner, a little uneasy at the prospect of dining alone
with her formidable host despite his slightly warmer
manner towards her. Some perverse instinct made her
choose her plainest dress, a shirtwaister in cinnamon
shantung, cut like a man's shirt, it's only gesture towards
frivolity the two gold tassels that swung at the end of the
hip-level sash. She brushed her hair back from her face
relentlessly, securing it in a knot on top of her head, made
up her face with a sparing hand, then hesitated and
weakened, choosing a pair of gold hoops to thread
through her earlobes rather than the tiny gold studs she
habitually wore.

When she was ready Claudia went quietly to look at
Becky, who lay on her back, arms outstretched, with all
the vulnerable beauty of a sleeping cherub. Claudia
gazed at the slumbering face for quite some time. If the
dead Elaine had been as lovely as her little daughter it
was hardly surprising Saul had become so embittered

when she left him for another man. Gently Claudia drew the sheet over Becky and tiptoed noiselessly from the room, hesitating in the corridor, wondering about Bea. Silently she crossed the polished expanse of the dark hall and very carefully opened Bea's door. The room was in darkness and quiet, even breathing seemed to indicate that the invalid was sleeping peacefully, so with no desire to disturb her Claudia backed out of the room and closed the door.

All at once Claudia was aware she was hungry. Lunch had been a long time ago, and her athletic, healthy body was in need of refuelling. Delicious smells came from the kitchen as she opened the door to find Maria busily occupied with preparations for dinner, with Lourdes in attendance.

'*O patrão está na varanda*, Dona Claudia,' said Lourdes shyly, and Claudia smiled her thanks, indicating how heavenly the food smelt, to Maria's obvious pleasure. Claudia would have much preferred to stay in the kitchen and watch operations, but realised her presence would only hinder, and went through the brightly lit dining room, with its attractively laid table, and joined Saul, who was leaning in his favourite place against the rail, glass in hand as he stared down at the lights of the town. A fat candle in the glass-shaped copper holder on the table gave a faint illumination, augmented by the light of the moon just rising over the peak of Morro d'Ouro, with its lighted cross at the summit.

Saul turned as Claudia joined him.

'You were remarkably swift,' he said dryly. 'I thought women generally took a fair time over their toilette, or whatever one calls it, so I told Maria to hold dinner for another fifteen minutes or so.'

'I can't answer for other women,' she retorted, 'but half an hour is positively lingering as far as I'm concerned.'

Saul moved over to the tray on the table.

'Gin and tonic?'

Claudia felt doubtful.

'I don't know that I should. I feel a bit empty, to

be truthful, and more gin might have a disastrous effect.'

He laughed, a sound as attractive as it was unfamiliar, and insisted on a small drink, handing her a dish of peanuts.

'Have some of these to keep the hunger pangs at bay,' he suggested. 'There are some olives here too, if you care for them.'

Claudia accepted the nuts with enthusiasm, but refused the olives.

'I've heard they're an acquired taste, but I've never had enough of them to acquire it.' She wandered over to the rail and looked out on the moonlit scene, shaking her head in wonder. 'This is unreal. It looks like a film set.'

Saul resumed his place beside her, and to her dismay Claudia found herself overreacting to the accidental touch of his arm against hers. Suddenly aware in every nerve of the large, lounging presence beside her, she began to eat peanuts with nervous speed, with the aim of keeping herself occupied.

'One gets used to it.' Saul's profile was clearly limned against the night sky as he looked down on the lights of the town. 'It looks unearthly from up here at this time of night, especially when there's a moon, I grant you, but in reality everyone down there is occupied with the serious business of the evening meal, eating enormous quantities of beans and rice, pork or *carne seca*, a type of salted, dried meat, and all kinds of dishes I can't begin to describe. I'll take you out to one of the substations one day and have the wife of the Power Engineer cook you a meal. An experience you won't forget, I assure you—the table literally groans!'

Claudia laughed, then looked down guiltily at the dish she held, realising all the peanuts were gone.

'Sounds like my idea of fun,' she said, glad of the excuse to move away to replace the dish on the tray. 'My appetite was famous in college.'

She turned to find Saul giving her a very deliberate appraisal, his eyes leisurely in their examination of her graceful, slim-hipped figure.

'It's hard to credit,' he said mockingly. 'You look as if you live on leafy green vegetables and yoghourt.'

'I do,' said Claudia, with a smile up at his definitely friendlier face, feeling reassured and more relaxed in the appreciably warmer atmosphere between them. 'But I eat stacks of other things as well. I'm lucky, I suppose, it's just metabolism.'

Lourdes's appearance signalled the arrival of dinner, and despite the warmth of the evening Claudia sat down to steaming julienne soup with gusto, aware of Saul's amused eyes on her, but in no way put out as she enjoyed the spicy, vegetable-filled liquid. There was little conversation while Claudia blunted the first edge of her hunger, but when the *camaroes baiana* appeared the dish itself was a conversation piece. King-sized prawns, cooked in a hot peppery tomato sauce, were served on a bed of fried rice and accompanied by runner beans, okra and marrow, or *quiabo* and *xu-xu*, as the latter were known as locally. Claudia was almost lost for words.

'This is absolutely fantastic—I've never tasted anything more delicious!'

Saul laughed outright, neglecting his own meal to watch the relish with which Claudia attacked hers. She looked up at him, her long grey eyes sparkling.

'You should laugh more often,' she said bluntly.

He went on with his dinner, the laughter fading from his strongly-marked face immediately, the dark blue eyes shuttered. Claudia cursed herself silently for a tactless idiot and searched for a neutral topic of conversation.

'Does Becky see much of the Fonseca children?' she asked in desperation.

'No, not all that much. She and Jamie are inclined to clash if too long in each other's company.' He clicked his fingers impatiently. 'A good thing you mentioned them. Luc said Emily would like you to go over there to visit. She's given you a day's grace to settle in, but will probably ring tomorrow. I'm sorry, it went clean out of my head.'

'Not to worry.' Claudia felt curious about the wife of

Luc Fonseca. 'What age-group are the Fonsecas? They
have young children, I know, but I assume that if he's
the owner Senhor Fonseca is an older man.'

There was a delay while Lourdes removed their plates
and put the cheeseboard and a compote of fresh figs on
the table.

Saul helped himself to cheese, his face wooden again.

'Why are you interested in Luc Fonseca?'

Claudia blinked. What had she said now?

'I'm not particularly, at least only in relation to
Senhora Fonseca,' she said carefully. 'I was interested
in her because she's British, I suppose.' Forget about
making conversation, Claudia, she told herself grimly.
Just get on with your dinner.

There was silence for a while as Claudia kept her eyes
on the fruit in her crystal dish, refusing to look up. For
once her pleasure in her food was impaired, and she
was obliged to abandon her dessert after only a
mouthful or two, deeply resentful that her appetite had
taken any notice of Saul's censorious attitude.

'Shall we drink coffee in the drawing room?' said
Saul, rising to his feet.

Claudia followed suit with reluctance. She had little
desire to sit à deux with him, even for the short time it
would take to dispose of a *cafezinho*.

'If you don't mind . . .' she began stiffly, but he cut her
short and held open the verandah door peremptorily.

'Oh, but I do,' he said with emphasis. 'Lourdes will
have checked on Bea and Becky, so there's no reason
why you can't spend a peaceful half-hour or so talking,
or listening to records if you prefer.'

Claudia stalked across the verandah and through the
open doors of the drawing-room, settling herself on the
comfortable couch as Saul entered the room. She
ignored the coffee-tray on the table in front of her and
took the bull by the horns.

'Before I pour out I must be honest and say a
peaceful half-hour, as you put it, would be very
pleasant. But, Mr Treharne—Saul,' she amended hastily
in response to his wagging finger, 'I don't care much for
conversations where I appear obliged to guard

constantly against putting my foot in it. It's wearing.'
Her grey eyes were bright and stormy as she locked
glances with the man who stood rock-still with surprise,
looming over her like a lighthouse.

'Is that how you feel?' His thick black brows rose
almost to the equally thick hair beginning to stray
across his forehead as he ran his fingers through it,
some of his imperturbability lost at her sudden attack.

Claudia nodded and poured out two cups of coffee,
rather triumphant to see how steady her hand remained
as it handed Saul's to him. He took it absently, and
drank it down in one swallow, apparently careless of
scalding his throat.

'Liqueur?' he asked.

She shook her head and sipped her own coffee with
more caution. I suppose that's torn it, she thought
despondently. Just as things were beginning to relax a
bit too. Oh well, in for a penny, in for a pound. 'There's
something else,' she added.

'Perhaps I'd better sit down,' he murmured, his blue
eyes expressionless as he sat opposite, his face all polite
attention. 'Do go on.'

'When I was at a loose end this afternoon I had
nothing to read. Bea had shown me your study briefly,
and as it was the only place where there seemed to be
any books I borrowed one.' Claudia paused, but he said
nothing, merely looking at her steadily. 'A snapshot fell
out of the book; someone so like Becky it must have
been your wife. I felt as though I'd trespassed, so I put
the book back without reading it. I'm sorry—I won't go
in your study again.'

'What was the book?'

Claudia looked at him uncertainly.

'Daphne du Maurier's *Rebecca*.'

Saul nodded, and held out his cup for more coffee.

'It would have been—it was her favourite. You might
say Elaine was obsessed by it; she even called our
daughter Rebecca.'

Claudia gave him his coffee and leaned back against
the sofa cushions, not sure if he was annoyed or merely
indifferent.

'You have absolutely no need for embarrassment, or sympathy,' he said, a sardonic twist to his mouth. 'I've no objection to your frequenting the study—borrow what you like. If you're concerned about my—er—feelings, for want of a better word, don't be. Any I had for Elaine underwent rather a violent metamorphosis when she left me for a wealthier man and took my child with her. And please don't imagine I'm nursing any secret sorrow,' he added. 'Elaine taught me a very valuable lesson. All women have a price. Someone else offered her a higher price than I could pay, and off she went.'

'It's surely not possible to generalise to that extent,' objected Claudia.

'The price varies, Claudia, that's all. Elaine's was a luxury life style, Becky was won over today by a present. You——' he paused, a mocking smile on his lips as she started, sitting bolt upright. 'You, Claudia, stood out for more money before you'd take the job. Admittedly it was in the name of security, a condition beloved by you above all else, as I heard it, nevertheless it was a price. Only the degree is different—the principle is more or less the same.'

Claudia sat very still for a moment or two.

'Miss Treharne said the extra sum would be something private; an agreement purely between herself and me,' she said quietly. All was now revealed, she thought fatalistically. At least she now had the key to Saul Treharne's attitude towards her.

'Unfortunately both my aunt and myself are B.S. Treharne. I opened her bank statement by mistake and the sum in question was large enough to be conspicuous before I realised my error.' Saul poured himself a brandy and sat down again, his eyes sombre on the liquid in his glass. 'I was worried, naturally, about Aunt Bea's need to spend such an amount, and asked about it when I apologised for opening the wrong letter. She was obliged to tell me how she prevailed upon you to leave England.'

There was nothing in the least condemnatory in his deep voice, yet Claudia felt guilty, degraded, like a criminal caught redhanded. There seemed no point in trying to vindicate herself, so she kept quiet, her cheeks burning.

'You don't spring to your own defence?' He sat relaxed, quite obviously enjoying her discomfiture.

Claudia raised her head and looked at him levelly.

'I don't have one. With no family behind me I needed the security a lump sum in the bank would represent before leaving not just England, but the very good job I had there. If there is any defence, as you put it,' she added, 'I would stress that I made this very clear when I turned down the post in the first place. There were, after all, several other applicants your aunt could have chosen.'

His answering look was saturnine.

'Yes, indeed. Any one of whom was older, more suitable, in my estimation, and had the advantage of being a damned sight cheaper!'

Claudia was stung.

'I may be younger than you wished, Mr Treharne,' she said tightly, 'but my teaching abilities are proven and above question. My qualifications aren't so bad, either. I intend to make a good job of Becky's education, in all departments; even my so-called youth is an advantage, surely, when it comes to games and swimming.'

'Oh, I grant you all the attributes,' said Saul mockingly. 'It's such a shame you happen to be so mercenary as well, don't you agree?'

'You can hardly expect me to agree to that!' Claudia's nostrils flared as she took a deep breath to steady herself. 'The extra money was a great incentive. I grant you that. Even so it wasn't the deciding factor. Apart from the instant rapport I felt with your aunt she said the one thing, quite unknowingly, which made her offer irresistible; the bit about being welcomed into your family in your home. You already know about the orphanage. I've lived in institutions of one kind or another for most of my life. My price, if you must think of it in that way, wasn't only the money, generous and tempting though it was. It was the idea of being accepted in someone's home as part of their family.' Her eyes were clear and cold on his. 'I'm sorry you consider me an unsuitable addition to your household, Mr Treharne.'

'I don't consider you unsuitable in the least,' Saul said surprisingly.

Claudia managed a crooked little smile.

'Just expensive! Don't worry—I'll do my utmost to prove worthy of my hire, Mr Treharne.'

'I'm relieved to hear it.' He rose to his full, towering height and drained his glass, then crossed to pour himself another brandy. 'Sure I can't persuade you to a liqueur?'

Claudia shook her head.

'No, thank you.'

' "Saul",' he prompted.

This seemed a night for clearing the air. Claudia looked up at him with an odd little smile.

'I'm afraid it doesn't come easily. In my mind you've been "Mr Rochester" from the beginning—my literary hang-up was *Jane Eyre*, not *Rebecca*.'

Saul stiffened and turned on her with an air of menace only half-feigned.

'Spare me any more unhealthy fixations on fictional characters, for God's sake—I've had enough of that sort of thing to last a lifetime!'

Something suddenly occurred to Claudia.

'If you knew about the money before I came why didn't you stop me coming? There would have been time—you could have engaged one of the others.'

Saul turned away to the open doorway, leaning against the lintel to look out into the night.

'Too many wheels had been set in motion by then,' he said. 'Besides, if Aunt Bea was sufficiently determined you were the only one possible, to the point of paying the added inducement out of her own pocket, who was I to go against her wishes?'

'I see.' Claudia looked thoughtfully at his broad back.

Saul swung round to look at her with a disturbing gleam in his eyes.

'Not quite, Claudia. You had your price, but I felt it was up to me to pay it, as Becky's father. So I reimbursed Aunt Bea for every penny. Contractually, at least, you are now my property.'

A trickle of cold apprehension ran down Claudia's spine, but her eyes met his unflinchingly, as clear and expressionless as panes of glass. The abrading quality of his tone flayed the outer skin of her composure badly, and she rose to her feet without hurry, even managing the suggestion of a yawn to mask her erratic pulse.

'There's really not a lot to say in answer to that, Mr Treharne,' she said evenly. 'Goodnight.'

'Goodnight, Claudia.' Saul was swift to open the door for her, his eyes hard and mocking on her face. 'By the way, if scraping your hair back like that is a gesture towards the Jane Eyre image, it doesn't really work—you're a damned sight too down-to-earth and contemporary to sustain the effect!'

Claudia glared at him for an instant, abandoning her careful inscrutability, then walked quietly away through the hall, her head in the air as she forced herself to walk slowly in the direction of her bedroom.

CHAPTER SIX

CLAUDIA was up by seven next morning, guiltily aware that in her vexation the night before she had quite forgotten to look in on either Bea or Becky before falling into her bed. After a speedy shower she dressed in black cotton slacks and a long sleeveless white tunic with a white-dotted black scarf tied at the waist.

A peep into Becky's room showed the child still fast asleep, and Claudia hurried along to Bea's room to find the door ajar and Bea sitting up in bed drinking a cup of tea and looking a great deal better. She smiled at Claudia in welcome.

'Good morning, you're an early riser. How are you today?'

'I'm fine, but how are you?' Claudia went in, her face

apologetic. 'I was so—tired—last night I forgot to come
and see you before I went to bed.'

'That's all right, my dear. Saul brought me some fruit
juice last thing, but my headache had almost gone by
then, and with the aid of yet more pills I had quite a
good night. He mentioned you were very tired. One's
inclined to forget about the altitude, but it makes a
tremendous difference, you know. You must be
careful.'

'I will. I'll just see if Becky has surfaced yet. She was
still sleeping a moment ago.' Claudia felt very guilty at
Bea's solicitude.

'I'll be with you for breakfast in half an hour.' Bea
smiled briskly. 'One day in bed in this heat is quite
enough!'

Claudia went back to Becky's room to find that
young lady sitting on the floor in her nightdress poring
over the contents of her beloved box.

'Hello. You're starting early this morning!'

'Hello.'

There was a marked lack of enthusiasm in the child's
greeting as she cast a careless look up at Claudia, but at
least she was not precisely hostile. Lourdes arrived to
dress Becky, so Claudia wandered off to walk round the
garden in the early morning sunshine, surprised to find
how warm it was even at that hour. She said good
morning to Afra, who was sweeping out the servants'
quarters, and strolled down the terraced lawns to look
past red roofs and clusters of greenery to the white
supports of the flume far below. The thought of
breakfast drew her back to the house, which she entered
through the kitchen, greeting the smiling Maria, who
told her the meal was waiting on the verandah.

Becky was already there, in a pale yellow muslin
dress, yellow ribbons at the end of her pigtails.

'Do I have to do lessons today?' she demanded, her
face belligerent.

'No.' Claudia sat down at the table, motioning Becky
to take her place. 'Your father says after Christmas is
soon enough.'

'When's Christmas?'

'In a week or so—not long.'

Bea came out to join them and poured tea while Claudia and Becky began their meal. She passed Claudia's cup and asked how they were going to spend the day, her eyes bright and clear, all traces of her migraine disappeared.

'I'm going to do more pictures,' announced Becky instantly, with a challenging look at both women to see if there was any opposition.

'Fine,' said Claudia casually, and helped herself to scrambled eggs and toast, hungry despite the excellent dinner consumed the evening before. She looked up at Bea enquiringly. 'Is this the hottest part of the year? It's very warm outside even at this hour.'

'No. January and February, even March, can be quite a lot hotter than this, and of course we get quite a lot of rain, too.' Bea looked at Claudia curiously. 'I hope your evening passed fairly amicably, my dear?'

'Yes, thank you. Reasonably so.'

'I'm glad.' Bea coughed delicately. 'You seem to—well, affect each other a little adversely. Saul really can be quite charming.'

Claudia smiled, shrugging.

'I'm sure a big part of the fault is mine.'

'You ring the little bell for Lourdes to clear away, Becky,' said Bea, avoiding Claudia's eye, 'and then you can start on your colouring.'

For an hour peace reigned on the verandah while Bea returned to her knitting and Claudia just lay relaxed in a long chair, chatting desultorily while Becky brought the full force of her attention to bear on a picture of Hansel and Gretel. The sound of the telephone eventually disturbed the quiet and Claudia got up to examine Becky's picture while Bea answered the phone.

'Is it nice?' asked Becky, her tongue curling out over her upper lip in her concentration on the tiles of the gingerbread house.

'I prefer to use the word "nice" for things to eat,' said Claudia. 'Your picture is very attractive, Becky.' She looked down on the bright gold head, wondering if the child still missed her mother. There had been tears of temper since Claudia's arrival, admittedly, but not of grief, though it was difficult to tell what went on in that complicated little brain.

Bea came back with a wide smile on her face.

'That was Emily. She announced that her curiosity has been contained long enough, and could Saul drop us off at Casa d'Ouro after lunch to spend the afternoon there.'

Becky looked up sharply.

'Can I take my box?'

'It might be a good idea to take just one or two things,' suggested Claudia. 'Otherwise there might be problems.'

'No,' said Becky instantly, an ominous frown darkening her face.

'Well, you could stay here with Lourdes and Maria, of course,' said Claudia reasonably. Something in her manner plainly told Becky discretion was necessary, and with a pout she returned to her painting.

Bea watched with admiration and patted Claudia's hand silently.

'Coffee-time, I think,' she announced. 'Becky, would you be kind enough to ask Maria to make coffee and tell her what you want; that is if you can?'

' 'Course I can,' said Becky loftily, and slid off her chair to run to the kitchen.

'I thought I'd take a leaf out of your book,' said Bea with a smile.

'I'm used to children,' said Claudia practically. 'By the way, it's kind of Mrs Fonseca to invite us over.'

'She would have sooner, she said, but she thought it best to let you get your bearings first.' Bea's eyes twinkled. 'Don't forget, we lead a quiet life here. Any diversion is welcome.'

'Thank you! I've never thought of myself in the light of a diversion.' Claudia laughed, then looked down at herself. 'Should I change?'

'Not unless you want to. You look very elegant as you are. How I wish trousers had been worn when I was your age!'

Saul was home to lunch promptly, Claudia feeling distinctly apprehensive as she heard his jeep arrive outside, but one look at his face as he ran up the steps lightly gave her reassurance. The forbidding manner was absent, and he smiled in a friendly fashion as he greeted all three, kissing his aunt, acknowledging Claudia casually and demanding to see the latest masterpiece from his artistic daughter. The agreeable change in his attitude made lunch a pleasant meal, at which Claudia had her first taste of brown Brazilian beans cooked with garlic and butter, and served with rice, a minute steak and salad. Becky, obviously fond of beans and rice, ate her portion with gusto, also the fruit salad that followed.

'Luc tells me I'm commanded to take you all over to Casa d'Ouro on my way back to the mine,' said Saul, glancing at his watch. 'I trust all you ladies are ready, as I need to be off in ten minutes minimum.'

There was instant activity as Bea and Claudia went to make necessary repairs, and Becky flew to her box to choose which trophies to take on her visit, and shortly afterwards they were all installed in the jeep and on their way down the hill towards the town, veering away from it to skirt the foot of Morro d'Ouro and follow the winding road that brought them eventually through open gates into a garden filled with poinsettias and bougainvillaea, the curving drive coming to an end in front of another square house, bigger this time, virtually nestling among palms, with a verandah running almost the entire length of the front of it. Saul sounded the horn, then jumped from the jeep to lift down his aunt before receiving his daughter from Claudia, finally holding up his arms to swing her to the ground in turn, his hard hands warm through the thin cotton of her tunic.

'Tell Emily I'm in a hurry,' he said, and leapt back into the jeep. 'I'm meeting someone in two minutes.' With a squeal of tyres he waved and turned the vehicle in a circle to shoot back down the drive out of sight.

A small, elderly lady with snow white hair came to meet them, her carriage imposing despite the stick she leaned on slightly. Sharp dark eyes gave Claudia an all-encompassing look even as she kissed Bea on the cheek and patted Becky's head. Bea drew Claudia forward.

'Thurza, this is Claudia March, Becky's new governess. Claudia, this is my aunt, Thurza Treharne Fonseca.'

'How do you do, Miss March. Welcome to Casa d'Ouro.'

Claudia smiled politely.

'How do you do, Senhora Fonseca. Thank you for inviting me.'

'To be accurate,' said Thurza Fonseca, with a slight smile, 'it was Emily who invited you, but at this moment she's involved in a minor crisis in the nursery. These crises happen several times a day, so it's not remarkable that one should occur just as you arrive. Do come in.'

Thurza led the way to a group of cushioned bamboo furniture very similar to those at Saul's house. She sat on a straight-backed chair and waved Bea and Claudia to the more comfortable seats, beckoning the little girl to her.

'And how are you today, Rebecca?'

Becky dropped her head and murmured, 'Very well, thank you,' obviously ill at ease with the old lady.

Thurza inclined her rigidly coifured head and told the child to run into the garden to look for Jamie, if she wished. Becky was off like a shot, only pausing long enough to give her painting book and pens to Claudia, with anxious instructions to take care of them.

Thurza turned her attention to Claudia, who was drinking in her surroundings with pleasure.

'And what are your first impressions of Brazil, Miss March?' The old eyes were observant, missing no detail of the slim figure sitting relaxed in the long chair.

Claudia decided the old lady possessed a far more astringent personality then her niece, and returned her assessing look with a direct gaze in her clear grey eyes that appeared to meet with Thurza's approval.

'Colour, light and warmth, Senhora Fonseca. I love England very much, but it was very cold and grey when I left Heathrow. This sunshine is a welcome contrast.'

'You were fortunate to arrive during a clear spell. At this time of the year one must expect frequent storms and heavy rain.' Thurza gave Claudia a shrewd look. 'I gather you taught at a girls' school. You'll find it different to concentrate all your energies on one small five-year-old, even one with as forceful a personality as Rebecca.'

'A great change,' agreed Claudia pleasantly. 'I shall enjoy the challenge.'

'She copes with Becky very well,' said Bea with satisfaction. 'My life is already becoming more relaxed.'

The sudden, ear-splitting cacophony of the macaws put an end to the exchange as a young girl emerged from the far wing, hand in hand with two small children. She came quickly along the verandah, light of step, her long, sun-streaked fair hair tied back with a red ribbon, the children breaking into a trot beside her. Blue eyes smiled in glad welcome at Claudia and Bea as the girl called.

'Hello, sorry I wasn't on hand to meet you.' She released the children and stooped to kiss Bea, looking up with undisguised curiosity at Claudia, who had risen to her feet. 'You must be Claudia. Welcome. I'm Emily Fonseca.'

Claudia smiled at her, somewhat at a loss. This serene, happy creature in the plain white sundress, though older than she had first thought, was still a far cry from the mature, sophisticated woman pictured as the mother of three children and chatelaine of this large, imposing house.

'How do you do,' said Claudia, her smiling eyes dropping to the two children. One was a boy of about four with a mop of dark curls and big dark eyes, in a tanned face with features already dominantly male. The other child was a girl, a year or two younger, with lint-white hair and her mother's blue eyes. They stared inquisitively at the newcomer, smiling shyly in response to Claudia's greeting.

'These are Mark and Lucy,' said Emily, and shooed her offspring away. 'Go and find Dirce, you two monsters, and ask her for a drink, then tell her to fetch a tray for us.' She turned to her guests. 'Where's Becky?'

'She went to find Jamie,' said Bea.

'And of course there'll be squabbling very soon as a result,' said Thurza dryly, 'so let us enjoy our peace and quiet while we can.'

Emily laughed and sat beside Claudia on the settee.

'We don't get too much peace here in the daytime. They all sleep well at night, thank God.'

There was a natural friendliness about Emily Fonseca that captivated Claudia instantly, and when a maid arrived with a tray of cold drinks the group split quite naturally into two parts, the older women enjoying a chat together while Emily unashamedly bombarded Claudia with questions about herself and her life in England, jumping to her feet after a while with the suggestion that the two of them took a stroll in the garden to find the children. She turned to Thurza and Bea with a smile of apology.

'You will excuse us, won't you, but I'm sure Claudia would like to see round the grounds.'

Thurza waved them off indulgently, presumably glad to indulge in a tête-à-tête with her niece.

Claudia followed the slim, white-clad figure down a flight of steps into the patio, past the aviary and out into the garden beyond, where clusters of palms and poinsettias gave pools of shade at intervals. For a while she and Emily wandered over the lawns, talking amicably on general subjects, eventually reaching a tall gate in the thick green foliage of a hibiscus hedge starred with brilliant coral-pink blossoms. Emily unlocked the imposing padlock on the gate and ushered Claudia through to look at a turquoise blue pool of impressive demensions, complete with diving boards and paved surround, sunbeds and garden chairs drawn up alongside it.

Mystified Claudia followed Emily to some white-painted chairs grouped around a table with a gay umbrella, out of sight of the verandah where the older women sat. Emily sat down, waving Claudia to another chair, a purposeful expression on the delicately-marked features of her attractive face.

'I want a private chat,' she said bluntly. 'I'm very fond of Thurza, but just this once I'd like to talk to you alone and sound you out.'

Claudia was intrigued.

'Fire away, Mrs Fonseca——' she stopped short as Emily shook her head.

'Thurza is Mrs Fonseca. I'm plain Emily.' She leaned her elbows on the table and said without preamble, 'I know it's a terrible cheek to ask, but I'm wondering if you'd consider teaching three children instead of one.'

Claudia drew in her breath, blinking, her first thought more concerned with Saul's reaction rather than her own.

'It's really not for me to answer that one,' she said frankly. 'Mr Treharne has put out a lot of money to get me over here to teach his daughter. I'm not sure how he'd feel about the idea.'

Emily nodded understandingly.

'I thought you might worry about Saul. Let's leave that side of it for a moment. The thing is, Claudia, how would *you* feel?'

Claudia thought it over carefully, watched anxiously by the other girl.

'Competition is good for children, of course. All three would probably do better academically with the stimulus of company.' She hesitated, her light eyes questioning. 'Correct me if I'm wrong, but do I gather Becky and Jamie don't get on too well?'

Emily smiled.

'Becky is a defensive, insecure child, and my elder son is a budding M.C.P.! He's never known anything but love and attention and behaves accordingly. The Latin in him takes over sometimes, even at his tender years. Becky secretly adores him, but he's at the age where girls are a nuisance, and orders her about, which she doesn't take very kindly to at all.' She made a face. 'I'm being honest, because there's no point in pulling the wool over your eyes. But from the point of view of lessons I sincerely believe they'd try harder together, and Mark could possibly do some simpler things too.'

'How old is Jamie?' asked Claudia, still somewhat taken aback by this new proposition.

'Six. So it means they are all different ages, but—not that I know anything about it, of course—I thought that might be an advantage. They could be doing three different things, but doing them together.' Emily's eyes were bright and persuasive, and Claudia knew perfectly well that were it left to herself to decide she would say yes on the spot.

'The numbers don't matter,' she said slowly. 'I'm obviously used to teaching fairly large classes. In some ways three would be better than one, in others I'm not sure. In any event it would up to Mr Treharne—I'm his employee.'

'Yes, I understand that,' persisted Emily, 'but if Saul's agreeable you wouldn't object?'

'No. No, I wouldn't.'

'Don't think we're trying to angle in on a good thing financially, of course,' Emily assured her. 'We're not trying to get something for nothing. We'd naturally pay two-thirds of your salary and give you an extra bonus on top.'

'My God, no!' Claudia looked at Emily aghast. 'No, please. Even if Saul does consent I don't *want* any more money. What I receive now is more than generous. Don't add to it. Your arrangements with Saul are naturally your own affair, but as far as I'm concerned I can't accept any additional payment.'

Emily stared at her in concern.

'I've obviously touched on a nerve.' She jumped up. 'Come on, let's find the children.'

They set off through the garden, Emily telling how Luc's idea had been to hire a tutor, but that Emily kept putting it off, not caring for the idea of a strange young man living with them. When Saul had announced Claudia's arrival as governess to Becky it had seemed like a splendid solution to everyone's problem. Emily cast a glance at the co-ordinated walk of the tall girl beside her and said frankly,

'With that figure you must be good at sport, which would be great, as I'm afraid I'm about to resign from the football team for the time being.'

Claudia halted, wondering if she'd received the right message.

'You mean——?'

Emily nodded, smiling serenely.

'I'm pregnant again. I had a miscarriage last year, so I shall have to watch my step this time.' She began to laugh softly at Claudia's expression. 'You look a bit stunned. Does my talent for reproduction embarrass you?'

Claudia found that it did, for some reason. As she looked at Emily she was beset by all sorts of feelings— wonder, anxiety, even envy. Envy? She caught herself up short. That was surely taking things a bit far!

'You seem very young to be the mother of several children, that's all,' she said. 'I thought you were a schoolgirl when I first caught sight of you.'

'I'm twenty-five.' Emily cast her a sidelong glance and said deliberately, 'Would it shock you if I said that my husband and I are highly compatible—in every way?' She laughed softly as the colour rose in Claudia's cheeks. 'Obviously it does. I'm sorry. How do you get on with Saul?'

Her sudden change of subject was a relief, though the question was a little difficult to answer, and Claudia had an uneasy feeling it was hardly the non sequitur it seemed.

'He was a little unbending at first,' she said carefully, almost tempted to confide in this charming, utterly natural creature. 'In fact I thought he actively disliked me on sight, but I gather it's not so much me personally, but his general attitude to most of the female sex.'

Emily looked at Claudia in astonishment.

'He's not in the least like that with me!'

Probably no one was like that with Emily Fonseca, thought Claudia sadly, following Emily to the source of noise near the servants' quarters at the back of the house, where the four children were milling round a perch, their voices raised in excitement.

When they all trooped up on to the verandah a long table was laid with a snowy embroidered cloth and set with dishes of dainty crustless sandwiches and tempting

small cakes and cookies. Tall pitchers of lemonade and
a silver tea service stood waiting on the trolley beside it.
Thurza and Bea looked up smiling as the warm,
perspiring group arrived.

'Say goodbye to peace and quiet now for a bit,
Thurza,' said Emily cheerfully.

'And very thankful I am to do so,' said the old lady
emphatically, to Claudia's surprise. 'The house had far
too much quiet for too many years. This is the way it
was intended to be.'

'I'd like to wash my hands,' said Claudia to Becky. 'I
wonder if you could show me the way to the
bathroom?'

The child nodded importantly and, with an apology
to the others, Claudia followed her to the bedroom
wing, where Becky showed her into a large bathroom
and even volunteered to wash her own hands without
being told. When they rejoined the others everyone was
settling down to a tea-party which had a decidedly
festive atmosphere.

Claudia was amused to notice Jamie's eyes on her a
great deal, also to find that Becky sat beside her
behaving with model propriety, a fact appreciated by
Bea, as she caught Claudia's eye in silent congratula-
tion.

Tea-time was a prolonged, noisy affair, after which
the two smaller children were taken off for their baths,
while Becky and Jamie sat at the cleared table and
became silently absorbed as they each coloured a
picture from Becky's book. The afternoon had grown
oppressively hot and humid, and Claudia was glad to sit
chatting with the other three women, smiling inwardly
as she looked at her watch and remembered what her
occupation had been a week or so ago at this time.
Trying to inject some enthusiasm for poetry into the
Lower Fifth, probably, she thought, then looked up at
the sound of the noisy arrival outside of two vehicles.

'Luc!' Emily sprang to her feet expectantly. At the
same moment Jamie cried 'Papae!' and slid off his chair
to run towards the two tall figures approaching from
the hall. Luc Fonseca was a little shorter than Saul, and

built on slightly less massive lines, but instantly recognisable from his startling resemblance to his sons, despite the grey streaks in his thick black hair. He swept Jamie up and kissed him, before setting him down in order to kiss his wife with the same lack of selfconsciousness. Claudia watched, fascinated, as he kept his arm close round Emily even while greeting his grandmother and Bea.

'And this is Claudia March, Luc,' said Emily, smiling warmly.

Luc bent and took Claudia's hand, raising it to his lips with a smile of great charm on his handsome, strong-featured face.

'Muito prazer,' he said.

Becky sat very still at the table, her eyes wistful on Jamie and his parents, and Claudia's heart was wrung as she saw the look on the child's face. Saul turned from greeting Thurza and Bea, acknowledging Claudia with a casual nod, his eyes narrowing as she tried to convey a silent message in her own. She gave an almost imperceptible turn of her head in Becky's direction, and relaxed as he interpreted it correctly and strolled over to his daughter, ruffling a hand over her head as he bent to examine what she was doing. Claudia met Emily's comprehending blue eye as she turned to Luc Fonseca.

'What do you think of Campo d'Ouro, Miss March?' he asked, sitting on the settee alongside her, his arm around Jamie.

Thurza laughed and wagged her stick in Claudia's direction.

'Your ingenuity will be taxed to find different polite answers, Miss March, as everyone will ask the same thing for the time being.'

Claudia smiled politely.

'I haven't actually seen Campo d'Ouro itself yet, unless one counts the view of it from the house. It looks very picturesque, Senhor Fonseca.'

Luc called over to Saul.

'When are you going to take Miss March on a tour, Saul——'

'We're going to use first names,' interrupted Emily

firmly. 'None of this "Miss" and "Senhor", if you don't mind!'

'One asks permission first, *carinha*,' said her husband reprovingly, then turned his smile on Claudia. 'You permit?'

She nodded, smiling warmly, responding automatically to his friendly charm. 'Of course.' She looked up to find Saul's eyes on her with a cold expression in them, and looked away hurriedly.

'Luc, you may offer our guests drinks while I take Saul away in private and have a little chat with him,' announced Emily, a statement which plainly surprised everyone present. Luc rose to his feet, frowning doubtfully at his wife.

'*Carinha*, don't you think I——' he began, but was silenced by the smile in the lambent blue of Emily's eyes. He shrugged gracefully. 'Very well. Saul, I apologise for my wife. She wishes to ask you a favour and firmly believes you will not refuse her.'

'She's probably right,' said Saul laconically, and followed Emily's small figure along the verandah.

'What is Emily up to, Luc?' demanded Thurza suspiciously.

'She will tell you herself in due course,' answered her grandson. 'May I give both you ladies your customary dry sherry, after which I shall attend to the requirements of Senhorita Becky and Senhorita Claudia.'

'And me!' said Jamie indignantly.

'And you,' amended his father indulgently.

Becky slid off her chair and came to stand silent at Claudia's side, her face brightening as Jamie jumped to his feet restlessly.

'Come on, Becky, let's play in the garden. You can have a turn on my bike.'

'Can I, Claudia?'

'Yes, of course.' Claudia was gratified Becky even remembered to consult her. 'Can you ride a bike?'

'She can with the balancing wheels on,' said Jamie with slight condescension. 'Come on, Becky, or it'll be time for you to go home.'

The children ran off together as Luc handed Claudia her gin and tonic, then two pyjamaed little figures appeared and hurled themselves, shrieking, at their father, who sat down with one in the crook of each arm and proceeded to devote himself to Mark and Lucy, while Bea drew Claudia into conversation with Thurza.

'Thurza's having a bridge evening tonight, Claudia, and to be honest it had slipped my mind. Would you think me utterly barbarous if I abandon you yet again?' Bea looked anxiously at Claudia, who was able to assure her quite honestly that she had no objection in the slightest.

'I'm sure a dinner alone with Saul holds no terrors for you, Miss—Claudia,' said Thurza, with a twinkle in her eye.

'None at all, Senhora Fonseca,' answered Claudia quietly. 'How could it?' She finished her drink slowly, wondering what Emily was saying to Saul, just as the two of them came back to join them, Emily's face triumphant, and Saul's wooden as his eyes met Claudia's.

Luc got to his feet, a child held in each arm.

'Who won?'

'I did,' said Emily, and relieved him of her small daughter.

'Saul, had you forgotten that I'm making up a bridge four with Thurza this evening?' asked Bea apologetically.

The navy-blue eyes of her nephew flickered for an instant, but he merely shrugged. 'I had, of course, but no problem. Have a pleasant evening.'

'You and Claudia stay, too,' said Emily immediately. 'Becky could sleep here.'

'That's kind of you Emily, but I need to get back—things to see to at home.' He raised an eyebrow at Luc. 'I'll have a word with you tomorrow.'

Luc put down his small son and shook Saul's hand, suddenly very formal.

'My grateful thanks, Saul. As you say, we will talk tomorrow.'

There was a flurry of leave-taking, a reluctant Becky

was fetched from her cycling, her belongings collected, and eventually Claudia was in the jeep with Becky on her lap as Saul reversed at speed all the way down the tortuous drive until they were outside the gates and headed in the direction of home. Becky lay sleepy against Claudia's shoulder and Saul was silent, giving Claudia time to think about the afternoon. Emily had presumably made her request, and obviously it had been granted, but it was hard to judge from Saul's withdrawn face whether the suggestion had met with his approval. He spoke once to ask Claudia how she had enjoyed her afternoon, but otherwise the drive was completed in silence.

When they reached the house Becky was surrendered to Lourdes for her bath and Claudia stood irresolute in the kitchen for a moment, wondering what to do next. The sky was overcast and heavy, the air warm and thick with no trace of breeze. It seemed fairly likely a storm was brewing—in more ways than one, and Claudia's heart sank as Saul came in from garaging the jeep and asked coldly if she would spare him a few moments on the verandah.

CHAPTER SEVEN

CLAUDIA followed the tall figure through the dining-room out on to the verandah where the air was, if anything, warmer than inside the house. She sat on one of the upright chairs and refused Saul's offer of a drink, her tension increased by the sound of thunder rumbling in the distance.

Saul leaned against the rail, glass in hand, his back to the lights of the town below, his face impossible to see in the darkness.

'Emily said you approved the idea of teaching her children along with Becky,' he began abruptly, his voice as impersonal as an answering machine, and considerably less friendly.

'Yes.' There seemed little else to say. Claudia sat quietly, one leg crossed over the other, and waited for him to continue.

'My idea in hiring you was as a personal preceptress for my daughter, not as a teacher for half the children in Campo d'Ouro.' Now his tone was biting.

'It was difficult to dismiss Senhora Fonseca's idea out of hand,' began Claudia carefully, looking down at her clasped hands.

'It would surely have been more politic to consult me first!' Saul tossed back his drink and crossed to pour himself another, dropping in ice with a force that threatened the safety of the glass.

'When she filled me in on the circumstances it would have been very unfeeling to voice my disapproval, surely,' she retorted, stung. 'Besides, I made it quite plain my consent was entirely subject to yours, naturally, when you'd gone to the expense of bringing me out here. As you so aptly put it, contractually I'm in your hands. You pay me.'

'And there, of course, we come to the crux of the matter,' he said bitterly. 'Finance. I gather Emily offered you a substantial reward.' The icy flash of her eyes must have got through to him even through the gloom as he quickly amended, 'Yes. I know you refused it, but can you deny that in your mind there is just the hint of a "great expectation" at some time or other?'

'Yes.'

Saul moved over to the table and lit the candle in the copper holder. He replaced the glass shade and sat opposite her, staring at her face in the soft glow. 'Yes what?' His voice was flat and hard, like a piece of slate.

'Yes, I deny it, of course.' This was impossible in Claudia's view. 'I said I wasn't concerned with the financial arrangements, that would be up to you and the Fonsecas. I, personally, have no wish for anything more than the substantial remuneration you already pay me. What else can I say?' Mutinously she threw back her head and stared into his face, more mask-like than ever in the light thrown up by the candle. For a moment or two she thought he would speak, but he kept silent. Claudia decided to have one last shot at appealing to him. 'I genuinely feel it might be the best thing for Becky if she did have company and competition at lessons. Most children do better this way. I gather Senhora Fonseca has been doing lessons with her children herself, but of course, now that she's pregnant again——'

'What!' He stared at her, eyes narrowed. 'Emily's expecting another baby?'

'Oh dear.' Claudia pushed her hair behind her ears uncomfortably. 'I thought she would tell you that as a means of persuasion. I'm sorry; I had no idea I was betraying a confidence.'

Saul got slowly to his feet and stood, rubbing his chin.

'I see. She could hardly have said anything more likely to enlist your sympathies. You know she lost a baby not too long ago? I see now why you agreed.'

'That was only part of the reason. I also genuinely happen to think it's a good idea. But if you wash out the whole arrangement I couldn't blame you after all. I am *your* employee,' pointed out Claudia. She was beginning to feel tired again and stood, facing him, squaring her shoulders unconsciously as she looked very directly into the dark, deep-set eyes above her. 'Mr Treharne, do you really consider there is much point in continuing with this arrangement? From my own point of view I firmly believe I could very soon establish a reasonable relationship with Becky. But, living as I do, as part of your household, life will be grim if you—well, if you find me unacceptable. Perhaps you should find someone else.'

Saul made a chopping motion of his arm in negation.

'How the hell am I to do that? I can't just take off for the U.K., and there's no way of engaging a person for this type of job without a personal interview. Besides, as you say, I've already spent a fair amount of money merely in getting you here—it goes against the grain to waste it.' He drew in a deep breath. 'Will it be of any use if I apologise? I had a tricky day in work, then when I got to Casa d'Ouro I found you and Emily airily disposing of my arrangements without a thought about my views on the subject, or at least, that was how it seemed.'

'Ah, but you were wrong,' said Claudia insistently. 'Believe me, they were my first thought! If the idea makes you unhappy, teaching the others, I mean, naturally it's your wishes that count.'

Saul sighed irritably.

'I can't go back on my agreement with Emily, even if I wanted to. As I may have said before, although Luc is my second cousin I never for an instant lose sight of the fact that he's also my employer. Besides,' he added, a softer note in his voice, 'I could hardly hurt Emily.'

Her own feelings, apparently, could go hang, thought Claudia acidly, then came to with a jolt as she realised she was listening to an apology.

'I'm sorry, Claudia,' said Saul shortly. 'Personal considerations apart, I have never been in any doubt about your ability to handle Becky, and to teach her, which is, after all, the important factor. Perhaps we could make more of an effort to understand each other's point of view.'

We, thought Claudia indignantly, but aware that this was the biggest olive branch she was ever likely to be offered she hastily opted for magnanimity.

'Very well, Mr Treharne.'

'Saul,' he said quietly.

'Saul,' she repeated with docility. 'I'll just go and see what Becky's doing. I'll read her a story after her meal.'

'I'll see you at dinner, then.' Saul sounded almost awkward, and Claudia gave him an uncertain glance as she passed him and retreated into the house in search of Becky.

That young lady was seated at the kitchen table, eating her supper and telling the maids about her afternoon, with much knife and fork waving. Claudia told Maria that Bea would not be in for dinner, and was surprised to see a look of dismay on the broad, genial face.

'*Tem problema*, Maria?'

It took a lot of hand-waving, plus the occasional

rough translation from the helpful Becky, before
Claudia was finally given to understand that Maria and
Lourdes would like the night off to attend a *festa*, an
anniversary party, at Maria's home. A cold meal had
been prepared in expectation of this, the food ready in
the refrigerator, and Maria would be grateful if Dona
Claudia would ask the *Chefe* for permission in Dona
Bea's absence.

Claudia went off to look for Saul, not over-disposed
towards asking the 'Chefe' for anything, despite his
apology earlier. The verandah was deserted, so was the
hall, and Claudia hesitated outside the door of his
room, not relishing the prospect of bearding the lion in
his den. As she stood, undecided, his voice could be
heard coming from the study, and she went towards the
half open door along the corridor, rather daunted by
the intense irritation only too plain in his raised voice,
even though his staccato, rapid Portuguese was
unintelligible. Claudia bit her lip and decided to retreat
and choose a moment slightly more propitious, but as
she turned away Saul strode through the door, almost
colliding with her.

'Ah, Claudia—good. I'm going out.' His face was
abstracted as he made rapidly for the kitchen. 'Don't
wait dinner, I'm needed at the mine.'

'Oh, but hang on a minute,' Claudia ran after him.
'There was something I wanted to ask—Maria . . .'

'Save it till I get back,' he interrupted impatiently,
and bent to kiss his daughter's cheek. 'Goodnight,
Becky.' Then he was gone within seconds, his jeep
roaring up the driveway and out on to the road.

Claudia spread her hands in apology and smiled
ruefully at the maids.

'*Disculpe-me*, Maria. *O Chefe tem problema na mina.*'
She searched desperately for the words, then appealed
to Becky, who was watching her struggles clinically.
'How do I say your daddy had no time to listen to me?'

Becky obligingly translated, then looked at Claudia
with a scowl.

'Can't Maria 'n Lourdes go, then?'

Both maids broke into voluble speech, the gist of

which seemed to be how early they would return in the
morning, the word '*aniversário*' repeated continually.
Claudia was torn. There was surely no harm in letting
them go. They seemed to think Bea's permission would
have been automatic, so eventually she shrugged and
nodded her head, rewarded with wide, white smiles of
joy as the two girls flew off to get ready, apparently
quite undisturbed by the menacing rumbles of thunder,
which Claudia noted uneasily were getting distinctly
nearer.

A wide yawn from Becky recalled Claudia to her
responsibilities.

'Bedtime,' she said firmly.

'I want to do more colouring.' Becky's face was as
stormy as the atmosphere, and she was plainly prepared
to do battle to stay up a little longer.

'Not tonight.' Claudia was immovable. It had been a
full day, and it was already some time past Becky's
normal hour.

With her father out of the way, and no one else to
intervene, Becky gave way to a regrettable temper
tantrum, pushing Claudia's patience to the limits.

'*Won't* go to bed!' She stamped a small bare foot,
wincing as it made painful contact with the hard marble
floor, tears starting in the great blue eyes. Claudia was
unimpressed, knowing full well they were tears of rage,
her own stomach contracting sickly as a roll of thunder
boomed with sudden violence, making the kitchen
windows rattle. Ashamed of her own cowardice,
especially in the face of Becky's apparent unconcern,
she spoke sternly to the sobbing child.

'If you stop that rather babyish display, Becky, I'll
read you a story, if not you can go to bed and settle
down straight away to sleep. I don't mind which you
choose, but either way you're off to bed right now.'

Becky rubbed her knuckles into her eyes, her tears
dying away almost at once as she gave Claudia a wary
look from behind her fingers, obviously deciding
Claudia meant what she said. She nodded, pouting, a
hiccup shaking the small body as she trudged along the
corridor to her room, making no objection when

Claudia suggested a detour to the bathroom to brush her teeth. The thunder was beginning to crash and crack around the house with growing ferocity by this time, and lightning flashed through Becky's room as Claudia drew the curtains, heroically suppressing her instinctive flinch away from it as she lit the little oil lamp which served as a nightlight.

Becky climbed into bed and submitted to being tucked in, her rebellion over for the time being.

'I like storms,' she said surprisingly. 'Sometimes the house jumps up and down when the thunder's loud.'

This piece of news brought no pleasure to the listener. Claudia loathed and feared thunderstorms, a weakness wild horses would never succeed in making her admit, and with iron control she fought a regrettable tendency to jump out of her skin at each clap of thunder, asking Becky which story she preferred.

Her own little storm forgotten, Becky sat up in bed, eager and bright-eyed.

'*Sleeping Beauty*—please. My books are in the toybox.'

Claudia began to read, acting out all the characters and bringing the story to life as much as she could, both to capture Becky's interest and to take her own mind off the ear-splitting elements outside. The child listened enthralled, sliding lower and lower in the bed as she fought against sleep. By the time Claudia reached the 'happy ever after' stage Becky was almost too drowsy to say goodnight. as the sheet was tucked round her again and she snuggled contentedly into her pillow.

As Claudia closed the door behind her the whole house seemed to shake on its foundations as lightning flashed end to end through the dark hall, the sky overhead simultaneously rent by a peal of thunder whose reverberations seemed to boom on and on for ever. Claudia stood flattened against the wall, her hands over her ears, her body vibrating with fright. After a moment she pulled herself together and made for the kitchen just as the whole house was plunged abruptly into darkness. She breathed hard, fighting for control of her stomach, which was displaying an annoying tendency to heave, and tried to remember where exactly the switch was she was supposed to turn off. Without light she had problems. Eventually her brain began to function again, despite the constant flashes of lightning and the almost continuous barrage of thunder. She remembered the candle on the verandah, and she had a book of matches from some restaurant in her handbag. The rain was sheeting down outside as Claudia dived through the dining room doors on to the verandah, which was lit brilliantly by the lightning as she retrieved the candlestick with a shaking hand and scuttled back into the house, bolting the glass doors and hurrying into her bedroom. She flung a hand in front of her eyes as a great fork of lightning seemed to earth just outside the open window, and, teeth chattering, she drew the curtains, and rummaged blindly in her bag on the dressing table, almost sobbing with relief as her fingers closed over the small matchbook.

Claudia managed to light the candle at the third attempt and immediately felt better, guilty at her panic. She took a cautious peep at Becky, who, amazingly, lay fast asleep, oblivious to the storm, the sight of the peaceful child making Claudia ashamed of her own shortcomings.

After locating the main switch and turning it off Claudia felt a little safer and found that by closing the door at each end she could make the bedroom corridor into a windowless tunnel where the lightning was shut out, if not the noise. She crouched on the floor with her candle, her clothes damp with perspiration, her hands over her ears, and prepared to sit out the storm. She lost count of the time as she sat there, moving only to check on Becky now and then, until the storm began to lessen and move away into the distance. Claudia was forced to leave her post finally by the sound of the telephone ringing she went to the instrument, picking it up with extreme care, her hand unsteady.

Emily's voice came unmistakeably through the static on the line.

'Everything all right, Claudia?'

'Fine,' croaked Claudia, and cleared her throat. 'Fine, thanks, Emily.'

'Look, the storm has brought Aunt Bea's migraine on again, so we've put her to bed here . . .'

The rest of her sentence was lost in atmospherics, and Claudia bit her lip.

'Yes, of course, Emily. I understand,' she said loudly.

'Crackle, crackle . . . so you'll be all right in any case. Goodnight.'

'Yes, thank you for ringing. Goodnight.'

Claudia was thoughtful as she returned through the house, the pitch darkness emphasised by the dim glow of the candle in her hand. Her whole instinct was to bolt to bed like a coward before Saul came home, but she had a feeling he would regard this in a worse light than waiting up to face the music. Her reflection looked eery and disembodied in the mirror as she brushed her hair by candlelight. The shadows emphasised her cheekbones, and miniature candle-flames danced in her eyes, their normal pale gleam obscured by the darkness of pupils still dilated by tension and fear. Claudia turned away in distaste, deciding her main problem was hunger. In the kitchen the refrigerator was still cold enough to preserve the food Maria had left for her dinner. There was even ice in the freezer compartment, which seemed to augur well, so Claudia made a sparing selection from cold chicken, some kind of fish mousse and a salad of red peppers and tomatoes. She found some bread in the big bin in the pantry and had a picnic on the kitchen table, washed down by milk, after which she felt a great deal better, though very weary. She washed her plates, then sat at the kitchen table, squinting at her watch in the gloom, noticing uneasily that the candle was burning down rapidly. It was almost ten. How long would it be before Saul came back, she wondered. She laid her head on her arms on the table. Just for a moment or two, she thought drowsily, and drifted off into sleep, worn out by the varying experiences of the day. She was rocketed to consciousness again by hard hands which shook her relentlessly, an all to familiar voice repeating her name loudly.

'All right, all right!' she mumbled crossly, then came back to earth with a bump as she realised the room was in darkness and only his voice made it possible to identify Saul.

'What the hell are you doing in the kitchen in the dark?' he demanded irately. 'The lights have been back on everywhere else for a couple of hours. Why didn't you ring the mine and tell me you had no power here?'

Claudia licked her dry lips, glad she couldn't see Saul's face.

'The switch,' she said huskily.

'What switch?'

'The main one you showed me. I turned it off.'

With a muffled curse Saul swung away from her and crossed the room, crashing into something in the dark before he found the master switch, most of the lights in the house springing to life as he turned it on. Irritably he went round switching them off, while Claudia ran silently on bare feet to Becky's room, relieved to find the child fast asleep by the light of her little lamp. Claudia covered her gently and went back to the kitchen to face the music.

'Are you hungry?' she asked politely. 'Maria left cold food before she went.'

Saul turned from the refrigerator with a bottle of beer in his hand, his eyebrows almost meeting his untidy black hair. The look in his eyes was enough to make Claudia quail.

'Maria isn't here? Lourdes?'

'She—she went with Maria.'

'Would it be too much to enquire where?'

Claudia leaned against the table, pushing her hair nervously behind her ears.

'They went to some kind of party at Maria's home. They'll be back first thing in the morning.'

'Aunt Bea gave permission, of course?'

Claudia looked at him with the calm of desperation.

'No. She wasn't here. If you remember, you were in too much of a hurry to listen when I tried to ask you earlier.'

'And what did she say when she came home?' Saul's

face held a look of polite enquiry, which chilled Claudia more than his anger.

'She didn't—come home, I mean. She's staying the night at Casa d'Ouro. The storm brought on her migraine again and they put her to bed there, as far as I can gather. The line was crakling so badly it was difficult to hear what Emily was saying.'

'Why didn't you tell Emily you were alone?'

'The line was very bad, and I couldn't see what could have been done about it. Becky was asleep by that time, and I knew you'd be home eventually, anyway.'

'That, Miss Claudia March, is the whole damned point. I *am* now home—virtually alone in the house with you. And in Campo d'Ouro this is just not permissible, strictly against the rules—contrary to what you might consider normal in England.'

Claudia glared at him with dislike.

'How do you know what's normal behaviour for me? Besides, the whole idea's archaic, apart from the fact that no one will know!'

He gave her a look of such contempt Claudia felt a streak of red-hot rage pierce her.

'Use your much-vaunted brain, girl! The servants, of course.'

'I'm sorry,' she said stiffly. 'When I gave them permission I had no idea your aunt would stay at Casa d'Ouro, and I never gave a thought to the fact of being alone here with you. To be honest, even if I had it wouldn't have disturbed me at all.'

'Why not?' There was a disturbing change in Saul's tone as he moved slowly towards her, finishing the beer in his glass without taking his eyes from her pale face.

Claudia frowned up at him resentfully.

'Well, you don't think of me like that—nor I you.' She leaned her hands on the table, secretly longing to make her escape, and turned her eyes away from the unsettling look in his. Saul put out a long hand and picked up a lock of her hair, sliding it idly through his fingers, a faint, cold smile playing at the corners of his mouth and deepening the cleft in his chin. He sighed.

'Surely, Claudia, with all those qualifications of

yours, you must have learned that if a man is alone in the middle of the night with a woman who's even halfway attractive, it's ten to one he *will* start thinking like that if he's normal.' He put out a finger to jerk her face up to his. 'And, believe me, I'm very normal.' He stood overpoweringly close, staring down into her stormy eyes.

'I think it's time I went to bed now,' said Claudia hurriedly. 'I'm sorry to have caused such trouble——'

'I had a feeling you were trouble the moment I laid eyes on you,' he muttered to her consternation, and pounced, backing her up against the kitchen table, held fast against him, holding her off balance so that her bare toes dangled just free of the floor. His mouth was so close to hers she felt, rather than heard, him murmur,

'After all, we might as well have the game as well as the candle.'

Something seemed to have robbed Claudia of all power of movement, even thought, as his mouth made contact with hers, not hard and punishing as expected, but subtle and persuasive, and infinitely more dangerous. It generated a trembling deep down inside her that increased as one of the arms holding her slackened its hold to allow a hand to slide rhythmically up and down her spine, slithering over the silk of her shirt in a lulling, hypnotic motion, relaxing her body, curving it against his as a little warm, sighing breath entered his mouth from lips she had opened in surprise as he seized her, remaining open in hesitant response to the insistent, demanding pressure of his.

Claudia forgot she hardly knew this difficult, disturbing man; no conscience prodded her to erect defences against the strong arms that held her in a security she dimly recognised to be almost sheer unalloyed comfort, save for an underlying warmth of some other, sensuous feeling, a flicker that grew and grew as his mouth became increasingly insistent, igniting to a flame as the stroking hand moved in a faster rhythm, accelerating the beat of her heart and taking away her breath as her head bent back beneath the pressure of his, her hair streaming down her back like a banner as his lips left hers to follow an inflammatory path down her arched throat to the point where the buttons of her shirt presented an obstacle to his progress. His stroking hand ceased its activity, only to find a new one as his fingers flicked the buttons from their moorings, her high, pointed breasts springing into ivory-white relief between the parted black silk, vulnerable and defenceless against his lips and fingertips.

Her feet still clear of the floor, Claudia's body arched like a bow, her arms held to her sides in the vice-like embrace of one of Saul's powerful arms, for the first time in her life utterly helpless before the dominance of male physical superiority, her own bemused senses his powerful ally as her erect, sensitised nipples experienced the onslaught of subtle, seeking lips and flicking tongue that sent streaks of fire much lower, to add fuel to the fire already raging where her hips were thrust against the unmistakable arousal of Saul's body as it ground against her own.

At this some half-buried instinct of common sense woke up in Claudia's brain. She gave a hoarse little sound of protest and shook her head, fighting suddenly to free her hands. Her whole body became a writhing, wriggling opposition to the lips and hands and rock-like frame, but Saul's only response was a laugh deep in his chest, vibrating against her, making her shiver. Abruptly she was free. Her eyes glittering like rock crystals with self-disgust and banked-down emotion, Claudia shook back her hair and frantically tried to match buttons to buttonholes, avoiding Saul's knowing eyes, furious with him, furious with herself. Raging inwardly at her spineless lack of opposition to his unexpected attack, she lashed herself unsparingly for behaving like a sex-starved fool. With cold distaste she realised the back of her thighs hurt from their contact with the edge of the kitchen table—the kitchen table, for heaven's sake! Like all the lewd, crude jokes she'd ever heard.

Saul stood, arms folded, not in the least disturbed and watched her disarray with apparent enjoyment.

'Why?' she spat at him, her voice unsteady.

He shrugged. 'You were so sure there was no harm in remaining alone in a house with a man at night, or indeed at any time. I decided to demonstrate how wrong you were.'

'There was no necessity for—for all that, surely!'

'All what?'

Claudia thrust her shirt into her slacks and looked at him with distaste.

'I would have preferred the point made verbally, not—not in a practical demonstration, like a cookery lesson!'

Saul threw back his head in a spontaneous laugh that altered his face so completely she stared at him with rancour at his lack of timing; hardly the moment to demonstrate that he was capable of mirth like any other mortal!

'I assume you were more annoyed by the motive than the deed?' He was obviously having trouble in recovering his gravity.

'I wasn't precisely thrilled by either of them,' she snapped, with a fine disregard for the truth, and made for the door with as much dignity as bare feet allowed.

'Claudia, Claudia, tell the truth!'

Unwilling she turned to look at him, her eyes icy.

'What do you mean?'

'Can you really place your hand on your heart and swear you experienced not one glimmer of response during our little—er—interchange?' Saul strolled towards the outer door of the kitchen, turning to look at Claudia's incensed face with a look in his eyes that made her drop sharply, the telltale colour tinting the taut skin along her cheekbones. 'Are you implying I was mistaken?'

'You took me by surprise,' she said woodenly. 'No one does that twice.'

'Always supposing they felt inclined!' Saul gave her a mocking little bow. 'Goodnight, Claudia, pleasant dreams.'

She stared at him blankly, her antagonism forgotten.

'Where on earth are you going at this time of night?'

'Back to my office to a hard, uncomfortable couch, where I shall ostentatiously remain until roused in the morning. Being last to leave tonight I might, with luck, get back without being seen. You won't be nervous on your own?'

'Less than if you stayed.' Claudia's chin went up defiantly.

Saul stood looking at her with infuriating indulgence, as if she were Becky in one of her tantrums.

'Not the nervous type, I gather?'

'No.' Claudia was back in possession of her much-tried composure.

'I'll wish you goodnight, then.' Saul sauntered through the door and Claudia crossed the room to lock it behind him, relieved to be alone again, leaning against it for several troubled minutes.

She had lied to Saul. She *was* nervous. The storm had moved away, and the thought of an intruder held no fears, but at the thought of what had happened a few moments earlier chills of apprehension chased up her spine. Her own emotions scared her to death. Or was emotion a rather fancy word for the feelings experienced by both of them a short while earlier? Claudia pushed a clenched fist against her mouth, mentally flaying herself for behaving like a—like a what? Alley-cat, or just woman? Claudia pulled herself together with an effort, turning out lights and checking on doors. Becky lay deeply asleep, arms outflung, the purity of her face so enchanting in the dim light that Claudia stayed, arrested, looking at her for quite some time. Elaine must have looked like that when she was asleep. The thought of Saul in bed with his wife sent Claudia off to her own room at the double. She stripped off her clothes and slid into bed, burying her face in the pillow in an attempt to blank out the memory of those few self-revelatory moments in Saul's arms; moments of discovery about herself that shook her to the very core.

There was only one course to adopt. No more thoughts of Saul Treharne in any way except as her employer; otherwise he meant nothing to her. Nothing.

Over and over again the words went round in her brain, nothing, nothing, like some hypnotic mantra that eventually had the desired effect and she slept.

CHAPTER EIGHT

AFTER her disturbed night Claudia woke only when Becky ran in to say someone was clapping their hands outside the kitchen door.

'I think it's Maria, Claudia!'

'Hang on a minute, Becky, I'm coming.' She pulled on her kimono and pushed her hair away from her face as she hurried to unlock the kitchen door and admit Maria and Lourdes, who both looked heavy-eyed and apologetic.

'*Bom dia*, Dona Claudia.' They both bade her good morning and Maria began preparing coffee at once while Becky ran off to dress, chattering with Lourdes, full of curiosity about the previous evening's festivities. Claudia decided to have a shot at explaining about the night before.

'Dona Bea *passou a noite na* Casa d'Ouro,' she began, her sleepy brain having trouble in finding the right words to tell the maid Bea wasn't in the house.

'*Donde?*'

Claudia nodded.

'*Com dor de*——' she hesitated and tapped her forehead. Maria nodded, her kind face creased with sympathy, obviously familiar with Bea's headaches.

Claudia went on doggedly, bent on establishing Saul's absence as soon as possible.

'*O Chefe ficou na mina.*' She knew very well Saul would have slept in his office, not the mine, but her vocabulary was limited at the best of times, and this morning it was nearly non-existent. She pointed to the light. '*Falta de luz.*'

Maria nodded vigorously.

'*E sempre assim em caso de relampago.*'

This was too much for Claudia's Portuguese, and the girl made a sizzling noise to indicate lightning.

Smiling in rueful agreement Claudia went off to dress, wondering how Bea was feeling this morning, and what sort of night Saul had spent in his office. She hurried into pink denims and a matching sleeveless shirt, and was tying her hair at the nape of her neck with a pink cord when Becky burst in, dressed in frilly blue organdie, her hair in a pigtail of rippling gold.

'It was Maria's birthday yesterday, Claudia,' she said excitedly. 'That's what "*anniversario*" means—"birthday". It was her party they went to.'

'What a pity we didn't know, Becky, we could have given her a present!'

'Oh yes, and cake and candles, like Jamie.' Becky was downcast.

Claudia thought for a moment, then rummaged in the suitcase that still remained unpacked. She drew out a smart box containing French soap and dusting powder, a parting gift from the Lower Fourths at Highdean.

'Do you think she'd like this, Becky?'

The little girl agreed with enthusiasm.

'But there isn't any wrapping paper, Claudia. Presents must have fancy paper.'

A further search produced a pretty paper bag which was pronounced suitable, and Becky tugged at Claudia's hand impatiently.

'Come on, let's give it to her!'

Claudia followed the flying figure into the kitchen, where the gift was received with rapture by Maria as Becky cried '*Feliz aniversário*, Maria,' turning with comic condescension to explain to Claudia that it meant 'happy birthday'. Claudia thanked her solemnly, then looked up sharply, her bonhomie evaporating as Saul appeared in the doorway, yawning, looking haggard and hollow-eyed from lack of sleep, a villainous growth of stubble on his chin.

'Good morning,' she said quietly.

'Good morning.' He peered at the package in Maria's hand. 'More presents? Quite a lady for handing out largesse, aren't you, Claudia?'

'No, not lar—not what you said,' said Becky
earnestly. 'Soap and powder for Maria's birthday.'

'I stand corrected. *Parabéms*, Maria.'

His sudden appearance threw Lourdes and Maria
into a frenzy of activity, and any awkwardness Claudia
felt at encountering him in the cold light of day was lost
in the barrage of instructions as Saul requested
breakfast as soon as he'd showered and changed and
sent Lourdes to ask José to clean some of the mud off
the jeep before it went back to the mine. Even breakfast
in Saul's company proved to be uneventful, as Becky
was unusually talkative, giving details of Maria's party,
and her father took full advantage of her uncharacteristic chattiness, leaving Claudia to hand round
food and pour coffee and juice without having to
contribute much herself.

The fleeting glimpse of her own face in the
bathroom mirror had shown shadows under her own
eyes equal to Saul's, and she stifled a secret giggle at
the thought that anyone watching would think they
had been engaged in an entire night of mutual
debauchery, instead of the short, sharp little episode
that actually took place.

'That was an odd little smile, Claudia.' Saul drained
the last of his coffee and stood up, stretching. 'It's just
possible I might manage to face the day now, thank
God—what did you find amusing?'

Claudia shook her head.

'Nothing of any interest. How soon do you think I
can ring to see how Bea is feeling?'

'Leave it an hour or so.' Saul stood at the top of the
verandah steps looking at her appraisingly. 'Did you
sleep well?'

She nodded coolly, busying herself by pouring more
tea.

'Once the storm died down I slept like a top. How
was your night?' Her eyes were unwavering on his,
pellucid with innocence.

'I spent the night on a three-foot sofa of leather as
slippery as glass. For one reason and another I've slept
better.' His own eyes returned her look with a

significant gleam. 'I won't be home for lunch, by the way.' He waved to Becky and ran down the steps, leaving Claudia to finish her breakfast in relative peace, quite satisfied with her own aplomb.

'Where's Aunt Bea?' demanded Becky suddenly. 'She's late.'

'Still at Casa d'Ouro. She had a headache, so she slept there.'

'Is she coming home this morning?'

'We'll ring and find out in a while.'

Becky showed no signs of animosity this morning, and after breakfast Claudia spent an hour helping her to use water paints to make a more ambitious picture, leaving the child deeply engrossed while she went off to look up the Casa d'Ouro number in the book beside the telephone. Emily answered and told her Bea was better, but was staying in bed a little longer, and would come home after lunch.

The rest of the morning passed without incident. Becky behaved like a normal child, with no tantrums to mar the oddly peaceful morning, with only two of them for lunch. Afterwards she even consented to lie on one of the long verandah chairs for a rest, cuddling the little koala bear somnolently while Claudia leafed through a couple of glossy American magazines.

The Fonseca chauffeur brought Bea back in the middle of the afternoon, while Becky and Claudia were engaged in a more complicated jigsaw puzzle. She apologised profusely for her absence overnight and kissed Becky fondly, giving Claudia a guilty smile.

'Advanced hypochondria, you'll be thinking, I know, and no wonder!'

'Nonsense! I know migraine is a terrible thing.' Claudia gave a conspiratorial wink at Becky. 'We managed, in any case, didn't we, Becky?'

The little girl nodded absently.

'Aunt Bea, it was Maria's birthday yesterday. She had a party.'

Bea looked stricken, gazing at Claudia in dismay.

'Oh dear! She mentioned it to me last week and I forgot—in fact I think she said something yesterday morning too, but it went clean out of my head. Age has an eroding effect on the memory!' She glanced at Claudia questioningly. 'Did you let her go?'

'Yes. Lourdes too.' Claudia smiled wryly. 'That was before I knew you weren't coming home last night.'

Bea collected herself visibly and asked Becky if she would order tea from Maria. When the child was out of earshot she turned to Claudia in agitation.

'Was Saul angry?'

'He wasn't pleased.' Claudia saw no point in dissembling. 'When he came home, which was in the early hours of the morning, he turned round and went back again when he found I was alone in the house with Becky. He slept, or rather didn't sleep, on a couch in his office.'

Bea groaned, then smiled brightly as Lourdes appeared with a tea-tray. Lourdes asked Bea something in rapid Portuguese, and Bea consented, with various instructions, telling Claudia Becky was going down to the village store with Afra to buy coffee.

'She loves it there—they generally give her a sweetmeat of some kind, and I need to talk to you, Claudia.' Bea's handsome face took on a look of resolution as she poured out tea and offered Claudia a piece of coffee-cake. 'I know you will probably find things a little behind the times here, my dear, but it wouldn't do for you to spend the night here alone with Saul. Oh dear, that sounds wrong! I mean merely under the same roof is sufficient. Normally the circumstances would never arise because the maids are usually here and I'm always here—last night was an unfortunate coincidence.'

'Please don't worry.' Claudia leaned over and patted the other woman's hand reassuringly. 'Saul turned up for breakfast after Maria and Lourdes arrived. They think he spent the entire night at the mine.'

Bea sighed with relief. 'Thank heavens for that!'

No more was said on the subject, and they talked of other things while they finished tea, after which Bea

took Claudia to her room and gave her a choice of
reading matter from a shelf of American paperbacks.

'I hope my trunk arrives before Christmas,' said
Claudia with a frown. 'Becky's presents are in it.'

'I'm sure it will. It may even have arrived already; we
must ask Saul this evening.'

Saul was late, arriving home long after his daughter
was in bed and looking gaunt with fatigue. Both women
had bathed and changed for the evening, and Claudia
felt at a decided advantage in her cool beige dress as he
came wearily up the steps and stood for a moment
leaning against the rail at the top as he greeted them
both and asked Bea if she were better.

'Yes, dear. Let me get you a drink——'

'For once I need a bath before I do anything,' he said
wearily, and rubbed a hand over his eyes. 'I'll only be a
few minutes.'

Claudia watched Saul leave with a more sympathetic
eye than usual.

'It's been a long day for him,' she remarked.
'Especially after that disastrous night.'

'Yes,' said Bea with feeling. She hesitated delicately.
'Perhaps we could keep the dinner-time conversation to
neutral subjects this evening.'

'Claudia laughed, her eyes dancing.

'I'm sorry. I hope our tendency to argue isn't causing
indigestion as well as migraine!'

Bea laughed with her and turned the conversation to
Christmas and the fourthcoming festivities at the
Fonseca household, assuring Claudia it would not be
necessary to take gifts. An early light lunch would be
eaten at home, then they would all arrive at Casa
d'Ouro well before dinner, Becky going with them and
sleeping with the Fonseca children.

'I understand Emily intends gathering up a few lone
bachelors for the occasion,' explained Bea. 'Tom Enys,
one-time Drill Doctor at the mine, and John Trelaur,
the retired Mine Captain. Both Truro men and
bachelors, so when they retired they decided to share
the next house down the hill from here. Oh, and Bob
McClure, the geologist, will be there too.'

Claudia was surprised. 'Sounds quite a party,' she commented.

Bea looked round as Maria came to the dining room door with a question, and rose to her feet.

'Some problem about the main course; I'll just investigate.' She looked at her watch with a frown. 'Saul's a long time. Just knock on his door and hurry him along, will you, dear?'

Claudia went through the hall with a marked lack of enthusiasm. She tapped on Saul's door and waited. Silence. She knocked louder and heard a muffled 'Come in.' She stood, undecided.

'Dinnertime!' she called.

'Come in, for God's sake!'

Startled, she obeyed, to find Saul lying face down on the bed, his magnificent body bare except for the towel tucked round his hips.

'Sorry!' Claudia backed away in dismay. 'I thought you told me to come in——'

'I did.' He twisted round and lay sideways, propped up on his elbow as he looked at her, examining her flushed face with clinical detachment.

'Your aunt sent me,' Claudia sidled nearer the door. 'Dinner's ready.'

Saul stood up and stretched, threatening the security of the towel.

'Don't be nervous,' he said lazily. 'I'm a damned sight too tired to be much danger at the moment. I merely wanted to know what you told Aunt Bea about last night.'

'The truth,' said Claudia succinctly, and turned on her heel.

'All of it?'

She halted in the doorway.

'Obviously not. I left out the worrying bit.'

'It worried you?' he asked, with exaggerated concern.

'No.' She stared up at him blankly. 'But I rather felt it might worry Bea.' She walked out and closed the door quietly, then went to Becky's room, standing for several minutes watching the sleeping child while she recovered her self-possession.

This was unshakeable during dinner while she complied with Bea's request and kept the conversation to neutral subjects, refusing to rise even when Saul's intention to aggravate was obvious. Only once her feelings threatened to get the better of her. When Bea asked Saul if Claudia's trunk was likely to arrive in time for Christmas his impassive face registered faint apology for once as he confessed it had arrived before Claudia, and only needed transporting from the company stores to the house. It gave Claudia enormous satisfaction to behave with saccharine magnanimity and display none of the irritation she felt inside. Saul could have saved her a great deal of anxiety if she'd known sooner. Claudia was allowed only a short time in the role of Pollyanna before Saul excused himself and went to bed immediately after coffee, and Claudia was quite glad when Bea suggested that an early night was a good idea all around.

Armed with a borrowed copy of *Princess Daisy*, Claudia read for an hour propped against her pillows, then settled down to a rather disturbed sleep. At some stage during the night she shot upright in bed, aware that something had woken her. There was no thunder, and after a while she realised that the sound she could hear was sitfled weeping coming from Becky's room. Claudia shot out of bed and into the child's room, to find the little girl burrowing her hot, sodden face into her pillow, her little body convulsed with sobs.

Claudia's heart was wrung. The child was probably having one of her periodic fits of longing for her dead mother. She sat on the bed and gently drew Becky on to her lap, cradling the feverish fair head against her shoulder, stroking the little girl until she quietened.

'What is it, poppet?' she asked gently.

A convulsive shudder racked the little body.

'B-bad dream.' Becky sniffed hard and pushed herself closer.

Claudia braced herself mentally.

'Can you tell me about it?'

Becky nodded blindly.

'I dreamed Father Christmas didn't bring me a bike

like Jamie's.' She hiccuped, and turned drowned blue eyes up to Claudia, her face blotched and swollen.

Oh boy! thought Claudia, blinking.

'Well, it's not Christmas yet,' she said soothingly. 'I expect he's waiting to see what a good girl you are.' God forgive me, she added silently.

'I'm a *bit* better, Claudia, aren't I?'

The appeal in the drowned blue eyes was irresistible. Claudia hugged her, hard.

'Yes, Becky today you've been great. But I think the idea is to go on trying hard pretty much all the time.'

'I will,' said Becky passionately, a stray sob shaking her hot little body.

'Then the first step is to go back to sleep now—only your pillows are sodden. Hang on——'

'Can I help?' Saul stood in the doorway in his dressing gown, watching them both.

Claudia got to her feet with care and handed her burden to him.

'Perhaps you'll cuddle Becky for a moment while I change her bed; it's a bit sweaty.' She gave an embarrassed glance down at her green nightie, which happily was a modest white-dotted cotton, nevertheless she ran to her own room for her kimono. Saul watched in silence, cradling his child closely as Claudia took fresh linen from the chest of drawers and remade the bed rapidly. Becky was fast asleep by the time she had finished, and Saul gently lowered her into the bed, tucking the sheet loosely round her with hands which looked incongruously large for the task.

Claudia smiled briefly and whispered goodnight, but before she could slip into her own room he said softly, 'Was she crying for Elaine?'

'No. She had a bad dream. Father Christmas came and didn't bring her a bike like Jamie's.'

He stifled a laugh, then whispered, 'Come into the study a moment, Claudia, please.'

Claudia followed him, standing just inside the closed door of the study as he switched on the desk lamp.

'Was that really the cause of all that sorrow?' Saul propped himself against the edge of the desk, his long brown legs stretched out in front of him, his long feet bare.

Nice toenails, thought Claudia irrelevantly, then recollected herself hurriedly, nodding in answer to his question. Saul frowned, scratching his chin thoughtfully.

'Tricky,' he said slowly. 'Bea bought a doll for her when she was over in the U.K., plus a typewriter as my present to her.'

'Oh dear,' Claudia bit her lip. 'I just brought various books for her. Without knowing the child beforehand it was a bit difficult to know what would appeal.'

'There's only one thing for it.' Saul looked at her questioningly. 'How do you feel about braving the road to Boa Vista one day next week?'

Claudia's face lit up. 'That would be marvellous!'

He raised his eyebrows. 'Tired of Campo d'Ouro already?'

She shook her head impatiently.

'No, of course not, but I couldn't think how to get the present for her I really know she'll like—apart from the bike. And please don't start on the subject of bribery!'

'Never entered my mind. Come on, it's late, let's go to bed.' He reached past her to open the door. 'Perhaps you'd prefer me to re-phrase that.'

She wasn't going to rise to that one. With an impersonal little smile Claudia wished him goodnight and left the room as he switched out the light. She listened to his almost soundless retreating footsteps as she did her best to get to sleep again, which was rather difficult after the disrupting little scene with Becky. The word to describe life here so far was leisurely, rather than quiet was her last thought. Even the nights were proving fairly eventful.

Events proved her wrong. For the next few days life went along serenely enough, with Becky trying hard to behave well enough to merit her much-coveted bicycle, and in the process finding she quite liked having Claudia around after all. Bea's migranes kept away in the absence of tension and upsets and Claudia settled into her new life with ease, writing to Liz on the subject at length. One of the reasons for all the serenity admittedly, was the absence of Saul for a few days over Claudia's first weekend. He and Luc went off on an inspection tour of some outlying sub-stations, and Bea took the opportunity of inviting Thurza, Emily and the children for the day on the Sunday they were away. Both ladies remarked on the difference in Becky, congratulating Claudia on her success with the child. Claudia disclaimed it, smiling, explaining that the angelic behaviour was merely advance payment on Becky's behalf for the hotly desired bicycle. Whatever the reason for Becky's reform, the result made life a great deal more pleasant for everyone in her vicinity, including herself.

When Saul came home he was unable to take a working day for the proposed trip to Boa Vista, and the following Saturday was settled on for the shopping expedition.

Boa Vista proved to be a modern city, its tall white buildings and wide streets raying out from a main tree-lined avenida. *Lotações*, the small local buses, scurried along crammed with people alongside big American limousines and dusty jeeps in an atmosphere of petrol fumes, roasting peanuts, coffee and cooking food, all blended together into a hot, foreign aroma by the fierce afternoon sun. Claudia breathed it in deeply, her eyes sparkling behind dark, white-framed lenses as she tried to take in everything around her at once. Advised by Bea to wear something on her head, Claudia had tied a white-spotted yellow kerchief over her hair, and chosen a double-breasted white overblouse and swinging pleated yellow skirt as both cool and suitable for the city.

Saul kept tight hold of her elbow as he steered her through the crowds thronging the wide pavements and pointed out various buildings of interest. A large department store was their goal, where they took the lift to the toy department and purchased the desired bicycle without fuss, leaving it to be picked up later.

'Would you give me a few moments to make a purchase of my own?' asked Claudia. 'I promise to be quick.'

Saul shrugged.

'No rush. I'll have a beer in the bar next door. Turn left as you leave the store, and join me when you've finished. Are you all right for currency?'

'Yes. Thanks a lot—I shan't be long.'

She watched his tall figure out of sight, then haltingly asked an assiatant for directions to the department selling children's clothes. Shaking her head at the enchanting frilly concoctions on display, Claudia eventually managed to make herself clear to the courteous, patient young man who served her, and bought three pairs of small jeans, the same quantity of shorts in vivid colours, plus half a dozen tee-shirts in every colour imaginable. A secret inspection of Becky's wardrobe had given her the right shoe size for two pairs of sneakers, and the final touch was several headbands in brightly coloured stretch-towelling.

Claudia had bought gifts in England for Saul and Bea, but when she left the elevator at the ground floor she noticed a kiosk selling cigarettes and saw the brand of cheroot Saul smoked and bought a large box to add to the framed antique map of Cornwall already chosen as suitable for an employer. It had taken quite an effort of armwaving and miming to buy the cigarillos, which she now knew was the Portuguese word, and feeling very pleased with her shopping spree Claudia left the air-conditioned store to emerge into the glaring heat outside, blinking in the brilliant light despite her sunglasses. She turned in the direction Saul had instructed and saw him immediately at one of the pavement tables just outside a small bar, his long legs stretched out under the table, his face absorbed as he read a newspaper, a half empty glass of beer in front of him.

Claudia stood silent, smiling down at his unconscious profile for a moment before Saul realised she was there and shot to his feet, a look of surprise on his face.

'My God, you were quick! I was all set for at least another half-hour's wait.'

'I said I wouldn't be long.' She grinned at him in such a friendly fashion he grinned back spontaneously and indicated a chair.

'Fancy a beer?'

'Not really.' Claudia eyed him hopefully. 'What I'd really sell my soul for is a cup of tea!'

'Why not?' Saul drained the beer in his glass and took her parcels, putting a hand under her elbow. 'If your soul can survive two blocks' walk in the sun it shall have its wish.'

He led her through the colourful crowd, past exciting shops selling tempting leather goods and jewellery, where Claudia would have given much to linger, privately promising herself a browse on some future occasion, until they reached a large, multi-storied building, the Hotel Paranà. Saul conducted her to the restaurant on the first floor, where half the tables were outside on a shaded balcony overlooking the Avenida. Claudia was delighted when Saul led her to one of these, able to gaze at the passing show to her heart's content while enjoying the tea Saul ordered, though rather wary of the plate of very ornate sweetmeats served with it.

Saul accepted a cup of tea but refused a pastry, urging Claudia to try one in her aim to experience the true flavour of everything Brazilian. She accepted one of the smallest, not because it was much to her taste but to please Saul, whose face today was without its habitual withdrawn expression. She disposed of the delicacy, a date embedded in a nest of marzipan, finding it over-sweet for her taste.

'Do these things have names?' she asked, wiping her fingers on her napkin.

'The one you ate is known as *Olha da Sogra*,' he said, with a sly grin. ' "Mother-in-law's eye" to you!'

Claudia's recoil was patently rewarding as he bent towards her with a mollifying look in his eye.

'Never mind, have some more tea, then we have one more call to make before we get the jeep and call back for the bike.'

'Where else are we going?'

'Just around the corner to a delicatessen where they stock imported products as well as very good food. Aunt Bea gave me a list of odds and ends.'

The delicatessen was a fragrant, dark Aladdin's cave of a place, where Saul was obviously well known, and the proprietor, a rotund personage in a white apron, greeted him like a long-lost son, sending minions scurrying in all directions while he himself presented Claudia with titbits of ham and cheese to taste, all of which were delicious. She watched, fascinated, as a box gradually filled with various delicacies, a kilo of hand-carved ham, another of Queijo Estepe, a superb local cheese, together with a slab of moist Mozzarella, special coffee from the city of Sao Paulo, jars of fat green olives, tins of anchovies, cashew nuts, walnuts, almonds, small biscuits like ratafias, and finally, carefully wrapped against the heat, some enormous chocolates were tenderly arranged before the lid was tied on the box surrendered to Saul with much quick-fire Portuguese, the gist of which Claudia understood to be Christmas wishes.

Soon after they were on their way back to Campo d'Ouro with the bicycle safely stowed beneath a tarpaulin with the other parcels in the back of the jeep. Saul drove at a less headlong rate than on Claudia's first, disastrous introduction to the scenic grandeur of the route to Campo d'Ouro.

'No troubles with your digestive system today?' he asked, with a gleaming sidelong glance.

'Nary a one,' she answered firmly, turning her mind away from thoughts of "mother-in-law's eye".

'I thought you were relaxed on the way in; you must be getting used to my driving.'

Even the scent of his cigarillo had no effect on Claudia this time, and she sat enjoying the breathtaking panorama of mountain peaks, her body swaying with the vehicle as it wound along the undulating route.

'You were in a towering hurry that first day,' she said. 'I was uncomfortably aware that you were hellbent on getting back, fast, and that fetching me from the airport was about the last on your list of priorities.

Today I'm getting different vibes. You don't seem in as much of a hurry.'

'I'm not.' Saul's eyes narrowed in concentration on a sharp bend ahead. 'I enjoyed our little excursion.'

'So did I.'

'Find everything you wanted? The shops here must be a bit different from the ones in England.'

'Very good, though. Figuring out the money was a bit tricky, but the shop assistant was patience itself with my fractured Portuguese and had just what I wanted, which is a relief.'

'Relief?'

Claudia nodded with satisfaction.

'Becky has done her utmost to be good lately and I wanted to buy her something I know she'll like—apart from the bicycle, of course. I've hit on the right thing, I think.'

Saul gave her a sharp glance.

'So your purchases were for Becky, not you? How do you know what she wants—another dream?'

'No. But I know she'd like shorts, jeans—things she can play in without messing up all those rather elaborate dresses she wears.' Claudia eyed him warily, unwilling to have anything spoil this pleasant outing, which had been notable for its lack of disagreement.

'I'm afraid my aunt just called in the village dressmaker, and she provided what she thought suitable for a little girl.' His face was bleak. 'I brought as little as possible from England when I collected Becky from Elaine's ménage.'

Claudia said nothing, inwardly sad for the child uprooted from everything familiar, not even her own possessions to cushion the strangeness of her new life in a foreign country with this unfamiliar father of hers.

'Thank God you heard Becky crying the other night,' Saul went on. Otherwise we would have had a very disappointed child on our hands on Christmas Day. What exactly had you in mind for me to do about the typewriter?'

A slight dryness in the last words made her smile.

'At the risk of being considered bossy, could I suggest

that you save it for her birthday, or some other appropriate time?'

'But of course, Claudia. I hired you for your educational qualities—I can hardly complain when you bring your talents to bear on the rest of the household as well.' This time the dryness was more marked.

'Just comfort yourself with the thought that you're getting your money's worth,' said Claudia tartly.

'That I intend to do, never fear.' Saul's teeth showed white in a grin that made Claudia uneasy and for the remainder of the journey she steered the conversation to more neutral topics until the conical peak of Morro d'Ouro came into sight, its cross already alight in preparation for the abrupt drama of sunset.

As the jeep came to a halt in the drive of the house a small figure danced up and down at the top of the verandah steps, the frills on her short pink lawn nightdress bobbing up and down as Claudia ran up the steps towards her.

'Clauida! Your box came. José put it in the *porao*.'

'Hollow, Becky, that's good news. Good evening, Bea.'

Bea Treharne was sitting near a drinks-laden tray on the table, an open picture book on her lap. She smiled as Claudia sank down on the settee beside her.

'How did you enjoy your afternoon, Claudia? What did you think of Boa Vista?'

'Very spectacular. The town itself was such a visual surprise. For some reason I never expected something so sophisticated and modern, and yet so very attractive. I think it's the contrast of the great interleaved double row of trees making an avenue of green shade in the middle of all that bright whiteness created by the buildings.'

Bea nodded, handing Claudia a long glass of gin and tonic.

'I find it utterly exhausting myself. It's the combination of the journey in, plus the impact of all that colour and noise, not to mention the different smells. I feel Boa Vista is a city for the young.'

'Nonsense!' Saul came springing up the steps with the

box from the delicatessen. 'Here are all your goodies, you poor ancient thing!'

'Splendid, dear. Now we can have a rather more special cold lunch tomorrow.'

Becky was examining the box Saul held, her curiosity plain to see, but with admirable self-control she forbore to enquire about its contents, to her father's amusement. He held out his hand.

'Come on, Becky, let's take this out to Maria to unpack, and see if we can find something in it for you.'

Joyously the child jumped up and took her father's hand without hesitation, chattering to him spontaneously as she skipped along at his side, watched with surprise and approval by Bea.

'You know, Claudia, I think you must be a catalyst. Since your arrival on the scene both Becky and Saul seem to be thawing.' She smiled kindly at Claudia, who shook her head instantly.

'It's early days yet. Perhaps the novelty of having someone come all the way from England for her sole benefit will wear off once lessons start in earnest. Perhaps she'll be more on her mettle with Jamie and Mark joining in.'

'Yes.' Bea gave a little cough. 'Has Saul recovered from his initial disapproval on that score?'

'I think so. Learning about Emily's pregnancy changed his attitude very quickly, anyway.'

Bea shook her head in vague disapproval.

'Personally I think it's too much for her—three children and a miscarriage already, and she's not even twenty-six yet. They should have waited a while before starting another.'

'Gossiping, Aunt Bea?' There was a slight warning note in Saul's voice as he reappeared suddenly from the hall, followed by Becky, busily engaged in removing the paper from an outsize chocolate.

'Thurza and I merely feel——'

'Surely it's more a case of what Luc and Emily feel!' His voice was crisp and dismissive as he helped himself to a drink.

Claudia jumped up and prepared to depart, reluctant

to listen in on any family disagreements, especially on this particular subject.

'If you'll excuse me, I must have a bath. The road wasn't nearly as dusty today after the rain we've had, but I feel a little scruffy, just the same.'

Saul looked her up and down with veiled amusement from his usual post at the verandah rail, but said nothing, downing the contents of his glass with enjoyment.

'Won't you feel like reading to me tonight, Claudia?' Becky's chocolate-daubed face was crestfallen.

'Becky!' Bea was indignant. 'I've already read you one story tonight—Claudia must be tired, after all.'

'Are you, Claudia?' Becky frowned earnestly as she turned apologetically to Bea. 'You see, Aunt Bea, Claudia makes different voices—like a really truly story!'

Bea held up her hands goodnaturedly, defeated.

'Oh well, in that case, how can I compete?'

'It comes of long practice in keeping young girls awake while I tried to cram some literature into their unwilling heads,' smiled Claudia. 'Come on, then, Becky, choose a dress for me while I shower, then I'll read you your story.'

All smiles, Becky ran to her great-aunt and her father, kissing them both goodnight without any prompting before dancing off with Claudia to her bedroom. Saul's eyes were thoughtful as they rested on the two departing figures, a fact secretly noted by his watchful aunt.

Dinner was ready by the time Claudia had showered, dressed and unleashed her talent for the dramatic on 'Red Riding Hood', to Becky's immense satisfaction. When Claudia said goodnight Becky opened her big eyes and stared up at her with anxious intensity.

'I've been a *very* good girl today, Claudia.'

'Well done!'

'Even though you weren't here, I mean. Cross my heart!'

Claudia smiled at her, touched.

'That's good news. Quite easy, really, isn't it?'

Becky nodded drowsily, the very picture of cherubic innocence. Claudia let herself out of the room quietly, smiling to herself, not a little doubtful about the ethics of good behaviour merely as a sprat to catch a mackerel, or bicycle in Becky's case. With luck Becky might adopt reasonable conduct as a life-style if practised long enough, bike or no bike. Aware that she was indulging in sophistry, Claudia joined Bea and Saul in the dining room, seating herself with anticipation before a tempting glass goblet containing large prawns in a sauce of delicious piquancy.

'Maria adds a dash of cream and brandy before serving,' explained Bea in response to Claudia's rapturous praise of the sauce.

'Did you come up to scratch with your rendition of Becky's bedtime opus?' Saul smiled blandly and leaned over to fill her wine glass.

'Red Riding Hood tonight.' Claudia gave him a mischievous smile. 'It's really quite difficult to read that one without histrionics anyway. It's quite surprising how children enjoy the ghoulish stories the best—they always did at the Home. I read somewhere that Eleanor Roosevelt was renowned for the drama of her bedtime stories and her family refused to allow anyone else to read to them.'

Bea shook her head regretfully.

'Definitely not a talent I posses. *And* I tend to stick to Cinderella and the prettier stories. No wonder Becky was bored—I honestly thought the more violent ones would frighten her.'

'Children are barbarians on the whole,' said Saul dryly. 'The fortunate grow up to be more civilised, but a great many never manage it, even in maturity.'

Bea looked rather smug. 'Claudia certainly seems to be civilising Becky—you must admit that, Saul.'

'Let's not get over-optimistic, Aunt Bea, perhaps we should wait a while before awarding accolades.' Saul gave Claudia a look that said quite plainly she had no reason to rest on her laurels.

Unperturbed, Claudia began on her Beef Stroganoff. Saul could put away his goad. She had no intention of

allowing herself to relax her vigilance with either father
or child. Her confidence in winning Becky over was
unshaken, but as far as Saul was concerned there
seemed little point in trying. Her mercenary proclivities
plainly had the upper hand in his opinion of her. Yet
the trip to Boa Vista had been pleasant, surprisingly so.
Her musings were interrupted by a question from Bea
on Claudia's opinion of the shops in Boa Vista, and for
the rest of the meal the conversation centred on
shopping and Christmas.

'I believe you drive,' remarked Saul later when they
were lingering over coffee in the drawing-room.

Claudia nodded, pleasantly tired after the strenuous
afternoon.

'Will she have to take another test, Saul?' asked Bea.

Claudia's sleepiness vanished.

'Another test?'

'I'm afraid so.' Saul's smile had a wolfish quality.
'No problem to an efficient lady like you.' He drank his
brandy, obviously relishing something more than just
the flavour of the spirit. 'They test several people, one
at a time down on the Praca, the square in the town.
It's a bit different from in the U.K. A fair crowd
usually turn out to watch.'

Claudia set down her coffee cup with care.

'It sounds more like an *auto-da-fé*,' she said acidly.
'What would I have to do?'

'The only thing that differs very much is the *balisa*.
This consists of reversing and backing acurately
through a pair of posts without touching them—
something like football posts, only a little closer
together.' Saul was clearly enjoying himself.

'Do I have to?' demanded Claudia.

'Well, you can't drive here without a Brazilian
licence, and it would certainly be a help for Bea and
Rebecca if you could act as chauffeur when I'm not
around.' Saul lit a cigarillo and watched Claudia's face
through the smoke with patient pleasure.

Defeated, Claudia said nothing, but gave him a look
that spoke volumes.

'Well,' he persisted, 'shall I put in an application?'

'I suppose so,' she agreed reluctantly.

'Cheer up, it won't be so bad,' he said patronisingly. 'Now, have some more coffee.'

With a sympathetic look Bea changed the subject and asked Claudia if there was anything she urgently required from her trunk, or could it wait until the following day.

'Having waited this long,' said Claudia sweetly, her eyes sending a barbed glance in Saul's direction, 'I'm sure I can hang on until the morning.'

Bea hid a smile as Saul looked defensive for once.

'I'm afraid it slipped my mind before I went away—you could have reminded me, you know.'

'I wouldn't have dreamed of bothering you with something so unimportant!' It gave Claudia great self-satisfaction to see the mighty Saul put out for a change. Her eyes were crystal-bright with conscious virtue as she watched him stub out his cigarillo with rather unnecessary force.

'Is your tennis gear in the trunk?' he asked surprisingly.

'Yes—the racquets anyway.'

'Fancy a game of tennis tomorrow?'

'With you?' asked Claudia, her eyes startled.

'Yes. I enjoy a game now and then, usually with Bob McClure, the geologist. Becky and Bea can watch.' The challenge in the dark blue eyes made it impossible to do anything other than agree.

'Fine,' said Claudia brightly. 'I'll look forward to it. In that case, though, perhaps I'd better get a good night's sleep in to prepare myself for the fray!'

CHAPTER NINE

CLAUDIA was awake next morning at the crack of dawn with the thought of the ensuing game hanging over her like a cloud. Worry about Saul's standard of tennis had made sleep harder to achieve than usual, and Claudia

grew quite irritable with herself, knowing very well that
she played a strong, workmanlike game, not brilliant,
but certainly good enough to give Saul a run for his
money, any day.

She dressed silently, putting an old denims and an
elderly rugby shirt in preparation for tackling her
trunk. It was very early, not long after six, and she
made herself some tea in the kitchen, taking it on the
verandah to lean against the rail, drinking in the
scene below her, the colours crystalline in the early
light. Gradually her sense of proportion was restored.
Back in England Sunday was a lonely day to pass as
well as she could, which at this time of the year
meant a long lie-in, a browse through the Sunday
papers while her solitary lunch cooked, then an
afternoon in front of the television with a pile of
marking, and if the quiet became too intense
sometimes an evening trip to the cinema. Whereas
here she had sunshine, company, the prospect of
tennis at the club, conversation and good food—in
fact, Claudia, she told herself impatiently, count your
blessings. She remained counting them for some time,
enjoying the relative coolness of early morning and
her moment of peace.

'You look happy this morning!'

Claudia turned to Saul standing behind her in the
dining-room doorway in jeans and sweatshirt, looking
more rested than at any time since her arrival.

'I was laughing at myself,' she said with complete
truth.

'What was so funny?' He strolled across and leaned
on the rail beside her. Claudia pushed her hair behind
her ears. 'Something bothering you?' asked Saul
casually. 'You do that when you're nervous.'

'Do what?'

'Push your hair behind your ears.'

'Do I? Great! Must be a dead give-away.'

'So what are you uptight about?' he persisted.

Claudia looked up at him for a moment, head on one
side, then opted for frankness.

'I was nervous about playing tennis with you.'

It was his turn to stare.

'Why, for God's sake?'

She shrugged. 'I have this insane feeling that if I don't measure up to your requirements in every department—give you value for your money, as it were—you'll pack me back to England at the first opportunity.'

'And you don't want that?' There was no mockery in his dark blue scrutiny for once.

Claudia shook her head and looked away.

'Your idea's nonsense anyway,' he said. 'I engaged you to teach my daughter, not entertain me. I merely thought you might enjoy some tennis today—it's the only one I have free.'

She smiled sheepishly.

'And you're perfectly right—I will enjoy it. I was being rather immature for a while, but at least I paid you the compliment of honesty.'

'A rare virtue among women!' The familiar mocking element was back, irritating Claudia.

'Sweeping generalisations are empty statements,' she said flatly. 'One might just as easily say all men are liars.'

'No doubt they are—ah, good! Here comes Maria and breakfast. Bea usually has a lie-in on Sundays.'

Claudia looked at him curiously. 'Don't you?'

'I wake at the same time each day. Habit——' he broke off as Becky ran towards them, her face accusing.

'You weren't in your bed, Claudia!'

'No, Becky, I woke early today.'

Becky turned to her father, demanding, 'It's Sunday. Are you staying home today?'

'Yes. You can come to the club with Aunt Bea and watch Claudia play tennis with me.' Saul smiled indulgently at the child and gave her a gentle push towards the table.

'Goody!' Becky prattled all through breakfast, then accompanied Claudia to the *porão* to open the trunk. Fortunately her racquets and tennis shoes lay on the tray on top, as Claudia had no intention of allowing Becky to see the contents underneath.

'I'll leave the rest until later,' she said, and relocked the trunk. 'Let's see if Aunt Bea's up and about.'

Maria and Lourdes departed after breakfast, not due to return until the following morning, and Bea took charge of Becky while Claudia went to change into her tennis gear. Her brief wrapover tennis skirt and tee-shirt top showed off her lithe, graceful figure and long legs to the best possible advantage, the white cotton knit of her shirt clinging to the curves of her high breasts and emphasising her neat waist. Claudia tied the laces of her tennis shoes firmly and secured her hair at the nape of her neck with a green ribbon, wondering if she needed a skirt for the short walk over to the club, and decided to play safe, adding the matching knee-length skirt and cotton blouson jacket that went with the outfit.

Bea examined Claudia approvingly in the kitchen where she was waiting for her.

'Saul's gone on ahead with Becky,' she said. 'You look very neat and businesslike, my dear.'

'I devoutly hope my game does the same!' Claudia's nerves were taut as Bea closed the door behind them and walked with her towards the gate.

'Don't be nervous, Claudia. It's not Wimbledon!'

The club bar was open, several people clustered round it, others sitting at the tables overlooking the courts, where a man's singles match was already in progress. All eyes seemed to turn in their direction as Bea and Claudia descended the steps and went towards the bar, where Saul, magnificent in white shirt and shorts, a light blue sweater knotted round his shoulders by the sleeves, was talking to two elderly men, Becky perched on a high stool beside him sucking orangeade through a straw. He looked up as he caught sight of Bea and Claudia.

'Ah, here they come!'

'Good morning,' said Bea. 'How are you John, Tom?'

Both men greeted her, short, dark, physically very similar, their kind faces creased in smiles.

'Claudia,' said Saul, 'meet John Trelaur, former Mine

Captain, Tom Enys, the best Drill Doctor west of the Tamar. This is Miss Claudia March.'

'She's my new gov'ness,' Becky informed them importantly.

Claudia received a warm welcome from both men, who began to tease Becky about having to watch her p's and q's from now on, then were obliged to explain to the curious child just what they meant.

'Ready?' asked Saul under cover of the conversation.

'As I'll ever be,' Claudia gave a little grimace. 'Where do I put my outer things?'

'Ladies' clockroom along there, just beyond the bar. I'll get on the court. Don't be long.'

'Yes, sir!' said Claudia smartly, and disappeared through the indicated door before he could respond. When she emerged Becky was loud in her praise of Claudia's outfit, embarrassingly so.

'You look smashing, Claudia, doesn't she, Uncle Tom?'

'A sight for sore eyes,' said Tom Enys, smiling in agreement.

'Saul's waiting for you on court, dear.' Bea smiled in encouragement. 'Good luck.'

Claudia's progress along the verandah and on to the court was made more nerve-raking by the knowledge that, added to the interested looks of the people sat at the tables, three pairs of male eyes were watching her cross the court with varying expressions; two with frank appreciation, the third blank as navy blue buttons as Claudia approached. Inwardly annoyed that Saul should subject her to this particular way of meeting two of his colleagues, Claudia's head came up proudly and she gave him a cool little smile as she reached the three men. One of them was a long-legged man with fair hair and gold-rimmed glasses, the same height as Saul but slighter and more rangy, with skin that showed a tendency to redden in the sun. His companion was younger, shorter by a head, swarthy and muscular with a thick black moustache and dark eyes that managed to convey respect and appreciation simultaneously as they rested on Claudia.

Saul took her by the arm.

'Claudia, I'd like you to meet Bob McClure, the geologist, and Manoel Araujo, one of the bright young engineers in my department. Gentlemen, allow me to present Miss Claudia March, who has been kind enough to leave the U.K. to teach my daughter and the Fonseca children.'

Feeling for the first time as though her exact function had now been clearly defined, Claudia smiled warmly at the two men, holding out her hand with a conventional 'How do you do.' Bob McClure shook it heartily, grinning in a friendly, disarming sort of way.

'Welcome to Campo d'Ouro, Miss March, I sincerely hope you'll like it here.'

'I already do,' Claudia assured him, and turned to give her hand to Manoel Araujo, who hesitated a second, then raised it to his lips for an instant.

'*Muito prazer, senhora*, allow me to add my good wishes to those of Bob.'

'Buy her a drink later,' Saul interrupted, 'but for the moment we'll all earn one with a little exercise.'

Claudia could see Becky on the edge of a chair at a table near the railing, with Bea and the two Cornishmen, all obviously prepared to watch with enjoyment.

With a fervent mental prayer to whatever patron saint had the job of looking after tennis players, Claudia began to knock up, sending balls back and forth over the net to Saul, whose sheer length of arm and leg augured only too plainly how difficult it would be to get a ball past him. Already familiar with his unexpected lightness of tread, it came as no surprise to Claudia to see the perfect co-ordination he displayed as he moved around the court with a speed not normally associated with someone of his proportions. At first her strokes were tentative, then eye and hand automatically began to function in unison, and Claudia grew bolder, hitting the ball at her opponent with a force Saul acknowledged with a raised eyebrow as he returned the compliment.

'Let's start,' he called, 'or the heat might get to you.'

Not if I can help it, vowed Claudia silently. She gave

him a nod and retrieved two balls in preparation for the
first serve. She threw the ball up high in a practised,
fluid motion, stretching every last inch of body and arm
as she came down on the ball with a strength many a
man might have envied, sending it over the net like a
bullet to land just inside the centre line of the service
court. Admittedly it was returned with interest, but
from then on Claudia's nerves steadied and she began
to enjoy herself, her brain cool as it automatically
calculated any weaknesses in Saul's game. There was no
weakness at all in his baseline play, and when she
slammed balls at his feet they came back with a force
that now and then defeated her, but doggedly she
stuck to her guns and the score went with service,
neither player conceding a break. Gradually she began
to introduce the occasional disguised little drop-shot
that fell just over the net, foiling Saul in his attempts to
reach them from the baseline despite his magnificent
bursts of speed. Nevertheless the score remained ding-
dong, with neither player gaining any advantage until
they reached a tie-break situation at the end of the set,
where Saul's powerhouse service prevailed, and Claudia
was defeated by means of three lightning-fast aces.

Saul vaulted across the net towards Claudia as a
spatter of applause sounded from the onlookers, to her
embarrassment, and Bob McClure and Manoel Araujo
came across from the other court, where they had
openly abandoned their game to watch. Saul gave her
an odd little bow, a smile of such genuine appreciation
on his normally impassive face that Claudia's heartbeat
might have quickened if it had not already been
pounding like a bongo drum with exertion, as she
suddenly realised she was very hot, very sweaty and
extremely tired.

'Claudia, I salute you,' he said simply.

She smiled shakily, her breath coming in laboured
gasps.

'Same to you, kind sir,' she panted.

Bob McClure loped up, the sun glinting on his
glasses, his face split from ear to ear in a grin of delight.

'Lady, you play a mean game! Before I beg the

honour of a game with you I guess I'd better get in some practice!'

'*Parabéms, senhora!*' The young Brazilian added his congratulations with sincere admiration.

Claudia felt embarrassed. Her aim had been to show Saul Treharne she was worth her salt in the sports department, not to make an exhibition of herself.

'I was stupid—I forgot to bring a towel,' she said apologetically, following Saul towards the exit gate, her legs like jelly.

'It's reassuring to find you have the odd little imperfection,' he said, with a barbed little grin. 'I had the forethought to bring two; Becky has them with her at the table.'

Claudia gave him an eloquent glance as she opened the gate to let her through to a rapturous reception from Becky, whose face was pink with excitement as she caught Claudia's arm in an excited grasp.

'I want to learn tennis, Claudia. Will you show me how?'

'Of course I will, then you can play with Daddy, too.'

The child's eyes sparkled as she ran to Bea to tell her. Bea's eyes twinkling merrily as she shook her head at Claudia.

'What in the world were you nervous about, dear girl?' She turned to look up at Saul. 'She almost beat you, my dear, your reputation is at stake!'

Saul grinned and handed a large blue towel to Claudia. She slung it round her shoulders, mopping at her forehead with one end.

'I'll have to resort to secret practice sessions with Bob to preserve my pride,' he said, straight-faced. 'Seriously, Claudia, you'd be wise to sponge yourself in the changing room and give yourself a good rub down before we claim the drinks Bob's about to stand us.'

Bea looked at Claudia's pale, perspiring face and said reasonably,

'It's only a step over to the house, Claudia. Why not run over and take a shower?'

Claudia agreed gratefully, and excusing herself to John Trelaur and Tom Enys, went to collect her skirt

and jacket from the cloakroom, Becky at her side
wanting to go with her to the house while she changed.
As they mounted the steps together Saul's voice halted
them.

'Claudia! What will you have when you come back—
your usual?'

Claudia nodded, smiling, and took Becky's hand to
walk jauntily back to the house, pleased at the
connotations of the word 'usual', which seemed to
indicate a permanency, a settled feeling, as though her
place in the Treharne household was an established,
welcome fact.

At lightning speed she showered and dressed,
hurrying into clean underwear and buttoning on a crisp
white cotton shirt which she tucked into the waistband of
the jade green trousers, which had been exquisitely
laundered and ironed by the invaluable Maria. Becky had
been delivering a running commentary about tennis up to
that point, but as Claudia tied the white rope belt and slid
her feet into white sandals she noticed Becky staring at
herself in the mirror with a black frown on her face.

'What's up, Becky?'

'This stupid dress is dirty,' grumbled the child,
pouting.

'Let's go and look for something else, then.'

Claudia rummaged through the hangers of exquisite
dresses in Becky's wardrobe until she found something
a little less elaborate, a sleeveless mint-green over
blouse with its own brief pleated skirt.

'How about this?'

Becky nodded unenthusiastically, but suffered
Claudia to strip off her dress and replace it with the
plainer outfit, in a fever of impatience to return to the
club. She danced on ahead as Claudia relocked the
house, but halted obediently at the gate in response to
Claudia's call, still very much on her mettle to show
how good she could be. Hand in hand they walked
more sedately back along the Club path, and descended
the steps to find Bea at a table, literally surrounded by
men, as Bob McClure and Manoel Araujo had now
joined John Trelaur, Tom Enys and Saul. They all rose

as one man as Claudia and Becky appeared, Bob instantly making for the bar, where a long gin and tonic materialised like magic from the cheerful, dark-skinned waiter in his immaculate white shirt and black bow tie.

Claudia sat down next to Bea amid a great deal of noise and cheerful teasing from the men as she took her first thirsty mouthful of her drink after acknowledging all the extravagant toasts aimed at her.

'Beginner's luck,' she said firmly, her face a little pink as she crossed one green-clad leg over the other and prepared to relax.

'You aren't trying to tell us that this was your first game of tennis?' said Saul severely. He hoisted Becky on to his knee, the startled look on the child's face evidence that this was not a common occurrence.

'It was my first game *here*,' said Claudia firmly, with a smile aimed at everyone in general.

'It surely won't be your last, Miss March,' said Bob with conviction. 'Where did you learn to play like that?'

'In college,' she answered, and turned to Tom Enys with a view to changing the subject, enquiring the meaning of the fascinating term 'Drill Doctor'. She was aware, out of the corner of her eye, that Saul was watching her as John Trelaur supplied the necessary information, as Tom Enys seemed a bit tongue-tied at explaining his special craft.

'The Drill Doctor's the chap who makes and sets the cutting-heads of the drills with diamonds——'

'Diamonds?' Claudia's eyes glittered in surprise.

'He means industrial diamonds, my dear,' put in Tom. 'I used to be responsible for forming new heads, or refurbishing existing ones, and not all had diamonds—some of them are made of special hard steel.'

'He was the best in the business,' said Saul, who obviously had great affection for the older man.

'Get on with you,' said Tom, embarrassed. 'Anyway, I trained young Sabino pretty well to follow me. I hear he don't do too badly.'

' "Young Sabino" must be all of fifty,' said Bob McClure with a grin, then looked at Saul expectantly. 'Feel like another game, old buddy?'

'Give me five minutes,' said Saul, and stood up, swinging Becky to the ground.

It was enlightening entertainment to watch the contrast in style between the two players. Bob countered Saul's fire and force with a game of craft and precision, placing his shots with as much care as his opponent allowed, endlessly retrieving and retrieving in a manner designed to wear down his opponent. At times it seemed he would succeed, but for Claudia the issue was never in doubt. She was certain Saul would win, and eventually the American conceded a service game and it was all over as Saul won the following game with four serves of devastating speed and accuracy Bob had no possibility of getting back over the net.

'Saul's on fine form today,' observed Bea, with a smiling glance at Claudia, who sat with Becky leaning against her shoulder, displaying signs of restiveness. The two men were hot and sweat-soaked as they came off court, the hot noonday sun having taken its toll. Bea rolled up her knitting and put it away, turning to her two fellow countrymen with a smile.

'Can I persuade you both to a pot luck sort of meal—you know I do it myself on Sundays, so you can't say you haven't been warned!'

They accepted with alacrity, as did Bob when Bea extended her invitation to include him.

'Yes, ma'am! With the greatest of pleasure. Be with you directly—just as long as it takes to shower.'

As the rest of the party made their way back to the house Saul gave a sly glance at Claudia and remarked,

'If you're stuck, Aunt Bea, perhaps Claudia might cook us something.'

There was a concerted laugh at the look of comic dismay on Claudia's face as she put up a hand in protest.

'I'm hopeless at quite a few things, but I must admit that cooking is my nadir!'

'What are the others, I wonder?' Saul's murmur was inaudible to the others as they followed more slowly.

'Don't worry, they'll become glaringly obvious the
longer you know me.' Claudia shook back her hair,
laughing, the shimmer of sunlight in her eyes prompting
an answering smile in his, attractive as it was rare.

The impromptu lunch was a very pleasant affair, cold
meats, including the delicious ham purchased in Boa
Vista the day before, various salads, and an enormous
pot of gnocchi, prepared by Maria the night before
ready for heating up next day. The atmosphere was
more like that of a picnic.

Bob McClure elected himself washer-up despite Bea's
protests, and he and Claudia made surprisingly short
work of the dishes while Bea put food away and
generally tidied up. Saul, seeming at a loose end,
lounged in the kitchen doorway and watched the
workers at their labours.

'Being a bachelor I don't have a maid that lives in,'
explained Bob to Claudia with a grin, methodically
washing and rinsing plates with a practised hand. 'So
I'm quite used to this sort of thing. Isilda always tells
me to leave my dishes overnight for her in the morning,
but my good New England upbringing considers that
kind of tacky, so I do them myself. She thinks I'm
weird, but no matter.'

'Well, aren't you?' said Saul lazily.

'I resent that, Treharne!' Obviously Bob didn't in the
slightest, and suddenly he swung round. 'Hey, Saul,
how about you and Claudia coming in to Boa Vista
with me, Christmas Eve? The American Consul's
giving a party. You'd be welcome.'

Claudia glanced at Saul, to find his eyes were fixed
on her in speculation.

'That's kind of you, Bob,' he said slowly. 'But as it's
Becky's first Christmas with me, I think I'd better be on
hand. Claudia's free to do as she wishes, of course.'

It was crystal clear to Claudia that acceptance on her
part was hardly likely to go down well with Saul, and
although a rebellious section of her mind resented this,
prompting her to say yes, the sensible side of her smiled
at Bob with sincere gratitude and declined.

'That's very sweet of you, but in the circumstances I

think it best for me to stay here too. I've been here a very short time, really, and I'm still working on this altitude factor. I need my sleep, I'm afraid. Another time, perhaps?'

Any slight awkwardness arising from Bob's well-intentioned suggestion was promptly dispelled as a familiar Mercedes turned in through the gate and came to a halt in the drive.

'Hold everything!' said Bob with a grin. 'Here comes the *Patrão*.'

Saul was gone instantly, running lightly down the descending concrete path at the side of the house as Luc Fonseca got out of the big car and helped his wife out of the passenger seat with tender care. Saul closed the big garden gates swiftly as Luc shepherded his children out of the car, Emily standing on tiptoe as she held up her cheek for Saul's kiss. Even from the kitchen window Claudia could instantly see the difference in his manner as he greeted Emily, a curious protectiveness in his manner as he smiled down at her.

'She's a very special lady.'

Claudia started. She had forgotten Bob was standing behind her.

'Yes.' She smiled, blinking. 'Utterly natural and charming.'

'No more than you, honey.' Bob's eyes were earnest behind his glasses. 'Different maybe, but you've got a lot going for you, Claudia.'

'You're nice, Bob. Good for my ego.' Her smile became carefully carefree. 'I must go and call Bea. She went to her room to tidy up.'

Claudia was glad to retreat along the corridor, leaving the American to join the group outside, as she tapped on Bea's door.

'Emily and Luc are here with the children, Bea.'

Bea emerged at speed, immaculate to the last hair, in her tailored pink linen dress.

'Then I suppose that means it's time for tea now we've just managed to dispose of lunch,' she said cheerfully, her eyes keen on Claudia's face. 'Does all this activity make you homesick for your quiet

Sundays in England? My dear! What have I said?' Her forehead furrowed with concern as Claudia blinked to keep back the tears that suddenly glazed her eyes.

In an agony of embarrassment Claudia sniffed prosaically, dashing away the tears with a careless hand.

'*Are* you homesick, Claudia?' Bea persisted gently.

'No—really. Quite the reverse.' Claudia accepted the proffered handkerchief with gratitude. 'In fact I was just thinking how friendly you all are, and—and how pleasant a day it's been.' She shook her head impatiently. 'My God, you must think me a right idiot—I never cry, honestly!'

'It doesn't hurt now and again, you know! Now pop along to the bathroom and wash your face,' said Bea practically. 'Give yourself a minute, then come and join us.'

In the cool privacy of the bathroom Claudia dealt quickly with repairs, her tears too transient to do more than brighten her eyes a little, the lids unaffected. As she added a little more shadow to them her eyes stared back at her, full of a sudden, unwelcome knowledge. Her tears had been caused by sheer self-pity. *She* wanted to be the one Saul looked at with such tenderness, not Emily Fonseca. His protective manner was one Claudia craved for herself, and what was more, she wanted the copyright on it. A tearing spear of jealousy had impaled her as she watched Saul smiling at another woman in a way she wanted him to smile at *her*. Claudia sat down suddenly on the edge of the bath, limp with revelation. This feeling was presumably love. And for Saul Treharne, for heaven's sake! And what's more, if this was how love made one feel she could very well do without it.

Claudia took a deep breath and stood up, squaring her shoulders, then, carefully arranging her features into a gay smile of welcome, she went back to join the party.

CHAPTER TEN

FOR the next two days life was an odd mixture for Claudia, uneventful on the surface, apart from a few leisurely preparations for Christmas, the entire thought of which seemed unreal against a backdrop of blazing sunshine. The nights were different. In bed alone she slept little, tossing and turning as she tried to keep her mind away from Saul, and failed miserably. She, who had once thought nothing of exerting discipline over classrooms full of children, now found that discipline over her own wayward emotions was impossible. She kept remembering the heated, illicit encounter on the night of the storm, at times wondering if it had been a figment of her own imagination in the face of Saul's attitude towards her, at others hot with shame at the thought that should such a thing occur again she would have difficulty in calling a halt to his lovemaking.

Claudia was almost piqued to find that she was unlikely to be put to the test. Granted Saul had mellowed towards her, especially since their game of tennis, for some reason. There was less sparring and more genuine conversation, to Bea's evident relief, as Saul probed Claudia's mind, crossing swords with enjoyment over politics, literature and sport at the dinner table, a change for the better, admittedly, from the brief, barbed skirmishes of the first days after her arrival, but with never a hint of anything more personal. Presumably he had forgotten the incident that remained so vivid in Claudia's mind.

Bea functioned in something of the role of Greek chorus when all three were together, and when alone with Claudia she dropped quite naturally into the role of surrogate aunt. Becky had her moments of mutiny and tantrums still, but these were shortlived and getting fewer and farther between, as the merest reminder of Father Christmas's checking-up activities acted like

147

magic on her ill-humour, and effected a hasty transformation into a child well behaved enough to merit the hotly-craved bicycle. Claudia stifled any feelings of guilt on this score, and resolved privately to think of some other means of curbing Becky's volatile temper once the bicycle was safely in the child's possession.

By day it was easy for Claudia to lock her new-found feelings towards Saul behind a door in her mind, constantly aware of their existence, but refusing to let them out to threaten the new temperate climate prevailing between herself and her employer. At night in bed it was different. At times she comforted herself with the thought that at least Saul was less hostile towards her, apparently no longer tarring her with the same brush that his memories of Elaine wielded over women in general—excepting Bea, Emily and Thurza, of course. As Saul made no attempt to put their relationship on a footing any closer than one of impersonal friendliness, Claudia sometimes wondered what would have happened if her reaction to his unexpected assault had been unconditional surrender instead of eventual rebuff. Would he have taken it on to its natural conclusion, or would he have just decided she was a fully paid up member of the permissive society and withdrawn even more abruptly in cynical affirmation of his cold-blooded little experiment? Not that Claudia ever managed to convince herself that the blood of either participants had been noticeably cool on that occasion which had been memorable to her at least, if not to Saul.

On Christmas Eve Luc Fonseca annually held a party for the children of his employees in one of the company's big store-rooms, emptied and cleaned for the occasion, and provided with long white-covered tables laden with potato chips and sausages on sticks and all the other delicacies de rigueur at these occasions, to be washed down with gallons of fizzy drinks before games were played and the excitement mounted in expectation of Father Christmas's arrival, complete with toys, carefully chosen by Emily in advance and labelled with the names of the recipients.

'I think I'll be extremely weak-spirited and deny myself the pleasure of this particular occasion,' said Bea, with an air of guilt. 'Emily says it's very noisy and gets extremely hot, and being a vinegary old spinster I find the prospect of so much infantile exuberance positively daunting.'

'This is where I finally start to demonstrate my usefulness,' said Claudia promptly. 'Think of all the sports days I've helped organise—the party will be child's play for me, if you'll pardon the pun.'

Bea smiled gratefully.

'I must admit I don't fancy it much——'

'No problem,' said Saul decisively. 'Claudia and I are more than enough escort for one small five-year-old. Besides,' he added as an afterthought, 'Emily will be very glad of Claudia's experience, and I'll be on hand to watch over Becky.' He eyed his aunt sternly. 'I think you'd better rest up all day tomorrow, Aunt Bea, or you won't enjoy the evening at the Fonsecas on Christmas Day.'

'Maybe you're right,' said Bea meekly.

'You've been doing too much in the kitchen,' said Claudia gently, 'all those mince pies, brandy butter and a chocolate log, not to mention dozens of sausage rolls for the party.'

'Well, apparently people tend to drop in over the holiday,' said Bea conciliatingly. 'I thought it would be nice for Saul this year if we fostered the Christmas spirit as much as possible.'

'And I'm very grateful,' said Saul, an expression of tenderness in his normally hard voice that Claudia noted wistfully. 'This Christmas will be the best I've had in years, I know, but I not unaturally want you well enough to join in all the festivities.'

'Amen,' said Claudia fervently. 'How about staying in bed in the morning with a tempting breakfast tray and one of the paperbacks I unpacked from my trunk?'

'Excellent idea.' Saul gave Claudia a warm smile of approval. 'Becky's in good hands now we have Claudia, so you can take it easy.'

'Oh, very well,' said Bea, obviously ensnared by the

idea. 'Only stop fussing now and let's have coffee in the
drawing room to let Lourdes clear away.'

Heavy rain overnight had damped down the dust,
but otherwise had done little to lower the temperature,
merely adding humidity to the heat next day. Saul
arrived from work in good time to change into
beautifully cut trousers of cream linen, worn with a
thin shirt in cream and black stripes. Claudia, who
had left changing until the last moment, sat down to
lunch feeling distinctly dowdy in a rather elderly
denim skirt and red tee-shirt, glad to see that Bea,
who had not long risen, looked a great deal better
after her rest. Saul's eyes rested on his daughter's
face, querying the look of frowning preoccupation on
her face as she disposed of her portion of meat loaf
with a marked lack of enthusiasm.

'Problems, Becky?' he asked.

She heaved a great sigh and abandoned her lunch.

'Is Father Christmas Brazilian?'

Claudia and Bea avoided each other's eye as Saul
blinked, searching for an answer.

'He doesn't really have a nationality, Becky,' he
began with care.

'What's a nasher—what you said?' Her frown deepened.

'Well, I mean he's not British or Brazilian, he—he's
just Father Christmas; a special person to all the
children in the world.' Saul cast a comic look of
anguish in Claudia's direction, but she merely smiled in
bland encouragement, feeling there were times when
fathers were best left to cope alone.

'How will he know my name?' persisted Becky.

'He knows everyone's name.' Saul spoke with the
hearty emphasis that denotes inward doubt.

'Can he say the Brazilian names?'

Saul was on firmer ground now.

'He doesn't have to. He just hands the parcels to
Uncle Luc and then Uncle Luc calls out the names.'

'Oh.' Becky gave this some thought and brightened.
Uncle Luc would know *her* name well enough. Then her
mouth drooped again. 'Will the other little girls wear
dresses?'

'You bet! They're hot on frilly party dresses here—they all look like a lot of pretty little butterflies.'

This idea held no appeal for Becky, from the expression on her face, and hurriedly Claudia asked,

'Should I be fairly fancy too, then? I'd rather thought of wearing slacks if I'm to help with the games.'

Saul grinned maliciously.

'Not on your life! It's a frilly party dress for you too—only I suggest you choose one that's easy to launder. Things get fairly boisterous.'

Casting a mental eye over her wardrobe, Claudia doubted she possessed anything in the necessary category.

'Something cool,' added Bea, 'not necessarily elaborate.'

'I don't go in for frills much,' said Claudia wryly.

Becky's attention was caught.

'You do, Claudia,' she said reprovingly. 'You've got frills on some of your nighties.'

'Oh yes,' Claudia ignored the gleam in Saul's eye, 'so I have. But that's only for bed.'

Saul rose, murmuring in Claudia's ear as he passed her chair.

'Do you think Freud might have found that significant?'

Luckily Bea was occupied in discussing Becky's choice of party dress with the child, and Claudia's sudden rush of colour went unnoticed as she made for her bedroom in undisguised retreat from Saul's unexpected veer to personalities.

Her choice of dress finally fell on one of silk-lined Tana lawn in apple green, sleeveless and falling straight to her hips where numbers of tiny pleats swung from a sash in lawn of a darker green. Not precisely frilly, she thought, as she added small green beryl ear-studs to her lobes and brushed her hair into a heavy coil secured firmly on top of her head. Hardly her own idea of suitable costume for the rough and tumble of a children's party! She grinned as she remembered the track-suit worn on her last visit to the Orphanage Christmas Party, and hoped none of today's party-goers were likely to run amok with the ice-cream in her vicinity.

'Claudia!' Becky's voice held a definite cry for help, and Claudia quickly slid into her plaited kid mules and went to investigate.

Both Lourdes and Afra were holding out dresses for Becky's approval, while Bea looked on rather helplessly.

'Claudia!' Bea smiled in relief. 'Come and cast your vote. What do you think Becky should wear?'

After some argument Becky finally consented to wear a white organdie dress cut like a slip and ending in three pink-scalloped frills at the hip-line, chosen because it vaguely resembled Claudia's. Claudia took over the hairdressing and brushed out the rippling waves of silver-gilt hair, sweeping it up and away from the flawless, impatient face, and tying it at the crown of Becky's head with a length of pink silk ribbon, allowing the shining waterfall to hang free down the child's back. Pink-edged white socks and white patent leather shoes were the finishing touches, and Bea heaved a sigh of relief.

'Both of you look very beautiful,' she said, an opinion obviously shared by the two maids, for whom the child's hair was a constant source of wonder.

'Want to show Maria.' Becky shot off in the direction of the kitchen for more compliments en route to her father on the verandah. Bea looked at Claudia and smiled quiltily.

'I feel quite terrible about not making the effort to go.'

'Nonsense,' Claudia said instantly. 'Just make sure Maria has gallons of tea ready when we get back.'

Saul was waiting with weary patience as the two women emerged from the house, Becky's hand in his as she jigged up and down, eager to leave.

'This was about as frilly as I could get,' said Claudia, sketching an irreverent curtsy. 'Will I pass?'

The impatience left Saul's face as he deliberately subjected her to a head-to-toe scrutiny.

'Not bad at all,' he said casually.

'Come on, then,' Becky pulled his hand. 'We'll be late—bye-bye, Aunt Bea!' She waved and scampered down the steps.

'Bye-bye, darling, Have a lovely time.' Bea stood waving as Saul ran down the steps to drive the jeep out from its cool sanctuary under the house. She put a hand on Claudia's arm, unexpectedly, a little smile on her forthright features. 'Don't mind Saul, Claudia, he's not one to deal in superlatives, you know. I think you look absolutely lovely—and suitable.'

'Why, thank you.' Claudia was touched. 'I was only asking approval, not compliments, you know. See you later—and mind you put your feet up while we're out!' She went down the steps, carrying a napkin-covered basket filled to the brim with sausage rolls for the party and accepted Saul's proffered hand to spring up into the vehicle in a whirl of pleats that revealed rather more of her long legs than she would have preferred.

'Sorry,' she said shortly, and turned to see if Becky was sitting on the clean linen sheet Maria had provided to protect the white dress for at least the time it took to arrive at the party.

'Don't apologise.' Saul twisted round to look behind him as he reversed up the drive. 'Since I've seen you in tennis kit——' his eyes looked full into hers for a second as he swung the jeep out into the road, 'and otherwise, it seems irrelevant anyway.'

Claudia sat dumb as the jeep made the descent down the winding hill. What was up with Saul today? Was he reminding her that he, too, still remembered moments when things had been a great deal less than impersonal between them? She was silent and thoughtful until they reached the party location, which was a big barracks of a place, halfway between Casa d'Ouro and the mine. As Saul parked on the stretch of gravel outside the excited chatter from a mass of voluble children came swelling from the open doors of the building, and Becky was noticeably quiet, her face tense as she looked towards the source of the hubbub.

'What is it, Becky?' Claudia took the small hot hand as Saul relieved her of the basket.

'Will anyone speak English?' Becky turned blue eyes full of panic on her father.

'Jamie and Mark will be there.' Saul handed back the

basket to Claudia and scooped up the trembling child in his arms. 'I'll give you a lift so those rather smart shoes don't get dirty,' he said, his eyes meeting Claudia's over Becky's head with a fierce expression in them she interpreted as a sudden violent urge to protect his child from anything and everyone.

'Good idea,' said Claudia, and pointed out her own white sandals to Becky. 'Aren't you lucky—I wish someone were here to carry me!'

'But you're too big to be carried!' A smile broke out on Becky's face at the thought and her moment of panic was forgotten as she arrived at the party safe in the strong arms that set her down gently just inside the door at the precise moment that Jamie and Mark spotted the new arrival and came tearing towards them, excitedly pulling Becky away to meet other children, who absorbed her into their midst without question.

'I thought we might have a problem there for a moment.' Saul let out his breath in an audible sigh of relief as he watched his daughter run off without a backward glance.

'You did exactly the right thing,' said Claudia. 'Becky needs security, in every shape and form—*and* a bit of discipline,' she added with a smile. 'She's so enchanting to look at it's an effort to be firm with her on occasion.'

'I don't think you I can teach you much in that department!' Saul's face softened as he caught sight of Emily near the raised dais at the other end of the room and took Claudia's arm to lead her over to a line of chairs occupied by ladies of varying ages, their dresses elaborate and elegant, their jewellery impressive. As one woman their eyes turned to watch Claudia as she crossed the room with Saul, the basket still in one hand. Emily was bending to talk to an elderly woman, unaware of the newcomers until something in the rapt attention of the women nearby made her straighten to look round with curiosity, a wide smile of welcome on her face as she saw Claudia.

'Hello, you two, I didn't see you come in.'

Claudia regarded Emily with undisguised admiration.

Today the artless girl with the long flying hair was
replaced by an elegant creature, every inch the wife of
the *Patrao*, her hair in an intricate coil low on her neck,
showing off magnificent aquamarine and diamond
earrings and a matching pendant above the neckline of
the intricately blue silk dress that swathed her slim
figure.

'You look very expensive and haughty today,' said
Saul smiling at her indulgently.

'I'm obliged to put on a show sometimes.' Emily
made a little face. 'You look like Red Riding Hood
with that basket, Claudia. Dump it somewhere and I'll
introduce you to all these ladies.'

Claudia quailed inwardly, but meekly allowed herself
to be led along the line of women while Emily
pronounced complicated names and each woman
politely welcomed Claudia to Campo d'Ouro. Saul went
off to join Luc and Claudia soon forgot him in her
efforts to keep track of Becky in the crowd of children,
finding an unexpected ally in Jamie, who proved to be a
very attentive escort. He took care that Becky found a
place at table, and looked after her with touching
diligence, seeing that she received her share of goodies
with all the éclat of a much older boy.

Claudia worked with a will, helping Emily pass laden
plates of food up and down the long table, pulling
English crackers, arranging paper hats on heads.

Soon the tables were cleared and removed and the
fun began in earnest. Emily took charge of the record-
player while Claudia organised the children for Musical
Chairs, Pass the Parcel and Grandmother's Footsteps,
but when it came to 'Simon Says' she merely eliminated
the transgressors while Luc roared out the instructions,
her Portuguese scarcely up to the task. Despite its size
the big room became very hot, and Claudia soon began
to feel uncomfortably warm and sticky from her
exertions, though none of this seemed to matter after
looking up at one stage to find Saul's eyes fixed on her
with undisguised warmth and approval.

There was a slight lull while drinks were consumed
thirstly and Claudia had a breather, taken aback to find

she was more breathless as a result of Saul's approval than from her participation in the games.

'I am much indebted to you, Claudia,' said Luc sincerely. He put an arm round his wife's shoulders. 'You have relieved Emily of much of the physical effort of the party.'

'I'm only too happy to help—I enjoy this sort of thing.' Claudia frankly mopped her forehead with a paper napkin, taking a surreptitious look across the room, but Saul had turned away to chat with some of the children's fathers. 'What happens now—more games?'

'The big climax,' announced Emily dramatically. 'The arrival of Papae Noel.'

'Ah!' Claudia leaned nearer. 'Who's in the starring role?'

'Tom Enys,' muttered Emily behind her hand, then broke off as her sons came running up with Becky in tow.

'Is Father Christmas coming yet,' Becky asked anxiously. 'They call him Papae Noel here, Claudia, did you know?'

Luc caught sight of Saul signalling near the far door and said triumphantly,

'He is arriving at this moment, *filinha*. Jamie, Mark, take Becky's hand.'

There was a great rush as all the children surged outside at the distant sound of bells. Saul caught up with Claudia as she followed.

'How are you doing? Everything all right?' he asked quietly.

Claudia nodded, smiling radiantly.

'Becky's having the time of her life.' Her eyes were alight with relief. 'I'm so pleased—I was very worried when we first arrived.'

'So was I!' He smiled down at her, taking her hand for a moment and squeezing it, to her surprise, but as they reached the door he stepped back to allow Claudia through with Emily and the moment was lost except for the pressure on her fingers, which still tingled from Saul's touch as she went outside and saw the reason for

all the excitement. Becky ran to her father, her face
white with anticipation.

'I can't see!' she said desperately.

Saul reached down and swung her up to perch on his
shoulder, and Claudia watched the child's eyes widen in
wonder, a lump in her own throat as she located the
source of the bells. A string of *burros*, little pack-mules,
were wending their way towards them along the red,
hard-packed earth road, a bell swinging from each
neck, a pannier on either side. At their head was a
larger animal, and astride it sat Father Christmas in all
his hot red and white glory, his face almost obscured by
his enormous white moustache and beard, sacks of toys
bulging from the panniers either side of his mount.

'Papae Noel, Papae Noel!' The cry went up in unison
as every child jumped up and down in a frenzy of
excitement before rushing towards the little cavalcade.
Instantly Becky struggled to get down in answer to
Jamie's imperious summons and ran off with him to
join the others as Father Christmas laboriously
dismounted, aided by dozens of willing hands as two
grinning young men bore the sacks of toys into the
building, followed by the burly figure in red, who led
the children into the big room like the Pied Piper.

Emily's maid had arrived by this time with a
wondering Lucy, who stared wide-eyed at all the
commotion from the haven of her mother's arms while
Luc distributed the presents as Father Christmas
handed them to him. Soon the room was a welter of
discarded wrapping paper as Becky stood hand in hand
with Jamie and Mark, the three faces tense and
expectant as they waited. Mark was soon the happy
owner of a sturdy truck, Lucy, a rag doll, and at long
last Luc handed Becky a large, flat box before passing
an identical parcel over to Jamie.

Becky tore back to Claudia, who helped her unwrap
a cowgirl outfit in white leather. Her eyes shone like
stars as she lifted out the brief, fringed skirt and bolero
and the miniature white Stetson, crowing with delight at
the finishing touch, a gun-belt with holsters and pistols.
Becky made a beeline for Saul, calling,

'Daddy, Daddy, look what I got!'

Saul spun round at her cry, his mask of restraint for once absent, revealing such a blaze of emotion in his eyes that Claudia turned away instinctively, unwilling for him to see she had witnessed the incident as he went down on his haunches to inspect his daughter's present. After such an emotional high it seemed only right that the party broke up soon after and Becky was driven home to recount the joys and triumphs of the afternoon to Bea until eventually even her inexhaustible energy ran out and she was persuaded to sleep after an extra long bedtime story from Claudia.

Claudia ate her dinner that evening in an atmosphere of euphoria, both from praise for her efforts at the party from Saul and from a definite rise in the temperature of his attitude towards her. Christmas spirit was high as all three enjoyed Filet Mignon and asparagus and a bottle of wine Saul had been saving for a special occasion.

'After all, what could be more special than Christmas Eve?' His eyes gleamed as he leaned across to fill Claudia's glass, a definite message in them she was at a loss to interpret, hoping it was something more significant than mere festive bonhomie. Whatever his intention, the result was a relaxed, happy atmosphere as Saul seemed intent on celebrating, pouring himself a mammoth brandy as they sat over coffee in the drawing-room afterwards. Claudia leaned back in her chair with a sigh of contentment as Bea confirmed the arrangements for the following day with Saul, wishing it were possible to crystallise and keep moments like this to store away and bring out in the future at less happy occasions.

'You look miles away, Claudia,' said Bea, smiling indulgently. 'Pleasant thoughts, I hope?'

Claudia blinked, flushing, and improvised rapidly.

'I—I was just remembering I have some odds and ends for Becky's stocking. Shall I fetch them to put with yours?'

There was a pregnant silence while Saul and Bea stared at her, their blankness ominous.

'My dear!' Bea put a hand to her mouth in consternation. 'I never gave a thought to a stocking!'

'One of those times when our inexperience becomes glaringly obvious.' Saul tossed off the remainder of his brandy and poured another, his eyes dismayingly shuttered once more as he turned back to Claudia. 'You might have mentioned it earlier.'

'I do apologise.' Claudia sat erect, her eyes glittering at him with offence. 'It never occurred to me that it would be necessary.'

'And why should it?' Bea regarded her nephew with surprised disapproval. 'The oversight is ours, not yours, Claudia.'

Saul shrugged impenitently.

'The fault is mine. Which doesn't alter the fact that Becky doesn't have a stocking. Knowing Elaine, I feel sure she bought one of those ready-filled affairs from Harrods and left it at that.'

'Which is hardly any help to us now,' said Bea with asperity.

Claudia intervened hastily.

'I have one or two little things, inexpensive odds and ends, really. I'm sure they'll be enough. At home one usually adds tangerines and so on, but out here where they grow in the garden they hardly seem appropriate.'

She watched with apprehension as Saul poured himself yet another brandy, drinking it in one draught before recollecting himself sufficiently to offer a liqueur to the two women. Neither accepted, more concerned with stocking-fillers, and Bea rose purposely to her feet.

'Fetch what you have, Claudia, and I'll just have a rummage through my room and see what I can turn up.'

Claudia went off to her bedroom and took the little bag of trifles from one of her suitcases, returning to Saul to find him alone at the verandah door, staring moodily out at the star-studded sky. He turned as Claudia put down her paper bag on the jacaranda table in front of the sofa, his face withdrawn and cold, his earlier mood vanished.

'I suppose you think I'm a bloody awful father,' he said morosely.

'No.' Claudia was cool and matter-of-fact. 'Just an inexperienced one.'

'You heard her say "Daddy" this afternoon?' Saul's tightly clenched jaw deepened the cleft in his chin as he scowled down into the contents of his glass.

Claudia nodded silently.

'The first time she'd ever said it.' He turned dark, bitter eyes on Claudia's watchful face. 'The only father she knew was Jack Connaught, Elaine's husband, though at least Elaine had some sense of fitness. Becky referred to him as "Uncle Jack".' He flung away and refilled his glass yet again before going on, his voice thickening perceptibly. 'What kind of father would forget that a little scrap like that would expect a Christmas stocking?'

Claudia was losing her patience. In a tone her former pupils would have recognised all too well she said, 'I think you're becoming maudlin. There'll be more than enough to fill a small stocking, and you've already bought her an extremely expensive bicycle, after all. Do keep *some* sense of proportion!'

Saul's look of blank surprise at her attack would have been funny at any other time, but it quickly dissolved into rage and Claudia quailed inwardly, deeply relieved as Bea appeared and he was forced to exert self-control with a visible effort. The mask was slipping a bit again, the result of an overdose of brandy, in Claudia's opinion. Bea sat beside her with her little haul, unaware of the tensions in the room as she produced her finds.

'I've done quite well,' she said with satisfaction. 'A little silver thimble I had as a child, two hair-slides I was keeping for her for tomorrow, a little pincushion in the shape of a mouse, and we could add one of those chocolates you brought from Boa Vista.'

Added to Claudia's contribution the result was pronounced extremely satisfactory, to Bea's relief.

'That's a load off my mind,' she said thankfully. 'I'll give them all to you then, dear, and you can pack them in a stocking. Will you creep in with it?'

'Why—yes, if you wish.' Claudia gave a quick glance

at Saul, but he was at the door again, his back to the room, the very set of his broad shoulders rancorous. Seething at the injustice of his attitude—after all, it was hardly her fault if the man had forogtten his daughter's stocking—she gathered up the little bundle.

'If you'll both excuse me I think I'll turn in; it could be an early start tomorrow.'

'Goodnight, dear. I shan't be too long myself.' Bea yawned. 'I'm quite tired.'

Claudia took her leave, winning only a wintry goodnight from Saul. And a Merry Christmas to you, too, she thought crossly. She dumped the bag on the bed and undressed with a regrettable lack of festive spirit, almost of a mind to keep back Saul's present next day, then decided to hand it over in the nature of coals of fire. Postponing the stocking filling for the time being, she decided to read for a while, lying against the pillows on top of the covers as the air cooled.

Claudia came to with a start, aware of having dozed. A look at her watch confirmed that it was only a little after twelve, and yawning, she got up to do something about Becky's stocking. She stood still as she realised she had no suitable stocking to put the presents in. Becky's socks were tiny, Claudia's own tennis socks still nowhere near large enough. She sighed in exasperation. The little haul would look silly and forlorn in a pillowcase—one of Saul's socks would be the answer. Not relishing her quest very much, Claudia tied on her kimono and went on silent bare feet to the drawing-room, but it was in darkness, the doors to the verandah locked. Damn! Saul must have gone to bed already. She crept cautiously past his room, grinning as she heard faint snoring. Hardly surprising after all that brandy. Her heart stopped as Saul's door flew open, then she turned to run, but a long arm shot out, a hand closing on her shoulder with a grip like iron, pulling her back.

It was difficult to fight without making a noise, and Claudia had no desire to wake Bea, who must have been the one snoring. She writhed in desperate silence, struggling to free herself from Saul's vice-like hold, but it was no use. For someone who prided herself on her

fitness it was galling to be drawn inexorably towards
that broad chest, even while her mind registered relief
that Bea's gentle snoring could be still heard,
undisturbed.

The previous time Saul had held her off balance like
this she had been bemused, incapable of thought or
movement, but now, as her head tilted back, she gasped
in brandy fumes so strong she panicked, kicking her
feet against his bare shins in a fury of resistance as he
carried her into his room, the door clicking quietly shut
behind them as she was slung unceremoniously on the
bed like a sack of potatoes. As she tried to escape the
weight of his big body descended on hers without
mercy, winding her temporarily and making her
prisoner, with no possibility of movement, let alone
escape unless he allowed it. Gasping like a landed fish,
she stared acrimoniously into the face above her, the
expression on Saul's face visible in the light from the
single lamp. Her mouth dried as she realised it was as
mask-like as usual, but it was a different mask. For the
first time in her life she saw a man's face devoid of any
feeling other than lust, insulting in its impersonal
intensity, and she began to feel the first stirrings of fear,
coupled with a sensation of burning injustice. At this
rate she was likely to be out of a job before it had really
begun. Her struggles renewed.

'Let me up!' she whispered fiercely.

'After you'd gone to the trouble of visiting me in my
room?' Saul's brandy-laden whisper terminated on her
mouth as he began to kiss her with hard, slow kisses
that took away what remaining breath she had. His
breathing grew rapid, rasping, his kisses rougher,
wilder, his teeth grazing her lips. One of his hands
relinquished its hold to begin exploring the curves
beneath her kimono, pushing aside the thin cotton of
her nightdress until it tore. Claudia's brain woke up, the
intruding hand provoking anger instead of passion in
response as she twisted in rage beneath his touch.
Miraculously she managed to free one of her hands and
thrust the palm flat against his chin, pushing with all
her not inconsiderable strength until Saul's head went

back with a grunt, his vertebrae grinding together at the back of his neck. The involuntarily slackening of his hold gave her the opening she was looking for and she slithered like an eel from beneath him and landed on the floor beside the bed. The wrong side of the bed, it was true, but she was free. They both stood staring at each other, panting, the wide expanse of brown crumpled bedcover separating them.

Saul drew his robe together, tying the belt slowly, his eyes, black in the shadow above the pool of lamplight, holding Claudia's as she fumbled to make herself decent, her fingers clumsy now that the crisis was over. The silence grew heavy, unbearable as she looked away from him with distaste.

'Say something,' he said quietly.

'What would you like me to say?' Her eyes returned to his, glacial and scornful.

He shook his head and ran a hand through his hair, giving a shrug that, in another man, would have been one of embarrassment.

'I heard a slight noise.' His deep voice was barely audible. 'I had too much to drink. When I heard you outside my door I thought—you know very well what I thought. I apologise. Hell, what else can I say? Except that I'm now stone cold sober.' He stared across the width of the bed to where Claudia stood, poised, ready to run at his first move, hugging her dressing gown across her like a shield. 'Why *did* you come?'

'Would you believe I needed a sock to use for Becky's stocking? I hoped you might still be in the drawing-room. When I found everything in darkness I was just going back to my bedroom when you came at me through the door.' To Claudia's intense irritation his shoulders began to shake and he raised a fist to press it against his mouth. She walked with dignity around the bed and waved him out of her way with a disdainful gesture.

'Goodnight,' she said stonily.

'Wait.' He moved over to one of the doors in the jacaranda unit and opened a drawer, taking a pair of new white tennis socks from it. 'Will one of these do?'

'Thank you.' Claudia took the sock from him gingerly, as though she were taking a bone away from a dog, then turned on her heel.

'Claudia!' His voice halted her. She paused and looked at him, unsmiling. 'I really am sorry. I was drunk, and I apologise.'

She nodded with silent indifference.

'Will this—episode make any difference?'

'To what?' she asked coolly.

'To whether or not you stay.' The light was too dim for her to see his face clearly, but she could have sworn his eyes held a trace of entreaty.

'As you said the other day,' she reminded him, 'I'm here to educate your daughter, not to entertain you. Perhaps you could bear that in mind.'

Saul took a deep breath as though her shaft had struck home.

'Would it make any difference if I said it was the last thing I intended to happen?'

Claudia frowned angrily.

'You mean I'm the last person you'd consider making love to if you were sober!'

With the sudden lightness of foot that always surprised her Saul was at her side, holding her by the upper arms, twisting her round to look into her startled grey eyes, an unreadable expression in his own.

'I'm stone cold sober now, Claudia, just as I said,' he whispered.

This is where I start struggling again, she thought, as his face came nearer, but whatever impulses her brain was sending to her body they had little to do with resistance. Quite the reverse; as his mouth touched hers she began trembling deep inside her, but not with fright. It was the feeling remembered so vividly from the night of the storm. Saul's hands left her arms and slid round her body, which melted into his as though the desperate, bitter fight of a few minutes earlier had never happened. Her lips opened to his as she gave herself up without reservation to an embrace that gave rather than took as his lips left hers to wander over her eyelids and nose, moving down her chin to her throat, where they rested against the pulse throbbing there before moving back up to her mouth to settle with increasing pressure. Claudia's heavy eyelids opened gradually to show eyes whose normal crystalline clarity was clouded by the intensity of the feelings aroused in her by his lovemaking. She stared at him, reassured when she saw that, for the first time, Saul's eyes were alight with warmth, his whole expression transformed as he looked down at her.

'I must go,' she whispered.

He nodded, releasing her reluctantly.

'See you in the morning.'

'It *is* morning!' She smiled, a limpid joy in her look. 'Merry Christmas, Saul!'

'Merry Christmas, Claudia.' He stooped and kissed her gently, then bent to pick up something from the door. 'Here's your sock. Isn't that what you came for?'

'I got rather more than I bargained for, didn't I?'

With an impudent smile she went quietly into the hall, relieved to hear gentle snoring still issuing from the next room.

'I thought it was you,' she whispered.

'I never snore,' he said into her ear.

'How do you know?'

'There's one sure way of finding out!'

Defeated, she fled with silent laughter, aware that he watched her out of sight.

CHAPTER ELEVEN

CLAUDIA opened her eyes on Christmas morning to find Saul standing in the doorway with his daughter in his arms, clutching her bulging stocking to her chest, her eyes incandescent with excitement.

'Claudia,' Becky whispered, 'can we sit on your bed to look in my stocking?'

Saul gave her a rueful grin of apology as Claudia sat up groggily, smiling into her eyes over Becky's head, silently sending a message that Claudia instantly understood, relaxing against the pillows, careless of her tumbled hair. Saul himself looked as though he'd pulled on the nearest garments to hand. His hair was wildly untidy above a white cotton sweatshirt and a pair of much-washed denims clung to his long legs like a second skin. A dark growth of stubble added to a piratical effect that appealed to Claudia strongly.

'We've come to wish you Merry Christmas, Claudia,' he said, with a flash of white teeth in a smile that did strange things to her respiratory system and set the mood for a day of unalloyed happiness, from the exchange of presents after breakfast with Bea, to the hospitality of Emily and Luc at a lavish, convivial Christmas dinner at Casa d'Ouro. To Claudia's surprise and delight Saul had given her a necklace made of three strands of gold in different colours twisted together in a heavy chain, and she wore it with pride, secretly treasuring his obvious pleasure when he opened her own gift to him. Not a little of the day's harmony was due to Becky's joy in all her presents, mainly the bicycle, naturally, but the child was also enchanted with her doll and the clothes Claudia gave her, instantly demanding to change into pink tee-shirt, blue jeans and pink sneakers, refusing to change into anything more formal for the visit to Casa d'Ouro, which, as her bicycle had to go along too, was probably just as well.

After dinner, when all the children were finally out for the count, Luc put some slow dreamy music on the stereo, and Thurza, Bob and John sat chatting while Tom danced with Bea, Luc with Emily, and Claudia had her first experience of dancing with Saul. To her surprise he was not the best of dancers, but under the circumstances on the dimly lit verandah, it was enough to be held in his arms, moving only the requisite amount in time to the music, both of them glad of the excuse for physical contact.

'Have you enjoyed your first Christmas Day in Campo d'Ouro, Claudia?' asked Saul softly, his mouth close to her ear.

The word 'first' elated Claudia, with its promise of more Christmases to come, a hint of permanence that reassured her questioning heart. She tipped her head back to look up into his face as he moved her out of earshot of the others.

'For reasons many and varied, Mr Treharne, this has been far and away the best Christmas of my life!'

Boxing Day was bound to be an anti-climax, quiet by contrast, except for a morning spent at the tennis club, where Becky cycled endlessly from one end of the verandah to the other while Saul and Claudia played two sets of tennis in far more leisurely fashion than their previous game. Bea sat watching them while Afra kept an eye on Becky. Bea sat idly, without her knitting for once, content to watch the tennis in silence, the club deserted on this hot, overcast day, with everyone else apparently indoors, sleeping off the excesses of Christmas.

Afra was sent home before lunch, which was a simple, cold meal eaten on the verandah. Saul and Claudia ate heartily after their exercise, and so did Becky, despite eyes that drooped a little after her disturbed sleep of the night before with a ride from Casa d'Ouro in the middle of it. Bea looked pale to Claudia's worried eye, merely picking at her food, and after the meal was over announced that she was going to lie down for a while.

'Not too good today, Aunt Bea?' Saul looked searchingly at his aunt.

'Just tired, dear.' She smiled brightly. 'Serves me right, dancing at my age. I'll take advantage of your good nature, Claudia, and leave you with the lunch dishes, if you don't mind.'

'Of course not. Have a good rest.' Claudia and Saul watched the older woman out of sight, then sat down again to finish their coffee, their unspoken anxiety mutual. Saul glanced at his daughter, who sat with her chin on her hand, making patterns in the cream left at the bottom of her dessert dish, her eyes heavy with sleep.

'Just for once, Miss Treharne, don't you think even you might have a little rest on your bed?' he suggested, ruffling the top of her hair. 'Then you'll be full of beans later on to ride your bike again.'

Becky heaved a great sigh and agreed, to Claudia's surprise.

'My doll's tired too, I think she'd better lie down with me.'

'Good idea!' Claudia jumped up and held out her hand. 'Come on then, let's tuck you both up for a little while.'

When Claudia got back to the kitchen Saul was washing dishes. He turned with a smile as she closed the door quietly behind her.

'Everyone out for the count?'

Claudia nodded, avoiding his eye, suddenly ill at ease as she began drying plates at speed. Saul put a wet hand on her wrist and turned her towards him, lifting her face towards his with the other, smiling down into her eyes.

'Afraid to be alone with me?'

'No.'

'Why are you shying away like a nervous horse, then?'

Claudia made a face at him. 'You might be a little more flattering with your similes!'

'I *was* being flattering.' Saul held her away, giving her a straight-faced considering look from head to foot. 'Long slim legs, a mane of hair, nostrils that flare a little when you're nervous—like now!'

'All right, all right,' Claudia tugged free from his grasp and began putting away plates. 'I'm *not* nervous of being alone with you, anyway.'

He leaned against the kitchen table, his legs thrust out in front of him, and lit a cigarillo, watching her as usual through the smoke.

'You should be.'

She swung round to stare at him, her colour heightened.

'Why?'

'Because, dear Miss March,' he said, his voice slow and deliberate, the look in the blue darkness of his eyes emphasising the subtle sensuality of his tone, 'because I, too, would like to go to bed right now. Only sleeping isn't what I have in mind, at least not for some time. I want to take you with me and make love to you with infinite patience and at infinite length until sleeping in each other's arms was the natural, inevitable conclusion.'

Claudia stared at him, her colour high and her eyes bright and blank. She turned to look at the abacata trees outside the window, their leaves motionless in the sullen humidity of the still afternoon. His words hung in the air between them. Pushing her hair behind her ears, she pulled her cotton shirt away from her back where it clung to the dampness between her shoulder-blades, deliberately willing herself to be calm.

'It might be best to pretend you never said that.' She picked her words with care. 'I think I may have misled you. You have every right to think—to assume that I'm only too willing to fall in with your suggestion.' She swallowed hard, her eyes still gazing blindly in front of her. 'I should have made it clear from the outset that I could never play a dual role. Becky's governess by day and your—your companion by night is out of the question for me.'

The silence in the room was ominous. Claudia could feel Saul's eyes on her back as tangibly as though he were touching her.

'I regret having given you the wrong impression,' she went on, her mouth dry. 'When you specified a proficiency at sport I had no idea that the field of activity would be extended to the bedroom.' The words sounded so much worse than she intended that she could have cried the moment they were said.

'Are you suggesting that all that warm response I've been receiving was a figment of my overheated imagination? Or possibly I am to believe it was perhaps a mere transient manifestation of the Christmas spirit!'

The icy sneer in Saul's voice made Claudia writhe inwardly, all his former hostility returned in full force.

Claudia turned and looked at him, chilled to the core to see the familiar mask of indifference in place once more, his eyes shuttered and bored.

'We misunderstood each other,' she said huskily. 'I
blame myself entirely. You had every right to think I—
to think I was willing to let things progress further. I'm
sorry, I'm just not in the market for——'

'That's enough,' he said savagely, and made for the
open door, hurling the butt of his cigarillo out into the
garden. 'You've made your point twice over. I'm not
one of your pupils, Miss Schoolteacher, I managed to
catch your drift first time round. Have no fear; you're
free to pursue your life of blameless instruction totally
unsullied by any male attentions.' Saul flung round in
the doorway, his head thrown back, looking down his
disfigured nose with a look of speculation calculated to
insult. 'Unless, of course, it's only *my* particular
attentions that displease. You may, of course, have
some other target in mind.'

'Saul, please!' Claudia felt stricken. She put out her
hands in appeal. 'Surely you can understand——'

'Of course I can.' Saul relaxed, his wrath abruptly
gone. 'Women are pathetically easy to understand—I
learned that early in life.' He gave her a mocking salute.
'I leave you to meditate on the joys of abstinence alone
and unmolested. Tell my aunt I shall be out for dinner.'

Claudia watched, dry-eyed, from the window as Saul
strode past the side of the house. He backed the jeep
out of the *porão* and reversed up the drive and out into
the road, sweeping the vehicle round in a noisy, brake-
squealing arc before gunning the vehicle down the hill
and out of sight. Claudia remained where she was for
some time, wondering just where he was going,
unheralded and unexpected at that time of day. She
knew nothing of his life before Bea came to live with
him. Perhaps there were several places down in the
town where he was sure of a welcome, and probably a
great deal more. Claudia gritted her teeth at the thought
that possibly there was just one place. Some beautiful
local lady who was accustomed to joining Saul in all the
activities outlined so temptingly in his proposed way to
spend the afternoon, and no doubt a great deal more
adept at it than his daughter's governess was ever likely
to be at this rate.

Claudia cursed herself for a fool as she sat at the scrubbed table in the big kitchen, chin on hand, wishing herself back to the day before with all its attendant joy and warmth. She should just have laughed at Saul, of course, and turned his sensuous words aside with subtle dexterity, leaving his self-esteem intact. Instead of which her attitude had been one of antediluvian rectitude, like some Victorian prunes-and-prisms spinster drawing her skirts aside from contact with man's baser instincts. He could hardly have been serious about taking her to bed with his aunt in the next room and his child likely to wake at any time.

The more Claudia thought about it the more she wished she'd kept her silly mouth shut. She was relieved when she heard Becky's call and her miserable reverie had to be abandoned for the joys of running round the garden paths after the intrepid cyclist, whose batteries had been recharged to an exhausting extent by her unaccustomed afternoon nap. When she joined them Bea was surprised to learn that Saul would be out for dinner, her curiosity as to his whereabouts increased when Claudia was unable to supply any details, only her obvious embarrassment leading Bea to change the subject out of sheer kindness.

Claudia felt little embarrassment in Saul's presence in the days that followed, for the simple reason that his household was graced by it very little. He was seldom home to lunch and often dined out, on the perfunctory pretext of pressure of work needing extra sessions with Bob McClure or Luc, or Manoel Araujo. When Bea suggested Saul bring his colleages home for some of these necessary working dinners he refused, on the plea of boredom for the ladies, and thereafter she held her peace. Luckily Becky was absorbed with her new toys and apparently found Saul's absence a familiar recurrence. Claudia, however, missed Saul's dominating presence with an intensity that it was difficult to hide.

She was relieved when, a couple of days after Christmas, the much-anticipated lessons actually began, though the schoolroom eventually chosen was in Casa d'Ouro, where so many rooms were at their disposal it

was considered impractical to use the only spare room
in Saul's house, so the books and equipment were
installed in a large, airy room looking out on the front
garden of Casa d'Ouro, away from the macaws, and
Claudia began to perform the function for which she
had been hired.

In the beginning the children found the regular hours
of schoolwork restrictive, short though they were, but
Claudia made their first lessons so much like play their
attention was quickly caught, and, as suspected, Becky
was a bright, intelligent child who absorbed knowledge
with an ease that put Jamie on his mettle to keep up
with her despite his slight seniority. Mark pottered
happily with less complicated lessons, and Claudia
found no difficulty in controlling three small children
after the numbers she had been used to teaching,
though the very youth of her pupils was a challenge to
her, and she never lost sight of her responsibility
towards shaping their entire future attitude towards the
discipline of education.

The new routine was welcome, passing the day very
effectively. Luc sent a car for Becky and Claudia
every morning, and again to drive them home in the
afternoon, and on days when Saul was out for lunch
Bea often went with them to Casa d'Ouro, and
passed the time chatting to Thurza and Emily. The
first week went by fairly uneventfully. Becky grew less
and less temperamental as her energies were concentrated on the lessons that proved to be far more
pleasurable than the child had expected, and Bea
became more relaxed as the responsibility of taking
care of a young, difficult child was taken out of her
hands completely. She was obviously concerned by
Saul's renewed absences from the house, but never
discussed the subject with Claudia, who was left to
think about it endlessly in private, on times heartsore,
at others angry at the lengths to which Saul was
carrying his displeasure.

Claudia and Emily lingered over coffee after lunch on
the day before New Year's Eve. Thurza had gone for
her rest, Bea had stayed at home, and the children were

playing in the garden, glad of the freedom after a morning of lessons.

Emily gave Claudia a thoughtful look.

'Bea says there's an atmosphere at home, Claudia; at least when Saul's there, which I gather is practically never.'

'I must have said something which offended him.'

'Must have been quite something!'

'Saul's behaving irrationally.' Claudia got to her feet restlessly and leaned her hands on the verandah rail. 'All right, so he's angry with me. Why should he let that deprive Becky of his company?'

Emily joined her, waving a hand towards the children, where Becky was playing quite happily with the others.

'Becky's doing very well, Claudia. She probably takes his absence for granted.'

Claudia lifted the hair away from her neck, her face troubled.

'Maybe you're right. I just hope it's not worrying Bea too much. I feel so guilty.'

'Well, stop it, you goose. I'm sure *you* aren't worrying her.'

'She doesn't seem well, Emily. I wish she'd visit the doctor.'

Emily nodded. 'Thurza has already broached the subject in her usual forthright way and I gather Bea agreed.'

Reassured, Claudia went off to chase up her reluctant pupils for their short afternoon session, secretly as little inclined for lessons as they were and comforting them with the thought that the next two days were holidays.

The following day was overcast and humid, with an oppressive atmosphere that intensified the uneasiness Claudia felt when Saul came home for lunch for once. She was relieved when the tall figure of Bob McClure loped up the steps behind Saul's forbidding figure, praying the American's relaxed company would lighten the atmosphere over the lunch-table.

'I've just been telling Saul here that you two ought to come into town with me tonight,' Bob said persuasively.

Saul shook his head, turning from something Becky was telling him.

'No, thanks—not for me.' He turned expressionless eyes on Claudia. 'There's nothing to prevent Claudia from taking you up on your offer, of course.'

'Good idea,' said Bea with approval. 'Why don't you, Claudia?'

'Oh, I don't think so.' Claudia smiled at Bob and went on doggedly with her chicken casserole. 'It's such a long way.'

'You went there with Daddy,' remarked Becky. 'Remember, Claudia?'

Claudia felt the colour rise in her cheeks.

'But that was for some necessary shopping,' she said hastily, and drank some ice-water, conscious of Saul's saturnine glance on her face.

Bob smiled goodnaturedly, giving a slightly baffled look at Saul.

'I promise to drive real slow, Claudia—come on, why don't you? If old stick-in-the-mud here won't budge, it doesn't mean you have to stay home too. What do you say, Miss Bea?'

'Oh, I'm in entire agreement,' said Bea heartily, then turned sharply as Claudia gave a sudden gasp and clapped her napkin to her mouth, rising precipitately to her feet with a muttered apology as she fled from the verandah, leaving the men staring after with varying expressions on their faces.

Bea followed Claudia to the bathroom in concern.

'What is it my dear? You're very pale—are you feeling ill?'

Claudia shook her head with a lopsided grin.

'I've broken a tooth.' Beads of perspiration stood out on her forehead. 'I think there was a fragment of bone in my chicken and I bit hard on it.'

'Oh, my dear!' Bea put her arm round Claudia's waist. 'Is it very painful?'

Claudia nodded dumbly, momentarily speechless with the agony of an exposed nerve-end, making an effort as Becky appeared in the doorway, large-eyed.

'It's all right, poppet. A spot of toothache, that's all.'

'Dentist for you, my dear,' said Bea with decision.
'I'll get Saul to organise it.'

'Oh, please——' Claudia gasped, but Bea had gone.
A small hand slid into Claudia's and Becky looked up
at her anxiously.

'Are you hurting, Claudia?'

'Don't worry, I'll live—let's go back to the others.'

Claudia could hear Saul on the phone in the study as
she and Becky went back to the verandah.

'Bad luck, honey. Is it grim?' Bob's pleasant face
shone with sympathy.

'One of my teeth just snapped in half.' Claudia smiled
with caution. 'The reward for filling my mouth too full!'
She looked up as Saul came back and stood over her,
his frown anxious instead of hostile.

'How do you feel?'

The slight warmth in his voice more than com-
pensated for sharp twinges in her jaw, and Claudia
smiled up at him gamely.

'Fine. Minus half a molar, that's all.'

'The earliest appointment I could get for you is at
five with my dentist in Boa Vista. I'll get back early and
take you in——'

'No need, old buddy,' cut in Bob. 'I was going in
anyway. I'll be glad to take Claudia.'

The fleeting warmth was gone from Saul's face
instantly and he moved back.

'By all means,' he said stiffly.

Claudia looked on helplessly as Saul provided Bob
with the dentist's address, her toothache almost
forgotten in her resentment. It was burningly obvious
that he was only too glad to shift the responsibility
for her on to Bob. Nevertheless, there was an odd
expression on his face when he looked down at her
before leaving after lunch. Staring mutely into his
face, Claudia could have sworn a flicker of emotion
showed in his hard eyes for an instant as he said
goodbye.

'I leave you in Bob's hands, then,' he said.

'So I see,' she said flatly.

'I was under the impression you'd prefer that.'

'Were you really?' The throbbing in her jaw cancelled out any effort at manners.

To Claudia's surprise Saul stretched out a hand, the clasp of his fingers tight on her own for a moment.

'Claudia——' he said huskily.

'Come on, Saul,' interrupted Bob cheerfully. 'I'll be back for you about three, honey.'

Saul dropped her hand and turned away with a jerk, making for the steps without a backward glance, and Claudia watched him go in frustration, barely capable of a polite thank you to Bob as he hurried off in Saul's wake. She could have wept. A toothache would have been a negligible price to pay for a trip into Boa Vista with Saul. Aware that she was losing her battle against tears, she made excuses to Bea and Becky and fled to her bedroom to cry hot, silent tears into her pillow, until the pain in her tooth drove her in search of aspirin to blunt the anguish, wishing there were some wonder pill she could swallow for the ache in her heart.

CHAPTER TWELVE

CLAUDIA emerged from her encounter with the dentist a new woman. The street lights glittered like baubles among the thick dark greenery of the trees lining the main Avenida as she strolled through the dusk with Bob, a temporary cap on her tooth, almost lightheaded with the relief from pain. Boa Vista was electric with the atmosphere of *festa* as they made their way along the crowded pavements, the passers-by in party mood and ready to celebrate New Year's Eve.

'I feel terrific. All the knots in my nervous system are delightfully unravelled.' Claudia smiled gaily at Bob as they crossed the wide thoroughfare. 'I hate dentists— they bring out the coward in me.'

'You look a whole lot better, honey.' He grinned down at her and led her in the direction of a small bar.

'How about a drink here, then a couple of hours in a nice air-conditioned cinema watching the new Dustin Hoffman film. Afterwards I'll buy you dinner.'

Claudia tried to hide her dismay, by no means overjoyed by Bob's programme.

'Oh, but I thought we were going straight back. I'll be expected——'

He shook his fair head, patently pleased with himself as he seated her at one of the small marble-topped tables in the cool, dimly-lit bar.

'Sort of depending on how you felt, I told Saul what I had in mind, and he was all for it.'

'He was?' Claudia's eyes gleamed like the ice-cubes in the drink the waiter set in front of her. She smoothed her heavy hair back from her face and smiled brightly. 'In that case how can I refuse? O.K., you're on.'

Claudia enjoyed the film, firmly controlling the wrath bubbling deep down at the thought of being granted permission by Saul to remain in Boa Vista to do so. She took less pleasure in the meal that followed. The dentist's injection had begun to wear off and chewing aggravated the slight throbbing that started up again in her jaw, and she demurred when Bob suggested going on to a party at the house of some American friends afterwards.

'That would make us very late, Bob. Besides, I'm not exactly dressed for it.' She flicked the skirt of her maize linen dress disparagingly.

'You look great, Claudia. Come on, honey,' Bob urged. 'Saul won't expect us back early. Anyway, we can leave straight after midnight, and Hank and Nancy are nice people. You'll like them.'

Her heart sinking, Claudia gave in, guilty at the thought that Bob's New Year's Eve would be affected if he was obliged to take her home early. From that point on her throbbing jaw made it difficult to focus on the rest of the evening, and she remembered very little afterwards of the noisy, highly animated party at a large white house in a lush tropical garden with a swimming pool. Strident music played while waiters circulated endlessly with drinks and mine host presided

over a barbecue with great good humour while his
guests lined up for the fruits of his labours.

Claudia was welcomed with open arms by Hank and
Nancy Riessen and introduced to many more people
whose names were difficult to catch above the noise.
With a determined effort to forget her sore mouth she
smiled and drank, smiled and chatted, smiled until her
lips felt stiff and Bob was delighted she was having such
a great time. What had been a moderately pleasant
evening turned into a marathon of endurance until
midnight when everyone screamed good wishes and
kissed everyone else, and still Claudia went on smiling
until she had grave fears her face would be set in the
same meaningless rictus for all time. It finally relaxed
when Bob was eventually persuaded to leave, almost an
hour later, by which time she was bone-weary, not
merely from aftermath of her dental ordeal but from
nagging worry about Saul's reception when she got
home. Taking herself to task for being so wet as to care
about the wretched man's opinions, Claudia settled
herself in Bob's Lincoln Continental with a sigh of
relief. It was more than likely that Saul was in bed and
asleep, utterly indifferent as to how her evening had
been spent or how late she was in getting back.

Bob was blessedly silent on the return journey, to
Claudia's gratitude. The temporary anodyne of champagne had quietened down her throbbing mouth, but
depression crept over her insidiously as the softly-
sprung car undulated its way around bends and over
ruts. To her surprise its motion was far worse for any
incipient nausea than the rattling of Saul's jeep. As she
thought of Saul she longed with a sudden passion for
his massive, dominant presence beside her instead of
Bob's kind, amiable company. It was no use. She stared
at what was visible of the road in the beam of the
headlights, as abruptly struck by the truth as though
this were the road to Damascus. Claudia sat upright,
her eyes narrowed. This was all so silly. When she got
home she would go to Saul with her pride in her pocket
and deliver herself up to him on whatever terms he
wanted. For her the battle was over. She settled back in

her seat with a sigh, her mind blissfully occupied with
the possibility that defeat might just turn out to be
victory after all.

'Are you all right, honey?' Bob sounded anxious.

'I'm fine, really. A bit tired, that's all.'

'I should have gotten away earlier,' he said
remorsefully. 'Just a few more miles now.'

They were precisely three miles short of Campo
d'Ouro when things began to go wrong. The car slowed
and began to make some very disquieting noises, finally
jerking to a halt plumb in the middle of a bend.

'Holy cow!' Bob leapt out of the car, torch in hand,
looking under the bonnet in frantic efforts to find the
fault. After a time he stuck his head back through the
window and looked at Claudia in agonised apology.

'I'm sorry, honey, but could you possibly help me
push the car off the road? We're obstructing any other
traffic like this.'

Other traffic! Claudia would have cheerfully sold her
soul for the sight of another car, truck, mule-cart,
anything, but aware that at this time of night it was
hardly likely. Balancing on the rough road surface on
the high heels of her fragile sandals, she pushed with a
will in response to Bob's shouted instructions until the
car was as much off the road as it was possible for it to
be. She held the torch and shone it under the bonnet in
the places Bob indicated until he was forced to give up
in frustration, to the accompaniment of a few highly-
coloured oaths.

'Forgive the language, Claudia, and me too for
stranding us miles from anywhere like this. I guess we'd
better sit in the car until——'

'No,' said Claudia forcibly. 'We walk.'

'Walk? You can't be serious!' Bob's glasses glinted in
the light of the torch, and Claudia smiled in spite of
herself, well able to picture the horror in the eyes
behind them. Her own mind was made up. Late they
might be, but no way was she sitting meekly in that car
until help arrived—if it ever did. If they set out on foot
at least she would have *tried* to get home. No doubt it
was a very faint hope, but Saul just might feel more

kindly disposed towards her if she had made some kind
of effort.

After only a few hundred yards of stumbling along
she deeply regretted her decision. Bob's torch helped a
little, but the road surface was rough and uneven, with
dangerous loose stones in abundance. Her sandals soon
began to rub blisters on her bare feet, but Claudia
trudged on doggedly, her hand in Bob's for support,
neither of them sparing the energy to talk apart from
the odd stifled curse from the American, whom she
could hardly blame for thinking it was madness even to
attempt to reach Campo d'Ouro on foot. Soon
Claudia's whole world became centred in her feet,
which grew rapidly more swollen and painful every step
they took. Several times she stumbled, wrenching an
ankle a little, but rigidly stopped herself from
complaining. Her concentration on just putting one
foot after another was so intense as they toiled up a
particularly steep incline she was past registering the
noise of a vehicle in the distance until it was almost on
them. Bob squeezed her hand with painful enthusiasm
as he saw the headlights of something large gaining on
them.

'Thank the Lord, honey—I think it's a truck!'

It was. A very ancient, battered lorry drew up
alongside them with a squeal of brakes, its cab
overflowing with a family from Campo d'Ouro
returning from festivities with relatives in Boa Vista.
Somehow Claudia was squashed in among several
children and their mother, everyone loud with
exclamations of sympathy as Bob explained their plight.
The driver was apologetic as he surveyed Bob's
dimensions and regretfully indicated the open back of
the truck as the only space available for one with so
long a leg. In no position to quibble, Bob scrambled up
into the lorry and they were off, the head of the family
goodnaturedly insisting on driving them right to the
gates of the Treharne house before setting them down.

Claudia flatly refused to let Bob see her inside the
house, wincing with pain as he set her on her feet after
lifting her out of the truck. After reiterated thanks to

their saviours she took off her sandals as the truck sputtered noisily away down the hill, turning down Bob's support as she prepared to hobble down the drive.

'No, really, Bob, thanks just the same. It's been a long night—God knows what time it is—so you go on home and I'll see myself inside. Goodnight, and thank you for taking me to the dentist.'

'I guess the last bit ruined the entire evening—I'm truly sorry, Claudia.'

Bob sounded utterly miserable in the darkness, but Claudia was too exhausted to essay much comfort.

'Don't worry, it couldn't be helped—I really must get off these feet. Goodnight, Bob.'

She crept gingerly down the drive on her abused feet, almost collpasing with fright as she cannoned into the figure that waited in the dark at the foot of the steps.

'Where in God's name have you *been*?' Saul shook her savagely, like a dog with a rat. 'Are you aware of the time?'

It was the last straw. Abandoning her earlier resolve to throw herself into his arms and pour out her love and devotion, Claudia slapped him hard across the jaw instead, connecting more by luck than science but making Saul's head jerk back, if only in surprise.

'And a Happy New Year to you, too, Mr Rochester!' There was pure venom in her voice as she hobbled up to the verandah, every step a victory of mind over matter. It had been her intention to keep on going until she reached her room, but once inside the drawing-room the lure of the nearest chair was too much and she sank down on it, her face screwed up in a ferocious scowl as a defence against the urge to howl like a baby.

'Why are you limping?' Saul stood over her in a towering rage, his mouth compressed as his eyes fixed on her feet. 'What the hell happened to you?'

'Where would you like me to begin?' Her eyes gleamed back at him in defiance.

'Did you manage to fit in a visit to the dentist, for starters!' He remained where he was, looming suffocatingly close, rubbing his jaw where her fist had landed.

He was still fully dressed, a half-full glass of whisky on one of the tables evidence of his occupation while he waited for her.

'Of course I did,' she snapped. 'It's the reason why I went in the first place. I've had a temporary cap and I have to go back next week.'

'McClure said he intended persuading you to stay in town for dinner,' he said bitingly. 'It must have been quite a meal!'

'Bob was set on going to a party afterwards—the last thing I myself wanted, but it *is* New Year's Eve, in case you've forgotten, and I knew I'd ruin Bob's evening if I insisted on coming back early.' Claudia's eyes opened wide suddenly, their clarity intense as they fastened on his. 'After all,' she said deliberately, 'I was fairly sure my absence would hardly be mourned very much.'

Neither moved, staring at each other angrily, their eyes locked as if trying to read each other's minds. Claudia lay in the chair, numb, her dress limp and crumpled, her eyes huge in her colourless face, her anger and defiance draining away to leave her defenceless before Saul's searching look. She winced as he went down on one knee and picked up one of her feet.

'How did you get these blisters?' He shook his head. 'Did McClure make you *walk* home, for God's sake?'

'No. I made *him* walk!' Claudia began to laugh softly, helplessly, her mirth submerging her until it was impossible to stop and tears ran down her cheeks. Saul bent and took her by the shoulders, shaking her again sharply, her laughter quenched in an instant at the touch of his hands. He released her and went across to the tray of drinks on the table, pouring a generous amount of brandy into a glass.

'Drink this.' He thrust it into her hand.

Claudia looked at it doubtfully. 'I don't know that I should—I had wine at dinner and champagne at the party.'

'What time did you leave?'

'Oneish.' Her eyes widened as she glanced at her watch. 'Good heavens, it's past three!' She gulped down the brandy, careless of any ill effects.

Saul stood, arms folded, his patience plainly at an end.

'Explain, Claudia. If you left the party at one, what happened between then and now?'

Her tongue loosened by the brandy, Claudia began on the account of the wretched journey, at first annoyed when Saul's lips began to twitch, then even to herself the sorry tale of the hike in the darkness with her reluctant escort began to sound ludicrous, and when she came to the part where she was squeezed into the cab of a rather vintage truck with a family of kind festive Brazilians while Bob finished the trip in more Spartan fasion in the back, she was grinning as widely as Saul.

'He was wearing such an elegant beige linen suit,' mourned Claudia. 'Heaven knows what condition it was in afterwards!'

'Hard luck.' Saul was unmoved. 'He should have checked the car before he went. In too much of a hurry to get you to himself, no doubt.'

'It wasn't Bob's fault the car broke down, Saul. Besides, he thought we should wait in the car until something came along.'

'I'll bet he did!' He raised an eyebrow at her, his eyes gleaming. 'Why didn't you?'

Claudia's eyes fell, her cheeks tingeing with colour.

'I wanted to get home.'

Saul looked pointedly at the sandals lying discarded by her chair. She glared at him.

'Next time I'll take my hiking boots!' Her shoulders slumped. 'Besides, I was afraid nothing *would* come along to pick us up, and three miles or so didn't sound too terrible in theory, only when we started to walk.'

'Was that the only reason?'

'No. But it's the only one you're going to get.' Claudia got up awkwardly, wincing as she put her weight on her feet.

'Oh, for God's sake!' Saul swooped and picked her up bodily, carrying her in silence through the hall and setting her down just inside the bathroom door. 'There should be some antiseptic in the medicine chest—pour a good dollop into your bathwater, then get yourself to

bed. I'll come and put something on those blisters when
you're ready.'

'There's no need,' whispered Claudia furiously. 'I can
manage!'

'You can't risk infection in this climate—be sensible,
woman!'

Claudia pulled a face as he closed the door softly
behind him, then did as he said, lowering her aching
body into the hot water gradually, gritting her teeth as
the antiseptic stung her feet and regretting it instantly as
her jaw gave a warning throb. She lay for only a minute
or two, much as she would have loved to linger, then
wrapped herself in one of the crimson bathsheets and
tiptoed to her room, shrugging her nightdress over her
head as a tap sounded on the door. Wrapping her
kimono round her she let Saul in.

'Lie on the bed,' he ordered. 'I'll put some antiseptic
salve on your feet—it might be as well to keep your
dressing gown on and lie on top of the covers tonight.'

Claudia obeyed, too tired for any protest as Saul
pushed pillows behind her head and slid the folded
towel beneath her feet. His hands were surprisingly
gentle as he smoothed on the cooling ointment, its
effect blissfully analgesic on the sore skin. Claudia
relaxed and closed her eyes with a sigh as he finished.

'Did I hurt you?' His deep voice was soft, without its
dictatorial note for once, and her eyes flew open to peer
warily at him as he leaned above her.

'No.' She managed a saucy little smile. 'Sorry to be a
nuisance. I don't need much medical attention as a
rule.'

Saul smiled at her spontaneously, his teeth white in
the darkness of his face, a glint in his eyes clearly visible
in the subdued light of the bedside lamp.

'How would you describe today's ailments? Foot and
mouth?'

Claudia clapped a hand to her mouth to stifle the
laughter bubbling up inside her, her body shaking
slightly.

'Hey,' he murmured, leaning closer, 'not hysterical
again, are you? Must I shake you again?'

She shook her head in disapproval, taking her hand away from her mouth.

'No way! Three times in succession is a bit over the top—in danger of getting hooked, in fact.'

The laughter faded from Saul's face and he leaned nearer.

'Too late, Claudia. I *am* hooked already.'

Her breathing felt constricted as she lay there, her eyes wary as she considered his undramatic statement.

'Did you hear me?' he persisted softly, and leaned lower.

She nodded, mesmerised, unable to look away from the disturbing warmth in his eyes.

'Well?' he prompted, his hands now on either side of her.

Her eyelids fluttered and she moved her head restlessly.

'I don't know what you want me to say,' she muttered.

'Liar!'

Claudia was torn. This would seem the right moment to tell him she was—was what? Available? The term seemed strangely vulgar in this particular context. She stared uncertainly into the strong face above her as Saul's broad shoulders blocked out the room, the scent of his skin enveloping her in a haze of excitement, his big body almost in contact with hers, yet not quite. She could push him away. The choice was hers. Before she could make it Saul suddenly levered himself up with one agile movement and left her without a word. Claudia lay deflated, her dilemma settled for her, wondering if her silence had been the reason for his departure. She would never understand this enigmatic, maddening man. So he was hooked, was he! It would have made her considerably happier if he had seen fit to explain just precisely what he was hooked *on*. Never end a sentence with a preposition, Claudia, she scolded herself, with an attempt at humour, but she seemed to have run the gamut of all the emotions she possessed, except for surprise, as the door opened again. Saul shut it noiselessly behind him and came over to the bed, looming large in the dim light.

Annoyed at his cool assumption that he was welcome to come and go in her bedroom as she wished, she demanded,

'Why are you here?'

She stared blankly as Saul merely smiled faintly and sat on the edge of the bed with his back to her and bent to take off his rope-soled shoes. He turned and lifted her farther over on the bed, then swung his legs up and settled himself comfortably beside her, sharing her banked pillows.

'You can't stay here!' She slid away from him in agitation, but he put out a hand and yanked her back, holding her against him in the crook of his arm. 'Saul—please! Becky——'

'Becky's at Casa d'Ouro. She was at a loose end after you left so I took her over to Emily when I drove Bea to see Dr Machado this afternoon.'

'What!' Claudia twisted frantically in his grasp. 'What was the matter? Was she ill—why didn't you say at once——'

'Calm down, sweetheart!' Saul pulled her wholly into his arms, smoothing her hair as he held her close. Claudia was silenced by the endearment, her body tense as he explained. 'She made the appointment days ago, but didn't want to worry any of us. She only told me yesterday when she asked me to run her up to the hospital.'

'But you offered to take me to the dentist at lunchtime.' Claudia raised her head from his shoulder to look up into Saul's face, something she found there making her pulse behave erratically.

'When you were in pain I forgot everything else,' he said simply. 'Even poor Aunt Bea's appointment went out of my head—which, I might add, amused her no end.'

Claudia forced her mind from this dangerously fascinating topic.

'But what exactly is wrong with Bea?'

'A touch of high blood pressure, but nothing some

medication and a lot of rest won't put right, I'm profoundly thankful to say.'

Claudia melted against him in relief, burrowing her face into his neck.

'Oh, Saul, I'm so glad! I had thoughts of heart trouble—all sorts of things. I've known her for only a short time, I know, but I've come to care for her very much.'

His arms tightened round her.

'You've known me the same length of time, Claudia.'

She nodded blindly. 'Yes.'

'What do you mean—"Yes"?'

She raised an arm and mopped her damp eyes with the sleeve of her kimono. 'Just yes.' She refused to look up at him, suddenly shy now that the moment of truth had arrived. 'If you mean do I care for you too, yes. Am I hooked on you, yes. Do I want you to stay here all night, yes!' She got no further as her face was turned up to his, their mouths coming together in a sweet violence that cancelled out the need to say any more for some time. They slid to lie full length, holding each other close with an aching need that grew more intense with each passing moment, his mouth caressing hers at first gently, then with heat and persuasion as their breathing quickened and their bodies began to move instinctively against each other in a rhythm as natural as breathing. As his mouth left hers to travel lower, a thought occurred to Claudia.

'Saul,' she said huskily, and shivered as his mouth moved lower.

Saul paused reluctantly and looked down into her eyes, his breath quickening as he saw the smoky tinge in their clarity.

'What is it, my lovely one?'

A tremor ran through her at his words, and she closed her eyes in wonder, unable to credit the light of tenderness in his.

'You can't really stay,' she said, her hands restless on his shoulders. 'Aunt Bea——'

Saul chuckled and held her closer.

'For the time being Aunt Bea is to take two sleeping

pills at night. Dr Machado says she needs undisturbed rest, and when I checked on her just now she was fathoms deep in sleep.'

'Oh.'

Even in the subdued light it was possible to see the great wave of colour that swept up Claudia's face. Very slowly Saul slid the kimono from her shoulders and followed suit with the ribbons holding up her thin white cotton nightdress. With infinite care he peeled it the whole length of her body, taking such an unconscionable time about it that Claudia lay in an agony of shyness, deeply aware of his eyes on her even though her own were tightly shut. She knew that this was what her words had invited, but now that it was all actually happening she felt diffident, ridiculously timorous for a woman of her age.

'Open your eyes, Claudia.' The caress in Saul's voice was as potent as the touch of his hands. Her lids lifted slowly, weighted by a new, consuming languor, then flew wide as she realised he was as naked as herself. Her eyes grew wild as they glittered at him in near panic, then the time for hesitation and doubt was over as he secured her against him in the seduction of skin on skin, the shock of it sending great ripples of feeling through her as his mouth and hands took possession of her body with a mastery that cancelled out fear, leaving only a pure refinement of longing that ignored the first painful instant as their bodies came together, and gloried in the wave upon wave of sensation that followed. For long, breathless moments he held her inexorably at the very brink of the unknown, then plunged with her into the fulfilment that lay beyond.

For long silent minutes they lay motionless in the aftermath of their loving, until, one by one, other senses began to reawaken in Claudia, reminding her that she needed to breathe, which was something of an impossibility under the circumstances. She stirred, and Saul rolled over on his back, holding her close against him.

'How are your feet?' he asked lazily.

'What feet?'

He chuckled, smoothing strands of hair away from her moist, hot forehead.

'Saul?' Claudia pushed herself up on her elbows to look down into his face. 'Is it always like that?'

The look of indulgence in his dark blue eyes was almost identical to the one usually reserved for Becky.

'It's a considerable source of wonder to me that somewhere among all that education you received this part was neglected.'

Claudia' s head lifted proudly.

'It was never compulsory on any of my courses.'

Saul held her away, shaking her slightly, his eyes suddenly serious.

'Do you think I'm complaining?' He brought her against him convulsively. 'To revert to your question, no. It is *not* always like that. This time it was our voyage of discovery and it will never be quite the same again. On the other hand, it was the merest foretaste— the best is yet to come.'

Claudia wriggled a little.

'I suppose it was painfully obvious that it was my maiden voyage!'

Saul pulled her head down to his, kissing her hard.

'Of course it was, you goose. Apart from that one unmistakable moment, you were so surprised by everything!'

'Stupefied, you mean!'

They lay together in contentment for a while before Claudia stirred unwillingly.

'It's almost morning. Shouldn't you go back to your room?'

Saul's head turned towards her on the pillow, his eyes filled with gratifyingly frank pleasure as they rested on her body, her skin luminous in the first pale glimmer of light filtering through the curtains.

'One or two things to clear up,' he said in a matter-of-fact way that caused a little curl of disquiet deep inside Claudia. She stiffened.

'Oh?'

'On the subject of value for money.'

Her mouth dried. 'Go on.'

Saul heaved himself up to lean against the carved headboard.

'I've hit on the very best solution possible.'

'So tell me.' Claudia turned wary eyes on his smug face.

'Certainly. Instead of employing you as governess I marry you instead. I get free tuition for Becky, Becky gets a mother as well as a teacher, Bea gains a niece and you get all the security you'll ever want.' He grinned in triumph at the expressions competing for mastery on her face.

Claudia slid off the bed and retrieved her kimono from the floor, aware of a need for protection as she tried to assimilate the statement made in such a casual manner. She pushed her hair behind her ears and sat on the dressing-table stool, looking appraisingly at the brown, relaxed body of the man on the bed. Saul drew the sheet over his lower half with blatant mock-modesty as he waited for her reply, wondering if she knew how different and how desirable she looked with her hair all anyhow, and her eyes diamond-bright in her flushed face as they examined his face in doubt.

'Is that a proposal, or a mere business proposition?'

'A proposal, of course. Surely it was obvious as such?' It was hard to recognise her grim, dour Mr Rochester in this elated male creature who was occupying her bed in such flagrant nudity.

'Not all that easily. Perhaps you could elucidate a little?'

'With pleasure.' Saul slid off the bed and stepped into his cotton slacks, zipping them up as he turned to her, the casual intimacy making her blink. He held out his arms. 'Come here.'

Claudia went. He shook her slightly.

'Saul!' Her tone was threatening.

'Sorry—I must break the habit. As I was saying, Miss March, will you marry me if I ask you very nicely, because in the short time I've been privileged to know you——' Saul paused, all his raillery abruptly gone, 'I've discovered that I can't for the life of me think how I ever survived without you before. I was joking about the teaching bit. You don't have to.'

'Of course I want to. I love teaching children.' A radiance was beginning to glow in Claudia's eyes, as she buried her face against him.

Saul shrugged, his arms almost cracking her ribs.

'The salient point I'm trying to make is that I love you,' he said huskily, 'and I hope to God you feel the same.'

'Of course I do. Why didn't you say all that in the first place?' She shook him crossly, or attempted to. She tipped her head back to look up at him with mock impatience. 'Why wrap it up in all that superfluity?'

'I wasn't sure how you'd answer.' To her astonishment she felt the arms round her tremble slightly.

'After last night? I'm afriad I must insist you make an honest woman of me!'

Saul drew back, his lips pursed judicially, his head on one side as he considered her demand, then he nodded graciously.

'Very well—on condition you make it worth my while.'

Claudia slid from his grasp and stood away from him, one eyebrow raised, hands on hips, the black silk of her kimono parting to give a glimpse of long slim leg. She ran her tongue round her lips and tilted her head back, her eyes narrowed to a sultry glimmer beneath half-closed lids as she stared into the dark face above her, unholy joy consuming her as she saw the colour rise in his face and his breathing begin to quicken.

'How do you propose I should do that?' Her voice was husky with provocation. 'Are you one of those chauvinists who consider woman's place is in the home?'

Saul pulled her back into his arms roughly.

'I'm not interested in other women, Orphan Annie. If you mean you're the woman I want in my home you're dead right. In my home and in my bed, for ever and ever, amen.'

Deeply satisfied, Claudia closed her eyes in rapture and slid her arms round his neck.

'Well?' he demanded, his hands hard on her waist. 'Nothing to say for once?'

She shook her head and eyed him questioningly.

'You mean that if I marry you I don't get a salary?'

Saul shrugged, his eyes dancing.

'The Fonsecas will pay you, the same as usual.'

'And how will you pay me?'

'In kind, my darling, in kind!'

GILDED CAGE

BY
CATHERINE GEORGE

MILLS & BOON LIMITED
Eton House, 18-24 Paradise Road
Richmond, Surrey TW9 1SR

*First published in Great Britain in 1983
by Mills & Boon Limited*

© Catherine George 1983

*Australian copyright 1983
Philippine copyright 1983
Reprinted 1983
This edition 1992*

ISBN 0 263 77775 8

*Set in Monophoto Times 9 on 10 pt.
19-9206-68793*

Made and printed in Great Britain

CHAPTER ONE

EMILY stood gazing out of the small casement window in Lady Henrietta's bedroom, her eyes absently on the last of the day's visitors as they left Compton Lacey. One man paused to take a photograph of the ancient house in the fading sunset light, and Emily smiled, knowing precisely the picture he saw through the viewfinder. Encircled by the green waters of its moat, the house had stood almost unchanged for the past six hundred years, dramatic, dreamlike, the embodiment of an illustration for some long-forgotten mediaeval romance.

This was the time of day Emily liked best, when left to itself again the old house seemed to relax and settle for a while before it was locked up and left to the solitude of the night. She stared dreamily down at the swans preening themselves on the moat, unaware that she was observed. To the man who stood silently in the doorway the girl looked like some wraithlike former occupant of the house, insubstantial in her grey dress, her long pale hair and finely chiselled profile only dimly visible in the gathering dusk of the small room. He held his breath, reluctant to disturb the girl's reverie, but something in his very stillness communicated his presence to her. She turned sharply, immediately reaching to switch on the lamps on the mantel as she saw him standing there.

She received a swift impression of a lean, darkly-tanned face with a prominent nose, and heavy-browed dark eyes beneath black hair that curled down into the upturned collar of a white trenchcoat.

'I'm sorry!' Emily smiled apologetically. 'Please come in; I thought everyone had gone.'

'I hope I didn't startle you.' White teeth gleamed in an answering smile as the man ducked his head to enter the room. He spoke with a trace of accent Emily found hard to place. She hesitated.

'Would you care to know about the contents of the room?'

'Very much.'

5

However, her companion seemed to take more interest in her face than the treasures surrounding him, and Emily found it more difficult than usual to concentrate on the details that were automatic to her by now from long practice. Deliberately brisk and prosaic, she launched into her account of the Charles I chest, the Queen Anne kneehole desk and the George IV toilet mirror, the man listening intently to her low, clear voice as she indicated the heraldic panes in the windows, the exceptional quality of the panelling and the ornate splendour of the fourposter bed.

'The lady in the painting,' asked her visitor, when she paused, 'is that the Henrietta for whom this room is named?'

'Yes.' Emily moved over the fireplace to look up at the smiling beauty in full court dress. 'She's Lady Henrietta Compton, who married Sir Giles Lacey in the reign of George IV, bringing with her a very large dowry which enabled her husband to make extensive restoration to various parts of the house.'

'If the artist was accurate, rather than flattering, Sir Giles was a very fortunate man.' The deep, rather harsh voice, with its faint elusive accent, held a mocking note. 'Heiresses seldom had beauty to accompany their fortunes, if one may believe all one reads.'

'No,' said Emily consideringly, looking up at the confident, beautiful face below the powdered curls. 'It hardly seems fair, does it?' Then she collected herself hurriedly. 'The other guides have gone from this floor. Would you like me to show you through the upper rooms? It's very nearly time to lock up.'

'You must do that?'

'No. Colonel Hammond, the custodian, closes up the house after he makes his final check-up. If you'd follow me.'

They moved slowly through the rest of the rooms, Emily's voice cool and concise as she pointed out features of interest in the chapel and the sacristy, also the barrel-vaulted ceiling in the great parlour, smiling at his expected amused reaction when she showed him the 'modern' improvement of closing in the upper gallery from the elements, its modernity dating from the time of the first Elizabeth. The approaching dusk invested the house with an even greater charm than the broad light of day, but she was not sorry when they reached the final room, the solar. The silent presence of the man beside her, listening with attention to her every word, was unnerving, different from her normal lecture, delivered impersonally to a room full of people.

'This is the final room, which, apart from its very fine collection of books, has a rather famous stain on the floor— over there near the fireplace. This is reputed to be where the owner of the house killed a priest he found making advances to his wife.' Emily smiled suddenly up at her companion. 'I suppose these days his reaction might be considered somewhat extreme.'

He shook his head, smiling.

'I think his reaction was perfectly justified. I would do the same if any man made advances to *my* wife.'

'Really?' Emily was determinedly impersonal as she led him down the narrow stone stairs and through the oak door that gave on to the formal Elizabethan garden. 'That's the lot, I'm afraid. It's quite a small house compared with some of the other National Trust showplaces.'

'Small, but perfect. A jewel in a beautiful setting.'

Some inflection in the deep voice made Emily's colour rise, and her manner was rigidly formal as she bade the stranger goodbye. Resisting the urge to watch the tall figure out of sight, she retreated to the gatehouse to say goodnight, and hand over her National Trust Warden badge.

Mrs Hammond, the custodian's wife, looked up, smiling.

'A bit late tonight, Emily dear. I'm sorry the rather exotic-looking gentleman held you up, but he appeared at the last minute and I hadn't the heart to turn him away.'

'No problem, Mrs Hammond. I had nothing better to do.' Emily smiled cheerfully as she collected her coat.

'Well, you should have. An attractive girl like you with nothing to do on a Saturday night—it's a crime!' Mrs Hammond's kind face wore its usual look of concern.

'Oh well, Mrs H., you know I'm a home bird.' Emily said goodnight quickly, promising to be back the following afternoon, then escaped before the other woman could expound on her favourite theme.

The shadows were lengthening as Emily crossed the bridge

over the moat, and a chill evening breeze eddied among the branches of the gnarled old trees in the parkland surrounding the house. Centuries before there had been a real drawbridge, and Emily liked to picture knights on brightly caparisoned horses riding gaily over it, though she smiled wryly to herself as she walked rapidly along the drive. These days girls were more likely to require their dream man at the wheel of a red Ferrari than on a white charger! Immediately she thought of the big dark man in the white trenchcoat. Emily had hardly liked to examine his face more than fleetingly, but the impression remained with her of dark good looks and strength, in both physique and personality. She wondered idly what sort of car *he* would drive—something long and fast, probably, certainly not a family car, despite the allusion to a wife. It was difficult to imagine him with little ones clustering at his knee. Emily's involuntary giggle changed to a gasp of fright as a figure detached itself from the gloom of the shrubbery leading to the car park.

'I startled you for the second time,' he said, standing foursquare in front of her. 'I am sorry, but when I saw no other car in the car park besides mine I waited to drive you home.'

Emily regarded the subject of her thoughts with mixed feelings.

'How kind,' she said coolly. 'I normally cycle back and forth, but I had a puncture this morning, so I walked.'

'Far?'

'No. A mile or so. I live in the actual village down the road, Compton Lacey; the same name as the house.' To her irritation Emily could hear herself beginning to chatter, put out by the way he stood so still and immovable, looking down at her. 'It's no distance—I don't really need a lift. Thank you just the same,' she added belatedly, wishing he would stand aside.

'Surely it is not a good thing for a child like you to walk alone along such a deserted road in the dark?' he asked harshly.

'I'm not a child—I'm almost nineteen.' Even to her own ears this sounded ridiculous, and Emily was hardly surprised to hear his soft laugh.

'So old! But in some ways that makes it even worse.'

'But it would be safer for me to accept a lift from a strange man, I suppose—a foreigner, I might add!' Emily was aghast momentarily at her own rudeness, relieved to hear him laugh again.

'You are quite right to be cautious. I applaud it.'

I *am* glad, she thought irritably, as he searched in his inside pocket and produced something it was too dark for her to make out.

'If you will come over to my car I will put on the lights and show you my passport,' he said persuasively. 'Then we may introduce ourselves formally and perhaps you will then allow me to drive you this mile or so to your home.'

Emily gave up. After all, there was little point in complaining about the dull monotony of life if one didn't take advantage of the smallest of diversions when it occurred. She inclined her head regally and walked with the man to his car, which was just as she'd imagined, long and speedy-looking.

'Not a red Ferrari, though.' To her horror she said the words aloud, and could have bitten her tongue in vexation. Her companion unlocked the car door and opened it, looking enquiringly into her face as the interior light shone on it.

'You accept lifts only in red Ferraris?'

'I never accept lifts at all,' snapped Emily, aware of the suppressed amusement in his voice as she unwillingly inspected his proffered passport. It showed his photograph, unmistakable and stern, giving his name as Lucas Antonio Jaime Guimaraes Fonseca, nationality Brazilian, age twenty-nine, hair and eyes black, no distinguishing marks. Stiffly she handed it back.

'How do you do, Mr—Fonseca.' She hesitated over the unfamiliar name. 'I'm Emily Harper.'

He took her hand solemnly, shaking it with grave formality.

'*Encantado*, Miss Harper. Now may I take you home?'

Emily had begun to feel more than a little ridiculous by this time.

'Thank you.' With dignity she settled herself in the comfortable passenger seat while he held the door for her and showed her how to use the seat-belt. She leaned back in luxury as he started the car, enjoying the way it glided slowly over the uneven surface of the long drive that wound its way for half a mile through the grounds of the house before reaching the narrow road that ran past the main gates in the direction of the village.

'Where do you live, Miss Harper?' asked her companion.

'It's the cottage just past the church.'

'Do you live with your parents?'

'No, they're both dead.'

'*Coitada!* How sad.' He was obviously affected by her words. 'But surely you do not live alone. You have relations?'

'Not many.' Emily wondered fleetingly whether she should be telling him all this. 'I have two old aunts in Scotland on my mother's side and I'm related, in a very distant way, to Major Lacey who used to own the big house. He's some sort of connection of my father's, and he lives in the Dower House now. He also owns the cottage I live in—there it is.'

Lucas Fonseca brought the car smoothly to a halt outside the gate of the cottage Emily indicated. Standing back from a small front garden, the house had obviously once been two separate dwellings, though the conversion had been effected with a care that did nothing to alter the charm of the black and white half-timbered building. A brass coach lamp was alight on the outer front wall.

'Someone is inside?' he asked, looking at the light.

'When my mother died I took in a tenant, Mrs Crawford, a widow with a small son. She's the local district nurse, a super lady and popular with everyone. Mrs Crawford—Lydia—lives in one half and I have the other, so although we're quite separate neither of us is really alone; a very convenient arrangement. Now I'll say goodnight, Mr Fonseca, and thank you for bringing me home.'

He put out a hand and caught hers as she turned to open the door.

'Wait a moment, Miss Harper, please. Now that we have formally introduced ourselves could you not take pity on a lonely visitor to your country and have dinner with me?' His dark eyes probed hers intently, and Emily felt suddenly shy, then she remembered something he'd said earlier and frowned.

'I believe you're married, Mr Fonseca, which is only one of the reasons why I can't accept.'

The dark face took on a baffled expression and one eyebrow raised in enquiry.

'Why do you think I'm married? I can assure you in all truth that I am not!'

It was Emily's turn to be confused.

'But when I told you the priest was killed for making advances to the owner's wife, you said you would do the same if it were *your* wife.'

He threw back his head and laughed, looking sideways at her with a wicked grin.

'I was speaking hypothetically—is that the right word? Alas, I have found no one willing to have me up to the present.'

Against her will Emily smiled back.

'Have you asked many?'

'None. I have never met anyone I wished to share my life with yet. Have you?'

'No,' said Emily regretfully, 'I haven't. I'm not likely to meet many likely contenders in Compton Lacey, either.'

'Well then, now that we have cleared up that point, I repeat: will you dine with me?' he said persistently.

'I said it was only one of the reasons. The other one is that I'm babysitting—Lydia's son.'

'Perhaps you merely do not wish to dine with me.' He frowned.

'Oh no, not in the least,' said Emily candidly. 'I would have enjoyed it very much; dinner invitations are few and far between. Never mind. Thank you very much for asking me. Goodnight.' She got out of the car quickly, but he was before her, opening the garden gate as she reached it. Lucas Fonseca loomed tall as he took her hand and raised it unexpectedly to his lips.

'*Até logo*, Miss Harper.'

'What does that mean?'

'The same as *au revoir* in French,' he said, smiling briefly before turning away to get in the Jaguar, waving a hand in farewell as he accelerated away from the kerb.

Emily watched the vanishing tail lights thoughtfully before hurrying up the garden path and round to the side entrance to Lydia's part of the house. She knocked and went in, to find

Lydia laying the table, dressed in all the glory of what she called 'the good frock', which was a well-cut silk shirt-dress in dark green.

'Hello, love, you're late tonight—come on in.' She looked up smiling, her serene face made up with unusual care beneath greying dark hair which had obviously recently enjoyed the ministrations of the hairdresser.

'I haven't held you up, have I, Lydia?' asked Emily anxiously. 'The bike had a puncture this morning——'

'And you've had to walk home? What a shame—not to worry, I'm not due at Celia's for a couple of hours, so I thought you could have tea with Tim and me and take the weight off your feet. Thank God it's my weekend off. How do you like my hair? Here, give me your coat.'

Surrendering to Lydia's forceful personality, Emily abandoned explanations and did as she was told, gratefully accepting a cup of tea and stretching out her feet to the blaze.

'Your hair looks gorgeous, Lydia, but why are you eating now? I thought it was a dinner party.'

'It's expanded and turned into a buffet supper; ergo, I'm lining my stomach with a little alcohol–absorbent insulation, otherwise the first glass of sherry will knock me flat.' Lydia grinned, then patted the generous curves of her hips. 'Not that I need the calories. You don't think this silk shows up the bulges too much, do you, Em?'

'Of course not,' said Emily firmly, 'you're tall enough to carry it off—not a shrimp like me.'

Lydia eyed her militantly.

'Don't put yourself down, Emily Harper. Your looks are the type to appeal to the discerning——'

'Which breed isn't exactly thick on the ground in Compton Lacey,' said Emily, giggling, then stopped, a faraway look in her eye. 'Mind you, I met someone today who was definitely different.'

Lydia was immediately all attention, settling herself in the armchair on the other side of the fireplace.

'Tim's still watching some programme on his television upstairs, so we'll wait a moment or two before eating,' she said comfortably, 'so tell me who you met.'

'He was late, after all the others had gone, so I showed him through the upper rooms on his own.' Emily paused.

'Go on,' said Lydia expectantly.

'When I'd finished he was waiting near the car park to see if he could give me a lift home. I wasn't too keen——'

'Why ever not?' Lydia looked at her in despair.

'Well, I didn't know him, did I? He could have been Jack the Ripper,' said Emily reasonably.

'But he obviously wasn't, so carry on.'

'He showed me his passport as identification, and he's a Brazilian called Lucas Fonseca—I think that's how you pronounce it, he's twenty-nine and quite good-looking, in a dark Latin sort of way.'

'Goodness!' breathed Lydia, impressed. 'Did he give you a lift home—what sort of car?'

'Yes, he did, in a white Jaguar XJS, very nice indeed. A whole lot better than my bicycle!' Emily laughed outright at the expression on Lydia's face.

'Well, surely that's not all, Emily!'

'Almost. He asked me to have dinner with him.'

'Then what on earth are you doing sitting there, you idiotic girl! Go and get ready,' said Lydia, exasperated.

'Oh, I didn't accept,' said Emily lamely. 'After all, I was babysitting for you. I could hardly let you down, especially on a Saturday night.'

Lydia jumped to her feet in frustration.

'I could have found someone else, silly. Or even have carted Tim along to Celia's party. He could have watched television there if necessary. You are the absolute end, Emily Harper! Too high-principled by half.' Lydia stopped short, then grinned at the younger girl. 'But then you wouldn't be you otherwise, I suppose. And after all, he knows where you live. Where's he staying?'

'I didn't ask him.'

'Oh, Emily!'

Later on that evening, after Lydia had departed for her soirée, and two games of draughts had been played with Tim, Emily shepherded her charge to bed and returned downstairs to make herself a cup of coffee and sit by the replenished fire with a book.

The fictitious characters in the novel fought a losing battle with thoughts of the man from Brazil, however, and Emily gave up trying to follow the story after a while. She sat daydreaming, her eyes on the flickering flames, wondering if Senhor Fonseca was dining alone, or whether he might have found some other companion to take pity on his loneliness. Not that he seemed the type to be disturbed at being left to his own company. A singularly self-sufficient type of personality, thought Emily, forceful even, and obviously used to having things all his own way. It was flattering, but scarcely credible that she could have had much interest for him. Emily had no illusions about her own attractions. As Lydia said, she had the sort of looks that would appeal to the discerning, or to anyone with the patience to take a second look, but at first glance she knew very well she lacked impact. Her hair was glossy and thick, hanging to her shoulders where it curled slightly at the ends, but it was a muted ash-blonde, though where it grew away from her forehead there were several lighter streaks, legacy of an unusually warm summer. Her skin was fair and transparent, all too inclined to show the ready colour that rose easily at moments of stress. Her features were all straight lines as though drawn by a delicate hand with a very fine brush and her eyebrows flared away in straight strokes from her delicate nose, the only curve in her face the lovely line of her mouth above a rather square, resolute chin. Added to this in her disfavour, as far as she was concerned, was a lamentable lack of what her mother used to term as 'presence', as Emily was only a little over five feet tall and her figure was slight and fine-boned.

Altogether not exactly front page stuff, she thought ruefully, overlooking the one vivid note of colour she possessed. Beneath the straight brows her eyes were a light, bright, translucent blue, a feature inherited from her remote connection with the Lacey family.

Wistfully Emily wished she were beautiful, fascinating, that at this very moment she was drinking champagne at some exclusive restaurant with Lucas Fonseca, dazzling him with her wit and charm. . . . Oh, come on, Emily Harper, she told herself crossly, forget about him. It's most unlikely you'll meet him again, so put him out of your mind. It was easier said than done, and irritably she jumped up and went upstairs to have a peep at the now sleeping Tim, then went back down to the fire, thinking for the hundredth time how fortunate she was to have Lydia to share the house with her.

Emily's parents had been surprised when after long childless years their daughter had arrived when Mrs Harper was in her forties and Professor Harper some fifteen years older. Already retired from lecturing at the local university, he had died when Emily was small, leaving her mother sufficient income to live very quietly in the cottage owned by Major Lacey and scrape enough to send Emily away to school. Laura Harper had herself been an only child and was in no way gregarious, content in the secluded life she led, only to succumb to cancer shortly before Emily was due to leave school. The disease had been arrested for a while, but six months ago she had slipped quietly out of life after a long, stoically borne illness, during which Emily had nursed her devotedly, with the aid of the district nurse, Lydia Crawford. The latter had been Emily's saviour during this time, with her cheerful common sense and compassionate nursing expertise.

Initially Emily was panic-stricken at being left virtually alone in the world, but a visit from Marcus Lacey after the funeral, assuring her that the house was hers rent-free for as long as she wished, did much to restore her balance. He advised her to divide the cottage again and find someone to live in the other half, using the rent to help support herself. Lydia had lit up with enthusiasm when she heard. Herself a widow with one small son, her present house was too big for her to maintain, and sharing Church Cottage with Emily was an ideal solution for all concerned.

Emily was still staring absently into the dying fire when Lydia returned home just before one, and after listening to a vivid account of the party over a cup of tea she retired to her own quarters and went swiftly to bed, still regrettably preoccupied with thoughts of the handsome Brazilian.

CHAPTER TWO

SUNDAY was the busiest afternoon at Compton Lacey and Emily, stationed in the Great Hall, had no time for thought as she supplied a constant stream of visitors with all the details of the Aubusson tapestries, the intricately beamed ceiling, the various paintings on the walls. She enjoyed answering the countless questions put to her, especially from overseas visitors, who were always impressed by the sheer antiquity of the building, which was one of the oldest fortified manor houses in the country. Its survival was largely due to its extremely remote location, deep within the Forest of Arden, where it had escaped the attentions of Oliver Cromwell. Emily considered herself very fortunate to have a job of such absorbing interest, especially as her expensive education had been cut short by the need to look after her mother, leaving her ill-equipped to find work of a more commercial nature.

Hard put to it to find a spare minute for a cup of tea, she found the afternoon flew by with no time to think of her foreign visitor of yesterday. Today the sightseers were mainly family groups and elderly couples, with the odd sprinkling of students here and there. The weather had turned colder, and Emily was glad of her black and white wool kilt and blue mohair sweater. Thick ribbed tights and knee-length black leather boots were a further precaution against the draughts that eddied through the old house, despite the modern central heating system. When the last of the visitors had finally gone Emily was decidedly weary and none too charmed at the prospect of walking home. Making a resolution to get her bicycle mended next day, she bade the Hammonds goodnight and huddled into her old sheepskin jacket. Twilight was rapidly giving way to darkness as Emily walked briskly along, her hands deep in her pockets, shivering slightly in the cool evening breeze. Her heart gave a great leap as she saw the tall figure waiting near the car park, instantly recognisable despite different, darker clothes. He started forward as she came into view.

16

'Good evening, Miss Harper.' The slightly harsh voice with its faint accent was unmistakable and, surprisingly, familiar. Emily made no pretence of a surprise she didn't feel.

'Good evening, Mr Fonseca. What brings you to Compton Lacey again so soon?'

He took one of her hands from its hiding place in her pocket and held it between both his own. Hard, almost rough hands, Emily noted absently.

'The need to see you again,' he answered simply, his unvarnished statement silencing her completely. Without a word she allowed herself to be installed in the white Jaguar, eyeing him cautiously as he came round the front of the car and sat in the driver's seat. Lucas Fonseca turned towards her, making no effort to start the car.

'You are not on the telephone,' he stated, frowning at her.

'Lydia has one in her half; for use in her job. I can't afford a separate one for me,' said Emily. 'Besides, it isn't necessary.'

'I could not reach you by telephone, so I came to see you.'

Her eyes widened.

'You came to the house?'

'At about four this afternoon. Your friend Mrs Crawford took me in and gave me tea until it was time to fetch you.' He grinned at her infectiously. 'We had quite a chat.'

'I'll bet you did!' Emily chuckled. 'She called me several kinds of idiot for refusing your dinner invitation last night.'

'So I gathered. So I hope very much you will give her no cause for complaint and consent to dine with me tonight.'

It was too dark to see the expression on the dark face turned towards her, nevertheless Emily was left in no doubt as to the urgency of his whole attitude, his body overtly tense.

'Well?' he prompted.

Emily threw caution to the winds.

'Yes, thank you, I'd be delighted.'

He relaxed visibly.

'I am glad,' he said quietly, switching on the ignition. 'Now tell me about your day.'

To her surprise Emily found it amazingly easy to do just that, and gave him a spirited account of the afternoon's visitors, including the American lady who thought the beams in the ceiling of the Great Hall should be replaced because they were 'warped and kinda rotten, honey, they must be dangerous'. Her companion told Emily gravely that she must make allowances for the opinions of misguided foreigners, and they laughed together, though Emily felt bound to add that the lady in question had been very charming, insisting on taking her photograph against the background of the imposing stone fireplace.

When they reached the gate of Church Cottage Lucas Fonseca left the car idling and glanced at the thin gold watch on his wrist.

'It is now six-fifteen, Miss Emily Harper. May I come back for you at seven-thirty?'

Emily nodded, frowning a little at a sudden doubt.

'Is it somewhere very grand? I'm afraid my wardrobe is a bit limited.'

His face held a curiously protective look as he smiled down at her.

'I am staying at the White Hart on the Birmingham road, and they do a reasonable meal. I am certain that anything you choose to wear will be appropriate.'

Reassured, Emily smiled at him and got out of the car.

'See you later, then.' With a little wave she ran up the garden path, practically colliding with Lydia, who had obviously been lying in wait and appeared round the corner of the house with suspicious promptitude.

'What happened?' Her face was alight with anticipation.

'Come and chat while I get ready, Lydia.' Emily unlocked the door, switching on lights recklessly and galloping up the stairs at a speed that left the other woman behind. 'I hear you had a visitor this afternoon!'

Lydia arrived in Emily's bedroom panting, and subsided on the bed, while Emily dashed to and from the bathroom, tearing off her clothes while the water was running.

'Can you imagine my reaction, love, when this gorgeous male rang my doorbell this afternoon, enquiring as to your whereabouts?' There was a giggle from the bathroom as Emily began soaping herself. 'You know, Em,' went on Lydia, a faraway look in her eye, 'I took one look at him and twenty years melted away like magic. What a smile, and that tan— did you see the quality of the suede jacket he was wearing?'

'Didn't notice,' was the blithe response.

'You're hopeless! Anyway, presumably you've actually consented to dine with him tonight—where's he taking you?'

'The White Hart,' called back Emily. 'That's where he's staying.'

'Nice and handy. What are you wearing?'

Emily came into the bedroom in a short towelling wrap, her hair pinned up in a knot on top of her head.

'Now that, Mrs Crawford, is a very good question. I just don't own the right type of clothes for wining and dining.'

Lydia bounced off the bed to inspect the contents of the wardrobe Emily was gazing into without much hope.

'You don't have to be done up too much, especially on a Sunday night,' she said practically, clicking hangers along the rail. 'What about this?' She drew out a plain slim skirt in fine black wool.

'I had that when Mother died,' Emily said doubtfully. 'I haven't worn it since. There's a black sweater I wore with it.'

'You must have something a bit more festive than that—here, what's this?'

Lydia produced a hanger from the end of the rail, inspecting the blouse on it with approval. Fine creamy silk with long full sleeves gathered into wide lace-edged cuffs and a yoke with lace-edged pin tucks below a high collar made a perfect accompaniment for the severe black skirt.

'I feel a bit guilty about that—I kept it for myself when someone brought it for me to sell on the Nearly New stall at the church fête—I put some money in, of course.'

Emily's confession amused Lydia inordinately, but she merely handed the garment to the guilty-looking girl and told her to get a move on.

'Now's your time to wear it, then—do you have any decent tights?'

'I think I still have the ones I wore with the skirt,' said Emily, searching in a drawer. 'Yes, here they are. "Black Coffee", extra fine.'

Well before the appointed time Emily was ready, her face made up with great care and her hair swept smoothly into a loose knot on the crown of her head. One slender leg, in its sheer dark covering, swung backwards and forwards nervously as she perched on the arm of a chair as she waited, wishing Lydia had stayed to shore up her confidence, but that lady had departed in good time, leaving Emily to wait alone, suddenly beset by all kinds of doubts about the approaching evening. Feeling jittery, Emily heard the slam of a car door with a feeling of doom. Looking wildly around the room as the doorbell sounded, almost wishing she could hide, she sternly took a deep breath, steadying herself forcibly before opening the door.

Lucas Fonseca, wearing a dark grey suit and dazzling white shirt, regarded her with open appreciation.

'*Que beleza!*' he said softly, taking her hand.

'Good evening,' said Emily a little stiffly. 'What did you say?'

'Merely how beautiful you looked. Are you ready to leave?'

She nodded, then collected her handbag and the crocheted black shawl Lydia had lent her before locking the door and following her escort down the path to the car. He handed her in with ceremony before getting in the driving seat.

'Are you nervous of me, Miss Harper?' he asked as the car moved off silently.

'Yes,' said Emily baldly, her fingertips white where they clutched her small handbag convulsively.

'I won't eat you, I promise.' The chuckle in his voice relaxed her a little, and she stole a shy look at his profile as they left the village and turned on to the Birmingham road.

He leaned down and switched on the car radio, finding some pleasant background music and turning the volume low.

'Now then, Miss Emily Harper, I am a lonely foreigner who is much honoured to have the company of such a charming young lady for dinner. I will behave with the utmost propriety, I assure you, and will bring you back home at whatever time you wish. Does that reassure you?'

Emily felt immediately sheepish, and relaxed in her seat with a sigh.

'Yes, of course. I'm sorry—it's just that I've always been a bit shy. In the beginning I found my job very difficult from that point of view, but I am improving—it's been very good for me.'

'Please, do not apologise. I find such diffidence very appealing.' He shot a brief smile at her. 'It is more than a little unusual in this country, also, where the ladies are reported to be all liberated.'

Emily thought this over.

'I rather think that being liberated is pursuing the course one wishes to follow. I do just that—so perhaps even I am liberated in a way. I suppose in your country things are different?'

'Many women follow professions, of course, but in the interior where I live some of the old customs still prevail. Some families adhere to the rule that a young lady of good family should not go out alone with a young man before she is married, not even her *noivo*—fiancé. She must be accompanied by a sister, or some other relative, or a maid.' He grinned at the expression on her face. 'You find this archaic?'

Emily nodded.

'I do, I'm afraid. I consider myself a bit of an anachronism, but, as you see, I'm out for an evening with you alone, and you're a complete stranger. What's more, you're a bird of passage. I hope. . . .' Her voice trailed off as they arrived in the forecourt of the White Hart, which was set back from the road in an attractive garden.

Lucas Fonseca was immediately out of the car and round to open her door, putting a hand under her arm to help her out.

'What do you hope?' he asked softly, looking down searchingly into her face. 'Do you hope you have not made a big mistake?'

'Yes,' said Emily honestly, 'and now that sounds extremely rude put into words.'

He led her through the hotel entrance, whispering into her ear: 'I promise—it is not a mistake.'

Seated in a secluded corner of the oak-beamed dining-room, Emily began to relax. By the light of the rose-shaded lamp on the table she looked up with undisguised curiosity at the planes and angles of her companion's face.

'Why are you looking at me like that?' he asked.

'Well, I haven't really had the opportunity before to see what you actually look like,' she admitted frankly. 'I didn't like to stare when we were up at the Manor House, and otherwise it's been too dark to see properly.'

His teeth and eyes gleamed in amusement.

'And now that you have made a study, do you like what you see?'

She nodded.

'Yes. You're extremely good-looking. But of course you know that.'

His smile changed to a startled frown.

'Why should you say that? I do not care for the sound of it.'

Emily examined him consideringly, head a little on one side, surprised and a little touched to see him shift slightly in his seat.

'I didn't mean to suggest you're conceited; but you have a certain aura about you.' She hesitated as his eyes narrowed. 'You're so—self-confident, absolutely in command of yourself. The way you dress, carry yourself; they're the mannerisms of a man sure of his reception, I think.'

Whatever he might have replied was forestalled by the arrival of the waiter, and it was only when they were both eating smoked salmon and tasting the dry white wine that accompanied it that he answered her.

'I do not think it is my looks that—engender this aura that you speak of.' He broke off and smiled at her persuasively. 'I would be very pleased if you would allow me to call you Emily?'

She nodded, smiling shyly.

'My family and friends call me Luc,' he went on, 'perhaps you will do the same?' Taking her acceptance for granted, he returned to his original statement. 'If—and I do not totally agree with you in this—I appear sure of myself it is more likely to be due to my circumstance in life than an accident of how my face is arranged. My family owns a gold mine in Minas Gerais in the interior of Brazil, and although I work hard in it and take my responsibilities seriously I have been brought up with total security, both in my family's wealth, and in my own place in life. This probably sounds feudal to you, but I am trying to be honest.'

Emily was very thoughtful as the main course of roast beef was set in front of them, accompanied by a different wine, a full, red Portuguese Dão. She sighed.

'You are pensive, Emily,' Luc said softly, filling her glass.

'I was thinking how very different our backgrounds are. We come from entirely different worlds rather than countries. Also,' she added, 'I'm not accustomed to drinking anything alcoholic at all, so forgive me if I'm a bit doubtful about all this wine.'

'Then do not drink any,' he said instantly. 'I have no wish to make you uneasy. And I do not see why our different backgrounds should prevent us from enjoying each other's company.'

'No, of course not.' Emily smiled and applied herself to her roast beef with appreciation. 'When you say "family", does that mean brothers and sisters?'

'Alas, no. I am an only child. My mother died at my birth and my father has never remarried, so my early upbringing was supervised by my grandmother, who is an English lady from Camborne in Cornwall.'

'So that's how you speak such good English!'

'I also received some education in England,' he answered.

'Oxford or Cambridge?'

'Neither, little—snob, I think you say.' He laughed as she flushed. 'I spent a year at Camborne School of Mines, otherwise I went to M.I.T. in the States.'

'Then you should have an American drawl,' said Emily, abandoning her plate half full.

'My grandmother would never allow it.' Luc regarded her plate with disapproval. 'Surely you can eat more than that!'

'Sorry.' Emily looked at the succulent meat with regret. 'My normal Sunday supper is something like cheese on toast, so I've done relatively well.'

He leaned across the table, his heavy brows drawn together in concern.

'You are too small, Emily, you should eat more and put curves on those fine bones of yours.'

She drew back instantly, the ready colour high on two of the bones in question, her clearly defined cheekbones.

'I hardly think I'll grow any more now,' she said distantly. 'Do tell me more of your home in—where in Brazil is it that you live?'

Obediently he abandoned his personal remarks and began to talk of Campo d'Ouro, high in the mountains of the state of Minas Gerais, where his family had mined gold for over a hundred years. He described the beautiful garden full of exotic plants and flowers where the palm-shaded house seemed to grow out of its environment, at one with its colourful surroundings where macaws screeched in the courtyard in the sun. The house was called Casa d'Ouro, and Luc lived there with his father and grandmother, and had come to Britain to inspect a new type of pneumatic rock drill manufactured in Cornwall.

'I was told I would consider the Cotswolds worthy of a visit,' he concluded, 'so I am spending a few days' holiday here before returning to Brazil.'

Refusing dessert, they both lingered over coffee while Luc asked Emily about her life in return. She found it surprisingly easy to tell him about the sorrow of losing her quiet, unassertive mother, and how her new way of life was just beginning to crystallise into routine.

'Of course, if it weren't for Marcus Lacey,' she told her attentive listener, 'I would have had quite a problem. My parents paid him rent for our cottage, but he insisted I live there free of charge when Mother died, or I don't know quite what I should have done; also he got the job up at the Manor House for me, so as things are I can manage quite well. Apart from boarding school, which I didn't enjoy very much, I've never been anywhere other than Compton Lacey.'

'Do you never have the urge to explore the world, do all those things other girls find so necessary?' he asked.

'Of course I do. I'm perfectly normal! But I like the tranquillity of the country, and to be honest, the glimpses of other people's lives afforded by television are alarming rather than attractive. I expect I seem like a timid rabbit to someone like you.'

'And what is your idea of someone like me?'

'Oh, someone cosmopolitan, travelled, highly educated—sophisticated, I suppose. But that's a very general sort of observation—after all, I hardly know you.'

Luc stretched a long-fingered brown hand across the small table and captured the restless fingers fiddling with her coffee cup as she talked.

'I would very much like you to know me better, Emily; just as I would like to know you very well indeed.'

'That's hardly possible,' she said coolly, disengaging her hand. 'You'll be leaving the country shortly, while I shall carry on here, firmly established in my bucolic routine. Which I enjoy very much,' she added defiantly.

Luc stood up abruptly, holding her chair for her, and they left the food and tobacco scents of the inn's warmth, to emerge into a cold, starry night. Emily shivered involuntarily as the wind cut through the thin silk of her blouse, submitting to Luc's swift ministrations as he wrapped the shawl securely round her and kept his arm round her waist as they walked swiftly to the car.

The drive back to Compton Lacey was accomplished in almost total silence, apart from an enquiry as to whether she were warm enough. Emily sat, tense and uneasy, stealing an occasional glance at the jutting profile of the man who drove swiftly and expertly, his expression hard to see in the darkness. When eventually they turned off the main highway down the twisting narrow road to Compton Lacey she slowly began to relax. This feeling was shortlived as the car continued past Church Cottage and through the village, almost to the gates of the Manor House itself, where Luc brought the car to a halt in a narrow layby near the entrance.

Before Emily could voice the startled protest that he obviously expected, Luc undid his seat-belt and turned towards her, capturing her cold hands which had suddenly grown icy with apprehension.

'Please, Emily,' he said huskily, 'do not fear me. I wished us to talk a little longer and I knew you would not care to invite me into your cottage as you live there alone. Please—do not tremble, I beg.'

'I don't seem able to help it,' she said irritably, staring down at their clasped hands. 'I'm not used to this sort of situation.'

'I did not think you were, *carinha*.'

The caressing note in Luc's voice did nothing at all for Emily's peace of mind, and she swallowed dryly, wishing herself safely home and in bed.

'What thoughts are hurrying around so frantically behind

those beautiful blue eyes?' Luc freed her hands and unfastened her safety-belt. 'There, now you are free.'

Emily's nostrils flared and she took a deep breath.

'Have you brought me here to—to make love to me?'

'I will do nothing against your wishes, *carinha*,' he answered obliquely, taking one of her hands and smoothing his thumb rhythmically backwards and forwards on the smooth skin. 'If you say to me now, "Start the car, take me home and go away for ever" I will do so, I promise.'

Emily found it quite impossible to say anything of the sort, and after a while he slid an arm very gently behind her, bringing her head down on his shoulder, his chin on top of her hair.

'I hope so much that you will not say this, Emily,' he went on quietly, 'because I want to stay here with you a little while, to come and see you tomorrow and the day after that, and every day until I leave.'

Emily lay against his chest, quiescent, all her instincts for flight lulled by the sincerity of the quiet deep voice she could feel vibrating against her shoulder.

'But if I let you do that,' she said doubtfully, 'If I do see you every day for a while, and then you disappear out of my life altogether, as you're bound to do, that same quiet existence of mine may not be so attractive to me afterwards. I shall perhaps be less content with my lot.'

'We shall write letters, and I shall come back before Christmas to see you again,' he said positively, his arm tightening. 'I do not intend to allow the mere fact of distance to be any obstacle. You will write to me?'

Emily turned in his grasp so that she was looking up into his dark eyes, intent on hers beneath the frowning black brows. She could feel the warmth of his breath on her cheek, and marvelled secretly at the wonder of being held so close to a muscular, male body, aware of the tautness of the arm around her, and the scent of him, compounded of some elusive male cologne, also tobacco, she thought, and something else, which could only be the particular personal aura of his own skin.

'You are very silent, Emily,' he said softly. 'But you are not trembling, at least. Does this mean you are not unhappy to be close to me like this?'

Luc's wide, well-cut mouth was only a small space away from Emily's and the nod she made in agreement reduced the distance to nothing. His lips touched hers almost imperceptibly for the space of a heartbeat, then, to their mutual surprise, both took fire, feeling blazing up in both of them simultaneously as their mouths fused and clung, parted momentarily as Emily gasped in wonder, then there was no more hesitation as both bodies sought closer contact, his mouth seeking, and finding, a response from hers that made her heart hammer as if it were trying to escape through the silk that covered it. She drew back momentarily, pressing her hand to her breast, but he replaced it with his own, holding her against him so fiercely it should have hurt, but she felt nothing except a wild gladness that sung through her veins in a triumphant paean of joy. Suddenly Luc tore himsef away, taking her face in both hands and staring down at her in a way that did nothing to decelerate her pulse.

'Has anyone ever kissed you like that before?' He sounded almost hostile, his breath coming unevenly, his accent more pronounced than usual.

Emily shook her head wordlessly, her eyes staring back wildly into his, which closed involuntarily as he brought her hard against him once more and they held each other tight, awkward in the confines of the car, until some semblance of calm began to return to them both. Eventually Emily disengaged herself and sat back in her own seat, noting vaguely that her hair hung around her shoulders in a wild tangle. Luc put out a hand and captured a lock of it, bending to kiss it as it slithered through his fingers, then he took her hand to his mouth and kissed each finger one by one, finally pressing his mouth into her palm, closing her fingers over it as he took his lips away.

'My hair came down,' said Emily faintly.

'I prefer it like that, leave it that way,' he said possessively. 'Now then, Emily Harper, there must be something else going on in that mind of yours besides the state of your hair?'

'Yes, there certainly is. So much I don't know how to put any of it into words.' Emily slid a sidelong look at him. 'Luc, do you always feel like that when—well, when you kiss someone?'

His shoulders shook slightly.

'No, *carinha*, I do not. Do you?'

'I've only been kissed a couple of times, at parties we used to have with the neighbouring boys' school at Christmas. And there was no comparison with—I mean it was nothing like— like the way you kissed me just now.'

Luc put out a hand and turned her face towards him, looking down into her questioning eyes with a tenderness that disarmed her completely.

'Emily, I kissed you because I could not resist the urge to do so. I had no idea that it would be such an explosive experience. You may take it from me that what we felt is not an everyday occurrence. Kisses can be very gentle and undemanding, I assure you—just like this.'

He bent his head to hers to show her. As a demonstration it was a failure, for as soon as their mouths made contact precisely the same reaction occurred as before. A great wave of heat enveloped them both simultaneously until they were clutching each other in a kind of desperation when their lips parted, both of them breathing in great painful gasps as they stared at each other blankly.

'Deus!' he panted, his hands bruising her shoulders, though Emily was totally oblivious to any discomfort. 'I should say I'm sorry, but I am not. You have an annihilating effect on me. It frightens me, almost.'

'It frightens me completely,' said Emily definitely, and detached herself firmly from his grasp. 'Please take me home right now, Luc Fonseca, while I'm still approximately in my right mind!'

Luc took a deep breath, running his hands through his hair, then he switched on the ignition.

'I suppose that now you will not let me see you tomorrow,' he asked, as they returned the way they had come.

'I don't think I should, in fact I know very well that I shouldn't,' she said, sighing. 'But I—I would like to see you again very much.'

At this touchingly honest little statement Luc crushed one of her hands convulsively in his, only releasing it as they drew up at the cottage.

'What time do you finish at the house tomorrow, *carinha?*'

He tucked her shawl round her shoulders and smoothed back her frankly untidy hair.

'It's my day off—no, don't get out.' Emily turned to leave.

'Spend the whole day with me then, Emily!' His hand held her captive.

Emily turned and looked at him for a long moment, then, reassured by what she saw in his eyes, she nodded. Luc smiled brilliantly, leaning instantly to kiss her, but she dodged, opening the car door and turning to laugh at him impudently from the pavement.

'Oh no, you don't!' she whispered, mindful of disturbing Lydia.

His teeth gleamed by the light of the street lamp, his eyes dancing with devilment.

'Coward!'

Emily nodded vigorously in agreement.

'*Até amanha*, Emily,' he said softly.

'What does that mean?'

'Until tomorrow, *carinha*. Goodnight.'

Emily lay awake for a long time in a state of excitement that refused to subside. The curtains were drawn back so that she could see the stars, wondering if Luc were watching them too, then laughing at herself for being so pathetic. As if he would! No doubt this was just a pleasant little interlude, a means of idling away his remaining time in Britain. After all, one evening together hardly constituted the basis of a relationship, by any standards. The problem was how little she knew of the opposite sex—the very minimum of experience would come in handy at the moment.

At school the staff had guarded their charges' purity with relentless fervour, and here in the village the few young people of her own age tended to treat her with caution because of her stay at boarding school. It would be nice to have a confidant, she thought wistfully, if only to talk things over and ask one or two pertinent questions. Much as she loved Lydia, somehow she was not quite the person to ask about Luc. Emily had a feeling she would disapprove strongly of some of the evening's events. Had her own behaviour been extraordinary, or was it normal to feel that overwhelming excitement? Luc had felt it too, that was patently obvious, but perhaps that was because he was male. Luc's maleness was something better banished from her mind altogether, she concluded, or it was more than probable she'd get no sleep at all.

CHAPTER THREE

ALL Emily's nagging doubts had vanished like magic next morning, and she was ready and waiting when Luc drew up in the Jaguar just after ten. She threw open the door and smiled shyly at the tall, athletic figure as he came swiftly up the garden path, his camel cords and silk shirt, both a shade or two darker than the supple suede of his jacket, making Emily very much aware of the shortcomings of her own chain-store skirt and sweater.

'Good morning.' She gave him her hand. 'I don't know quite what you had in mind for today; will I do as I am?'

Luc bent his dark head and kissed her fingers, then looked at her in surprise as though her question was unnecessary.

'You are quite perfect, Emily,' he said in a matter-of-fact manner that restored her confidence immediately. 'And in a quite different way, so is this room. Your parents had great taste.'

Emily looked around the room, following his gaze, trying to see it with a stranger's eyes.

'They were fond of antiques, and took great pleasure in tracking down various finds. I believe the sofa table is quite valuable, according to Mother, and the two matching velvet chairs are late Regency, but I'm not very knowledgeable on the subject myself. I just love this room because it's home, I suppose.'

She became aware of Luc looking down at her with such an air of amused indulgence she was annoyed.

'Am I boring you?'

'Not at all, little one. But I think you are trying very hard not to let the events of last night embarrass you in the cold light of day, am I right?' Luc put an arm round her waist and lifted her reluctant face to his with the other hand. 'Let me reassure you, Emily. Today we will explore all the beautiful places you can think of, and we shall talk, and learn about each other, find somewhere interesting to eat, and try to forget that very special something that occurs when we kiss. I shall not lay even one finger on you again, unless you say I may.' He stopped, looking down enquiringly into her troubled face. 'What is it?'

Emily released herself deliberately and backed away a little, smiling at him ruefully.

'Well, I thought perhaps you might think that I—well, that it——'

'That last night was a common occurrence for you, *carinha*?' Luc laughed outright. 'Not at all. It was very obvious that it was not.'

'Why?' demanded Emily, inexplicably nettled.

'Because, my innocent, coupled with the warmth of your response was an unmistakable sense of astonishment. You were very surprised, I think—don't be upset, *carinha*, you were no more surprised than I!'

'Why should *I* surprise *you*?' she asked quietly.

'Not you, Emily, it was I that surprised myself.' Luc's teeth gleamed white in his tanned face. 'I don't think that sounds quite right, but you must be lenient with my English. It is not the language that comes easiest to me.'

Suddenly happy, she put on her coat.

'You speak English perfectly—as you well know. That trace of accent is just enough to be fascinating.' She grinned at the look on his face. 'Well, it is; I'm sure it's an enormous asset as far as the opposite sex is concerned.'

Luc opened the door for her.

'But does it affect you that way, Emily?' he murmured into the back of her neck as they went down the path.

'Oh yes,' she said carelessly, 'but I'm working on it. Oh, Luc, isn't it a lovely day?'

'It is a perfect day,' he agreed gravely, settling her into the car seat. 'And it's going to stay that way all day,' he added as he started the car. 'I shall personally ensure that it does.'

He was as good as his word, and took her for a leisurely drive through narrow roads leading to little Cotswold villages

that basked in the light of a mellow autumn sun. They had
lunch in Moreton-in-Marsh and then wandered around the
small town for a while before driving to Broadway and
Chipping Campden and exploring the very different attractions of each. Finally they came back to Stratford for dinner
and Luc booked seats at the Royal Shakespeare Theatre for
'Much Ado About Nothing' on the following night, lucky to
get two cancellations.

'I have never been to the theatre here,' he told her as they
lingered over coffee in the riverside restaurant. 'Have you?'

'Only when I was in school,' said Emily. 'They used to
organise at least one trip a year; more if one was doing A-level
English.'

'You studied English, Emily? What did you wish to do?'

'English and History were my particular thing. I wanted to
teach History, actually, but as you know, fate took a hand
and I had to leave school early.' Her eyes dropped, then she
raised her chin resolutely and smiled at him. 'However, I do
impart quite a lot of historical knowledge about Compton
Lacey to anyone who'll listen, so I could have been a lot less
fortunate.'

He stretched out a hand to take hers.

'*Coitadinha!* Poor little one, you have been left alone very
young.' He frowned at her, his eyes full of concern. 'Is there
no one you can turn to should you need help?'

'Well, I have Lydia close at hand,' Emily smiled
reassuringly. 'And Marcus is in constant touch. You should
meet him, he's a very charming man, though he doesn't enjoy
the best of health.'

'Is he young?'

'In his forties. Why?'

'I wondered if he might have more than a cousinly interest
in your welfare.' Luc's frown deepened.

Emily withdrew her hand swiftly and stood up, leaving Luc
no choice but to do the same.

They left the restaurant and walked back towards the
theatre in silence for a while.

'I have offended you, Emily?' Luc's hand held hers captive,
even though she made an attempt to free it.

'It just seems so tawdry to reduce everything to this

man/woman thing,' said Emily distastefully, leaving her hand where it was rather than wrestle childishly. 'Marcus regards me as merely a distant connection in awkward circumstances who needs a helping hand, nothing more.'

Luc stopped in his tracks, bringing her close against him. The narrow pavement opposite the park was deserted in the limbo when most people were at home in front of the television, or out wining and dining, and before the end of the performance when Stratford would be thronged with the after-theatre crowd. Emily stared up mutely into Luc's scowling face, aware that the contact of their bodies, though they barely touched, was producing the same effect as the night before, and she resented the fact that her physical responses were functioning in total independence from her mind, which was furiously trying to remain aloof.

'I'm jealous of the thought of any man in your life,' Luc said through his teeth, his nostrils flaring as he felt her instant recoil, his hands biting into her upper arms through the sleeves of her coat. Emily swallowed, her breath quickening as she looked up at him in disbelief.

'That's ridiculous,' she said jerkily. 'We've only just met. I don't know you. You don't know me. Besides, I'm not—not exactly Helen of Troy. Hardly the type to bowl a man over at first glance. I'm too ordinary——'

'Be quiet,' he said forcibly, and cut off any further protests by stopping her mouth with his own and taking her wholly into his arms. After only a moment or two he raised his head at the sound of approaching voices, and in silence they began to walk again, his arm close round her waist as they wandered slowly back to where the car was parked.

In a trance Emily got in the Jaguar and watched Luc walk round to seat himself beside her. He leaned over to fasten her seat-belt, kissing her nose as he did so, and started the car without a word. For some reason the tender little caress made Emily wildly happy, and she leaned back in her seat perfectly relaxed while the car ate up the miles on the road to Warwick where they bypassed the lovely old town and took the Birmingham road for Compton Lacey.

It was still comparatively early when they reached the cottage, and Emily was racked by indecision, eventually giving a mental shrug as she turned to Luc when they drew up outside the gate.

'Will you come in for a cup of coffee, Luc?'

He gave her a surprised look.

'Is that wise, Emily? Apart from your fear of my intentions, would you not mind that my car is at your gate for all to see?'

'It's only half-past nine—hardly the middle of the night,' she pointed out. 'I should think my good name could stand it if you stay an hour. And, of course, you did promise not to lay a finger on me without my permission!'

'Then I accept with pleasure, before you change your mind.'

Once indoors Emily lit the small gas fire in the living room and retired to the kitchen to make the promised coffee. Luc lounged in the doorway, watching her graceful, economical movements with pleasure while she chattered away to him happily.

'It's only instant, Luc—can't afford the real stuff, I'm afraid,' she apologised as she set a small tray.

'Now that is a commodity we can offer in abundance in my country,' he laughed. 'You must come and see my home and taste our coffee, feel the warmth of the sun.'

Emily giggled as he took the tray from her and placed it on the beautiful old sofa table.

'Now that really is an unlikely proposition—unless I win the pools.'

He looked blank.

'What are these "pools"?'

They sat close together while Emily explained the complications of filling in football coupons and the rewards it was possible to reap. The coffee in their cups grew cold while she talked, her small face animated until she realised that her companion was silent, watching her changing expressions with unwavering eyes.

'I'm boring you,' she broke off abruptly, shifting a little further away from him.

'On the contrary, Emily, I am fascinated by every word you say, even more by the way the expressions on your face change by the second, like the kaleidoscope my grandmother has at home.' Luc's smile faded as their eyes met and held, but he remained where he was, tense and still. 'Do you not consider me admirable, little one? I am keeping my promise, and a very difficult one it is to fulfil.'

Emily made no pretence of misunderstanding him.

'I had noticed,' she said, turning away, 'and as I've no intention of giving the requisite permission perhaps I'd better bid you a fond farewell and see you off the premises.'

Luc rose to his feet instantly, his manner a shade formal as he raised her hand to his lips.

'I will be waiting at the Manor House at five-thirty tomorrow, Emily, to take you to the theatre; will that be convenient?' He kept her hand in his. 'I will bring you back here to change, if you wish, of course.'

'That's not necessary, Luc—I'll wear something suitable to the house.' Emily smiled up at him gaily. 'I warn you, none of my clothes really suit your sort of life.'

He smiled down indulgently into her face.

'You know nothing of my normal life, *carinha*. I spend the greater part of it in dusty drill trousers and shirts, heavy boots. Not in the least elegant, I assure you.'

Emily studied him deliberately, head on one side.

'I think it's very possible that you look elegant whatever you wear, Senhor Fonseca.'

He drew in his breath and reached for her instinctively, but checked himself sharply and made for the door.

'That's not what you English call "cricket", *carinha*. If I am to keep to the rules, so must you.'

'Spoilsport,' said Emily impenitently, and waved him goodbye vigorously as he strode rapidly down the path. After he had gone she closed the door behind her dreamily, then suddenly seized one of the sofa cushions and did a mad polka with it all round the room before sedately washing up the coffee cups in a less zany frame of mind.

For the next few days Luc waited for her to emerge from Compton Lacey each evening and took her to the theatre in Stratford, the cinema in Leamington Spa, to a French restaurant in Kenilworth. Emily felt like Cinderella before the fateful stroke of midnight, and did her best to treasure each moment they spent together without thinking that shortly he would be gone and her life would revert to its former uneventful routine.

How am I going to bear it? shrieked a strident mental voice. She closed her mind to it frantically and spent some of her special hoard of savings on a new outfit she saw marked down in a very select dress-shop in Warwick. Lydia had given her an early lift into the town on her rounds and Emily was really supposed to be buying groceries, but instead of concentrating on baked beans and breakfast cereal she was irresistibly drawn to the elegant window where the creation lay cleverly draped against a wicker screen. Basically little more than a skirt and sweater, really, she told herself, but her hand was pushing open the door even as she thought. The charming lady who owned the shop looked at the size while Emily held her breath, and, sure enough, it was a size ten. A very small fitting, she was warned, which was why it was reduced, but when she had hastily scrambled out of her jeans and sweater to try the suit on it had quite obviously been made with Emily in mind, a Mary Farrin model spun from yarn fine as a cobweb in a mulberry shade that threw up Emily's fairness and brought a glow to her cheeks. The skirt had been knitted to give the impression of countless tiny pleats which swirled at the hem, and the top was short-sleeved with a deeply slashed neck opening.

'Should it have a button or something?' Emily eyed the faint hint of cleavage visible with doubt, but was assured that it was meant to look just like that.

Without further persuasion she consigned caution to the winds, paid for the suit, then rushed round the shops at top speed buying food in record time in order to catch the bus back home early enough to start a casserole. Tonight she intended to entertain Luc at home in some small return for the past few evenings. Taking her courage in both hands, she rang the White Hart from the callbox in the village, and asked for Mr Fonseca, praying he would be there. He was, his voice tense when he answered.

'Emily? What is it? Is something wrong—are you ill?'

'No, no, Luc, nothing like that. I just wanted to make a suggestion,' she explained apologetically, touched to hear his audible sigh of relief.

'Of course, *carinha*—or do you mean I may not see you tonight?'

'No—or rather yes,' said Emily wickedly, making a face at herself in the small mirror above the telephone.

'Emily, please make yourself clear!' Luc's voice was satisfactorily anxious, and she hurried to explain.

'You've been entertaining me royally all week, so I thought it would only be proper if I cooked dinner for you here tonight.'

There was a lengthy pause.

'Do you think that wise?' he said at last.

'Probably not. My repertoire consists of only three recognisable dishes, so you're probably taking a great risk,' she said flippantly. 'I'll expect you at eight, Luc.'

She rang off before he could protest any further, and ran home to start the recipe she liked best, humming happily as she browned succulent cubes of beef in a heavy pan, seasoning them with a teaspoon each of curry, ginger, sugar and salt, adding sliced onions, Worcestershire sauce and stock and transferring the lot into a cast-iron casserole to simmer in the oven while she tidied up and gave some of the lovely old pieces of furniture a loving polish. The garden yielded some branches of bright beech leaves to arrange in a copper pot with the last few rust-red chrysanthemums. When these were placed with care on the sofa table Emily ran an eye round the room, sniffing the fragrance of lavender-scented polish mingled with the tantalising aroma from the kitchen, and, satisfied, decided it was time to turn off the oven and cycle to the Manor House for her afternoon stint.

It was a fairly quiet afternoon, and she was jubilant to get home by five-thirty to switch on her casserole to finish cooking while she washed her hair. As she blew the long pale strands dry the thought of drinks suddenly struck her. She opened the sideboard without much hope to see one bottle of sherry, of excellent brand, but half empty, and the remains of another of brandy, kept for emergencies by her mother. Emily shrugged. Luc would just have to slum it for one evening, she decided, and turned her attentions to her casserole. The meat was fork-tender by this time. Adding a generous dollop of creamed horseradish and a carton of sour cream, she left the pot to sit on top of the stove to blend its flavours together while she dressed.

She was quite pleased with herself when she was ready. The new outfit clung and swirled simultaneously, giving her a look more sophisticated than usual, added to by her hair, which she left down, on Luc's instructions, but caught at the nape of her neck with a tortoiseshell comb. Her one expensive pair of black slender-heeled shoes had to do, though she yearned for something strappy and frivolous. Making a face at herself in the mirror, Emily ran downstairs to envelop herself in a large apron while she prepared the rice, mushrooms, corn and green beans to accompany the main course.

Fifteen minutes before Luc was due to arrive everything was ready, and Emily stood in the kitchen checking on her fingers that all the tasks she had set herself were done. There was no table to lay, regretfully, as the dining room had been in the other half of the cottage and was now Lydia's sitting room. They would have to eat from trays on their knees in front of the fire, which Emily had lit earlier, and was now flickering invitingly round the two huge logs arranged carefully in the cowled stone fireplace. No way could she fit someone of Luc's dimensions at the table in the minuscule kitchen. Besides, it would be a change for him, decided Emily—picnicking off trays would hardly be routine in his life-style at home. Wondering what Brazilian food was like, she checked the contents of the various pots and pans, then halted at the sound of the old iron knocker on the front door. Luc was five minutes early.

Emily opened the door to find him standing there with his arms full of bottles, a smile of warm admiration on his face as he examined her from head to foot.

'How very elegant you look, Emily—or should I say Miss Harper? May I please put these down somewhere, *carinha*, or I shall lose the lot.'

Emily swiftly relieved him of two of the bottles, scolding.

'It isn't a party, Luc—you shouldn't have brought so much; but thank you anyway. I'm afraid I was too engrossed in providing the food to give a thought to the drinks.'

As Luc came into the firelit room Emily looked at him with undisguised pleasure. Instead of the more formal clothes he had worn previously he was dressed in tight-fitting black cord jeans, a shirt in fine cream wool and a black suede waistcoat.

'You look elegant too, Luc,' she said, smiling happily at him.

'But not nearly enough to match that very charming dress, Emily.' Luc raised her hand fleetingly to his lips. 'I thought something casual would be appropriate for an evening at home—but I see I was wrong, you look like a princess.'

'It's new,' said Emily candidly. 'I saw it in a shop in Warwick this morning when I was supposed to be buying food, and I couldn't resist it. So I was extravagant. I'm a bit fed up with my usual things.'

'To me you are enchanting whatever you wear—but you know that.' He was purposely brisk as he turned to the array of bottles. 'I had no idea what you were cooking, so I brought one red, one white, one rosé, a bottle of dry sherry and one of champagne.'

Emily looked at him ruefully.

'You do realise that we shall be eating from trays, Luc Fonseca? Our erstwhile dining room is next door with Lydia, and somehow I just couldn't picture you in my little kitchen!'

'Just to be with you, Emily, is of infinitely more importance than what I eat, or where I eat it!'

There was silence after his words, broken only by the crackling and spitting of the logs in the fireplace.

'We're having beef in horseradish sauce,' said Emily finally, her eyes held fast by his.

'Then perhaps we should drink the red wine,' he answered softly, moving closer.

She turned abruptly, blinking, and opened the sideboard to take out two crystal goblets.

'Will these do?'

'Perfectly. Perhaps you can find two sherry glasses also and we'll have an aperitif.' He was deliberately casual as he helped her to her feet. 'I like my sherry dry, but perhaps you do not?'

Emily shook her head vigorously.

'I warn you now,' she said gaily, 'I have absolutely no palate, so I'll have some of my own bottle in the sideboard. I shall drink it while I put the vegetables on.'

Luc stationed himself in the kitchen doorway while Emily put the finishing touches to the meal, watching her as she tasted and seasoned, his eyes indulgent as she carefully

brought the casserole to the correct heat without curdling its
creamy contents.

'No first course,' she said cheerfully over her shoulder, 'and
no serving dishes. I'm just putting everything on your plate,
so if there's something you don't like just leave it.'

'*Carinha*, from the heavenly smell coming from that pot
that will be highly unlikely,' he assured her. 'Besides, I'm
starving. I didn't have any lunch.'

'Neither did I.'

Without further ado Emily drained the vegetables and filled
two plates generously. Settled on the comfortable rubbed
leather sofa in front of the fire, they both fell on the food
avidly, Luc flatteringly extravagant in his praise. In a
gratifyingly short time he had cleared his plate, insisting that
he help himself to more, his mouth inelegantly full.

'Did you learn to cook at school, Emily?'

'Yes, but not things like this, really—more in the Sole
Véronique and Chicken Florentine style. Sort of upmarket,
but not what my mother considered suitable for a hungry
man. This dish was my father's favourite. I enjoy cooking, but
my usual cuisine alone is more in the mince and bacon and
egg area, and lots of salads. I'm not terribly good at puddings
either, I'm afraid, but I've noticed you don't eat sweet things.'

'I am touched that you remembered.' He smiled at her
tenderly. 'You are quite right. Creamy concoctions are not at
all to my taste. But you are, little *cozinheira*.'

'What's that?' Emily's colour was high as she took his empty
plate with hers and whisked them off to the kitchen. 'No, stay
where you are—I'll just put the coffee to perk while we have
our next course.'

Luc leaned back against the velvet sofa cushions, watching
her indolently as she came back with a cheeseboard and a
bowl of crisp apples.

'*Cozinheira* merely means "cook", suspicious one.' He
grinned at her and looked appreciatively at the fine piece of
Stilton she offered him. 'Now *that* really is to my taste,
Emily. No biscuits, thank you, just one of those tempting
apples and a large slice of that noble cheese.
Gostoso—delicious, to you.'

Emily found she was drinking a third glass of wine as they

finished their cheese, and felt rather alarmingly weightless as she got up to collect the coffee tray.

'I've had much more to drink than I should have,' she said solemnly as she poured two cups of black coffee with infinite care. 'It's a bit risky serving coffee at all to a Brazilian, I suppose, but if you don't like it you'll just have to lump it.' She grinned at him cheekily over the rim of her cup.

'What is this "lump it"?' Luc frowned ferociously.

'Never mind.' Emily patted his arm condescendingly. 'I forget you're a poor misguided foreigner!'

Without warning he took her cup from her and put it down on the tray with a bump that threatened the delicate china's safety, then pulled her roughly into his arms, looking down into her startled face with an evil smile lifting the corners of his mouth.

'Misguided foreigner, am I?' He was almost too quiet for her to hear. 'Tell me you're sorry.'

'I'm sorry,' said Emily instantly.

'How sorry?'

'Very sorry, Luc.'

'Show me,' he demanded.

'How?'

He closed his eyes, his voice unsteady as he held her close.

'You know how, *carinha*. Put me out of my misery.'

Emily's mouth reached his before he finished speaking and there was silence in the small room as their lips came together, clung, opened, welcomed, and communed with each other in a frenzy of delight that was at once an immense relief and a sweet torture. Luc pulled her across his lap and sank back with her against the velvet cushions, never taking his mouth from hers as Emily gave herself up joyfully to the insidious warmth that lapped them both, enclosing them in a cocoon of pleasurable sensation. Sensation soon became much, much more than pleasurable, as his hands slid slowly into her hair, removing the comb and playing with the long shiny strands, winding them round his wrist to bind her to him, as the other hand smoothed rhythmically over her back and shoulders, lulling her hypnotically into something approaching a trance. When Luc lifted his mouth from hers she sighed, turning her face blindly into his neck as he released her hair and slid his hands over the gossamer fabric covering her small, pointed breasts. The convulsive shiver that ran through her at his touch was purely sensuous, no thought of rejecting his hands entering her head. With a gasp Emily sought his mouth urgently with her own, the ardour of her untutored response driving him wild. He crushed her to him, burying her head against his chest murmuring incoherently into the tangle of her hair.

'*Querida*, forgive me—I promised, but it is almost impossible—I should not have come—*Deus*, Emily. . . .'

Luc trailed into silence as she pushed herself away from him and stared up into his eyes, her face transformed from its usual delicate aqua-tinted charm. Colour flared along her cheekbones and her eyes burned with a brilliant, lambent blue, their expression blank and unfocussed as she pushed her hair from her face with a careless hand. Something in her unwavering stare was causing Luc's breath to come faster, his nostrils to flare, and as the signs of his disturbance became increasingly more evident, her mouth curved in a smile as old as Eve. Whatever shreds of self-control Luc had left deserted him suddenly and completely. Teeth clenched, hands trembling, he threw the velvet cushions on the floor and drew the silent, unresisting girl to lie full length before the dying flames of the fire. Taking her face between his hands, he began to kiss her again, his whole body trembling in an intense effort to be gentle as he laid his lips on her eyes, her cheeks, her throat, returning to her parted lips again and again as though he would never be satiated by their sweetness. Emily curled her body against his, instinctively arching against him to get closer and closer, to soothe this new burning ache that was consuming her, possessing her, so that nothing in the world mattered but the assuagement of her longing. She pushed her hands inside his shirt, wanting the touch of his skin, putting her open mouth against his chest, kissing all of him she could reach, while his hands grew frantic, removing her clothes, then his own, with an awkward haste she barely registered until their bodies came together, skin against skin, the dim light of the fire the only illumination as it washed over the dark copper of Luc's body against the fair, pale fragility of hers. There was no one to

hear as Luc's English deserted him and a torrent of
Portuguese poured into Emily's ear as, caution engulfed in
raw need, he initiated her into the first painful pleasure of
love. The faint, hoarse cry of pain she gave was lost against
his mouth, and her struggles stilled by the sheer superiority of
his body as it subdued hers, then all was utter silence as he
lay, still holding her tight, his face pressed against hers in an
agony of immediate remorse.

After a long, long time Luc felt a shudder run through
Emily's body and he raised his head. Her eyes refused to meet
his and she kept her lids lowered. He swallowed.

'You are disgusted with me, Emily?' Bleakly he turned her
unwilling face up to his. 'You shuddered. Am I abhorrent to
you, *carinha? Deus*—say something!'

Emily surprised him with a little sidelong smile.

'It's only that I'm shy, I think, Luc—and a bit cold. Not
very romantic, I know, but I'm not used to lying about
without any clothes on.'

With a sound suspiciously like a sob he got to his feet,
jerking her up with him.

'Forgive me, little one—shall I dress you first, or put more
logs on?'

Emily began to laugh.

'I think it's best if I put my own clothes on, if you'll just
turn your back—oh, and if you'd just let me go for a
moment.'

He relaxed a little.

'Then you are not angry?'

'No.' Her eyes slid away from the urgency in his. 'How
could I be? It was every bit as much my fault as yours—more.
You did try to fight against the inevitable, after all. I just let it
knock me flat without a struggle.'

His dark face still troubled he turned away and pulled on
his jeans, then made up the fire, his eyes averted as Emily
tried unsuccessfully to locate various items of clothing.

Luc stood staring down into the fireplace, resolutely
keeping his eyes on the flames beginning to curl round the
fresh logs.

'You are very slow,' he said gruffly at last, then turned at
the sound of a smothered giggle, to see Emily standing

barefoot in a brief half-slip, clutching the top half of her new suit to her chest.

'For pity's sake, cover yourself, Emily!' A reluctant grin spread over his face.

'Well, I would,' she said apologetically, 'but you seem to have disposed of my clothes with such energy that I can't find some fairly vital items. They're all over the place.'

Luc laughed outright and joined in the hunt, discovering her bra tangled in the folds of his shirt, handing the beribboned trifle to her in apology.

'I have behaved in a very barbarous fashion, Emily—you have every right to throw me out here and now.'

She had her back to him and was struggling in vain to do up the clasp of the offending item of underwear.

'Not before you do this thing up for me,' she panted in frustration.

Luc bent his attention to the small task, frowning as he discovered the problem.

'To add to my sins, Emily, I'm afraid the—the hook?—has come off. I must have torn it in my—my——'

'Enthusiasm?' suggested Emily, abandoning any efforts at modesty and turning to face him, her sweater still bunched in front of her, an irresistible smile lighting her whole face. Luc's teeth gleamed in an answering smile, a light growing in his eyes that resembled the flames beginning to flicker in the fireplace.

'I love you, Emily,' he said simply, and held out his hand.

Without hesitation, ignoring her dishevelled state, she walked into the circle of his arms and he stood holding her quietly, his chin on top of her head, one arm close round her waist while the other hand stroked her hair.

'I hurt you, *carinha*?' he whispered.

She nodded her head vigorously.

'It will not hurt like that the next time.'

Emily trembled at the note in his husky voice, her vibration communicating itself to Luc and his grasp grew tighter, her arms going round his waist in response as he held her fast against him, her face against his bare chest, his buried in her hair.

'Is this the next time?' she said, her voice muffled.

He took a deep breath.

'Only if you want, *querida*,' he said unsteadily.

'Oh yes, I want!'

All thoughts of modesty were cast to the winds as this time it was Emily who threw her remaining garments to fall carelessly where they would in her haste to be close to Luc, glorying in the touch of his mouth and hands that were leisured and lingering in their quest to give her all the pleasure that his previous frantic haste had not allowed. She twisted and turned beneath his caresses, responding to him with all the untapped warmth of her nature, returning kiss for kiss, learning to caress and touch him so that some of his unhurrying care was abandoned and his mouth and fingers became urgent as their bodies surrendered to the force that overwhelmed them both.

Some time after, when their breathing had finally slowed to something approximating normal, Luc said roughly,

'Do you love me, Emily?'

'I think I must,' she said honestly. 'I can't imagine doing what we did unless I loved you.'

'Oh, Emily!' He cradled her to him protectively. 'One does not need to love to want to *make* love.'

'You may not. I do.'

He shook her hard.

'You know that was not my meaning. My English is not colloquial enough. But you must believe I love you, Emily. From the moment I saw you——'

'That was only five days ago,' she said practically.

'Five days—minutes—years—what does it matter? Will you marry me and come to live in Campo d'Ouro with me?' Luc's face was deadly serious, his dark eyes glowing and anxious as he took her face in his hands. 'Are you willing to leave your life here and come to live in Brazil?'

Emily gazed back unflinchingly.

'Yes, I am. But for the moment I think I should put my dressing gown on and you should get dressed too. I feel extraordinarily vulnerable like this.'

Luc drifted his mouth down over her eyes and nose, lingered a moment on her mouth, then deliberately dropped a kiss on each small breast before lifting her to her feet.

'I prefer you like this,' he said, eyes glinting, 'but I would not wish you to catch cold.'

Emily grinned back, then a sudden wave of colour washed over her face and she shut her eyes.

'What is it?' he said, alarmed.

'It just swept over me,' she said faintly, 'that my behaviour tonight was not precisely what I was taught as fitting at the school I went to.'

'What behaviour?'

'Well, standing here like this and doing—well, doing what we just did.' Emily kept her eyes closed tightly, to Luc's amusement. 'And—well, I've never seen a man without any clothes on before.'

Luc threw back his head and roared with laughter, a joyous sound that instantly drove away the embarrassment that had suddenly overtaken Emily. He turned her round, gave her a gentle slap on her bottom and proceeded to make himself decent again while she rounded up her scattered garments and went upstairs for her robe. Then they went into the kitchen and washed up the dinner things together and made coffee again, eventually settling themselves in front of the fire to drink it and make plans.

'I must fly back on Sunday,' he told her, holding her close in the crook of his arm. 'Then I shall tell my father and grandmother and make some necessary arrangements. I shall return here for you in about a month, *carinha*. Will that be suitable for you?'

Emily gazed into the fire with bemused eyes.

'I can hardly take it in, Luc,' she said hesitantly. 'Won't your family think that this is all a bit sudden?'

'All I am concerned with, Emily, is whether *you* think I am in too much of a hurry. If I lived in this country I would take more time to court you properly, let you become accustomed to the idea more slowly; but as things are I must—what is the phrase—sweep you off your feet.' His voice dropped a little, roughened with sincerity. 'I cannot chance losing you, *querida*.'

Emily twisted in his hold, throwing her arms round his neck and pressing her face hard against his.

'No chance of that,' she said unsteadily. 'I'll be ready and waiting when you come back. And anyway, this is not goodbye tonight, Luc, we've another day tomorrow.'

Emily was wrong. She woke to knocking on the front door early next morning. Pushing her tousled hair out of her eyes she threw on her dressing gown and ran barefoot down the stairs to find a white-faced Luc on the doorstep, formal in dark suit and tie.

'Darling, what is it?'

Emily drew him hastily into the living room, her arms going round him as he took her into a bonecracking embrace.

'It's my father,' he said, swallowing hard. 'I received a cable an hour ago. He has suffered a major heart attack—I must go at once. I was able to get a cancellation on a plane today.'

Emily looked at him with aching compassion, longing to give him comfort yet at a loss to know how.

'Let me make you coffee——'

'No, *carinha*,' he interrupted, refusing to let her move. 'I must go now. I'm driving down to London where I will take back the car, and there are several things I must see to while I'm there before I catch the plane. I do not have much time. Now. I must be practical.' He released her for a moment and took a leather-covered diary from his breast pocket. 'You said Mrs Crawford has a telephone. She will not mind if I ring you at her home?'

'No, of course not.' Emily manfully battled with the lump in her throat and give him the number, which he noted alongside her address.

'I will ring as soon as I have seen my father, Emily,' he said, taking her by the shoulders and looking deep into her eyes. 'I will write also, and when—when my father recovers I shall return for you. Until then, remember that I love you, I love you, Emily.'

Tears began to trickle down Emily's face, and he pulled her roughly against him, murmuring comfort in a mixture of Portuguese and English, none of which registered. The stark fact of Luc's departure dominated her completely for a moment until her natural common sense began to return. Emily drew away from him a little, her eyes on a pulse that was beating violently in Luc's throat. She gave an inelegant sniff and smiled damply up into his strained face.

'I hope you won't carry a picture of me in your mind the way I look at the moment,' she said, striving to lighten his despondency. 'My dressing gown is a relic of schooldays.'

Luc bent his head and kissed her quivering mouth hard, his hands bruising her shoulders.

'I shall hope to see you many times like this,' he said huskily, 'with your hair untidy and your body warm from bed—our bed, *carinha*. Soon I hope there will be no more painful goodbyes.' He broke off, looking at his watch. '*Deus*. Emily, I must go. *Até logo, carinha*.'

'Goodbye, Luc.' Emily's hand clung to his as she saw him through the door. 'I hope very much you find your father recovered when you arrive home. And please drive carefully down to London.'

They stood for a long moment, hands clasped, while Emily fought to keep back the tears and they looked at each other in anguish. Then Luc bent and kissed her swiftly, literally tearing himself away, striding down the path to the gate, his head bent. He turned once before he got in the car, and Emily smiled valiantly in response to his wave, then he was gone.

The next couple of days went past like years. Emily did her stint at the Manor House, glad of something to pass the time, spending the rest of the day listening for Lydia's knock to summon her to the phone. By the end of the fourth day after Luc's departure Emily was hollow-eyed from lack of sleep, and beginning to lose weight from lack of appetite. She attacked the garden, reducing it to neatness for the winter with a violence that helped a little to relieve the pent-up state of anticipation mixed with bitter disappointment that was her waking state of mind. Lydia was very concerned, but Emily refused all offers to spend time with her next door, as she couldn't bear to be in the house where the phone rang frequently, but the caller was never Luc.

Frantic with anxiety, she rang the airline to see if the plane Luc took arrived safely in Rio, and after a momentary feeling of relief on learning it had, she was beset by a new anguish as to the cause of his silence. Every morning she ran downstairs to see what the postman had brought, but no airmail envelope ever dropped through the letter-box. In the haste of his departure Luc had forgotten to give her his address. Besides, she thought proudly, no way am I going to write to ask why he hasn't contacted me. And, to be fair, heaven knew what sort of situation had waited for him on his return. His poor father could have been worse, or even have died. His grandmother would need looking after. Luc himself would be worried out of his mind, utterly grief-stricken, if the worst had happened. On and on went the list of possibilities in Emily's mind, giving her no respite from the endless speculation as to the reasons for Luc's silence.

Of course, thought Emily, after two agonising weeks had dragged by, it is very possible that he is a consummate actor, and our pitifully brief time together was merely a pleasant way of whiling away his holiday. All that line about coming back to marry me was probably a bit of sugar to sweeten the fact that he had relieved me of my much-vaunted virginity. No doubt a commonplace occurrence to him, but he was considerate enough to try and infuse a little respectability into the incident by conning her as to his intentions. Emily laughed silently, her face mirthless. 'Intentions' was rather an outdated word, used in that context. It was more than possible that Luc Fonseca had intended nothing more than a diverting little interlude, and the marriage bit had been a sop to her sensibilities.

'Look, Emily, I think it's about time you had a square meal,' said Lydia severely one morning, as she saw her yanking up weeds viciously in the front garden.

'I'm all right, honestly,' said Emily, smiling brightly as she sat back on her heels.

'Well, you don't look it, to be frank. Come in and have some lunch.' Lydia helped Emily to her feet with a peremptory hand. 'No excuses, now. It's Monday, so you don't have to dash up to the Manor House, and you'll just have to try to ignore that blasted phone.'

Emily gave in and allowed herself to be fussed over and cosseted, plied with shepherd's pie and trifle and all the latest news from the neighbourhood. She ate obediently, though less than her hostess wished, and sat docilely by the fire with a cup of tea afterwards, somnolent with warmth and food. Lydia noted her pale face and shadowed eyes with a professional eye.

'Not sleeping too well, Em?'

'No, not too well at all, to be honest.' Emily sighed, staring into the cheerful crackling fire. 'Silly, really—sort of arrested development, I suppose. I should have been nursing a broken heart a lot earlier than this, judging by the girls at school.'

'Very understandable, love,' said Lydia. 'If this is your very first stab at romance you did rather choose a high-powered subject to cut your teeth on.'

Emily frowned, nibbling her bottom lip.

'I didn't choose, Lydia. Luc just happened. And after all this time without hearing from him I imagine I can just write him off to experience.'

'It's only just over a fortnight, love.'

'It may be a fortnight to you, Lydia. To me it's been a little private eternity.' Emily heaved herself up out of her chair. 'I'll wash up so you can get back to work.'

'Thanks, love.' Lydia put on her blue overcoat and the matching uniform cap, looking at Emily with troubled eyes. 'It *will* pass, Em. All hurts heal in time. I thought I'd never get over Tom's death, but I did. You've had a rough time, losing your mother and trying to sort your life out for yourself. I could ring Mr Fonseca's neck for him!'

Emily smiled wearily.

'That makes two of us. I've just about reached the stage where I'm angry instead of—well, desolate is the word that springs to mind.'

'That's the spirit,' said Lydia approvingly. 'Try to put him out of your mind.'

'That's going to be difficult.' Emily sighed, then grinned. 'Not impossible, of course. I shan't allow a few short days in my life to ruin the rest of it. One thing I'm resigned to, though.'

Lydia turned, her hand on the latch.

'What's that, love?'

'I know I'm not going to hear from him now, somehow. This morning as I was fighting with the weeds a feeling of certainty took over, so I'll stop looking for the postman, and I'll make friends with your phone again.'

When Lydia had gone Emily turned to the lunch dishes

with a sigh. Her last assurance to her friend had been sheer invention to reassure Lydia. And now, by some means, she would have to make it come true, banish Luc from her mind and forget the fateful few days that had been such a colourful interlude in her humdrum existence. And perhaps Colonel Hammond would be kind enough to let her avoid Lady Henrietta's bedroom in future. It had no record of being haunted, but for Emily it had acquired a very personal ghost, tall and dark, with a glinting smile she found impossible to erase from her mind.

CHAPTER FOUR

ON a cold, blustery March day, some eighteen months later, Emily closed the door of the Dower House on the last sorrowful, sympathetic face and leaned against the heavy oak panels for a moment, limp and drained. For the count of ten she stayed where she was, eyes tightly shut, then pushed herself upright, irritated by the melodrama of her pose. As she crossed the polished wood floor of the hall her face brightened at the faint sounds of exuberant bathtime coming from upstairs, and she hurried to join in. She was barely past the newel post when the doorbell rang yet again. Emily slumped against the banister rail in despair. Surely there was no one else to come? It was past six o'clock on this endless, harrowing day, and human nature could only stand so much.

Sighing, she retraced her steps, automatically smoothing a stray strand of hair back into its smooth chignon, schooling her pale face into a polite, social expression. She switched on the porch light and shot back the great iron bolt, opening the door for what seemed like the hundredth time that day. The light from the ancient, wrought-iron porch lamp fell on the dark, sombre face of the tall man who stood, silent, waiting for her to speak. The polite smile on Emily's face died, the last vestige of colour in her face dying with it. Her visitor's face was instantly familiar, and she stared up at him in incredulous

hostility. She struggled to take a deep breath and failed. Her
hands fluttered in a feeble effort at warding him off, then she
gave an odd, stifled little moan and crumpled abruptly into
the outstretched arms of the man who sprang forward to
catch her.

Luc Fonseca shouldered the door closed behind him and
stood looking down at the fine-drawn face that lay so still and
white against the dark cloth of his coat. His lips tightened as
he estimated the weight of the small limp body in his arms, his
head jerking up as he heard a horrified exclamation from the
stairs. Lydia Crawford came running down into the hall, her
kind face worried.

'Mr Fonseca! What happened? Poor child—I suppose it
was the shock of seeing you. Bring her in here.'

She directed him through an open doorway into the rather
shabby elegance of the drawing-room, motioning him to lay
the still girl on one of the faded brocade sofas flanking the
marble fireplace, where a log fire gave out light and warmth
into the high-ceilinged room.

'Why is she taking so long to come round?' Luc's voice was
harsh with anxiety, the social niceties ignored. 'What has
happened to her, Mrs Crawford? *Deus*, she looks so thin and
exhausted!'

Lydia poured some brandy from the tray on the low table
between the two sofas, handing the crystal tumbler to him.

'Try to get that down her if you can,' she said, then looked
over her shoulder, forehead furrowed. 'Look, can you cope on
your own for a moment—there's something I must see to
upstairs.'

'Of course.'

Luc put down the glass while he shrugged himself out of his
coat, oblivious to Lydia's departure, all his attention for the
alarmingly quiet figure which lay as though lifeless. With
infinite care he slid his arm behind Emily's shoulders and
gently began to stroke her cold white cheek with his other
hand, holding her close and talking quietly in a soothing
monotone.

'Wake up, *carinha*. Open your eyes. I know you are not
pleased to see me, but wake up so that I may talk to you,
explain . . .'

To his relief Emily gave a faint sigh and stirred a little. Luc held the brandy to her lips and trickled a little of the spirit into her mouth. She swallowed, gagged, opened her eyes and stared blankly into the face bent over her. Her lids shut instantly and she turned away from him in repudiation.

'No, Emily,' Luc said urgently, refusing to loosen his grasp. 'You must drink just a little more of this. You will feel better.'

He tilted the glass against her lips and automatically Emily swallowed some of the brandy before pushing the glass away and struggling to sit upright.

'You may take your arm away,' she said, her voice barely above a whisper, but its icy distaste unmistakeable. Silently the man obeyed and rose to his feet, standing over her with sombre eyes fixed on Emily's face, where the leaping flames reflected a slight, borrowed warmth. She refused to look up.

'I don't know why you're here,' she went on, with complete composure, 'or how you knew I would be here at the Dower House. Nor am I interested. So perhaps you would leave. At no time would you be welcome, but today is inopportune in the extreme. Please go.'

Her head fell wearily back against the sofa, as though the effort of her frigid, stilted speech had drained her of her last resources.

Luc Fonseca looked about him for the first time, noting trays with half-empty plates of canapés and sandwiches, the remains of an enormous fruit cake and a number of sherry glasses still bearing traces of their recently consumed contents. He looked down into Emily's withdrawn face.

'You were entertaining?' He frowned. 'I had not thought—I mean, it is so soon after your husband's——'

'Death, you mean.' For the first time Emily looked directly at him, her blue eyes glacial as she swung her feet gingerly to the floor and sat upright with care. 'I know nothing of customs in your country, but in Britain it's normal courtesy to offer refreshment to those people civil enough to come to a funeral on a cold March day. This afternoon my husband was laid to rest with his ancestors in the family vault.'

Luc stared down at her in disbelief.

'But I was informed of his death a week ago. I assumed all

would be over by now. In Brazil burial takes place in twenty-four hours.'

Emily rose to her feet, looking at him with suspicion.

'How did you know about Marcus's death?'

'I read the notice in the paper.'

'You said you were informed.'

'A slip of the tongue, no more.'

'Even so, how did you know he was my husband? My name wasn't mentioned.' Her breathing became agitated and Luc pushed her gently back down on the sofa, where she sank unresisting against the cushions, her eyes cold and questioning as they tried to pierce the armoured expression in his.

'For the time being just let us say I knew. I have always known. But now is not the time for explanations which can only add to your distress.' Luc dropped to one knee in front of Emily and took one of her flaccid hands in his. 'Please believe me, Emily. I would not have come today if I had realised it was such an unsuitable time to choose. I will go away now, with the hope that you will allow me to return tomorrow.'

Emily shook her head immediately, but her protest was halted as Lydia came back into the room, and she brushed Luc aside, getting to her feet anxiously.

'Is—is everything all right, Lydia?' Her eyes communicated silently with the other woman and Lydia smiled cheerfully.

'All settled in happily for the night,' she said reassuringly, then cast a professional eye over Emily. 'You don't look too marvellous, though, young lady.'

'I fear the blame is mine. I gave her a shock,' said Luc grimly.

Emily ignored him.

'Are you in the neighbourhood for long, Mr Fonseca?' asked Lydia hurriedly.

'My plans are uncertain. I shall stay at the White Hart for a short time.' He turned and bowed formally to Emily. 'Allow me to offer my condolences. Perhaps you will spare me a few minutes tomorrow afternoon? I hesitate to intrude at such a time, but my time in England is limited.'

'No!' Emily bit back the violence of her protest. 'I mean,

would you make it tomorrow evening, if you really feel your visit is necessary.'

'I do,' he said formally, picking up his coat.

'Seven-thirty, then,' said Emily, unsmiling.

There was silence for a moment as the two looked at each other like antagonists, the pale slender girl in the stark black dress and the tall, grim-faced man in the dark, formal suit, his shirt-collar startlingly white against the dark tan of his skin.

'Thank you, Mrs Lacey,' he said gravely. '*Até amanha*. Goodnight, Mrs Crawford.'

'I'll see you to the door,' said Lydia swiftly, and ushered him into the hall while Emily sat down again abruptly, her legs unable to support her any longer. Head in hands, she tried to assimilate this additional shock. For eighteen months she had heard nothing at all of Lucas Fonseca; vanished from her life as though dead, or departed for another planet. As well he might have done for all she had known. She had regarded him as dead. Almost she had accustomed herself to the idea. To see him standing there this evening, like a spectre from the past, had been an affront, an outrage. Dead he was out of her life, alive he was a challenge, a threat. I refuse to allow it, she thought fiercely. My life is mapped out. Marcus helped me make a future. I will *not* let Luc come back and ruin everything a second time.

She looked up earily as Lydia returned.

'I must go up to Jamie.' She rose unsteadily to her feet.

'No need,' said Lydia firmly. 'Sit down and put your feet up, he's fast asleep. I gave him his supper early and he went off quickly. He's a good little lad.'

Emily's face softened, and she sank back thankfully on the sofa, motioning Lydia to sit down. They both sat staring into the flames in silence for a while before Lydia sighed and looked across at Emily, her kind face troubled.

'It's no good, Em. There's no point in trying to ignore the fact that Luc appeared tonight.'

'No. How right you are.' Emily's mouth curled. 'Right little melodrama, one way and another, wasn't it? Stupid, passing out like that—quite the Victorian heroine! But Lord, Lydia, the very sight of him standing there like an apparition was just too much after the rest of today.'

'It was perfectly understandable, I would say. You've eaten practically nothing since Marcus died, and there's been such a lot to see to. After all, love, you're very young to have all this on your plate. Luc should never have reappeared like that without warning.'

'I don't feel young,' said Emily wearily. 'I feel old, ancient, as though I mislaid my teens somewhere.' She paused, eyes narrowed, considering Lydia in speculation. 'Do you know, Mrs Crawford, I have this strange feeling. Somehow or other Luc's dramatic reappearance wasn't quite the cataclysmic shock to you that it was to me.'

'Well, it wouldn't be, would it?' Lydia said reasonably. 'He was your pigeon, not mine.'

'Mm,' Emily was by no means satisfied. 'Nevertheless I rather think you knew he was coming.'

Lydia sighed.

'Yes. At least, I knew he would some time. I really had no idea it would be today. He should have waited a bit.'

A strange feeling was creeping over Emily, as though the ground were shifting beneath her feet.

'Lydia!' Her blue eyes were dark and enormous in her white face, as she stared at her friend incredulously. 'You've known what happened to Luc all along, haven't you? No——' as the other woman started to speak, 'don't bother to deny it. My God, why didn't you say something? You knew the agony I went through . . .' Great tears started to roll down Emily's face, the first since Marcus's death, and at the sight of them Lydia jumped to her feet.

'Now for heaven's sake don't upset yourself, Emily. It was agony for me, too, to keep quiet about it, but he swore me to silence—oh dear—look, love, let's be sensible. I'll tell you everything, I promise, but not until you've had something to eat.'

Emily jumped up, wavering a little on legs that were still unsteady.

'How can you bother about food——'

Lydia put up an inexorable hand, and began to gather up the used plates and glasses, quick and efficient as always.

'I'm going to wash these while that pan of soup in the kitchen heats up,' she said firmly. 'Then I shall make a pot of tea, set a tray and we'll have a little snack in here. In the meantime you can go up and check on your son, change into your nightie and dressing gown, and not a word will you hear from me until then.'

Recognising the finality in Lydia's voice, Emily helped clear the debris of the funeral refreshments, carrying trays out into the big old-fashioned kitchen. Leaving Lydia up to her elbows in suds, Emily climbed the shallow treads of the oak staircase and entered the nursery, which, unlike the rest of the house, was completely modern, with Winnie the Pooh wallpaper and white-painted furniture with nursery-rhyme stencils. Her son lay in an untidy heap at the foot of his cot, and Emily felt her usual surge of love at the sight of his rosy, sleepy face. She straightened him out gently, tucking the covers round him. His eyes opened drowsily and looked straight up at her in the soft dim glow of the nightlight.

'Mum—mum,' he muttered indistinctly, his mouth curving in the smile that rendered Emily helpless. She bent over him and kissed him and he sighed, turning over to settle into sleep once more. She tiptoed from the room to her bedroom next door, averting her eyes from the closed door of the room where Marcus used to sleep. He had left that for ever. She dashed the tears away from her eyes and concentrated on taking off the unbecoming black dress and brushed out her hair from the confines of the severe chignon.

When Emily returned to the kitchen, snug in high-necked nightgown and fleecy aquamarine wool dressing-gown, Lydia turned away from the pan of soup she was seasoning and looked at her with approval.

'That's better. You look terrible in black.'

'I'll never wear it again if I can help it,' said Emily fervently. 'Let me do something to help.'

'You take the tea-tray with the bread and cheese, etc., I'll bring the soup bowls and the cutlery.'

Before they settled down to their simple meal Emily added a couple of logs to the drawing room fire and they sat opposite each other, the trays on the long low table between them.

'Right, Lydia, I'm eating, so fire away,' said Emily, finding she was hungrier than she'd thought after the first appetising mouthful of onion soup.

Lydia ate for a while before starting to speak.

'I've known that Luc was all right since just after you married Marcus,' she began without preamble.

Emily stared at her blankly, opening her mouth to interrupt, but Lydia held up a hand.

'I think it's best if I tell you the whole story, Em, then you can have your say afterwards. Not that I have much to tell.'

Emily heard her friend out in silence, as advised, and poured out tea after they finished their soup, cutting two slices of fruit cake to eat with it. She remained surprisingly calm throughout the little tale, though inside she felt a burning rebellion at the callous way the gods take up poor mortal lives and tangle up their destinies with all the carelessness a kitten might bring to snarling up a ball of wool.

'It was only about a fortnight after you came back to Compton Lacey with Marcus and announced that you were married,' began Lydia. 'The phone rang one night and it was Luc, from his home in Minas Gerais. He was very agitated and his accent was much more pronounced than usual, also the line wasn't too clear. One way and another we had quite some difficulty in getting a clear picture of events on either side. To be brief, when Luc went back to Brazil the taxi taking him from one airport to the other in Rio was involved in an accident. Luc suffered concussion from a blow on the head, and though not unconscious for long, was the victim of temporary amnesia when he came round in hospital. He could remember things in the past, more or less right up to his trip to England, but the time immediately prior to the accident had been wiped clean from his memory.'

Emily stirred restlessly at this.

'Sadly,' Lydia went on, 'he was not in time to see his father alive. Senhor Fonseca Senior died from a second coronary before Luc was well enough to return to Campo d'Ouro. The experts had predicted that Luc's recall would be total in time, and little by little everything did return to him—hence the frenzied telephone call to me for news of you. I had to tell him that you were married, of course. He—well, he took it badly, to say the least. I heard no more for quite a while, then he wrote to me, asking me to write to him regularly, giving him reports on you and to let him know should you need help in any sort of way.'

Emily was dumbfounded.

'Do you mean that all this time you've been sending off bulletins about—about everything that's happened to me? My God! Something like a school report, I suppose. "Emily tries hard, but needs more application" used to be a favourite comment. What were yours, Lydia?'

'Don't be too hard on me, love, I was sort of pig-in-the-middle,' begged Lydia. 'Luc made me promise faithfully I would never tell you. I could never decide whether he was right.'

'He wasn't,' said Emily bitterly. 'Is there anything else I should know?'

'When I wrote about Jamie's birth there was complete silence until three months ago, when he began writing again. I subsequently told him Marcus was terminally ill, and eventually informed him that he had died. I admit I knew he was here in the country, but I had no idea he would turn up today, of all days.'

'They bury people within twenty-four hours in Brazil,' said Emily dully.

'I see.'

There was silence while they both sipped tea, staring into the fire. Lydia sighed.

'When he comes here tomorrow are you going to freeze him out like you did tonight, Em? To be fair, it wasn't his fault things happened as they did.'

'I realise that. Or at least, one part of me does, the sensible, logical side. But the other part feels a terrible, burning resentment. The fact that it's entirely unmerited doesn't seem enough to send it away.'

'Do you resent my part in it, Emily?' asked Lydia anxiously.

'No, of course not, Lydia.' Emily smiled in reassurance. 'How could I? You did what you thought was best. Besides, you know very well that I could never have survived these last months without your help and support, I don't know what I would have done without you.' She yawned suddenly, exhaustion finally overtaking her like a tidal wave. 'God,

Lydia, I'm tired! I think it's time for bed. I know it's early, but it's been a long, long day.'

Lydia rose, piling up the trays.

'I wish you'd let me stay here tonight, Emily. I could easily have packed Tim off to one of his friends.'

Emily smiled gratefully as they went into the kitchen.

'You've done quite enough in having Jamie all day and putting him to bed for me. Besides, I'm not nervous. And anyway, you're back to work tomorrow. Thank you for everything, Lydia, I don't know what I'd have done without you.'

When the sound of Lydia's departing car had died away the old house seemed very empty and still. Emily locked up hurriedly and went upstairs to peep at her soundly sleeping son before settling herself down in her wide bed in the adjoining bedroom. Despite her weariness it was a long time before she could stop her mind from going round and round on an endless treadmill of speculation about Luc's reappearance. She wondered how he would have got on with Marcus, then the thought of her husband's kind face with the weary eyes opened the floodgates and she turned her head into her pillow and wept bitterly in a storm of pity, and a futile rage against the injustice of life.

CHAPTER FIVE

JAMIE was a very good little boy about settling down to sleep at nights, but he was equally good at waking up bright and early. Emily was glad of her early night when she heard him banging against the bars of his cot at six-thirty next morning, reiterating his usual litany of 'Mum—mum' until she went in to him.

'Who needs an alarm clock with you around?' she said ruefully, as the little figure in the red stretchy sleeping suit held up his arms, confident of being picked up, his mouth wide in an irresistible grin that displayed his six milky-white teeth. 'O.K. Out you come!'

Thank heavens it would be just a normal, peaceful day today, thought Emily, as she stripped and changed Jamie. She dressed him in warm sweater and dungarees and carried him down to the kitchen where the big Aga stove was still alight, filling the room with warmth against the raw chill of the morning. She installed the wriggling little figure in his highchair and gave him a rusk to occupy him while she made porridge and boiled eggs, joining Jamie in making a good breakfast for the first time in months. Towards the end she had been too involved in nursing Marcus to have much appetite, and had become noticeably skinny, even to herself. Her daily woman, Mrs Giles, would be in at nine to help clear up after yesterday, so for an hour or so she could actually read the morning paper in comparative peace while Jamie played in his playpen. The only abnormality about the day would be the meeting with Luc this evening.

Emily sighed. What was she going to say to him? What could he want to say to her, if it came to that? Their brief relationship had blossomed and died a long time ago. The Emily who had been hit for six by the charm of the handsome Brazilian just didn't exist any more. She had been transformed into the chatelaine of the Dower House of Compton Lacey, a very different proposition from the naïve, inexperienced girl whose defences had been unequal to Luc's charm. Poor man, she thought dispassionately. He'd had a hard time of it too, losing his father like that coupled with his own traumatic experience. She had thought of many reasons for Luc's complete disappearance from her life, but had never come within any distance of the truth.

After Mrs Giles arrived and they had worked together to set the old house to rights, Emily wrapped Jamie up well and took him for a walk in the grounds of the Manor House in his pushchair. The day was grey and blustery and she walked briskly, trundling the chair along at a fine pace, to Jamie's delight. Emily felt uneasy. She wished Luc weren't coming tonight. She should have put him off for a day or two, even if his time were limited. She had every excuse, after all. And now she came to think of it, seven-thirty was an idiotic time to suggest. Perhaps he thought she'd asked him to dinner. Emily's 'dinner' usually consisted of something like scrambled

eggs or soup eaten with her son before she put him to bed.
Not really the sort of meal she could offer Lucas Guimaraes
Fonseca. Still, there was a well-stocked drinks cabinet.
Perhaps his visit would be brief. Emily bent to retrieve the
woolly rabbit Jamie had hurled from his chair and turned for
home. At least Jamie could be depended on to settle down to
sleep promptly, and with luck should be well away before
Luc's arrival. Emily felt suddenly depressed. Not so long ago
the prospect of seeing Luc would have transported her into
the seventh heaven. Now it was merely another chore to be
disposed of as painlessly as possible.

'Come on, Jamie,' she said brightly. 'Let's go and have lunch.'

The rest of the day was taken up in writing acknowledge-
ments of all the letters of condolence on Marcus's death. She
played with Jamie for some time afterwards to restore her
balance, then gave him his supper. While Emily fed her son
with fish in cream sauce she became nervous about whether
she would have to offer Luc a meal. Depositing Jamie in his
pen for a while, she rummaged in the freezer and produced a
quiche Lorraine, setting it on the rack above the Aga to thaw.
There was no lettuce, but she found a firm white cabbage,
shredding it and mixing it with sweetcorn, onion and sliced
red pepper for salad. Finally she put some potatoes to bake in
the oven after making up the fire and checked on the contents
of the pan of soup at the back of the hotplate. Mrs Giles
always 'knocked up' a pan of soup when she came to clean,
and today it was vegetable, thick with winter roots, celery,
leeks and onions. That should do, thought Emily, then if he
doesn't stay nothing will be wasted.

By this time Jamie had tired of his blocks and was
beginning to droop, so Emily scooped him up and cuddled
him in her arms as she took him up to the cheerful, brightly lit
nursery. He went down without a murmur, hugging his
rabbit, and Emily gave thanks, as she did most nights, for
such a sunny dispositioned child. She stood looking down at
him lovingly for some time, then tiptoed out, leaving only the
nightlight to keep him company.

Emily had a swift bath and thought dispiritedly what to
wear. Not the black dress of yesterday; Marcus had hated
black and she had worn it merely as a sign of the respect she

knew the mourners at the funeral would consider mandatory. Marcus had bought her quite a lot of clothes, and had appreciated the subtle, muted colours that suited her best. She took out a dress of ginger-pink suede, draped cleverly across her breasts, the skirt bias-cut to swing gracefully as she moved. She brushed her hair back from her face and let it hang loose, screwed small pearl studs into her earlobes and made up her face with care. She might as well meet Luc with all flags flying. The pathetic creature of yesterday was ousted by a poised young woman who looked back from the mirror with confidence. Marcus would have approved. Her full lower lip trembled for a moment, then she held her head up high and went down to turn on all the lights and make up the drawing-room fire.

Emily had just finished setting a tray with sherry decanter and glasses when the doorbell jangled. Her stomach muscles contracted for a second and she took a deep breath, annoyed with herself, before crossing the hall to open the heavy door to her visitor.

Luc Fonseca came into the hall carrying a sheaf of pink roses, which he handed to Emily as he closed the door.

'Good evening, Emily,' he said gravely. 'I trust I find you recovered today.'

She accepted the flowers and took his sheepskin jacket.

'Thank you, Luc. They're very beautiful. And yes, I'm perfectly well today.'

They exchanged looks for a long moment before Emily turned away.

'Please go on into the drawing room while I put the roses in water. Help yourself to a glass of sherry; oloroso or dry, whichever you prefer.'

'Thank you.' Luc bowed his dark head formally and did as she suggested while Emily laid the coat on the settle in the hall and took the flowers to the kitchen. Her pulse was more rapid than usual. Which was only to be expected under the circumstances, after all, hardly the result of realising how very attractive Luc still was, especially in the black velvet jacket and silver-grey trousers and shirt he was wearing. When she went back to the drawing-room he was standing before the blazing fire, a glass of sherry in his hand.

'May I pour one for you?' he hesitated. 'I'm sorry, I should refer to you as Mrs Lacey. I'm afraid I forgot when I arrived.'

'No,' said Emily quickly. 'I'd rather you didn't. Emily will do. I'll have the oloroso, please.' She took the glass he filled for her and drank deeply, glad of the warmth of the wine, which had an immediate calming effect.

'There is something very comforting about an open fire,' he remarked quietly, leaning against the mantelpiece. 'Something we rarely have in Campo d'Ouro, except on the coldest of nights.'

'It's a necessity here.' Emily seated herself in the corner of one of the sofas. 'We do have central heating, of course, but the rooms are large and high-ceilinged—in winter we need the fire to make this room habitable.'

There was silence for a while, prolonging and stretching until the room was filled with tension.

'This is a very difficult situation,' said Luc finally. 'I came to give my reason, Emily, for what happened and did not happen, after I left you that last time. It is not easy. You were a shy young girl then, and now you are the poised lady of the Manor.' He looked at her searchingly. 'Though I sense none of the hostility you displayed last night.'

'No,' she admitted. 'I—well, I suppose I bullied Lydia into telling me a few pertinent facts after you left. Apart from that I was not precisely myself, as you can appreciate. I'm sorry if I was unreasonable. After all, you weren't to know it was the day of the funeral. Also I'm not the "lady of the Manor", as you put it. This is merely the Dower House, where Marcus lived after he handed Compton Lacey to the National Trust.'

'Will you continue to live here?'

'No. It was part of the bequest to the Trust. Marcus had an agreement that he would stay here until his death, then the Dower House becomes Trust property too.'

Luc frowned.

'But what will happen to you and—your son?'

'We're moving away from the district.' Emily held out her glass to be refilled and Luc did so abstractedly.

'Should not the child have inherited this house?' he asked, his heavy brows meeting in perplexity.

'The arrangement was made before he knew of Jamie's advent, and I wouldn't allow him to alter it in any way' Emily stood up quickly and changed the subject. 'Will you have dinner with me, Luc? It's the simplest of meals, but you're quite welcome to share what I have.'

Luc was plainly taken aback.

'If you are sure I do not intrude. I had expected to return to the White Hart to dine, but naturally I would prefer to remain with you.' He paused, holding her eyes with his. 'I remember with utmost clarity the last time we dined together.'

Emily kept her face blank.

'I'm afraid I can't remember what I gave you to eat,' she lied, smiling politely. 'Tonight it's what we call "pot luck" in this country.'

He gave an oddly formal little bow.

'As a foreigner I am hardly likely to understand, but am more than happy to find out by sharing this "pot luck" with so charming a companion.'

With the feeling that Luc was deliberately turning on the Latin charm, Emily led the way to the dining room, which by day gave a splendid view of the Manor House from the long windows, but tonight was elegant by candlelight, its atmosphere very much that of the third George when it was built. The dead white of the paintwork on the pilasters and cornices was in direct contrast to the soft mushroom-brown paint of the walls, and the straw-coloured heavy satin curtains drawn against the chill of the night.

Emily waved Luc to the chair opposite her at the oval table and went to fetch in the tureen of soup. Luc watched her ladling the savoury mixture into Royal Doulton bowls, her delicately cut face closed and concentrated on her task.

'You do not have servants?' he asked, as they began their meal.

'Not in the way you mean. I have a daily woman who comes in some days, otherwise I manage alone.'

Luc accepted a piece of the crusty French loaf she offered.

'And your son? You have no help with him?'

'I don't need any. In this country one looks after one's own children, unless the mother has a career. My career at the moment is bringing up Jamie.'

'Does this content you?'

'Yes, indeed. He's a happy little soul, which is—only to be expected.'

Luc obviously noticed her hesitation but said nothing, applying himself to the soup and merely commenting on its excellence.

'Do have plenty,' urged Emily brightly. 'The second course is not over-exciting.'

However, when she set the piping-hot quiche on the table, flanked by the crisp winter salad in a crystal bowl and a platter of baked potatoes, their skins slit and stuffed with sour cream and chives, Luc was adamant that the White Hart could not have provided anything more delicious than Emily's pot luck.

They chatted generally while they ate, both deliberately avoiding every subject which might become emotive. Gradually Emily began to relax and recapture some of the ease she had felt with Luc during their brief time together long before, and by the time they were once again seated in front of the drawing room fire, drinking coffee, the atmosphere was a great deal more cordial than prior to the meal. Emily scanned the contents of the drinks cupboard and brought out a bottle of Remy Martin fine champagne cognac, handing the fragile balloon glass to Luc with no constraint when she told him the brand had been Marcus's favourite.

'You are brave for one who must be grief-stricken,' said Luc, finally deserting the impersonal and plunging back into the sphere of relationships.

Emily sipped the very small quantity of Grand Marnier in her glass and considered a little before she answered.

'I don't think bravery comes into it,' she said reflectively, then impulsively leaned over to touch his hand, 'and please don't think I'm insulting your command of the niceties of the English language!'

Luc's hand tensed beneath the touch of her fingers and Emily removed them hastily, taking refuge in refilling their coffee cups.

'I became accustomed to the fact that Marcus would die, because I was aware from the first that this would be sooner rather than later in his case. He had leukaemia, and there were several recessions in the progress of the disease before the final, terminal stage, which made it easier to be resigned to the eventual fact of his death when it finally occurred. I did a lot of my actual grieving in the days before his death, which makes my present behaviour possibly more explicable to you.'

Luc was sitting with one long leg crossed over the other, displaying the fine black leather of the half-boot he wore, one elbow on the arm of the settee, his chin on his supporting hand. The brooding look he turned on her hinted at an inner disquiet at odds with his outer appearance of relaxation.

'He was fortunate to have you by his side at the end,' he said quietly. 'He must have taken great delight in his son, though you must be very tired after coping with an invalid and a baby. You are very thin; motherhood has not changed you much.'

Emily flushed, ignoring the last part of his comment.

'Jamie was always a source of happiness to Marcus, though, of course, towards the end it wasn't possible for them to be together for any length of time. More cognac?'

Luc declined and there was silence for a while.

'Emily,' he said eventually, sitting up straight, bracing himself for what he was about to say, 'I have come six thousand miles to talk to you, and though I began badly by presenting myself on the day of your husband's funeral, I would be glad if you could bring yourself to hear me out.'

'Of course,' agreed Emily, settling herself to listen. 'That was the reason I allowed you to come tonight, as I imagine your time in this country is restricted.' Silently she marvelled at the formality of their conversation. No one listening would ever have suspected that for a fleeting few days they had once been so close.

'When I left you that morning, Emily,' he began huskily, 'I was torn apart I was—shattered at the news about my father, agonised at leaving you so precepitately when we had just—just——'

'Become lovers,' suggested Emily calmly.

'As you say,' he agreed. 'The flight back to Rio was one of the least enjoyable experiences of my life, to make an understatement. My mind was in a—turmoil?—the whole

way, half of me frantic with concern for my father, the other
half unable to forget the moments when I held you in my
arms, when——'

'Perhaps you could cut out the more emotional bits,'
interrupted Emily restlessly.

'I'm sorry. I have no wish to offend you.' Luc took a deep
breath before continuing. 'In Rio I took a taxi from the one
airport, Galeao, to the other, internal airport, Santos
Dumont, and the cab was involved in an accident. I was
thrown against the window and hit my head. I remember
nothing else until I woke up in hospital with no recollection of
my trip to the U.K., or that my father was ill. My amnesia
was temporary. Little by little things began to return to my
mind, but only in fragments. I knew there was something
wrong—badly wrong. When I found that my father had died
before I even reached hospital I thought that this was the
cause of the terrible feeling of anxiety that consumed me. But
back in Campo d'Ouro, with all the aftermath of my father's
death to deal with, my grandmother to console in the loss of
her beloved only son, this feeling, this almost insupportable
feeling, still persisted. My grandmother was highly sensitive to
my distress and did her best to help me remember the missing
gap in my time in England. One day she remembered the
name of the hotel they cabled to call me home, and as
soon as she mentioned the White Hart everything fell into
place.'

Luc took out a fine lawn handkerchief and passed it over
his forehead. Emily got up and fetched the bottle of Remy
Martin.

'I think you'd better drink a little more of this, Luc.' She
looked at him levelly. 'There's no need to go on. Lydia put me
very loosely in the picture last night. I mean, she just gave me
the bare details.'

'I am being too Latin and undisciplined for you?' he said, a
wry smile at the corners of his mouth. He pushed a hand
through his crisply curling hair, accepting the cognac Emily
offered him with appreciation.

'I'm not knocking you, Luc, but it was a long time ago, and
it's all over now. I was bitter at the time, but not now.'

'You were bitter yesterday,' he reminded her, frowning.

'I had no idea you were even alive until yesterday,' she retorted, sitting down again. 'You could have been in orbit round the moon for all I knew—that is until I pressurised Lydia into telling me about your little arrangement.'

'Then I think I should put you "in the picture", I think you said, even more accurately,' he went on relentlessly, his emotions obviously now well in hand. 'I immediately telephoned Mrs Crawford, not even remembering the time difference. Did she tell you it was in the middle of the night for her?' Emily shook her head. 'I could hardly take it in when she told me you were married. It was impossible to believe that you had married your cousin so short a time after we had—we had——'

'Had sex together?' said Emily brutally.

The colour left Luc's face, leaving him grey beneath the tan. He stood up slowly, setting his glass down on the tray with great care, his mouth compressed, rigid with distaste.

'I do not feel——' he began, but was interrupted by a sharp cry of anguish from upstairs.

Emily tore out of the room with a muttered apology over her shoulder, running upstairs at top speed to the heartbroken sounds coming from her son's room. Jamie was sitting up in his cot, his arms held out in piteous supplication, the reason for his distress immediately obvious. He had been very, very sick. Emily grabbed a towel from the low chair she used to change him and enveloped her sobbing little son in it, cradling him to her fiercely while she looked for somewhere to lay him down for a moment.

'Mum—mum—mum,' hiccuped the flushed little boy, clutching her convulsively, his sobs beginning to subside.

'Never mind, my lovely boy,' she crooned, 'it was that nasty old fish, I expect.' She laid him gently on the furry rug beside his cot, still in his cocoon of towel, while she gathered up the sheets from the cot and ran into the bathroom to dump them in the white pail kept for nappies. She flew back into the bedroom and gathered up her son, taking him into the bathroom to remove his sleeping suit and sponge him down. When he was comfortable and dry Emily stood irresolute for a moment.

'I'm going to have to put you down for a moment while I

do your bed,' she said to the drowsy baby, then jumped as a voice spoke from the doorway.

'Perhaps you had better give him to me,' said Luc softly, holding out his arms, his eyes on the child's face. Emily clutched Jamie to her breast instinctively.

'No, really, he'll ruin your jacket—I can manage.' She was breathless with embarrassment, and something else, which could only be fear.

'Emily.' Luc spoke without inflection, and silently she surrendered the relaxed little body of her son to him. She turned away sharply and began to sponge the plastic-covered cot mattress, drying it energetically and fetching fresh sheets and blankets from the white chest of drawers beneath the window. In complete silence she remade the little bed, then turned back to Luc for Jamie, who was now fast asleep. Without a word he brushed past her and laid the little boy on the mattress, tucking the fleecy blanket gently round him. They both stood in silence, looking down at the mop of black curls against the white sheet. The child gave a great sigh, then opened bright dark eyes amd smiled up at Emily.

'Mum—mum,' he murmured, then his thumb went into his mouth and he settled down in his usual little curled-up ball, fast asleep before the two looking down at him turned away to tiptoe quietly from the room.

They went downstairs still enclosed in the same chill shell of silence until they reached the drawing room, where Luc pointed out a silver-framed photograph on a glove table between the two long windows.

'Marcus Lacey, I think,' he said quietly.

Emily nodded, looking at the coloured photograph of the slim man in a tweed jacket and riding breeches, his labrador alongside him gazing up in adoration at the man who smiled at the camera, his eyes narrowed a little against the light, but their colour perfectly visible for all that. They were the same shade of light, bright blue as the girl who looked up in apprehension at the man staring fixedly at the photograph.

CHAPTER SIX

THAT night Emily lay twisting and turning in the grip of a terrible cold anxiety that sent her several times into the next room to hover over Jamie's cot, looking yearningly down at the soundly sleeping baby.

If only Luc had said more, she thought wretchedly, getting into bed for the third time, but he had just gone on looking at the photograph of Marcus without moving a muscle, as though mesmerised by the sight of the thin, aristocratic face. Something in his stance told Emily very clearly that he was consumed by rage. Whether it was directed at herself personally she found difficult to tell. She had stood there, hardly daring to breathe, expecting him to turn on her with a torrent of accusation, demanding explanations, but Luc remained silent, eventually wishing her goodnight, thanking her for the meal, ignoring the incident upstairs as though it had never happened. She had followed his lead, behaving like the conventional hostess, and they had taken leave of each other like two polite strangers. Emily's hand had been on the door, ready to close it behind Luc's tall, elegant figure, her whole body beginning to relax with relief, when he had turned almost casually and smiled, a mere muscular movement of his mouth that left his eyes cold.

'I shall be back in the morning, Emily. Early. I would like to make the acquaintance of—our son.'

Emily had stood at the open doorway long after Luc's car had accelerated down the gravelled drive, until the realisation that she was shaking with cold and reaction had galvanised her into life again, and she had locked the house and cleared away the dinner things in a frenzy of haste, desperate to get to bed and try to come to terms with a situation she had never imagined would exist.

Instead of being Latin and emotional Luc had shown all the animation of a block of granite. The sight of the baby seemed to have rendered him speechless and icy. What did she expect?

71

thought Emily, burrowing into her hot pillows. A great dramatic scene, with cries of 'My son, my son!' and 'Why did you not tell me?' would have been embarrassing in the extreme. Of course, it was her own fault; sheer stupidity not to have hired a babysitter and met Luc outside somewhere. The very next day after Marcus was buried? enquired a polite inner voice; a marvellous story for the village that would have been! If only Jamie hadn't been sick, poor baby, then Luc need never have laid eyes on him. He could have said his say and gone on to Cornwall, or wherever, to transact whatever business had brought him to this country, and that would have been that. Finis. Nothing would convince Emily that he had come all this way solely to see her. And now what? Luc was coming back in the morning with what purpose in mind? she wondered. Would he demand that she hand over his son? But he could hardly do that, when, as far as the world was concerned, Jamie was Marcus Lacey's son. If anyone suspected any different from the sheer genetic impossibility of two fair, blue-eyed people producing an olive-skinned, black-eyed baby, no one had ever mentioned it to Emily's face.

None of her thoughts gave Emily any comfort, and it was a pale, wan mother with dark shadows under her eyes who got wearily out of bed next morning in response to the urgent cries of hunger from her son's room.

All through dressing Jamie and giving him his breakfast, Emily was tense and worried, anxious in case she communicated her state of mind to the little boy. But he sat happily in his high chair while his mother disposed of the laundry and cleared away the breakfast things, banging on the tray in front of him with a spoon, and drinking the milk Emily gave him without a murmur.

Giving thanks that this was not one of Mrs Giles's mornings, Emily defiantly set up the playpen in the drawing room. Luc might as well make Jamie's acquaintance first as last, and the baby sat gurgling happily amongst building blocks and various furry animals while Emily lit the fire, and whisked round the room with a duster in a fever of impatience to be ready and waiting when Luc arrived. God only knew what Luc meant by 'in the morning'. She should have asked him to be more specific, but it couldn't be helped. By nine Emily was doggedly pushing the electric polisher over the parquet floor in the hall, one eye through the open door of the drawing room on Jamie, when the doorbell rang. She took a despairing look down at herself, pushed her hair out of her eyes and yanked the door open on a blandly smiling Luc, who stood there affably, in a heavy cable-patterned white sweater and black cords over the leather boots of the previous evening. His comprehensive survey of her own dishevelled appearance did nothing to improve Emily's disposition, and conscious of her faded denims and much washed, rather tight pink jumper, her 'Good morning' was scarcely brimming over with warmth.

'You were not expecting me so early?' he enquired as Emily shut the door with a rather unnecessary bang.

'You said "morning", not the crack of dawn,' she answered irritably, and directed him into the drawing room. 'Well, here's the person you've come to see, I presume, so let me introduce you to—my son, James. Only I call him Jamie.'

Luc stood with hands on hips smiling down at the little boy, who, not in the least shy, shuffled nearer on his bottom and offered Luc his woolly rabbit, displaying his milky teeth in his usual irresistible smile. Luc squatted down on his heels and accepted the toy solemnly, stretching out a hand to touch the dark mop of curls gently, his dark eyes tender.

'He is beautiful, Emily,' he said huskily, not turning his head.

'Yes.' Emily's irritation evaporated. 'He's so happy and cheerful, I'm amazed at my good fortune sometimes. The only roaring I get is when his lunch is overdue, or just a bit when he's teething, and of course for something like last night. Though he's never been sick like that before.'

Luc detached his fingers reluctantly from Jamie's and stood up, his handsome face cold as he looked squarely down at Emily.

'Perhaps we may regard Jamie's sickness as an act of God, Emily, for I have the distinct impression that otherwise I might never have made his acquaintance. Am I right?'

She nodded dumbly, the colour flooding her cheeks, her eyes dropping before the accusation burning in his.

'Why, Emily? *Deus*, tell me why!'

'Until two days ago I didn't know you were even alive!' She flung it at him like a gauntlet. 'Lydia did. You made her keep silent. But all the time you knew everything that happened to me. Why could I not have known that you were at least alive——'

'But you were married to another man,' he cut in, nostrils flaring. 'So how could it have made any difference?'

'How can you be so obtuse!' Emily flung away to one of the long windows looking out into the winter chill of the garden, and with a swift glance at Jamie, who appeared quite unaffected by the emotions seething in the room, Luc followed her and stood close behind her, his voice low in her ear.

'When Lydia told me that you were married to Marcus Lacey, I presumed that you were merely carrying on with an arrangement understood before you met me. I knew he allowed you to live rent-free in the cottage; I suspected then that he took more than the remote interest in you that you insisted was all he felt.'

Emily took a deep breath and turned on him, her eyes cold and bright, like acquamarines in the pinched pallor of her face.

'When I didn't hear from you, through the agony of those hours and days after you left, I felt I had experienced the ultimate in unhappiness. I was wrong. In my sheer ignorance and grief I ignored certain messages that my body was trying to transmit. It wasn't until one afternoon up at the Manor after the visitors had gone that all became hideously clear. Colonel Hammond, the custodian, was in America on a lecture tour, and Marcus had taken over pro tem. He found me in the solar, desperately trying to get downstairs to the garden door before I was sick or fainted. Happily the latter overtook me first, which saved messing up National Trust property, and Marcus brought me here to the Dower House to recover.' She broke off to return to the fire to warm herself before the blaze, absently picking up a teddy bear Jamie had pitched out of his pen. She handed the toy to her son, smiling at him reassuringly before looking at Luc.

'Come and sit down, Luc, and I'll try to finish my little tale in a more reasonable manner.' Emily sat down on one of the sofas, waving Luc to the one opposite, but he sat beside her and took one of her hands.

'Go on, Emily,' he said quietly, and after a moment she took up her narrative, her face averted from him.

'That little incident took place about two months after you were here. In the face of Marcus's kindness I poured out my tale of woe, and he was obliged to point out that it was just possible I might be pregnant, even though he was a bachelor, and not really fitted to pass judgement on such things.' Emily turned a wry smile on Luc. 'Talk about stupid! After a little hasty basic arithmetic I realised how right he was, and felt as though the sky had fallen in. Up to now it had been tragedy as far as I was concerned, but the new development spelled disaster plus. Marcus was a tower of strength. He took me home and told me to sleep on it while he thought things over. Needless to say, I didn't sleep very well, but somehow having someone else involved in my problem made things marginally easier to bear.'

Luc shifted restlessly.

'*Deus*—if only I had known!' He shook his head as if to clear something from his vision. 'Go on, Emily.'

'Marcus came next day and suggested two courses of action he thought open to me. The first was that he tried to trace you. I couldn't even remember the name of the town where you lived, let alone what area it was in, and besides——' Emily paused.

'And besides?' he prompted, squeezing her hand gently.

'Put yourself in my place. I didn't know if you were alive or dead. There was every possibility that your father, poor man, *had* died. Even if we were able to make contact with your grandmother, how could I possibly burden her with a sorry tale from an unknown girl who claimed to be expecting her grandson's child?'

'But I was not dead.'

'No.' Emily's head lifted proudly. 'But the silence from you hardly encouraged me to acquaint you with my little problem. If you were alive I thought you'd just forgotten me.'

'Which I had, Emily. I had forgotten everything, or nothing in the world would have kept me from returning to you,' he said passionately.

Emily withdrew perceptibly.

'Possibly. But at the time begging had no appeal for me, even in my rather desperate circumstances. So Marcus suggested I marry him then and there. He told me about the leukaemia and how his life expectancy was not great. He had dreaded spending his remaining time alone, and somehow managed to convince me that I would be doing him as great a service as he was doing for me. I might add that his quiet way of describing his death sentence brought everything into proportion with an almighty click. My problem seemed suddenly minimal when compared to his.'

Luc moved to restore Jamie to a sitting position after the baby had fallen over on his back like a stranded duckling. He paused to look at Marcus's photograph before returning to sit by Emily.

'I would have been honoured to know him,' he said quietly. 'I apologise for my previous attitude.'

Emily shrugged.

'You weren't to know. We went off to London the very next day, and returned to Compton Lacey after two weeks with our marriage a fait accompli. It was the usual village nine-day wonder, of course.'

'But how——' Luc hesitated. 'Forgive me, but Jamie's arrival in the world was a little early by conventional standards.'

'Normally it would have been. Lydia and the family doctor knew the truth, of course. Up to then I had said nothing about my pregnancy to Lydia; after all, idiot that I was, I hadn't realised myself until my system gave me a nudge. I had the baby right here at the Dower House, with only the doctor and Lydia in attendance after a miserable waiting period when I felt nauseated the whole time. Poor Marcus swore that he had no time to get on with his leukaemia because he was so busy trying to keep me in one piece.' Emily's eyes filled with sudden tears and Luc's hand tightened on hers while he fished in his pocket and produced a folded white handkerchief.

Emily blew in it prosaically, mopping herself before going on.

'Jamie only weighed four and a half pounds, so it was very easy for Lydia to give the merest hint to Mrs Giles, the daily woman, that he was premature. He was so small that no one questioned it—I almost believed it myself, except for those black eyes of his that left me in no doubt. His appearance was the one thing neither Marcus nor I could do anything about. But with Marcus suddenly progressing to the terminal stage of his illness I haven't really taken Jamie out and about much except for walks in the grounds, and possibly Mrs Giles isn't too heavily into genetics to question any doubt about Jamie's parentage.'

Luc looked over at Jamie, who was absorbed in trying to balance one block on another. He smiled with a gleam of pure possession in his eyes.

'It is good that I am not known locally. Jamie looks exactly like me.'

Emily nodded in agreement.

'Carbon copy. It's been a bit painful lately as he's begun to grow out of the indeterminate baby stage and started to develop more strongly marked features. I've seen you looking at me out of his eyes.'

'And that was unwelcome to you?'

'Can you blame me?'

'No, Emily,' he said heavily, 'I cannot blame you. I know very well it does not lessen your love for him. Last night you stood like a tigress at bay when I came upstairs. I thought for a moment you would refuse to give Jamie to me.'

'I didn't want to,' said Emily honestly. 'But something about you commanded instant obedience.' She stood up as a wail came from the playpen and went to scoop the little boy up in her arms.

'What is the matter?' Luc's voice was alarmed as he stood close behind her. 'Is he ill?'

'Don't you know anything about babies?' Emily grinned at the worried frown on his face. 'Jamie has a little internal alarm clock which goes off mid-morning. It means his nappy needs changing and it's time for milk for him and coffee for us.'

Luc's face altered dramatically at the word 'us' and he reached for her, baby and all. But Emily dodged out of reach, Jamie in front of her like a shield.

'No, Luc,' she said softly. 'Nothing's altered.'

His mouth tightened and he stood back, his arms folded across his chest, glowering down at her.

'I do not understand,' he said, with a sulky look so like his son's that Emily had to restrain a smile.

'You've been extraordinarily good over all this,' she said reasonably. 'I appreciate what a remarkable restraint you placed on yourself last night when you were obviously thunderstruck by seeing Jamie.'

'Thunderstruck?'

'Well, astonished—shocked,' amended Emily hastily. 'Now I'm going to make my son smell a little less anti-social and when I come back down I'll make us some coffee. Would you like the morning paper?'

Luc shook his head emphatically.

'I will come with you and watch.'

'It's not exactly enthralling watching me change a dirty nappy!'

'For me it is. You forget, I have missed nine months of my son's life already. I have much to make up.' Luc relieved her deftly of his unprotesting son, striding swiftly from the room with a protesting Emily in his wake.

'Be careful of your sweater, Luc. Jamie, stop it!'

The latter had a handful of his father's thick black hair, and was pulling it gleefully, giving way to ecstatic giggles at the shouts of mock anguish issuing from this large new playmate.

'*O bichinho feio,*' panted Luc as they reached Jamie's bedroom. 'I shall be bald! Where do I put him?'

He laid the wriggling little body on the wide padded surface of the chest of drawers as instructed, and anchored him there with one long hand while Emily produced nappy, cream and a clean pair of dungarees.

'He is a handful for you, Emily, and will get more so as time goes on. No wonder you are so—skinny, I think you say.'

'That's right. How kind,' said Emily composedly, quickly undressing and cleaning up her son. 'But he won't always be in nappies—I should have potted him this morning, but I was so wrapped up in my woes I forgot. Now, up you come, you rascal!' She buried her face in the little boy's neck, blowing against the silky soft skin. 'Come on then, Jamie, I'll go and make coffee and you can go to——' She stopped, while her eyes met and clashed with Luc's above Jamie's unsuspecting head.

Luc took the child from her and held him in the crook of one arm while his other hand held Emily's wrist as he marched her from the room. The trio descended the stairs in silence, pausing at the drawing-room door.

'Your mother will go and make coffee,' said Luc, addressing his son, who gazed back at him attentively as though he understood every word. 'while you come in here and talk to—your daddy.'

Emily's wrist was released and she was left, feeling oddly forlorn for a moment before she went into the kitchen and put coffee to percolate. She glanced down at herself with distaste and ran back upstairs, hurriedly stripping off her jeans and sweater and pulling on a cream silk double-breasted shirt and soft charcoal flannel trousers which she tucked into calf-length grey suede wrinkly boots. She brushed her streaky fair hair and caught it away from her face on one side with a mother-of-pearl barrette, sprayed on some 'Chloe', added a touch of beige-pink lipstick and ran back down to the kitchen just as the thermostat light on the percolator went out.

Breathless, she set a tray with coffee cups, warmed some milk for Jamie, poured it into his lidded, spouted mug, and took the lot in to the drawing room to join the men. Luc was standing by the window with Jamie in his arms, pointing out the distant cows grazing in the parkland and various other objects of interest, including his hired car, which was parked just outside. He swivelled as Emily came in with the tray, his eyebrows shooting up into his hair at her transformation.

'Look, Jamie, *que Mamae bonita*,' he said softly in the baby's ear, and as though he was quite conversant with Portuguese the little boy promptly held out his arms with his usual 'Mum—mum.'

Emily's cheeks were pink as she put the tray on the fireside table and took Jamie from Luc.

'He goes back into his pen now for his drink,' she said hurriedly, giving Jamie a smacking kiss as she sat him down in the playpen and handed him his mug.

She seated herself sedately behind the coffee tray and poured a cup for Luc, telling him to help himself to sugar.

'I was hoping for something sweeter,' he said gravely as he accepted the cup. 'You gave Jamie a kiss with his.'

To Emily's annoyance she went scarlet, her poise shattered momentarily.

'Please, Luc,' she said repressively, 'let's keep things impersonal. It will be much easier that way.' She drank her coffee rapidly, heedless of whether it scorched her throat on the way down.

'For whom, Emily?' he mocked her silently across the long table. 'Not for me. I remember a different Emily, one who allowed me to become very personal indeed.'

'That's a very underhand sort of crack to make.' Emily kept her voice level by sheer will-power. 'That's all in the past. Things are different now.'

Luc leaned forward, his attitude implicit with menace.

'It is *not* in the past, Emily. We have a living reminder sitting there looking at us right now. *Deus*, can you imagine how I feel, when I have a son who is my image, and yet he bears another man's name?' He flung himself back into a corner of the settee, one booted ankle flung across his knee, his face black with anger.

'That's not exactly my fault,' retorted Emily, stung by the injustice of his words.

'I know,' he said more reasonably. 'It is no one's *fault*. But just to look at Jamie gives me such a surge of feeling—I had no idea how much I craved fatherhood until I saw him clutched in your arms last night. I was not trying to take him away from you, Emily, but the urge to hold him in my arms was irresistible.' He thrust an impatient hand through his hair, looking at her in entreaty. 'Do you understand?'

'Oh yes, I understand.' Emily sighed, then glanced at her watch. 'Look, do you want to stay to lunch? I must give Jamie his shortly, then he has a nap. Or do you have to get back to the hotel?'

'May I spend the day here with you—and Jamie?' Luc leaned forward, his hands clasped between his knees. 'Today is Tuesday; I must go back at the weekend. There is not much time.'

'When do you go to Cornwall?'

'Cornwall?' Luc looked blank. 'I am not going to Cornwall. Why do you ask?'

'I thought you must be on a business trip like last time.'

'Emily, I thought I had made myself clear. I came to England solely to see you.' Luc's voice was passionate in its sincerity and Emily moved restlessly, discomfited.

'I find it difficult to take in,' she said tonelessly. 'You knew me for such a brief while. Why should it have had such an effect on you?'

He closed his eyes for a moment, jaw clenched, as though hanging on to the last shred of patience.

'Nossa Senhora!' he said violently, then opened his eyes, glaring at her so fiercely Emily instinctively shrank back into her corner of the settee. 'I was almost thirty when I met you—not exactly a boy. I had known other women, of course, even considered one or two as prospective brides, but never with sufficient enthusiasm to do anything about it. My father and my grandmother kept dropping broad—hints?—about marrying and producing sons to carry on the name, but always they hoped I would find someone to love. I did.' Luc jerked his head violently towards the window. 'Across the park, in that old house, I found a girl daydreaming one afternoon, and instantly I knew why no other woman had ever appealed to me for long. You were what I wanted. God knows why—you are not stunningly beautiful.'

Emily was well aware of this, but it hurt to hear him put it into words so baldly. Luc smiled derisively.

'You do not have a voluptuous figure, even now after giving birth to a child. But one look from those dreaming blue eyes and I was lost. Now are you beginning to understand?'

Emily refused to comment, her eyes falling to her tightly clasped hands.

'When I knew you'd married someone else,' he continued bleakly, 'I did my utmost to forget you. But I could not. When Mrs Crawford wrote to me to say you had borne a child last August——'

'It was June, actually,' murmured Emily.

Luc's expression softened a little.

'Yes, of course—it must have been. But I did not know that then. For a while I tried to put you out of my mind, worked an eighteen-hour day and drove everyone mad, but eventually I gave in and started writing to Mrs Crawford again. It was like some sickness that was incurable.'

'Hardly.' Emily's voice was cold.

'No,' he agreed soberly. 'I am sorry, that was a gauche thing to say. But I am trying to make clear how I felt—how I still feel. And yet you say that is all in the past. How can you expect me to agree? Is that really how *you* feel?'

'It's not as clear-cut as that.' Emily collected the coffee cups and rose to take Jamie's mug from the corner of the playpen. The baby automatically held up his hands.

'Mum—mum?' he said hopefully.

'In a minute, darling.' Emily smiled at him lovingly.

'May I pick him up, Emily?' Luc was beside her, an unexpected humility in his request.

She looked at him consideringly, then smiled faintly.

'Yes. You don't need to ask permission.'

'I would not like to upset any routine you and Jamie have, Emily.'

She laughed outright.

'We don't have any. I don't know whether Jamie's a good baby because of the way I've looked after him or in spite of it. He seemed to sense that I had to devote a lot of time to Marcus in the end, somehow. It was odd, now I come to think of it, how I never felt torn between the two.'

Luc picked up the eager little boy, rubbing his nose against the child's, which was a miniature version of his own. Emily watched indulgently while the tall man tossed the laughing child into the air, then carried the tray to the kitchen, stopping short as she laid the tray down on the big deal table. Guilt flooded her abruptly as she suddenly remembered how short a time had elapsed since the day Marcus died, but in the wake of the guilt came a feeling of serene certainty. Her heart lifted. Marcus would want her to be happy in any way she could. Emily frowned anxiously. The problem was that for the time being she had no idea which way that was.

When Luc appeared with Jamie Emily surprised him by asking what he had had for breakfast.

'Er—coffee, that's all,' he answered. 'Why, what did you have?'

'The same, I'm afraid. I was merely sounding out what to do about lunch. What do you say to some of last night's soup followed by good old bacon and eggs?'

'I'd say *"otimo, senhora"*—perfect, splendid, whatever translation you like.' Luc's sobriety of a moment ago was replaced by a gaiety that Emily found infectious.

'Right. How about having a go at feeding Jamie?' She took a ladle of vegetable soup from the pan at the back of the stove and poured it into a small bowl, directed Luc in strapping in the eager baby and tying on his bib, then handed Luc a spoon and provided him with a tea-towel to put in front of him.

'He'll try to grab the spoon,' she warned, 'but I'm not letting him feed himself just yet. Not until he's a bit more co-ordinated.'

It was hard to decide who enjoyed lunchtime more, Jamie or Luc, though by the end of it there was a great deal of soup on the floor, joined by some of the scrambled eggs that followed.

'Piglet!' scolded Emily as she mopped the tray and the rosy face above the bib. 'Though, to be fair, you're not entirely to blame!'

'I could play with him all day,' said Luc ingenuously, grinning at her with an expression so like Jamie's that Emily failed to hang on to her reproving frown.

'Would you like to have a shot at putting him to bed while I cook lunch—or will the nappy defeat you?'

Luc looked startled for a moment, but he bore Jamie off obediently after a few basic instructions.

'If I get nervous at a vital stage I shall yell for help,' he said over his shoulder.

'Don't worry, Luc, I'll come running,' said Emily reassuringly.

He stopped short in the doorway, his face suddenly serious. 'Always, Emily?'

'Don't push your luck,' she said shortly, and turned away. It seemed a very long time before the expected cri de coeur came from upstairs, and Emily sprinted up to find a very smug Luc holding a drowsy baby dressed in pyjama top and a fairly adequately fastened nappy.

'Will that do?' The anxious look on Luc's face made Emily giggle as she handed him plastic pants and pyjama trousers.

'Fantastic!'

They ate lunch at the kitchen table and tacitly avoided any personal matters. They discussed the problem of dinner, and Emily apologised that there was very little in the house she considered suitable for a hungry man without doing some shopping.

'I don't think I should go out myself so soon after the funeral,' she said diffidently, 'but otherwise I shall have to call on Lydia to help me out by fetching some groceries.'

Luc jumped to his feet instantly.

'No problem. Just tell me what you want and where I should go to buy it, and I'll come back and even cook for you as well, if you would like.'

Emily looked at him doubtfully.

'Are you sure? I can hardly believe that you're used to shopping, somehow. Besides, English food's probably a lot different from Brazilian.'

'You will write a list. I will take it to the shop and pay for what I receive. What could be simpler? Where is the nearest town?'

After thinking of the easiest way for Luc to tangle with the intricacies of British shopping Emily sent him into Knowle, a pleasant little town not too far away. Provided with the necessary list and scornfully turning aside Emily's attempt to hand over some money, Luc set off in the Daimler Sovereign he had hired, and she was left in the sudden tomb-like quiet of the empty house. Hurriedly she cleared away and went to have a bath while Jamie was asleep. She had just finished drying her hair when the doorbell rang, and checking to see that Jamie was still out for the count she ran downstairs to admit a Luc laden with plastic carriers.

'That looks like a great deal more than I asked for,' said Emily suspiciously when all the bags and packages were lined up on the table. Luc threw his black leather jacket carelessly on a chair, grinning at her with such a sheepish, guilty look she hadn't the heart to protest as, in quick succession, he produced with the air of a magician taking rabbits from a hat, a potted azalea, a large box of chocolates, a glossy magazine and a bottle of Guerlain's 'Mitsouko'.

'Luc! You were very naughty really—I had no idea you'd go raving mad!'

'There was no insanity involved,' he returned with dignity, his eyes sparkling with pleasure at the expression on her face as she opened the perfume. 'You look like a little girl on Christmas morning.'

'That's more or less the way I feel,' she confessed, then leaned over to kiss his cheek. 'Thank you very much, Luc.'

He tensed beneath her touch, and Emily drew back instantly.

'Do not worry,' he said quizzically. 'I will not step over the barrier you have placed between us.'

'Thank you,' said Emily quietly, then turned to the other bags cluttering the table. 'I must put these things away.'

'Where is Jamie?' asked Luc, springing to his feet.

'Still sleeping—good heavens, it's half past three, he'll never go down again tonight!' Emily groaned.

'I'll get him up.' Luc made for the door.

'No, Luc, wait—he might be nervous if a strange man is there when he wakes up.' Emily hastily caught him by the arm.

He shrugged her restraining hand away.

'Nonsense, Emily, I am his father, after all. He must get used to me.'

A very thoughtful Emily was left in the kitchen to begin preparations for dinner. There was something the matter with her, she decided. Any normal female would be over the moon at the way things had turned out, but it all seemed too easy, too pat. Luc had not stated any intentions to the letter, but it seemed pretty obvious that he thought they could just take up where they had left off. Her eyes troubled, Emily considered this with care, and found that it was not a prospect that pleased. Not that Luc was vile, of course, as the hymn went on to say, but neither he nor she were the same people who had come together for such a brief time eighteen months before.

As she removed the newspaper wrapping from some celery, Emily's eye was caught by the picture above an article on a sheet from the week-old *Daily Clarion*. She smoothed out the newspaper, frowning. The journalese in the tabloid-style

paper was very expressive; quite different from the sober
broadsheet delivered to the Dower House. Perhaps she should
change her order to the newsagent. She folded the paper
automatically and put it in a drawer.

By unspoken consent for the rest of the day both of them
avoided any descent into the personal and contented
themselves with playing with Jamie and seeing to his simple,
easily provided needs. It was dark very early and Luc fetched
in a large supply of logs from the woodshed to make a
substantial blaze which gave the drawing room an air of
warmth and comfort when the rose-shaded lamps were
switched on and the curtains drawn against the chilly March
day that was more like midwinter than the forerunner of
spring. After his prolonged nap earlier on Jamie was less
inclined for bed than usual, and Luc gave him his bath while
Emily prepared the supper. When she went upstairs to put an
end to the noisy, prolonged hi-jinks going on in the bathroom
she found Luc stripped to the waist endeavouring to wrap a
wriggling, excited little boy in a bath towel, both faces flushed
with their exertions.

'I can only hope he'll settle down to sleep after all this
disturbance,' said Emily, casting a cold eye on them both.
'Come along, young man, let's get you into your sleeping suit
and ready for supper.'

Luc surrendered his burden and put his sweater back on.

'He's an energetic little bundle,' he said breathlessly,
'though I repeat, Emily, he must be quite a handful for you to
cope with on your own.'

'I manage,' she said shortly, as he followed her from the
room. 'Some people have a lot more than one to cope with,
after all.'

Some time later, when Jamie was fast asleep and both of
them were seated at the dining table, Luc poured out the wine
purchased that afternoon, and said seriously,

'It's time we had a talk, Emily.'

'Not over dinner,' she said instantly. 'I've taken great pains
with this pork fillet, not to mention the apricot and chili
sauce, so I don't want any tension spoiling my appetite.'

'It was not my intention to upset you in any way,' he said
stiffly, his brows drawn together in a black bar across his

forehead. 'I merely wished to clarify the situation in which we find ourselves.'

'Later,' she insisted, and began to discuss the history of Compton Lacey, giving him details of the old house's occupants down the years. He listened with polite attention, but from his rather tense attitude Emily was well aware that his mind was only half on her words.

Eventually the moment of truth could no longer be postponed. They were settled opposite each other in the drawing room, drinking coffee, before Luc launched into the discussion he had been waiting to start for some time. He looked at Emily, curled up quietly in the corner of the settee, her face washed a pale gold by the leaping flames, and said the last thing she expected to hear.

'I do not like your dress,' he said harshly.

Emily looked down at herself defensively.

'It's not unusual for someone in my position to wear black,' she said distantly. Some perverse instinct had prompted her to wear the dress bought for the funeral.

'I do not need to be reminded that you are another man's widow,' he went on, then broke off abruptly. 'May I have a brandy?'

'Of course. Help yourself.'

The truce was suddenly over. Hostility crackled between them as she refused a liqueur, and Luc sat down again, asking her permission to light a cheroot.

'I want my son, Emily.'

'Quite possibly.' Her breathing quickened, but her voice was calm and cold. 'However, he is *my* son first and foremost. Your part in his existence was minimal.'

Luc's eyes narrowed through the smoke curling up in front of him.

'Nevertheless, I want Jamie. The obvious course is for you to marry me and come back to Campo d'Ouro as soon as possible. After all, there is nothing to keep you here in Compton Lacey any more. Very soon, presumably, you will not even have this house.'

Emily's head lifted proudly.

'I don't intend to live in Compton Lacey. I'm going to buy a house somewhere else, possibly further north, and bring

Jamie up away from this area.'

Luc sprang to his feet, his eyes glittering like jet in his fury.

'What are you saying? What is to keep you from marrying me? And why should you want to move away from here? *Deus*—if you are not to stay here then what is to prevent you coming to Brazil?'

'The simple reason that I don't want to!' Emily glared back at him.

He sank down on the sofa, staring at her in disbelief.

'Emily,' he said, slowly and distinctly, his accent more pronounced in his agitation, 'I am offering you a life in a beautiful house, where the climate is very good, where Jamie can have everything he wishes, and where he will be my heir.'

'Very tempting. But no, thanks.'

'*Deus me livre!* Why not? What is your objection?'

Emily raised her chin.

'What precisely is to be my part in all this?'

He closed his eyes as though summoning the last of his patience.

'I thought I had made myself clear,' he said wearily. 'I want you for my wife. I can give you security, even wealth to a moderate degree. You will want for nothing. Now I have seen you again I realise how very suitable you will be. You are poised and adult now, attractive, a very good mother—what more could a man wish?'

'I'm afraid I'm not concerned with how I fit into your specifications,' said Emily, looking him squarely in the eye. 'I don't want to leave this country.'

'But, woman, you know I cannot leave Campo d'Ouro—my livelihood is there——'

'I'm not asking you to,' she interrupted. 'I don't think joining our lives together now is a good idea.'

Luc stared at her in blank incomprehension.

'Why, Emily, why?'

She hesitated, then sighed.

'I don't love you, Luc.'

CHAPTER SEVEN

FOR several minutes the only sounds in the room were the spurt and crackle of the flames and the ticking of the grandmother clock in the corner. Eventually Luc got up and helped himself to another cognac, gazing down into it morosely for some time before he put the glass to his lips and drank the contents in one swallow.

He returned to the sofa, legs stretched before him, his eyes on her face in brooding fixation, which made Emily inwardly restive, though outwardly she remained composed, sitting quietly with one sheer black-clad ankle crossed over the other, her small hands folded in her lap, her head turned to gaze into the fire.

'Do you mean that, Emily?' he said quietly after an unbearably long interval.

'Yes. I'm sorry if it's hurtful, but on an important issue like this I think one can only deal in the truth.'

'But you loved me once?'

She nodded.

'But you were the knight in shining armour who came and swept me off my feet. How could I not imagine myself in love with you?' Emily's eyes were candid as she tried to explain logically. 'But all the other emotion I felt afterwards, the bleak disappointment, the hurt, the panic when I knew I was pregnant, the gratitude I felt for Marcus, then the grief, and of course my love for Jamie. Such a long list, Luc, that I think it used up everything I'd felt for you.'

He flinched and raked his hand through his hair until it was a wild, curling tangle above his colourless face.

'Very well,' he said curtly, 'I accept that. But why must you take Jamie away from here? Is it that you wish to conceal him from me?'

'Oh no!' Emily leaned forward urgently. 'I shan't stop you visiting him, Luc, if that's what you want.' She stopped for a moment, then went on resolutely, 'I told you that when

Marcus and I returned to Compton Lacey after a fortnight in London we announced that we'd been married there. This was sheer falsehood. Marcus was set on marrying me, but I felt it was neither fitting nor possible.'

Luc jerked bolt upright, staring at her.

'You mean . . .?'

'Yes,' said Emily levelly. 'To all intents and purposes Marcus made everyone believe I was his wife. The only person who knows I'm not is the family solicitor. I had enough knowledge about the family to know that if I presented Marcus with an heir the complications would have been endless. As it is, everyone believes that the bequest to the National Trust was irreversible and I'm more or less obliged to seek a new home. And I'm going to live somewhere else where I'm going to be Mrs Harper and her son James. It's on his birth certificate. James Marcus Harper.'

Luc sat like a statue, his face blank and cold. Emily waited a moment then rose to her feet.

'I'll make more coffee, Luc. Do have another cognac—you look as though you need it.'

Out in the kitchen as she waited for the percolator, Emily's heartbeat began to slow down to normal. Underneath her outward calm she had been terrified of the effect on him of her disclosure. Poor man! He had obviously taken a body blow, but she was very certain of one thing. No way was she willing to trail meekly off to Brazil just because Luc wanted his son. Unreasonable, childish, Emily admitted it all to herself as she carried the coffee tray back to the drawing room, nevertheless a quiet little cottage near a good school somewhere was infinitely more tempting than some mountain fastness in the wilds of Brazil.

Luc was on his feet to relieve her of the tray, and she examined his face in trepidation, but he seemed to have recovered somewhat, and sat opposite her with a reasonably civil expression on his dark face while she filled their cups.

'If you were not married to Marcus Lacey,' he began, 'why will you not come with me? Surely you cannot wish Jamie to grow up with the stigma of illegitimacy. God!' Suddenly he banged one fist into the other, his anger at flashpoint again. 'My son a bastard! You felt it was neither "fitting" nor "possible" to let Marcus Lacey father my son; I agree. But neither is it "fitting" nor "possible" for you to bring him up alone.'

'Don't be so old-fashioned, Luc. There are plenty of one-parent families these days.'

'But those families don't have any choice!' he almost shouted. 'I am offering you my name, my home, a proper background for our son.'

'And that's what it boils down to, Luc. Tell me the truth.' Emily stood up to face him, hands on hips. 'You haven't really come all this way to see me. I think you suspected all along that this child just might have been yours, ever since you knew of his birth. While Marcus was alive there was nothing you could do about it, but once he was dead it was different.'

'I admit that it all seemed a little suspect to me—the hasty marriage, the premature birth. It all fitted in with what might be possible.' Luc ground his teeth impotently. 'I *wanted* it to be true; prayed that it was. When I followed you upstairs last night I cannot find words to describe how I felt at my first sight of Jamie. He is the living image of a photograph Thurza has of me at the same age.'

'Thurza?'

'My grandmother. I have always called her by her name,' he said impatiently. He poured himself a generous tot of brandy. 'Please sit down so that I may also do so.'

My God, thought Emily, with a wild desire to laugh, never mind the fact that we're in the middle of a blazing row, we must preserve our tribal rules and customs to the last letter.

'I think I'll change my mind,' she said. 'Perhaps you would please pour me a glass of Grand Marnier.'

'*Pois é.*' Watching his tall, graceful figure as he measured out a far larger quantity of liqueur than she normally permitted herself, Emily braced herself for further skirmishes, the warmth of the fire making her a little flushed above the uncompromising black of the high-necked wool crêpe dress. Luc strolled back slowly and handed her the glass, and with a faint feeling of alarm Emily realised his hand was the slightest bit unsteady as she took the drink from him.

'I am amazed,' he said, scowling at her. 'What can I say to make you change your mind?'

'The truth?' suggested Emily.

'What do you mean!' His eyes narrowed.

'Wait a moment.' She rose and went out of the room, returning almost immediately with a piece of crumpled newspaper. Luc took it from her gingerly, his face growing grim as he read it.

The photograph above the piece was a little blurred, but the headline below it left no room for doubt. 'Attractive young gold magnate arrives to address Anglo-Brazilian Society at banquet'. The date of the paper was two days before Marcus's death.

'So you came especially to see me,' said Emily quietly.

His eyes dropped before her limpid blue look, and he moved restlessly.

'Very well, I embroidered things a little. Would it help to know that I contacted Mrs Crawford as soon as I arrived in this country?'

'Not really. However, I now see how you knew about Marcus so quickly.' She drank her liqueur in one draught recklessly and set the glass down with a click on the silver gallery tray. 'Do you know why I feel so—unenthusiastic?'

He shook his head bleakly.

'I loathe the feeling that I've been watched, that you were receiving information about me as though I were some sort of criminal. Can't you see, Luc? If I'd known you were alive it would all have been so different. Yes, yes, I would have been upset, but at the same time I would have known that you cared. Even if we had had no direct communication I could have been rid of that awful uncertainty about you that hung over me until you appeared two days ago. It would have altered nothing as far as poor Marcus was concerned, but at least I would have felt a little less like a cheap, casual push-over who'd been taken for a night and immediately forgotten.'

'*Deus*, Emily!' Luc sprang to his feet, glowering at her, his eyes like two coals glowing in his livid face. 'How could I communicate with another man's wife?'

'The same way you did all along,' spat Emily, 'but Lydia could have been allowed to tell me—oh, what's the use!' She flung away, her head on her hands, and tried in vain to hold back the tears.

Luc's face convulsed with pain and he knelt beside her, touching her shoulder gently.

'Do not cry, Emily!'

Emily shrugged his hand away violently, ignoring the torrent streaming down her cheeks.

'I'm not crying!' she said fiercely, then looked up sharply in dismay as a familiar sound came from upstairs. 'Oh God, Jamie, and I'm crying! Have you a handkerchief—he's never seen me cry—I mustn't upset him——'

'Stay here,' said Luc gently. 'I shall go to him. If it is something I cannot manage I will call you.'

Emily sat tense, rubbing her face fiercely with Luc's handkerchief, listening for his call, but none came. Wearily she went to the dining room and cleared the table, an intermittent sob still shaking her and her head aching from emotion and wine as she began to wash up. Suddenly too lacklustre even to worry whether Luc was coping with Jamie, she doggedly washed and dried plates, careless of the delicate dinner service that was now National Trust property. She was storing them away in the sideboard when Luc came downstairs to find her.

'What was the matter?' she asked dully.

'I changed his nappy and gave him some orange juice. Was that correct?' Luc looked at her face with concern. 'I think he really wanted to play, but I resisted that smile and settled him down. Are you all right, Emily?'

'Just tired,' she said wearily. 'I've had very little sleep for some time now.'

'Come into the other room for a nightcap,' he said persuasively, 'then I must go. It is late.'

Emily complied docilely, accepting another glass of Grand Marnier, too listless to raise any objection when Luc sat beside her, glass of cognac in one hand, her own cold hand in the other. She stared mutely into the dying fire, a random sob still catching her occasionally. They sat in a not un-companionable silence, each one lost in thought as the fire died away, and the levels in both bottles of spirit grew decidedly lower.

'Must go to bed,' muttered Emily eventually, realising with vague surprise that her head was on Luc's shoulder, and sitting up muzzily.

He made no answer, getting slowly to his feet. Emily was in no fit state to register the unnerving fact that Luc was not entirely steady on his feet, not even to protest when he picked her up in his arms, turned out the lights and slowly mounted the stairs. Luc looked round him as he reached the landing, then made for the open door nearest Jamie's, and laid his somnolent burden on the bed without troubling to switch on the light.

Almost asleep, Emily was hardly aware of hands that slowly undressed her and slid her between the sheets. She flinched a little as her bare skin came into contact with cold linen, then she gave a little sigh and relaxed into deep, sweet oblivion.

At some time during the night she came near enough to consciousness to be aware of a long, hard bare body pressed close to hers. She opened her mouth to protest, but was silenced by the mouth that covered it instantly, any rebellion her body might have attempted instantly quelled by hands that restrained, then caressed, then moved over it in gentle, ceaseless, cumulative pleasure that moulded the lifeless clay of her body into a warm, willing vessel fashioned to receive the rushing, molten, surging tribute of the body that engulfed and encompassed her own. Gasping, fulfilled, she subsided helplessly back into blessed sleep once more, locked in the warmth of arms that refused to loose their hold.

'Emily, is there anything wrong—Oh, my God!'

The door closed with a thud, and Emily sat bolt upright in bed, blinking like an owl. She looked down at her nudity aghast, then at the brown back of the man who lay fast asleep beside her, his face buried in the pillow.

She tore out of bed, making little moaning noises of horror, threw on her dressing gown, vainly smoothing back the tangled mess of her hair.

Jamie! Emily closed the bedroom door firmly behind her and flew into her son's room to find him still fast asleep in his cot, neatly tucked up beneath the coverlet. She ran down the stairs and into the kitchen to find Lydia filling a kettle.

'Lydia!'

The other woman spun round, her face a picture of mingled remorse, laughter and embarrassment.

'What can I say, Emily! I do apologise. I called round before work to see what I could do for you, and the back door was unlocked, no Jamie in evidence—I thought perhaps you were ill.' She screwed up her eyes in repentance. 'I'm so used to barging into people's bedrooms unannounced I just didn't think.'

'Why should you?' Emily groaned and collapsed into a chair at the kitchen table, head in hands. 'You'd hardly expect to find anyone in mine, after all. Oh, my head!'

Lydia made a large pot of tea, then stirred the embers in the stove and set the fire to draw.

'I came along the back lane, otherwise I would have seen his car, I presume, and avoided embarrassing you like that,' she said ruefully.

'It really doesn't matter, Lydia,' said Emily apathetically.

'You seem to have settled your differences fairly quickly, anyway!' Lydia's eyes twinkled naughtily.

'But we haven't—I didn't—oh, God, how can I explain——' Emily wailed.

'You don't have to explain anything to me, pet. It's your business entirely.' Lydia poured out two mugs of fragrant tea and sat down opposite.

Emily opened one eye.

'Come off it, Lydia, you and Luc have been pen-pals all along, so you can hardly start playing the disinterested bystander! Mmm, what heavenly tea; my head is splitting.'

'At the risk of appearing nosy, what on earth did you get up to last night? And how come Jamie is still fast asleep at eight in the morning?'

'He had such excitement yesterday he didn't settle down properly last night. Luc and I had rather a rich dinner—he went shopping—with a large bottle of wine, followed by a flaming row and a great deal too much Grand Marnier on my part—ugh!—and cognac on Luc's. As for the rest of the night's events, I can only plead diminished responsibility, m'lud. I don't know why I'm joking—I feel ghastly!'

Lydia stifled her amusement with difficulty.

'I take it Luc has seen Jamie, then?'

'Oh yes; mutual love at first sight. They're besotted with each other.' Emily turned a mutinous look on Lydia. 'He tried to make out he came to England just to see me.'

'Can't blame him, love!'

'No. But I feel very bitter about what I can only consider as an infringement on my personal privacy. Don't be upset—I'm not blaming you, only Luc. And I deeply resent the fact that he thought he could just walk in and commandeer us both as if we were items on a supermarket shelf! Besides, you know what I'd planned, Lydia.' Emily looked at the older woman in appeal.

'Hardly much of a comparison for Jamie, though, is it?' said Lydia unanswerably. She searched in her bag and produced a couple of tablets. 'Here, take these. You'll feel better. Luc *is* offering marriage, I presume?'

'Oh yes.' Emily swallowed the pills obediently. 'One look at his son and you could see the covetous light in his eye, and unwelcome though the idea is to me, he feels he has to take me along with the package deal.'

'Oh, Em, come on!'

'I object to being played along like a fish. Anyway, I found out he was already in London, socialising, when Marcus died. You telephoned him at his hotel, I presume?'

Lydia nodded guiltily.

'Why couldn't you have told me, Lydia?' asked Emily sadly. 'It would have made life so much more acceptable for me.'

'Oh, darling, I'm deeply sorry, but I agreed with Luc that it would be infinitely harder for you. We just didn't understand.' Lydia coughed delicately. 'If—er—if things weren't very cordial last night how did—well, I mean——'

'How did we end up in the hay?' said Emily baldly.

'Emily!'

'I had too much to drink and fell asleep on his shoulder after we'd simmered down a bit. He must have taken me to bed and undressed me. I was out for the count, anyway. I half woke up in the night and he was in bed with me, and—well, I don't have to draw pictures, do I?' Emily stopped dead, her eyes on Lydia's in horror. 'Oh, Lydia—oh no! It was only once last time and that was it! Jamie. What if—Oh God, not twice!' She buried her head in her hands in despair.

'Have some more tea. I'll put the kettle on again.'

Both women swung round as a deep voice spoke from the doorway.

'What a good idea. We are both very hungry.'

Luc stood watching them, a slight smile on his face, wearing only his black cords, his beaming son in his arms in all the glory of white sweater and red velveteen dungarees.

'You've dressed him!' Emily stood up unsteadily, trying to smile at Jamie, while Lydia looked from father to son and whistled softly as she sat down abruptly.

'Oh dear, oh dear,' she said slowly. 'I don't think you should let anyone see those two together if you want to keep your affairs private, Emily. Talk about a chip off the old block!'

'Good morning, Mrs Crawford,' said Luc, surrendering his son to Emily. 'A "chip off the old block"—what is that?'

'It means Jamie looks just like you,' said Emily impatiently, inserting the baby in his highchair.

'What about Mrs Giles?' asked Lydia. 'Doesn't she come in today?'

Emily groaned and rounded on Luc.

'You must get out of here. She'll be here in an hour. And if she sees you we might just as well put an announcement in the paper.'

'And what is wrong with my being here——' Luc began stormily, but Lydia interrupted soothingly.

'Why don't I call in at her place now on my way to the clinic, and tell her you don't need her for a day or two? You can ring her when you want her.'

'That would be a great help, Lydia, thank you.' Emily smiled, wincing as it aggravated the throbbing in her head. 'I'd rather be on my own for a bit. All right, young man, I shan't be long.'

Lydia made her farewells, leaving a strained silence behind her.

'Right,' said Emily purposefully. 'Porridge and a poached egg for Jamie. How about you?' She studiously avoided Luc's eye, busying herself at the stove.

'What are you having?' He sat at the corner of the table,

one leg swinging, his eyes on what he could see of her averted face.

'Just coffee.'

'That's not enough. I shall make us some omelettes.' Luc sprang to his feet, caressing Jamie's cheek as he passed.

Emily closed her eyes and swallowed, nauseated at the mere thought.

'No, thank you,' she said hurriedly. 'I'll have a—a piece of toast. Perhaps you'd care to feed Jamie his oatmeal while I do his poached egg.'

'Of course.' Luc accepted the small bowl from her and began to spoon porridge into the eager mouth impatient to receive it. 'Not so fast, *filinho*, one mouthful at a time. Is he always as hungry as this?'

'Mostly. He's late this morning. He overslept.'

'We all did.' Luc grinned unrepentantly at the wave of colour that washed over Emily's face.

She resisted the impulse to throw something at him and carefully cut fingers of bread and butter to accompany Jamie's egg, handing Luc the plate and retrieving the porridge bowl.

'If you'd cope with this I'll just dash upstairs and brush my hair while the coffee perks.' Emily looked at his bare chest with dislike as she passed. 'Shall I bring down your sweater?'

He smiled in obvious enjoyment of her disapproval.

'Does the sight of my bare chest offend you?'

'Now that you mention it, yes!' Emily flounced out of the room and retired upstairs to the bathroom for a sketchy wash and a vigorous brushing of teeth, noting with affront that Luc had obviously borrowed her toothbrush earlier.

And why not, she thought bitterly, he's had the use of practically everything else!

When she returned to the kitchen a few minutes later, neat in caramel cord jeans and matching sleeveless sweater over a black wool shirt, Luc had washed up his son's breakfast things and Jamie was contentedly pushing a solid little wooden engine round the tray of his highchair.

'Where did he get that?' Emily pointedly handed Luc his sweater.

'I bought it yesterday.' He pulled the sweater over his head, his face emerging dark and smiling at her pained expression. 'What's the matter, *carinha*?'

'Don't call me that!' she snapped viciously, then put a hand to her head. 'I'm sorry, but I think I must be experiencing my first hangover. I feel terrible!'

He pushed her gently into a chair.

'Sit down and I'll make breakfast. What should I do with Jamie?'

'Leave him where he is for the moment.'

Emily sat, her head throbbing, while Luc made toast and laid the table with the yellow pottery mugs and plates Emily used in the kitchen. She knew she ought to be feeling outraged and indignant, but it seemed like too much effort. The new engine clattered to the floor and Jamie pointed to it imperiously.

'Mum—mum!'

'Let your mother sit quietly,' Luc told him firmly, retrieving the engine himself. Jamie beamed happily at him, Emily noted with resentment. She looked glumly at the slice of toast on her plate.

'You will feel better if you eat,' said Luc, in much the same tone of voice that he'd used to Jamie.

Emily sighed, but it was less effort to munch the toast than to argue, and after the first cup of coffee went down she actually did feel better.

Luc sat opposite her and they both ate in silence while Jamie patiently pushed his engine from one side of his tray to the other.

'Better now?' Luc asked softly.

'Yes, thank you.'

'You are angry?'

'Angry?'

'You must surely remember last night? If only because I was in your bed when you woke up!'

A quick rush of colour burned in Emily's cheeks and she bent her head, a great lump rising in her throat. She dropped her piece of toast on her plate and stumbled blindly from the room, running upstairs to cast herself down on the rumpled bed, which still seemed warm from the heat of their bodies.

How could she have allowed such a witless thing to

happen? You were a tiny bit smashed, said a hateful inner voice. Even so. It was disgusting to give in without a murmur, even allowing for the fact that she was half asleep. Her instincts ought to have reared up and made her fight tooth and nail, but they must have been drowned in a sea of Grand Marnier. A great shudder ran through her, and she sobbed harder than ever until she was hauled up to rest against a wool-covered shoulder, while Luc stroked her and whispered unintelligible comfort into her ear.

'*Coitadinha, faz isso não!*' He rocked her gently until her sobs began to lessen.

'Where's Jamie?' she asked, sniffing.

'I put his pen up in the kitchen. He's still playing with his train.' Luc tilted her face up to his. 'Was it so terrible an experience?'

'That's not the point.' Emily pulled away from him. 'It's not the point at all. Why on earth did you do it?'

Luc cast his eyes heavenwards.

'You need to ask such a question? I am a man.'

'I had noticed.'

'Than you must make allowances for the baser side of my nature.' He gave an exasperated sigh. 'I did not mean to sleep with you, but after drinking too much of that excellent but potent cognac, I was not fit to drive. When I put you to bed suddenly I could keep my eyes open no longer and I just slid in beside you, then pssst, I knew no more until I became conscious of a delectable little body wriggling against mine somewhere in the small hours. I could no more have resisted what followed than tried to stop breathing.'

Emily got up decisively.

'This doesn't alter anything, you know.' She looked at him militantly. 'I shan't alter my plans.'

'Very well.' He got up unhurriedly and went from the room, leaving Emily to trail behind feeling decidedly deflated.

Luc collected his leather jacket and went to the kitchen to plant a kiss on Jamie's cheek.

'Bye-bye, Jamie.' He turned formally to Emily, raised her hand and kissed it. 'Goodbye, Emily.'

'Goodbye,' she said faintly, then saw him to the door, watching the long car out of sight.

Closing the door with an irritable bang, she returned to the kitchen, flopped down in the carver chair at the head of the table and sat looking at her son blankly.

'Mum-mum,' he said, beaming at her as usual.

For once the smile failed to strike its usual chord.

'I'll have to teach you a new word,' she said huskily.

The little boy shuffled on his bottom to the side of the playpen, looked at the bars, then, frowning furiously, he pulled himself upright, grinning at her in triumph as he stood unsteadily upright for the first time.

'Oh, my lovely boy,' said Emily, a catch in her voice. 'What a cleversticks!'

Jamie wavered on his feet, looking towards the open doorway.

'Da—da?' he said questioningly, then sat down abruptly, a look of such comic surprise on his face Emily had to laugh in spite of the lump in her throat.

'Well, my lad, you're learning quickly all of a sudden,' she said ruefully. 'Da—da, indeed!'

CHAPTER EIGHT

SUCH a feeling of anti-climax swamped Emily for the rest of the day that she was hard put to it to keep even moderately cheerful for Jamie's benefit. She took him out in his pushchair later in the morning, but the park was enveloped in chill damp mist after only a short walk, and she was glad to get indoors and light the fire in the drawing room. While Jamie was having his nap Emily doggedly worked her way through a pile of ironing, trying to map out her next course of action. She was a little stymied by Luc's sudden volte-face. The last thing she had expected was Luc's abrupt departure like that, without any further persuasion. Her face flamed. Perhaps he had changed his mind after sleeping with her—possibly she had been tried and found wanting. She tossed her head angrily. It hardly mattered, after all, as there was no likelihood of the incident recurring. She didn't *want* to marry Luc, and the thought of uprooting herself to go to Brazil filled her with antipathy. Suddenly she sat down, thoroughly depressed. The thought of uprooting herself to move anywhere else at all was giving her nightmares. Oh, Marcus, she thought despairingly, what ought I to do?

She jumped up as the phone rang, annoyed with her own disappointment when the caller proved to be Lydia.

'Everything all right, Emily? Just thought I'd check.'

'Oh yes, just fine.' She gave a forced little laugh. 'I told Luc he was wasting his time, so he just went.'

'Oh, Emily—and here was I thinking it was happy-ever-after time!' Lydia was obviously distressed. 'Look, love, shall I pop in for an hour this evening? I don't like to think of you alone up there.'

'No, it's all right, thanks. I thought I'd get an early night. I'll see you tomorrow, perhaps.'

The afternoon seemed interminable, and for once Jamie was fretful and disinclined to amuse himself. Twice the phone rang, and each time it was someone offering condolences. Emily was thoroughly out of sorts by the time Jamie had eaten his evening meal and the bathtime ritual had been observed. All the attention given him the day before had had a considerable effect, and it was much later than usual before he finally consented to sleep. Emily decided to get into her dressing gown and have her supper on a tray by the fire with a book. There had been precious little time for reading lately, so she would enjoy what was an unaccustomed luxury. She made herself concentrate on a novel set in the time of Henry II, or Fitzempress, as the book called him, ate the cheese sandwich and drank her coffee absentmindedly, her mind switched off from her personal problems for the first time in days.

The doorbell cut through her absorption and she jumped nervously to her feet, looking at the ormolu clock on the mantelshelf. Nine-thirty was a bit late for Lydia. The bell rang again as Emily crossed the hall, then she heard Luc's voice faintly through the door.

'It is I, Emily.'

She drew back the heavy bolts and opened the door to let him in, though with some reluctance. He brushed past her into the hall, taking off his trenchcoat and shaking it, his hair glistening with rain.

'It's a little late for calling,' said Emily coldly. 'You might have rung first to ask if it were convenient.'

'You would have refused to see me, I think.'

Emily bit her lip. All day, ever since his departure, she had hoped he would come back. Now he was here all she could feel was animosity. What was the matter with her? she thought irritably.

'You'd better come in by the fire,' she said ungraciously, tightening the wide satin girdle of her dressing gown. 'I'm afraid I'm not dressed for receiving visitors.'

She led the way to the drawing room and sat down, pulling the folds of the pale blue robe securely over her knees. Luc smiled and seated himself opposite.

'You look charming. The colour is just a little lighter than your eyes.' He looked at the open book beside her and the tray on the table with the remains of her supper. 'Is that all you had for dinner?'

'It was what I wanted.'

'You do not eat enough.'

'Fascinating though the subject may be,' said Emily sarcastically, 'I am sure you didn't come here to discuss my eating habits.'

'No, you are right, I did not.' Luc leaned back and fumbled in his pocket for a cheroot. 'With your permission?'

Emily nodded impatiently.

'How is Jamie?' Luc lit the cheroot, inhaling deeply as he settled himself more comfortably.

'He's been thoroughly disagreeable. All the attention and fuss he enjoyed yesterday must have gone to his head. I was expected to dance to his bidding all day. For once I was heartily glad to get him finally settled down!'

Luc laughed. 'I apologise for disturbing him.'

Emily shrugged indifferently. 'He'll be back to normal tomorrow.'

'Emily, I have left you to yourself today to give you time to think. Have you done so?'

She laughed shortly.

'What do you imagine? My mind has been somewhat agitated, as you might expect, but it isn't changed in any way, if that's what you mean.'

Luc sighed. 'I had hoped you would have become more reconciled to my proposal.'

'Sorry.' Emily was immovable. 'I don't want to be your wife, and I don't want to go to Brazil. I just want to find somewhere quiet where no one knows me and where Jamie and I can live in peace.'

Luc leaned forward, his brows in the familiar black frown.

'For "peace" don't you mean isolation, Emily, and might not "quiet" turn out to be loneliness?'

Emily drew her breath in sharply.

'I will just have to take that chance,' she said stubbornly. 'I must go away from here—indeed it's better that I leave. This place is full of painful memories now.'

'Then marry me and come home with me,' he said promptly.

'No, I won't! I don't want to marry you. I don't want to marry anyone!' Emily's voice cracked. 'I just want to live in peace with my son.'

'*Our* son, Emily,' he said inexorably, his eyes glittering. 'I will take you to court for him if necessary.'

Emily froze, her heart hammering.

'You couldn't do that,' she whispered, her eyes enormous on his implacable face.

'You think not?' Luc sat back and crossed his legs, smiling faintly.

'But no court would give you custody. As far as the world is concerned I'm Mrs Marcus Lacey. Jamie is Marcus's son.' Emily felt sick.

'But he is not. You told me yourself that the birth certificate gives his name as Harper; the family solicitor could be called as witness—no possibility of perjury or collusion there. Then there is the undeniable likeness of Jamie to myself.' Luc's face was hatefully smug.

Emily sprang to her feet and stood over him.

'You'd never win,' she said passionately. 'No court in the country would let you take Jamie away from me. I'm his mother.'

'And I am his father. I am offering you marriage and Jamie the security of my name, a home and an eventual inheritance of some magnitude.' He sat looking up at her, all quiet reason. 'I might not win, Emily, but think of the publicity such an emotional case would attract. Imagine newspaper pictures of Jamie and me together. I might lose the case, granted. But the possibility of your quiet life in some rustic Utopia would have dramatically diminished, I think.'

'You bastard,' said Emily quietly.

'That is what you insist on making my son, Emily. My own birth was above reproach.'

Wounded beyond reason by this last sally, Emily was unable to stay in the room with Luc a moment longer. She seized the tray and stormed out to the kitchen. In the grip of an anger so great she shook from head to foot she set up the percolator with trembling fingers. So this was why he had left her so meekly this morning! This had been his intention ever since last night, when her idiotic confession had handed him all the trump cards in the pack. And after all that he had slept with her, made love to her, and for all she knew made her pregnant again. What kind of defence would she have if any court knew about that? Emily shuddered. The tabloids would have a field day!

When she was calmer she went back to the drawing room with the coffee tray, which Luc sprang to take from her. He looked at her warily as he set it down. Emily refused to meet his eye and began to pour coffee, as composed outwardly as though this were one of the charity coffee mornings in aid of the church.

'Very well,' she said conversationally, holding out a cup. 'You win. I could never cope with the type of distasteful notoriety such a court case would give. It would be beyond me to subject an innocent child to such a traumatic experience. Victory is yours, Senhor Fonseca.'

Luc's eyes narrowed.

'Do you mean that, Emily?'

'It's hardly a subject for levity,' she said distastefully.

'Then you will marry me?'

'Yes.'

'And you are reconciled to coming with me to Brazil?' Now that Emily had capitulated Luc's implacability had gone, and he looked at her with concern.

'No,' said Emily flatly, 'I am *not* reconciled to it. I dislike the thought of a strange house in a foreign country, where presumably my company will consist of a husband I don't want, and your grandmother, who will no doubt be somewhat suspicious of your wife when she's in possession of a son already nine months old. You expect me to relish the prospect? However, you've made any other course impossible for me.' She rose to her feet with dignity. 'I think you should leave now. You may return some time tomorrow to make whatever arrangements are necessary.'

Luc got up instantly, looking down into the pale, proud little face with something like admiration in his eyes.

'Of course; you must be tired. I will return in the morning.'

'Not too early, if you don't mind,' said Emily, unsmiling. 'I would like to make one or two things clear. You've made your position quite plain, so perhaps you will bear with me if I make one or two trivial conditions?'

'What are they?' he demanded, instantly suspicious.

'I will marry you, as you wish, and come and live with you in Brazil, thus allowing you to attain your goal—Jamie. However, the only capacity in which I'm prepared to function is as Jamie's mother. For anything else, Luc Fonseca, you'll just have to whistle—though I don't suppose you know what that means?'

'I think I understand the general meaning, Emily.' He smiled frostily. 'Jamie's mother, but not my wife.'

'Oh, I didn't say that,' said Emily ingenuously.

Luc raised an eyebrow.

'What, then?'

'I'll play hostess, housekeeper—even cook, if you wish. But I won't sleep with you.'

'In that case,' he said coolly, 'you are more or less superfluous. My grandmother has been hostess at Casa d'Ouro for many years, I have several servants, including an excellent cook. But as I realise I cannot have Jamie without having you too, I shall just have to make the best of things. Goodnight, Emily.'

CHAPTER NINE

IN a shorter time than Emily would have thought possible the dreaded day had arrived and she sat in the Pan-Am V.I.P. lounge of Heathrow Terminal Three, waiting for the flight to be called for Rio de Janeiro. For the moment she sat alone, an untasted cup of coffee on the small table at her side, unopened glossy magazines in her lap, her eyes fixed unseeingly on her new Kurt Geiger sandals that matched so perfectly the beige knitted silk coat thrown down on the seat beside her. Luc was roaming around with Jamie in his arms, keeping him amused until the time came to board the plane. Emily wished it never would. She was ill at ease at all the discreet attention shown her, and had refused various offers of refreshments and drinks, wanting only to sit alone in her misery.

Perhaps if she closed her eyes for a while all this would disappear and she would wake up in the Dower House, plain Emily Harper again. She knew very well, really, that nothing could alter the fact that a special licence had made it possible to transform her into Emily Fonseca in an amazingly short time. The Dower House had been vacated, painful farewells made to Lydia; Emily's whole life turned upside down. The past three days had been spent in London, where Luc had insisted on looking after Jamie while Emily bought some clothes. Brushing aside her objections that she had enough, he had given precise instructions as to what would be suitable and ignored her protests that Marcus had provided her with sufficient clothes already. Submitting, after several clashes of will, she had followed his instructions with a reckless extravagance intended to dent his bank balance. Her eyes followed his tall figure, elegant in brown and black striped jacket and brown trousers, worn with a cream shirt and fawn silk tie. Emily looked at him dispassionately. Very, very attractive, no doubt; and he was her husband, unbelievably, though this fact had failed to sink in yet. The antique keeper Marcus had given her had been replaced by a plain wide gold ring which looked oddly stark on her slim finger. It weighed heavy, like a fetter. She sighed, and craned her neck to see Jamie, in the crook of his father's arm, attracting not a little attention from a group of cooing, elegant ladies. Dressed in a smart yellow cotton jumpsuit, he looked particularly adorable. It was to be hoped he would be good on the plane. Oh lord, the plane! thought Emily, her eyes down on her shoes again, her heart right down there with them. It was immature to be so uptight. She was quite normal, heaps of people were afraid of flying, she was by no means the only one. But did everyone else feel as if all the blood was draining from their bodies, the ice in the stomach and the teeth that would have chattered like castanets but for the fact that her jaw was too tightly clenched together with tension to give them the chance.

'Surely you are not asleep, Emily?'

Her eyes opened guiltily, to see her husband and son in front of her.

'No, of course not; just relaxing for a moment.'

'Relaxing! You look as though every part of you is tied up in little knots.'

Luc's smile was teasing, then his voice changed as he saw how white she was.

'Are you not well, Emily? No, Jamie, you may not go to your mother just now. Stay with me.'

Jamie looked crestfallen and laid his head on his father's shoulder, his thumb in his mouth.

Emily smiled with stiff lips.

'Jamie must be a bit confused with all this upheaval.'

'He will be fine. You are the one who's giving concern. What is it, Emily? Do you feel ill?'

'Luc, I'm terrified!' It burst from her.

'Terrified? How is that?'

'Of flying,' she said desperately. 'I've never flown before.'

'Ah, I see.' He shifted Jamie a little and took her cold hand in his warm one. 'There is nothing to fear, I promise—try to relax. It will be just like sitting in a comfortable armchair, and much less dangerous than trying to cross a busy street. Look at Jamie, he's not a bit worried.'

'Blissful ignorance,' said Emily ruefully, then started violently as a flood of Portuguese came through the tannoy, followed by a cool English voice calling Varig passengers for the Rio flight. Glad in one way that the waiting was over, Emily picked up handbag and coat, smoothed down the skirt of her brown linen dress and received Jamie in her arms, leaving Luc to follow with the hand luggage. Once on the plane the first-class section surprised her with the luxury and space of its accommodation, and some of her panic at take-off was lessened by her interest in the surroundings, and all the attentive care given by the air hostesses, who, without exception, were dark, glamorous and looked like entrants for the Miss World contest.

It was only when the plane was actually airborne, and Emily began to believe that possibly it actually might not plummet straight down again, that she was able to relax just a little. Jamie was fast asleep on her shoulder, and despite Luc's desire to detach him from her, something in the warmth of the small body against hers gave her comfort. Fear shortly gave way to boredom, and she was glad when Jamie woke up with his usual 'Mum—mum' and seraphic smile for her. As she shifted him to her knee he saw Luc and held out his arms.

'Da—da,' he said quite distinctly, and Emily could see a pulse throb at the corner of Luc's mouth as he heaved the little boy over into his lap, where the intricacies of the seat-belt kept him occupied for a while.

Luc's eyes met hers.

'He learns quickly,' he said softly, his hand stroking the black curls.

Emily nodded silently, feeling oddly forlorn.

The plane landed at Lisbon for an hour for refuelling, and when it took off again Emily was slightly less petrified this time. There was a tempting dinner and a film she had always wanted to see, but the hours passed slowly, despite all the attention given to her, the stewardesses so charmed with her son—and possibly her husband—that one was always discreetly on hand to take over for Emily to eat the delicious food served to her, or visit the washroom. In answer to her shy request they brought her tea instead of coffee in an effort to woo sleep, but Emily found this impossible, and was glad when the interminable journey was over and it was time to land.

Her impressions of Rio were confused. After the first breathtaking glimpses of the Corcovado, the great mountain-top figure of Christ, and the Paõ de Açucar, the conical mountain with cable cars for access to its summit, the plane came in low over the island-studded blue waters of Guanabara Bay in the early morning sunlight. They had arrived. They were through the hassle of Customs and baggage in a remarkably short time, its brevity due in part to Jamie, who was a tremendous asset, the Brazilian nation en masse seeming to idolise babies.

'I will show you Rio properly another time,' Luc promised when they were in a taxi en route for the city. Emily craned her neck this way and that in an effort to see as much as possible. It was very hot. Her linen dress soon felt as heavy as wool, and she was very glad she had taken Luc's advice and changed Jamie into brief cotton rompers on the plane.

'You're not obliged to treat me as a visitor, Luc,' she said coolly. 'I don't intend to be any trouble.'

'Do you not, Emily?' Luc eyed her sceptically until she turned back to what glimpses of the beautiful city the short drive afforded.

It was necessary for Luc to visit his Rio office before finally flying to Boa Vista, and Emily spent what seemed like several exhausting hours on the nineteenth floor of a multi-story office block, trying to amuse Jamie while Luc consulted with his Rio agent. Breakfast was sent in, but this only resulted in Emily's dress being splashed with milk and coffee, despite willing help from two pretty secretaries, as Jamie began to get more and more fractious.

After an eternity of courteous farewells another taxi was called, their luggage loaded up and they headed for Santos Dumont, the internal airport, where they caught the plane for Boa Vista by the skin of their teeth, Emily speechless with fright at their spectacular take-off from a runway which seemed to head straight into the sea. She endured a short but terrifying flight through an electric storm over mountainous country, where the peaks were illumined by constant flashes of lightning and the plane bumped constantly owing to turbulence, making her sick with fright. After they had landed Emily was almost numb when Luc told her they still had a journey of some sixty kilometres by car.

They were met by a smiling, dark-skinned chauffeur who stowed the luggage in the capacious boot of a large Mercedes, and drove them along a road that wound through bare, high mountains, at times with sheer drops on either side of it down to ravines many feet below. The assault on Emily's nerves of so many ordeals in quick succession finally took their toll, and she fell asleep against Luc's shoulder.

Oblivous to the beauty of the palm-shaded house at the end of a long, curving drive through a lush tropical garden, she made her first entrance into Casa d'Ouro carried over the threshold by her husband in traditional manner, but fast asleep. Her son was

borne along behind her, also slumbering deeply, in the arms of
the woman who had taken him from his father, her face tender
as she cradled her great-grandson to her breast.

Emily began to surface slowly, aware she was in a blessedly
still bed, but her eyelids felt too heavy to open and let her
look at her surroundings. Vaguely she was aware of a
whispered conversation near at hand, but the voices died
away again. After a long interval while she just lay enjoying
the comfort of the bed, she opened her eyes cautiously to find.
herself in an enormous, cool, high-ceilinged bedroom with
white filmy curtains moving gently at two large casement
windows screened by wire mosquito netting. Emily pushed
herself up gingerly, propping the pillows behind her, admiring
the beautiful white embroidery on the sheets. She was lying in
a wide bed, almost the size of a British double bed, but this
one had its twin a short distance away with a small table
between the two on which stood a beautifully carved wooden
lamp with an amber silk shade.

The furniture in the room was massive, made of some black
wood with great wrought-iron hinges on the two huge
wardrobes, and intricate carving on the high headboards of the
beds. A dressing table with a swivel mirror stood diagonally
across one corner near the windows, and a large chest was
placed between them. The floor was a gleaming expanse of
wooden boards polished to a glass-like finish, punctuated here
and there by fluffy rugs the same dead white as the walls and
ceiling and the thick fringed cotton of the bedcovers.

Emily was unwillingly enchanted. Unwilling because she
had intended to hate anything Brazilian. Enchanted because
the room, despite its absence of colour, was quite the most
attractive bedroom she had ever seen. She looked down at
herself. She was wearing one of her own cotton lawn
nightgowns, but there was no sign of any of her belongings,
except her handbag on the table beside her. She knew she
should get out of bed and go in search of Jamie, but she was
consumed by a nervousness that held her in the safe cocoon of
the bed, unwilling to venture into whatever—and whoever—
awaited her in the unfamiliar world beyond the closed door.
She glanced at the other bed. Had Luc slept there last night?
If he had there was no outward sign of his occupancy

anywhere. She put that thought, and all its attendant problems, firmly from her. She would cope with one thing at a time in this new life fate had thrust upon her. This sensible decision was unable to stop her sitting bolt upright, heart thumping, as the door opened to admit the tall figure of her husband, looking subtly different in white cotton narrow trousers and a collarless white cotton-knit shirt.

Luc closed the door quietly and came over to the bed, looking down at her with a faint smile at her first words.

'Jamie? Where is he?'

'In very good hands, Emily, I assure you. Do you feel rested?'

'Yes, I feel fine. What time is it? Are my clothes here? Have I held you up for breakfast——'

'*Calma, calma,* Emily! It is nearly noon. Breakfast is long over, your luggage is outside, the maids will unpack while you have a bath, then I shall come back and take you to lunch. My grandmother is waiting to meet you.'

Emily had been afraid of that. She stirred restlessly beneath the sheets.

'If you'll leave, then, Luc, I'll get out of bed.' She flushed, her eyes falling before the amusement in his.

'Are you afraid that the sight of you in that prim little nightgown will drive me to bestial deeds in the full light of day?' The jeering note in his voice rubbed Emily raw. 'After all, who do you imagine undressed you and put you to bed last night?'

She looked at him in horror.

'Couldn't—someone else have done it?'

'Who would you suggest as more appropriate?' Luc sauntered nonchalantly to the door. 'You forget, I am your husband. Besides, I must confess I have rather a preference for undressing a woman when she is fully aware of what I am doing.'

This was too much for Emily. She threw back the bedclothes and slid to her feet from the rather high bed, her chin lifted, ignoring the unkempt tangle of her hair and the brevity of the lawn nightgown.

'If you would please send someone with my clothes I'll do my best to keep you waiting as little as possible. I am anxious to see my son,' she said with dignity.

Luc's black eyes flared momentarily.

'*Our* son!' He opened the door and called loudly. 'Maria, Dirce, *vem ca, faz favor.*'

Two dark-skinned girls wearing print dresses and white aprons came into the room carrying Emily's suitcases. They smiled shyly as Luc introduced them by pointing to each one in turn and saying their names, and busied themselves with unpacking Emily's clothes. She took out a dressing gown, one of her new purchases, café-au-lait heavy satin cut like a kimono, and wrapped it around herself, tying the girdle tight with a yank, and pushing her feet into matching mules.

'If you'll show me where the bathroom is?'

Luc took her outside into a cool corridor, floored in the same gleaming wood, which caught the sun from regularly spaced windows which appeared to give on to a verandah. He opened the door next to theirs.

'I'm afraid the house was built long before bathrooms en suite. You have to share this one with Jamie and me. Thurza sleeps in the other wing, and has a bathroom to herself. I'll return in, shall we say, twenty minutes?'

He left her with a formal little bow, and Emily flew into the bathroom, hardly with time to take in its marble floor and old-fashioned white suite with gleaming brass taps. She made for the huge separate shower stall, protecting her hair with one of the snowy white towels piled on a bamboo chair. In desperate haste she returned to the bedroom to find one of the maids quietly waiting, all Emily's clothes put away except for a change of fresh underwear laid out on the bed. Emily smiled tentatively at the girl.

'Maria?'

'*Não, senhora;* Dirce.' The girl giggled in confusion, opening the door of one of the wardrobes to indicate Emily's clothes hanging in an orderly row, obviously asking which of the dresses was required.

Emily shed her robe and pulled on briefs and bra, any embarrassment at Dirce's presence eclipsed by the thought of what Luc's grandmother would consider suitable. She wanted very much to make a good impression, but had no idea what would help most towards it. After a few moments' hesitation she pointed to her choice, and Dirce helped her into it, fastening it at the back and helping her tie the sash. The dress was off-white, cut like a gymslip, sleeveless and pleated, hanging straight except for a wide aquamarine silk scarf slotted round the hips and tied loosely. Emily hastily put on the sandals worn to travel in, brushed her hair furiously and coiled it in an uncompromising knot on top of her head. A touch of lipstick was all she had time for before the door opened to admit Luc, carrying Jamie.

Forgetting her appearance, Emily held out her arms to her son and hugged him fiercely, to the accompaniment of ecstatic gurgles and incoherent noises, interspersed with 'Mum—mum' and, quite definitely, 'Da—da'.

'You diplomat,' she muttered into his neck, yielding him up reluctantly to his father under the wide, adoring eyes of the maid, who was unable to restrain an outburst of Portuguese which Luc translated to Emily as being a mere outpouring of baby adulation.

'This young man has disrupted the whole household this morning,' he said severely, scowling fiercely at Jamie, who merely chuckled and tried to grab his watch.

'Has he been naughty?' asked Emily anxiously.

'Not in the least, but everyone wishes to play with him instead of whatever they should be doing. Now let us go and have lunch.'

Luc led the way across the corridor on to a wide verandah which ran round three sides of a patio filled with flowering plants. The verandah obviously served the house behind it as a great, three-sided extra room, and had a view through the patio on to a garden which gave the impression of such lush profusion that Emily exclaimed in wonder.

There were palm trees everywhere, giving shade to the house without in any way dominating it, so that Emily received the impression that the building and the trees were interdependent. From what she could see of the garden beyond, roses and azaleas predominated, interspersed with beds of multicoloured coleus, before a glossy green hedge, alight with scarlet blossom, cut off the rest of the garden from view. Suddenly Emily jumped at the raucous noise from one end of the patio, where macaws with brightly-coloured plumage shrieked a strident welcome from a gilded metal aviary which glinted in the noon sunlight.

The middle section of the verandah was obviously used as an extra sitting room, with bamboo furniture padded with cushions covered in cool green and white batik, and a glass-topped bamboo table set for lunch, Luc waved Emily to the settee, plumping Jamie alongside her, and turned to a trolley laden with bottles and glasses.

'What may I give you, Emily? You should have had some coffee, but you seemed in a hurry to dress.'

'I won't have anything just yet, thank you,' she said politely. 'Don't let me stop you, of course.'

Luc poured himself a long gin and tonic, added ice and lemon and sat down on the other side of Jamie, his glass out of reach of his son's inquisitive investigation.

'No, you don't, *bichinho*. He's had his lunch, by the way.'

Emily was startled.

'What did he have? How did you know what to give him?'

'He just had what any child in this country might eat—we manage to raise quite a few children successfully here, you know.'

She felt foolish.

'Of course. I was just interested in his menu, that's all.'

'He had *canja*—chicken soup with rice—then vegetables and minced beef, followed by a fresh fruit salad.' Luc looked at her in enquiry. 'Satisfactory, I trust?'

'Sounds delicious.' Emily was aware that her own stomach was in need of food also, despite her nerves. 'This house is beautiful, Luc. I had no idea it would be so large.'

'You showed very little interest in your future home before you left England.' Luc stared down into his drink. 'I would have described it to you—but perhaps it was better to view at first hand. The wings of the house which form the three sides of the square at one time each had a separate function. Where you slept was all bedrooms, the main wing behind us was the reception area, and over to the right, kitchen, dining room and servants' quarters. Now my grandmother has her rooms in the main wing, and we are alone in our wing—except for Jamie.'

Something about the way he said the last words chilled Emily, though she was saved from comment by the need to hang on to Jamie as Luc jumped to his feet to greet the small figure of his grandmother, who was walking towards them along the polished wooden boards, her erect, graceful carriage giving the lie to her seventy plus years.

Emily picked up Jamie and rose to her feet, wishing suddenly that she were anywhere in the world but where she was at this precise moment.

Thurza Treharne Fonseca, the daughter of a Cornish landowner, had been swept off to Brazil by Luc's grandfather, Jaime Fonseca, at the tender age of seventeen, where she had taken to her elevated position in this exotic, beautiful country like a duck to water. After more than fifty years she was the complete autocrat, and to her servants her word was law. The only person who treated her with any degree of normality was her grandson, who held a unique and unassailable place in her affections, and the only one, since the death of her husband, who ever called her Thurza.

To Emily's surprise Thurza Fonseca was barely the same height as herself, her body slim and erect, grey hair expertly, if a little rigidly, coiffured above a discreetly made-up face with piercing dark eyes that examined her grandson's wife with detached interest. Her grey and white dress was severely tailored but made of finest silk, her only jewellery a string of perfectly matched pearls and the huge diamond on her left hand above her wedding ring.

'Thurza, this is my wife, Emily.' The slight emphasis on the word 'wife' was lost by neither woman, and Thurza gave her grandson a swift amused look before touching her cool, powdered cheek to Emily's pale, smooth one.

'How do you do, my dear, please sit down again. Has Luc not given you anything to drink?' She seated herself gracefully in the chair nearest to Emily and stretched out her arms imperiously to Jamie. 'Come to Vo-vo, then, my darling.'

To his mother's surprise Jamie happily accepted the invitation and was instantly enthralled by his great-grandmother's pearls, to Emily's trepidation.

'How do you do, Mrs Fonseca. Are you sure Jamie won't be a nuisance—he's not very civilized about grabbing whatever he fancies.'

'Men are like that,' Luc murmured softly as he turned to the drinks trolley.

'What was that, Luc?' Thurza looked sharply at him, but he merely turned a bland smile on her and asked what she wanted to drink.

'Just a small dry sherry as usual. I'm sure Emily will enjoy the same.'

Emily meekly accepted the unwanted drink and sipped a little, trying not to wince at the astringent assault on her uneducated palate, aware that Luc was watching her with amusement.

'I trust you slept well,' said Thurza Fonseca, settling Jamie more comfortably. 'When you were still asleep at eleven I was becoming anxious, but Luc wouldn't allow anyone to disturb you.'

'I'm sorry if I inconvenienced you——' began Emily defensively.

'Of course not, my dear,' interrupted Thurza smoothly, 'but we are early risers here, so naturally I was a little concerned. However, it gave me an admirable opportunity to make friends with this captivating young man—no, little one, not Vo-vo's pearls.'

'Emily has been under a great deal of strain recently,' said Luc evenly. 'Coupled with our rather daunting journey I think things rather caught up with her. She is feeling some reaction.'

'Yes, of course,' said Thurza guardedly. 'Luc has been telling me. To have been widowed and them married again in such rapid succession would tax the strongest of constitutions.'

Emily's head came up with a proud lift. She drained her glass and handed it casually to Luc, then rose to her feet.

'How kind of you to be so understanding,' she said sweetly 'Now I think I should put Jamie down for his afternoon nap, if you'll excuse me for a short while, Mrs Fonseca. I trust I haven't held up lunch too long.'

Thurza waved a hand gracefully, a look of reluctant admiration in her eyes for a fleeting instant.

'Lunch will wait on your return, my dear. Go to Mamae, then Jamie. *Dorme bem.*'

Emily bore her son off with dignity, her back very straight, Luc following in her wake.

'I think the score was about even, don't you think?' he

grinned as they turned in to the wing where Emily had slept the night before. 'You haven't asked where Jamie's room is.'

'You said it was in the same wing as us, so I presumed he would be next door, or at least near at hand.' Emily ignored the sally about scoring, still ruffled by Thurza Fonseca's remark.

Luc opened the door beyond Emily's room and disclosed another bedroom of slightly smaller dimensions, furnished with beautiful, modern nursery furniture, complete with toybox, playpen and a single bed ready for when Jamie outstripped his cot. Emily was surprised.

'This is all new!'

'I telephoned Thurza as soon as you—agreed to come back with me. This is all her doing.'

'How very kind.' Emily handed Jamie to Luc. 'Hold on to him a minute, please, while I investigate.'

The chest of drawers was filled with her son's clothes, neatly folded, some new toys lay in the playpen, and, best of all, when Emily turned down the cot sheet, there was the old woolly rabbit, ready to accompany Jamie for his nap.

'I'll cope now,' she firmly said to Luc. 'You go back to your grandmother and I'll come as soon as I've undressed him.'

'You can find your way back?' Luc laid Jamie on the single bed and straightened, his eyes searching Emily's face. 'Do not worry about anything. You will soon settle down here once you're used to us.'

'And once everyone's used to me!' Emily waved him away and set about preparing her son for bed.

When she returned to the others, her high heels clicking on the hard wood floor, Luc sprang to his feet.

'Did Jamie settle down fairly well? He seems quite happy in his new room.'

'How could he not be?' Emily fumed inwardly at the unnecessary jog to her manners. 'You've been to a great deal of trouble, Mrs Fonseca, Jamie's room is charming. Thank you very much.'

Thurza Fonseca got to her feet with surprising agility.

'I had a great deal of pleasure in choosing it, Emily. Luc had to put up with his father's things, but I thought it was time to get something new. The only piece we kept was Luc's highchair, but it was hand-carved specially for him and it seemed a shame to discard it. Now, let us begin. They brought in the first course while you were away.'

They sat down to chilled avocado halves stuffed with huge prawns in a pepper sauce, and went on to succulent slices of filet mignon served on pâté-spread rounds of crisp-fried bread, eaten with a puree of potatoes and a green salad. They finished with some of the fresh fruit previously enjoyed by Jamie, or in Luc's case, cheese; finally lingering over coffee.

'This is Emily's very first taste of Brazilian coffee, Thurza.' Luc lit a cheroot and watched his wife lazily through the smoke as she took her first experimental sip.

'Good gracious, child, didn't Luc send for any when you woke up?' Thurza frowned at him in exasperation.

'She was too concerned with getting dressed,' Luc smiled at Emily. 'What do you think of the coffee, *carinha*?'

Emily finished the diminutive demi-tasse almost in one swallow.

'It's different from what I expected,' she admitted, 'but delicious. Yes, thank you, I'd love another cup.'

Thurza manipulated the heavy silver pot with dexterity, looking at Emily expectantly as she laid it down.

'And what do you think of Brazil, now that you have come to live here?'

Emily waved a hand around her.

'Apart from the road through those rather terrifying mountains I've seen only this, which is very beautiful. But the one thing I'm very aware of is the smell.'

Both faces turned to her in amused query.

'Smell, my dear? What do you mean?' Thurza seemed to thaw a little.

Emily thought carefully.

'I think it must be the earth that smells different here— nutty, is the nearest I can come to it. Possibly the vegetation contributes to that, and the smell from Luc's cheroot, and now I've sampled it, the coffee too, also a faint hint of perfume. It's all mingled in a general pervasive scent that's new and foreign, though very pleasant.'

'I think I know what you mean.' Thurza rang the little silver bell beside her. 'Though one becomes accustomed to it, especially after over fifty years. Shall we sit over there and let the maids clear away.'

Luc pushed a cushion behind Emily's back before seating himself beside her on the settee.

'What time can we expect Jamie to surface? When he wakes I thought we'd go for a drive and show you the town.'

'Perhaps I'd better check on him now,' began Emily, but Luc put a restraining hand on her knee.

'Stay there. I will go.'

Thurza Fonseca watched her grandson stroll along the verandah, then cast a watchful eye on the verandah table to see that the maids had fulfilled their duties satisfactorily before turning purposefully towards Emily.

'Well, my dear, and how do you think you will cope with making my grandson happy?' she asked, without preliminary.

Emily took her time before answering, wondering suddenly if Luc had told his grandmother anything of their artifical situation, or was she under the impression that theirs was an idyllic affair merely disrupted for a while by circumstances.

'I hadn't really considered it in the light of an occupation, Mrs Fonseca,' she said at last. 'I don't think one can "make" another person happy, but I believe that two people can work together as a team to make a good marriage and a good background for one's child.'

'H'm. Do you not intend to have more children?' The dark eyes were eagle-like on Emily's downcast face. 'I was blessed with only one—Antonio—and he had only Luc. Antonio refused to marry again when Helenita died giving birth. I would like to think that you and Luc might do better; though you don't look particularly strong to me.'

Neither had noticed Luc's return and his voice was coldly reproving to his grandmother.

'Emily has been through a great deal lately, Thurza, enough to make anyone look a little fragile. There is time enough before thinking of any further additions. We have only just met Jamie, after all.'

'Through no fault of ours——' began Thurza sharply.

'Nor of Emily's,' said Luc with finality. 'Now, let us plan what we shall do this afternoon. Jamie was showing faint signs of stirring, *carinha*, so let us get him ready and then I

shall show you Campo d'Ouro—everything you missed by
falling asleep yesterday. Will you accompany us, Thurza?'

The older woman refused.

'Show her the sights alone while I have my rest, then you
may bring my great-grandson back for me to play with later.'
She paused, then looked at Emily with something approaching
kindness. 'You have done well with him, my dear. He is a
delightful child.'

CHAPTER TEN

WITH Jamie enthroned in the back of the large Mercedes, in
the car seat thoughtfully included by Thurza in the rest of his
new belongings, Luc took Emily for a tour round the steep
little town of Campo d'Ouro, with its two churches, a cinema,
several shops and many streets of houses all built to house
employees of the mine. Nearer the mine he showed her the
aqueducts that were such a physical feature of the town,
passing right over the narrow main street. She saw the
hospital on a quiet hillside, where treatment was given for all
ailments from the common cold to major surgery. The general
effect of red-roofed white-painted houses clinging to the steep
hills of the town among lush greenery and the rich, red earth
of the region was very picturesque, the postcard effect
mitigated by the mountain rising above the town, surmounted
by a great cross which was illuminated at night.

Emily looked about her with intense interest. Everything
was so foreign and different from the quiet Warwickshire
village of her upbringing that she felt Campo d'Ouro might
disappear like Brigadoon if she as much as blinked. As they
returned towards the big house, Luc told her to close her eyes
for a moment as they reached the main gates, which stood
permanently open in welcome.

'Now look,' he instructed, as he drove slowly through the
gateway.

At first the house was hidden, as the driveway curved
through the green lawns and clustering palms, a blaze of

colour here and there from scarlet poinsettias and the
tumbling pink and purple of bougainvillaea, until a final bend
brought it into view, beautiful and complete, at one with the
tropical beauty of its surroundings. Only the reception wing
was visible from this part of the garden, and Emily realised it
had a verandah on the outward side as well as the inner one
looking over the patio.

Luc brought the car to a halt at the foot of the flight of
steps leading up to the verandah and through a main hall out
to the section where they had had lunch.

'I'm sorry you had to carry me all that way,' she remarked
apologetically. 'You should have woken me up.'

Luc leaned over and undid her seatbelt.

'I enjoyed it. After all, if you will not allow me the
normal pleasures enjoyed by a husband you must expect me
to gather up what crumbs of comfort I can whenever
possible.'

Emily opened the door with a jerk and got out, leaving Luc
to extricate a clamouring Jamie from his seat, while she
marched into the house, nose in the air.

Thurza laid down a book and removed gold-rimmed
spectacles as she greeted them from one of the bamboo chairs
on the verandah, her smile warm as Luc brought Jamie to her.
A tray with a jug of lemonade floating with ice-cubes and
fruit was on the table beside her and she waved Emily towards
it while she held up her arms to Jamie.

'You do the honours, my dear, I expect you're thirsty after
your drive, though you look very cool in that clever little
dress.'

'Thank you.' Emily smiled politely, filling Jamie's mug and
two tall glasses, then looking at Luc in enquiry.

'Thank you, no, *querida*. I'll get myself a beer.' Luc kissed
her cheek casually as he passed on his way through to the
kitchen, leaving Emily in no doubt as to how their
relationship was to seem as far as the rest of the world was
concerned.

'I hope he won't tire you out, Mrs Fonseca,' she said
doubtfully as she sat down, watching with concern the way
the little boy was bouncing up and down energetically on the
old lady's lap.

'He's a lively boy,' said Thurza indulgently, though somewhat breathlessly, 'but a little of this won't do me any harm.'

Emily looked over her shoulder as Luc reappeared.

'Darling,' she said demurely, noting gleefully how his face went suddenly still at the unexpected endearment, 'perhaps it might be a good idea if you brought that smart new playpen out here until Jamie's suppertime, then he can be part of the fun without wearing out your grandmother.'

'Good idea, *carinha*,' he answered instantly, smiling down at her so fondly Emily was almost ready to believe he was as besotted with her as he obviously meant Thurza to believe.

His grandmother watched him go with such an intense look of love on her face that Emily looked away with a feeling of intrusion.

'The Fonseca men have the knack of reproducing themselves with great exactitude,' said Thurza. 'Luc is the image of his father and grandfather. I have often wondered what my other children would have been like if they had survived.'

'You had others?' asked Emily gently.

'Two miscarriages before Antonio, and a girl born after him who only lived a day.' Thurza laid her cheek on Jamie's curly head. 'Childbearing was not my forte, to my great disappointment. I wanted very much to give Jaime a large family, but my size was against me.' She looked across at Emily, a look of delicate enquiry on her face. 'You had a difficult time with Jamie?'

Emily tried not to feel antagonism at the thinly-veiled feeler as to her prospects as a brood mare.

'All my troubles were in the months leading up to his arrival,' she said lightly, 'the actual birth was surprisingly straightforward. Of course he was rather small, which helped.'

Luc arrived at that moment, laden with the playpen and an armful of toys. Emily jumped up to help him.

'You never told me how it was when Jamie was born,' he said shortly, frowning as he put the pen together.

'No. Men aren't usually interested in the boring details.' Emily took Jamie away from Thurza. 'Come on, you bruiser, leave your poor——' She shot a look at the other woman. 'What was the word you used?'

'*Vo-vo.* Grandma, roughly, in Portuguese,' explained Thurza, smiling in approval. 'And what are *you* going to call me, Emily? Mrs Fonseca sounds rather a contradiction in terms.'

Emily was a little flustered, avoiding Luc's eye.

'I hadn't thought——'

'You will call her Thurza, as I do,' said Luc firmly, and sat down on the settee beside her, taking her hand in his. 'That will be acceptable, Thurza? I presume you do not require Emily to say Dona Teresa, like the maids?'

'Of course not.' Thurza was unruffled. 'Of course in England one is not generally on first name terms with one's grandmother, but that hardly concerns us, I feel. I shall be very pleased to have Emily use my name—oh, by the way, my dear, the maids will probably convert your name into something easy for them, so I expect you will become Dona Emilia.'

Emily smiled.

'That sounds very pretty.' She turned to her husband. 'What do they call you, Luc?'

'When my father died I inherited his title.' He grinned at her mockingly. 'I am referred to as *"O Patrão"* '

'Which means Lord and Master, I presume,' said Emily sweetly.

Very deliberately Luc raised the hand he was holding to his lips, kissing it with a flourish, gazing at her with an expression in his glinting black eyes that brought the colour to her cheeks.

'Exactly,' he agreed solemnly.

Emily was aware of Thurza following the little exchange with interest, and turned to her with determination.

'I enjoyed the trip round the village,' she said brightly, 'though I gather it's referred to as a town.'

'I rarely venture down there these days,' said Thurza regretfully. 'The local hairdresser comes to the house once a week, and now and then I'm driven into Boa Vista for a little frivolous shopping, but generally speaking my life is spent within the confines of the house and garden. I quite enjoy a little gardening, though José, the gardener, strongly disapproves. You haven't shown Emily the garden yet, Luc. Leave Jamie here while you take a stroll.'

As Luc raised Emily to her feet, Jamie's face crumpled a little and his attention wavered from the toys in the pen Laboriously he hauled himself to his feet, with such an imploring look on his face Emily's heart was wrung.

'Couldn't we——?' she began tentatively, but Luc shook his head.

'Leave him with Thurza for now. You'll see why in a moment.'

With misgivings Emily left her objecting son to be soothed by his 'Vo-vo', while she accompanied Luc down in to the patio with its plants; ferns and rubber plants and many more that were strange to her. The gaudy macaws shrieked at them as they passed the aviary and emerged into the garden proper with its beautifully tended lawns and beds of roses, some of them taller than Emily, but all of them scentless. A great expanse of coleus of all colours edged the brilliantly green grass, and Emily smiled in amazement.

'One of those in a pot costs quite a lot of money at home,' she said pensively. 'They had a big brass pot full of them on the staircase at Compton Lacey—I used to look after the houseplants.'

Luc's hand closed over hers and he turned her to face him.

'This is your home now, Emily. Do not dwell in the past.'

She looked up at him squarely.

'You want me to forget that I lived in another man's home and existed for eighteen months without knowing what had happened to you?'

'Yes, I do,' he grated, bruising her fingers, his eyes cold and implacable. 'You are now Emily Guimarães Fonseca, Dona da Casa d'Ouro, mother of my son and my wife. Do not forget it.'

Emily's head lifted with hauteur.

'I am hardly likely to, am I? But I refuse to put my past life, especially Marcus, out of my mind. They are a part of me every bit as much as this place is part of you. I have a heritage too, Luc Fonseca, so don't browbeat me.'

He grinned suddenly, disarming her completely.

'I am beginning to realise that "browbeating" you, as you put it, is not as easy as one might think. You may look gentle as a gazelle, but behind that façade beats the heart of a tigress!'

They walked on slowly, the sudden flare of animosity dissipated a little.

'Nevertheless, Luc,' said Emily thoughtfully, 'how will you explain a new wife with a ready-made son who is pretty obviously yours?'

They had reached a white-painted garden seat, and Luc motioned Emily to sit down. He sat close and slid an arm along the back of her shoulders, which stiffened at his touch.

'Just think what a picture of felicity we present to Thurza,' he murmured in her ear. 'She can just see us at this point.'

'And is it so important that she believes our marriage is all sweetness and light?' Emily felt resentful at this nerve-racking game of charades she seemed to be playing with Luc.

'Oh yes, indeed, Emily. If she believed for one moment that you were anything but a normal, loving wife to me she would make your life a misery. She can be a tyrant as far as her family is concerned; or indeed about anything that does not fall in with her way of thinking.'

'I *had* suspected as much,' said Emily dryly. 'You haven't answered my question about your somewhat precipitate rise to fatherhood status.'

'Everyone knew of my amnesia,' said Luc bleakly. 'Failing to get here for my father's funeral, and the reasons for it, were naturally highly publicised. What no one knows, except Thurza, is how completely my memory returned. I was very cagey—is that right?—about claiming full recall, as frankly I felt that if I had forgotten about you, God knew what else had been erased from my mind. So the general message to those that matter is that we had a lightning romance and wedding the first time, cut short by the tragedy of my father, and that I only remembered about you just before I went to England this last time.'

'What was I supposed to be doing in the meantime?' demanded Emily.

'You thought I'd been killed, and had too much pride to apply to my family for support, which is not too different from the truth.'

'And people are going to believe that?' Emily was sceptical.

'I care little whether they do or not,' said Luc indifferently 'I am answerable to no one but God and my family.' He squeezed her shoulders hard. 'Do not worry. Whatever anyone thinks privately, to you they will behave with the utmost circumspection, or they answer to me.'

The menace in his deep, quiet voice made Emily shiver, and she got up quickly.

'The sun's going down. Show me the rest of the garden, then it's time to give Jamie his bath. What lies beyond this spectacular hedge, Luc? What lovely blossoms!'

'Hibiscus. We go through this narrow opening at the end and—*o piscina*.'

Luc ushered Emily through the gap in the hedge with the air of a conjuror, and laughed at her gasp of pleasure at the sight of a large swimming pool paved with turquoise tiles, complete with a high-diving board, garden chairs scattered along the grass beside it.

'Oh, Luc, how fantastic! I haven't swum since I was in school——' her glowing smile faded. 'Oh, but——'

'Exactly,' he agreed. 'Our son will soon be walking, so I must arrange for a high gate in the opening back there so that he can never accidentally get through to the pool.'

Emily shuddered, white to the lips at the thought.

'But how did you manage when you were small?'

'It's only seven years old,' he explained. 'It was made for me when I came home for good after college. Now you see why I don't want Jamie to see it before I can get this part of the garden closed off. I shall teach him to swim as soon as possible.'

'But he can't walk yet!'

'No matter, Emily. He can learn both at once.' He grinned at her doubtful face. 'Come, let us go back, *carinha*, Jamie will be growing impatient.'

'I'm *"carinha"* in private again as well as in front of your grandmother?' Emily looked up at her husband's handsome jutting profile mischievously.

'Not if you dislike it, Emily.'

For some reason Luc's quiet answer made Emily deflated. again, an annoying little habit of his, she thought irritably as they went back to the house.

Bathtime was its usual lively but exhausting pastime, with Thurza a delighted spectator a little distance from the inevitable splashes hurled around by the exuberant Jamie. He had been provided with a new boat which his father helped him sail while Thurza conducted Emily to the kitchen to discuss the little boy's supper. Emily inspected the large square room with pleasure. A window in two of the walls gave maximum light, and the same marble floor as the bathroom gave a coolness she assumed would be very welcome in the middle of the day. The double cooker, refrigerator and freezer were obviously up to date, as were various gadgets like blenders and food mixers, but the rest of the kitchen looked unchanged, its cupboards and large table very much in keeping with the rest of the house.

'You probably find such a kitchen somewhat antiquated,' said Thurza.

'No indeed,' Emily laughed. 'The Dower House kitchen was more or less in its original condition of three hundred years earlier, except for the basic modern appliances, cooker, etc. But it was a bit dark and dismal. And my kitchen in the cottage was minute.' Her face clouded. 'Luc wants me to forget all that, though, and just live in the present.'

Thurza laid a hand on her arm, her face softening.

'Try to bear with him, Emily. He has been brought up as a Brazilian, despite his cosmopolitan education, and the thought of the woman he loves, and his son, both belonging to someone else is abhorrent to him. I had great reservations myself, I admit freely, until you arrived, but I am sure we will all learn to live together in harmony if we each of us do our best.'

Inwardly Emily had grave doubts, but she smiled at Thurza, nodding, and both of them turned to thoughts of supper.

Jamie settled down very well in his new bedroom, and, not for the first time, Emily gave thanks for his equable disposition.

'It's surprising how easily he adapts himself,' she said to the other two when they were eating the cold meal prepared earlier by Dica, the cook, and left ready for them to serve themselves.

'I wouldn't describe Luc as the most placid man in the

world,' said his grandmother dryly, 'so Jamie must have inherited your nature, Emily.'

'Don't make the mistake of thinking her meek and mild,' warned Luc, smiling evilly at Emily. 'She has claws that scratch when she's roused.'

'Then stop trying to provoke me,' said Emily calmly. 'I think Jamie learnt very quickly that roaring his head off was no use, as often I was—well, unable to come running just when he wanted. And during the time before he was born, of course . . .' She trailed away, embarrassed, and took one of the crisp nut cookies Thurza offered with the coffee.

'What were you going to say?' asked Luc gently

'Well, I merely meant that I wasn't too happy myself, so one would think it might have affected him adversely, instead of which he's always been a happy little soul.' Emily looked away, unable to meet his look.

'A fortunate compensation for you, my dear,' put in Thurza smoothly. 'Now shall we repair to the morning room and discuss plans for a little reception I intend to give next Saturday.'

Luc scowled.

'Reception?'

'Of course, dear.' Thurza smiled at him blandly. 'We must introduce Emily to our friends, and some of the mine officials. It will be expected. Come along.'

Emily gave Luc an agonised look as they followed the small, regal figure to a pretty room, with chintz-covered furniture, a pastel Chinese rug on the floor and several watercolours on the walls. There was a large fireplace, to Emily's surprise, and a wall devoted to shelves holding books and records and hi-fi equipment.

'This is the morning room,' said Thurza.

'*Your* room, you mean, Thurza,' said Luc. 'Sit down, Emily, and I'll fetch us a drink. What would you like? Grand Marnier?'

Emily refused to rise to his bait, wishing his memory were less efficient.

'A soft drink, please.'

'I thought about thirty people,' went on Thurza inexorably 'A buffet, of course, and we'll have drinks down in the patio first. For some reason people adore those noisy macaws; then we'll serve supper on the side verandah and repair to the drawing room afterwards.'

Luc sighed, handing her a small Benedictine, then giving Emily a glass of chilled orange juice. He sat on the floor beside Emily's chair, leaning against her knee with a familiarity she resented fiercely, but took care to hide. He drank some whisky, regarding his grandmother with resignation.

'I suppose it is really necessary?'

'You know it is,' she answered firmly. 'A Fonseca bride is not an event that happens often. As there was no wedding reception to attend everyone will be agog to meet her, therefore we shall present Emily in style. I believe—and you will forgive me for being outspoken, I know—that the best way to deal with any possible rumours or gossip is to behave as though they don't exist.'

'If I hear anyone make so much as a reference to my wife or son in any derogatory way——' began Luc harshly, the sudden tension in his body communicating itself to Emily where it touched her thigh.

'You will ignore it!' Thurza's arrogance faded as she looked at Emily's white face. 'What is it, my dear? Does the prospect of a little party frighten you?'

Emily smiled valiantly, her eyes glittering in her pale face.

'No, of course not, it's just that suddenly I feel a little tired. It's very embarrassing. I've done nothing at all today, and yet I'm sleepy again. I promise to be more lively tomorrow.'

'Drink your orange juice, then bed,' said Luc, turning his face up towards hers. 'I must turn in, anyway, back to normal tomorrow.'

Emily felt a little pang.

'Are you starting back already?'

'He spent an hour or so down at the office this morning, while you were sleeping,' said Thurza tartly. 'He has a lot to make up after spending the additional time in England with you, after all.'

Luc rose to his feet in one lithe movement and held out his

hand for his grandmother's glass, looking down at her unsmiling.

'I think perhaps it would be a good thing for you to retire also, Thurza. Tomorrow you may introduce Emily to the rest of the servants and familiarise her properly with the house.' He paused significantly. 'I am sure that you will do your best to see that Emily settles in comfortably. I shall not be home for lunch, I have to visit Congonhas dam, so take care of my wife—not to mention my son.'

Obviously a message was received and noted between the two, thought Emily with interest, as a very slight flush mounted Thurza's well-modelled cheekbones.

'Goodnight, Emily,' she said with dignity. 'Sleep well. Goodnight, Luc.'

She presented her cheek to Luc, but merely nodded to Emily as she passed through the door held open by Luc.

'Oh dear,' said Emily faintly, downing the rest of her orange juice with a gulp. 'I think she was put out. She was beginning to thaw towards me, too.'

Luc stood leaning against the carved wood mantelpiece, kicking a suede-booted foot irritably against the curb.

'She will ride roughshod over anyone if they don't stand up to her. She likes to aim those little barbs just when one is lulled into thinking what a sweet old lady she is. It doesn't work with me, nor did it with my father, but I have been told she made my mother's short life none too happy on occasion.'

'Did she not approve of your mother?'

'Oh, very much so. She more or less arranged the match. Helenita de Carvalho was a great matrimonial prize. The family is old Portuguese colonial, owns vast areas of land in Minas, and my mother was beautiful and sweet in to the bargain. But she had been brought up in true, high-class traditional Brazilian style, obedient, ornamental, waited on hand and foot and protected from everything. My father never saw her alone before their wedding day.' Luc's wide mobile mouth twisted at the look of horror that Emily turned on him.

'But that's barbaric! I mean, it isn't human to expect people to—to——'

'Sleep together when they have never even held hands?'

'Well, yes, it takes time to get used to someone in that way——' Emily stopped dead, but it was too late.

'You mean that they should have waited at least five days first.' His voice was silken and cruel. 'It took you all of that, Emily, if I remember accurately.'

Emily sat still and silent, cursing herself for a fool. She had led with her chin, so had only herself to blame for the inevitable coup de grâce. Utterly drained and exhausted by this strange, quiet yet wearing day, she rose to her feet and handed Luc her empty glass, silently turning towards the door.

'Would you like some more orange-juice, Emily?'

Did she detect a faint note of contrition?

'No, thank you. Perhaps the oranges are different here, but I thought there was a strange aftertaste,' she said politely.

'I put some vodka in it,' he confessed, face straight. 'If I remember correctly, alcohol—er—relaxes you.'

Emily suddenly and completely reached the end of the very frail tether she'd been hanging on to. Taking Luc off guard, she gave him a vicious swipe on his cheek with the flat of her hand, all the conflicting emotions of the day compressed in to one great wallop, which gave her enormous satisfaction.

'Goodnight,' she said flatly, and left the room unhurriedly.

Luc caught up with her immediately, his hand reaching out to catch her elbow in a painful grip as they went to Jamie's room in a pulsating, tangible silence that was loud with things unsaid. Emily straightened out the crumpled heap at the foot of the cot into a tidily disposed little boy, tucked the satin-edged cellular blanket round him and left him peacefully sucking his thumb, blissfully unaware of the dark, violent currents that eddied back and forth between his parents as they silently left the room.

Luc followed her in to their bedroom and closed the door with an ominous thud. Emily rounded on him, eyes like chips of blue ice in the glow from the bedside lamp.

'You can't sleep here!'

'Indeed I can, *minha esposa*, this is *my* room, you are merely sharing it.'

He stood with arms folded across his chest, such

malevolence on his dark face that Emily suddenly knew fear, and drew in her breath sharply.

'Then tell me where *I* may sleep,' she said desperately. 'How can you expect me to get any rest in these circumstances?'

'You managed very well last night!'

'That was different. I knew nothing of where I was, or indeed anything else.'

'Nevertheless, this is our room, and this is where you, and I, will sleep. Nothing goes on in a Brazilian household that is ever concealed from the servants.'

'And you care for servants' gossip!' Emily bit the words out, shaking with rage.

'Not particularly. But my family is one subject that I do not care to be discussed intimately all over Campo d'Ouro. There is enough subject matter for speculation already. I do not intend that there will be one iota more.' Luc spoke quietly, yet with a deadly emphasis that chilled Emily to the bone.

She took a deep breath and flung her head back defiantly.

'I said in England that I would act as your wife in public— and I use the word "act" intentionally—but I will not sleep with you.' Her breathing was ragged as she got the last words out, and she recoiled instinctively as Luc moved.

But it was only to sit on the far side of the other bed, however, where he leisurely removed his boots, then his clothes, getting up casually to open his wardrobe and take out a white towelling dressing gown. Emily watched him, hardly breathing, paralysed by nerves and apprehension. He strolled indolently towards the door, turning to look at her before he opened it.

'Perhaps you should wait until you are asked,' he said cruelly, then sauntered out, closing the door softly behind him.

CHAPTER ELEVEN

To say Emily spent a miserable night was an understatement. Her rage and frustration at Luc's Parthian shot made her shake so violently her fingers were all thumbs as she got out of her clothes and into the fresh nightgown laid out for her. She feverishly wrapped the satin robe round her tense body and brushed out her hair vigorously, trying to calm down before Luc returned.

If he *is* returning, she thought viciously. Tears came to her eyes as she pulled the bristles through a particularly tight knot. But of course he was returning. The servants might gossip if not. The reputation of *o patrão* must be upheld at all costs, especially if there were any danger of his machismo being in question. There were doubtless numbers of well brought up Brazilian maidens who would give their solid gold pedigrees to be in her place right now. Emily forced back a choked little sob. None of them had her supreme advantage, however, one ready-made firstborn son, created in the exact image of his sire, with not one feature of his mother to mar the effect. She started as the door opened. Luc came in quietly, his hair wet from the shower, and with complete disregard for Emily's sensibilities, stripped off his dressing gown, stretched, and slid into bed.

'*Boa noite,*' he said with a yawn, and rolled over on his side, with his back to her.

Emily's temper boiled up again and it took every last ounce of self-control she possessed to get herself quietly into the bathroom and make her preparations for the night. Conflicting emotions were poor bedfellows, and hours of tossing and turning passed before Emily finally slept, hours made all the more unbearable by the quiet, even breathing of the deeply sleeping man in the bed next to hers.

It was almost seven when she cast a bleary eye at her watch next morning. She rolled over quickly, but the other bed was empty Yawning and heavy-eyed, she tiptoed next door to

134

look at Jamie, but he was still asleep. A quick shower revived
her a little, and she dressed rapidly in a denim skirt and
sleeveless shirt, brushing her hair to hang loose to her
shoulders. Emily arrived at her son's cot in time to see him
dragging himself upright by the cot-rail, unusually dis-
gruntled.

'Mum-mum,' he said predictably, a scowl on his face
laughably like Luc's.

'What's the matter with you, grumpy?' As Emily lifted him
out it became all too evident. Jamie was in crying need of a
bath and change of apparel.

'*Bom dia.*'

A shy voice behind her made Emily turn round, as the maid
who had helped her the day before stood there, her white
teeth displayed in a wide smile.

'Dirce?' said Emily tentatively, and the girl nodded
vigorously. 'Good morning, Dirce.'

With gestures and smiles the girl indicated that she wanted
to help, and Emily soon found it a great deal quicker to bathe
and change a little boy when there was someone at hand to
dispose of soiled linen, pass towels or hold a wriggling little
body still while it was dressed. Jamie palpably enjoyed having
this admiring addition to his handmaidens, and gurgled as she
clapped her hands in compliment to the picture he made
finally dressed in smart pale blue towelling shorts with
matching blue and white striped tee-shirt. He immediately
tried to imitate her, flapping his hands and laughing
uproariously. No language barrier here, concluded Emily,
with the guilty thought that it was really very pleasant to walk
away with Jamie on her shoulder, leaving Dirce to dispose of
all the unpleasant bits.

It was a beautiful morning, already quite warm, and as she
wandered slowly along the verandah to the kitchen she
breathed in the air deeply, remembering that last night there
had been a definite perfume in the air that was missing this
morning. But last night had hardly been very opportune for
asking about trivia like that in the midst of their quiet, furious
little altercation. Emily dismissed this from her mind as she
entered the kitchen to a chorus of '*Bom dias*' from Maria, the
housemaid, Dica, the large black cook, whom she greeted for

the first time, also a thin, wiry little man who was introduced
a little unintelligibly as José. Ah, the gardener, thought Emily,
surrendering Jamie willy-nilly to the arms of Dica, who
poured floods of baby worship over him while Maria
presented her new mistress with a large cup of milky coffee.
Ambrosia, thought Emily, watching her son's installation into
his father's ornate rosewood highchair. Everyone suddenly
sprang to attention as Thurza Fonseca came into the room,
immaculate to the last hair, dressed in crisp pale green linen.

'Good morning, Emily.' A cool kiss was bestowed on
Emily's surprised cheek, then Thurza greeted her staff, finally
bestowing her attention on her grandson, who smiled cheerily
at this other member of his court. Spoiled rotten, thought
Emily with resignation; what else could one expect? Still, Luc
had obviously survived the same treatment. Yes, and look
what it had done for him—used to having his own way in
everything, she thought acidly.

Thurza suggested Emily leave her son to breakfast with
Maria in attendance while the two of them took theirs on the
verandah.

Emily was reluctant, looking at her son with misgivings.

'I really don't feel I should leave him yet just like that.'

'He managed perfectly well yesterday morning,' said Thurza
tartly. 'You'll probably find he eats more with the girls than
with you. Come along.'

Powerless against Thurza's bracing personality, Emily
allowed herself to be shepherded out on the verandah, with an
anguished look over her shoulder at Jamie, who ignored her
completely, entirely wrapped up in his new adoring entourage.
Maria was spooning porridge into his mouth while Dica
prepared scrambled eggs for his next course.

Emily sat down at the breakfast table opposite Thurza
feeling forlorn and superfluous. The other woman smiled at
her not unkindly as she raised the delicate china teapot and
poured tea into matching Spode cups.

'No guilt is necessary about leaving him to the maids for a
little while now and then, Emily. Motherhood need not be
quite as draining an occupation now that you're living here at
Casa d'Ouro. Not that I approve of children being left to the
care of servants too much. On the contrary. But delegating

nappy-washing and the occasional meal to Maria or Dirce
will do Jamie very little harm, and you a great deal of good.
You're much too thin and there are shadows under your eyes.
You obviously need feeding up.' She passed Emily's cup to
her briskly. 'There, enough lecturing, I think. Now while you
try some of this *mamão*—perhaps you know it better as
papaya?—you shall tell me something of this historic house
where Luc found you.'

Emily tasted her melon-like slice of fruit with interest,
enjoying the smooth, peach texture very much, deciding it had
a flavour all its own.

'I rather thought Luc meant me to put all that behind me,'
she said, 'and concentrate on my life here.'

'Men are not always reasonable. I think it would be a great
mistake to forget your heritage. I never lose sight of the fact
that I was once a Treharne, a family every bit as good as the
Fonsecas in their own way, and I never allowed my Jaime to
forget it. Strange that you should give his great-grandson the
same name.'

'My father's,' explained Emily, 'a happy coincidence, as it
turned out.'

'He has a second name?'

'Marcus.' Emily looked levelly at the other woman.

'Your—former husband, I presume,' said Thurza, touching
her lips delicately with her hand-embroidered napkin. Emily
nodded and changed the subject swiftly.

'I didn't even hear Luc get up. Does he start very early?'

'Six-thirty. He likes to be down at the mine before the
others, just like his father,' said Thurza proudly. 'He comes
home for lunch at noon, though he's away today, and his
hours rather vary after that. I'm never sure when to expect
him home in the evening—any time between five and eight.'

Emily stared at Thurza in surprise.

'That's a very long working day!'

'Luc is a very hard-working man. But now he has a wife
and son to attract him home perhaps he will come home
earlier.'

Maybe to see his son, thought Emily, but certainly not his
wife.

After breakfast the two women strolled in the garden, with

Jamie in his pushchair, Thurza taking pleasure in pointing out
many plants strange to Emily, in particular a small flowering
tree with mauve and white blossoms.

'I expect you've noticed its perfume once darkness falls. Its
name is *dama de noite*—lady of the night; scentless by day, but
heavenly once the sun goes down.'

There were also some gnarled trees with damson-like dark
fruit growing directly out of the greyish bark. These were
apparently called *jaboticabas*, and the fruit made excellent
jam, some of which Emily had enjoyed on her toast for
breakfast. She could have wandered around the fascinating
garden indefinitely, but before long the heat of the sun drove
them back to the shade of the verandah and a pause for coffee
while the little boy was installed in his playpen. For once he
was not too happy about being left to his own devices, and
clung to the bars shouting 'Mum-mum' in a very imperious
tone indeed.

'I think His Highness is letting all this new attention go to
his head,' said Emily ruefully, and turned her back on him
until he gave up and sat down with his toys.

'Well done, my dear.' Thurza smiled in approval. 'He must
realise that you're not always at his beck and call.'

'It's understandable. After all, I have been until just recently.'

'You must both find it strange.' Thurza was surprisingly
understanding. 'But I hope you will both settle down quickly.
Now let's make plans for my little reception.'

Emily listened with growing disquiet as plans for Thurza's
'little reception' revealed that it was to be quite a large, formal
affair.

'People have so few reasons to dress formally these days it's
pleasant to give them an excuse for doing so.' Thurza looked
up at Emily over the top of her spectacles. 'You have a
suitable dress?'

Emily nodded, almost wishing she could truthfully say no,
but then it would have made little difference as without doubt
she would have been packed off to the nearest town to buy
one if Thurza thought it necessary.

'I did a little shopping in London before I left,' she said. 'I
can only hope that what I have will be in keeping with Campo
d'Ouro standards.'

'Don't be meek, Emily. If *you* think it suitable that should be all that matters.'

Emily laughed.

'I presume that's the rule you live by!'

'Yes, indeed. It has served me in very good stead.' Thurza smiled and returned to her list. 'There, I think that will do. Not much point in confusing you with a string of names, but generally speaking it's a handful of mine officials, and the rest are local people with the odd relation or two mixed in. And some of Luc's Carvalho relations really *are* quite odd, in an aristocratic kind of way. What Fonsecas are left live in Sao Paulo, so we'll just have to leave them out.'

Emily was intrigued, and would have liked to hear more, but Thurza was bent on showing her round the house properly, so with Jamie settled on one hip Emily followed the older woman through a succession of large, high-ceilinged rooms filled with beautiful furniture, the two largest of which were connected by wide double doors and would be used for the party. Some rooms were kept closed now that the family had dwindled in size, but Thurza intimated that this would all be changed if Emily would kindly turn her thoughts to producing several more little Fonsecas. One long room was lined with portraits and photographs, more like a small museum than a private room. Rock samples were displayed on shelves, with various mounted animal heads on the walls between family portraits, the men all possessed of thick dark curling hair, heavy black eyebrows and dominant noses, quite irrespective of the characteristics of the relevant spouses hung alongside. Emily stopped before the photograph of one girl, and stood looking at it for some time, shifting Jamie to her other hip. Thurza Treharne Fonseca looked out at her, a proud smile on her lovely face beneath a misty cloud of dark hair, slender as a reed in a white, bias-cut satin evening dress with a great white rose on one shoulder, one hand touching the long rope of pearls that hung to her waist.

'How lovely,' said Emily involuntarily.

'Thank you, my dear. That was taken in 1930, soon after my marriage.'

'And this is your husband?'

Thurza looked fondly at the photograph.

'Yes, of course, though it might equally be Antonio, or Luc. As you see, it's only the clothes that change. The men are more or less identical. The Fonseca genes must be very powerful, they overcome all others with unfailing inflexibility; although I believe some Treharne blood contributed to Luc's height. My brothers were quite tall for Cornishmen.'

Emily moved to the next portrait, a mere head and shoulders of a girl with flawless white skin, huge dark eyes and an other-worldly look of purity and innocence more in keeping with a nun's habit.

'Luc's mother, Helenita.' Thurza sighed. 'Antonio worshipped her, but sadly she proved very delicate and the rigours of childbearing were too much for her. Like me, she had miscarriages, then finally gave birth to Luc only at the expense of her own life. Ridiculous, isn't it, when down in the village women regularly produce a baby once a year with no fuss at all. Come along, then.' She chucked Jamie under the chin as the little boy grew restive, bouncing up and down on Emily's hip. 'Leave your poor *mamae* alone and come and have your lunch.'

Emily was made to rest on her bed after a light meal, and to her surprise slept soundly for two hours. She woke up with a start to find it was nearly four o'clock. I'm lotus-eating, she thought, hurriedly putting on her blouse and skirt. This life of sloth will become all too addictive if I don't watch it—I must find something to do with myself. Jamie's room was empty and she hurried along the verandah to find Thurza enthroned behind the tea-tray and Jamie being pushed around the garden by both Dirce and Maria, each taking turns to pick up his woolly rabbit as he hurled it at them with shrieks of delight. The macaws set up a great sqwawking which the little boy tried to imitate to the laughter of the two maids and Emily smiled. How different Jamie's life had become in such a short time!

'You look much better.' Thurza examined Emily's face critically. 'You obviously need rest. Now have some tea and some of Dica's delicious coconut biscuits.'

After tea both women applied themselves to the invitations embossed in gold on thick white cards. Thurza kept a supply which merely needed filling in with the correct date and name, ready to be delivered by hand next day.

'Isn't it rather short notice for Saturday?' asked Emily.

'Not for an invitation to Casa d'Ouro,' said Thurza grandly.

Insisting on giving Jamie his bath and supper herself, Emily passed the time until Luc arrived home by keeping herself as occupied as possible, scarcely admitting to herself how ill at ease she felt after the rather less than cordial interchange of the night before. When Maria called her to the telephone as Jamie was finishing his supper Emily felt a start of surprise, not even remembering where the telephone was. She followed the girl to the morning room, where Thurza was speaking into an elegant onyx and gilt instrument which stood on the small rosewood escritoire. She handed over the telephone to Emily and tactfully left the room.

'Hello,' said Emily cautiously.

'Hello, *carinha*,' said the startlingly caressing voice of her husband, 'I've just arrived from Congonhas and I shall be home in about half an hour. Will you please keep Jamie up until then?'

'Yes. I'm sure he'll be delighted,' said Emily blankly.

'How has your day been, darling?'

'Er—fine; very pleasant. And yours?' She looked at the instrument with suspicion.

'A little hectic. I greatly look forward to a relaxing evening with my wife.' In the background Emily could make out the sound of other voices, and she raised a sardonic eyebrow.

'Keeping up appearances—"darling"?'

'Of course, my love. *Até logo*.'

The telephone looked too ornamental and costly to treat with any disrespect, so Emily laid the receiver carefully on its cradle, scowling at it with irritation. Hypocrite! She turned, arranging a smile on her face as Thurza came back into the room to say Jamie was in the playpen under Maria's watchful eye and Emily had just nice time to bathe and change before Luc arrived home.

Complying mutinously, Emily felt thoroughly put out. Everything must revolve around the wishes of the *patrão*—no matter if Jamie was tired or not. The incontrovertible fact that Jamie was as bright as a button made it even more annoying.

Emily had to admit that she looked a lot better this evening than she had for some time. Her eyes shone as she applied a little silvery blue shadow to them, and her face was definitely less drawn. Her aquamarine cotton dress, cut low and square like a sundress, with wide straps, had a matching loose jacket in the same colour, checked in citrus and white, and there were new backless white kid sandals with four-inch heels to go with it. She was hurrying to play with Jamie just as Luc arrived home. They met head-on in the middle of the verandah, and to her annoyance he held her close for a moment and kissed her hard. She opened her mouth to protest, then saw Thurza smiling indulgently at them both.

'You look better, *carinha*,' said Luc, examining her in some detail. 'Good evening, Thurza.' He bent to kiss his grandmother's delicately rouged cheek and gave a stifled yawn. 'Forgive me, it's been a long day. Did you keep Jamie up?'

'Of course,' said Emily meekly. 'You told me to.'

He shot her a glinting look.

'What a compliant little wife! Then let me see him before you put him to bed.'

'He's in the kitchen in his playpen,' said Thurza, following him and leaving Emily to bring up the rear.

The scene in the kitchen as Luc entered was comic enough to dispel Emily's ill humour. The maids fluttered like doves in a cot and Jamie hauled himself up to his feet with a huge smile, saying 'Da-da' quite clearly before subsiding with a thump when he released the bars to reach up to his father.

Luc instantly bent to scoop him up, disregarding the dust on his khaki shirt, holding the small pyjamaed figure close, his face buried in his son's curls.

Emily turned away from the unashamed tears in Thurza's eyes and the worshipful expressions on the faces of the maids, prey to a mixture of emotions herself.

'Come and sit on the verandah with your Da-da while he has a drink,' Luc said to his son, 'and perhaps Mama and Vo-vo will come too while Dica gets on with the dinner.'

Both women followed in his train to sit on the verandah, where candles in glass-shaded copper holders shed a soft glow to augment the light of a new moon in the warm, still evening sky. As Luc was preoccupied with Jamie Emily felt obliged to pour the drinks in deference to Thurza's seniority. She gave the older woman her habitual sparing quantity of dry sherry, mixed a double gin with a large tonic and placed it in Luc's reach on the table, then had a swift look at the rest of the drinks for something she herself fancied.

'Try a Cuba Libre, Emily. You will enjoy that.' Luc took his attention away from Jamie for a moment. 'A small quantity of white rum, plenty of ice, the juice of a fresh lime and as much cola as you like.'

After carrying out his instructions Emily was pleased with the resulting concoction and sat down on the settee next to Luc in response to his imperious gesture.

'You look very charming tonight,' he said gravely. 'I like your dress.'

'Thank you.' Emily felt embarrassed and put out a finger to tickle her son's ribs.

'Mum-mum,' said Jamie immediately, and held out his arms, but Luc laughed and restrained him, turning his son's attention to his watch, holding it to the small ear for Jamie to hear the tick.

'I have been showing Emily the family portraits,' said Thurza, watching the little family tableau with bright eyes.

'A little repetitive on the male side, don't you think?' Luc grinned.

'*You* aren't there yet,' remarked Emily, enjoying the flavour of her drink.

'I thought I would create a precedent. You and I shall have our portrait taken together in a few weeks' time, when you are completely rested, and your new life has restored the bloom to your cheeks.'

Emily flushed, oddly put out.

'I'm not photogenic,' she muttered.

'Have you had a photograph taken recently?'

'Well, no, not since I was at school——'

'I thought not. This will be different.'

Privately Emily considered this last an understatement, every instinct in rebellion at the thought of her own unremarkable features cheek by jowl with the beauties already on the wall in the gallery.

'Perhaps you should be thinking of changing for dinner, Luc,' suggested Thurza quietly. 'I think one small gentleman has finally fallen asleep.'

Luc looked down tenderly at the small drooping head and rose carefully to his feet, Emily going on before him to Jamie's room to turn down the cot sheet and make sure Rabbit was waiting. Luc laid his son down with care, watching in silence as Emily tucked the cover round him, then following her out quietly as they left the room.

'I'll be as swift as I can,' he said softly, some of the tenderness still in his face.

Emily shrugged.

'No rush,' she said casually, and walked unhurriedly away, aware that two coal-dark eyes were boring into her back.

Dinner was a leisurely meal in the long, cool dining room, Thurza's presence ensuring that an atmosphere of reasonable cordiality prevailed. Emily found Dirce's cooking very much to her taste and enjoyed the minute steaks fried in crisp batter with their accompaniment of green beans and crisp salad, also the compote of chilled fresh figs with delicious creamy coconut ice-cream that followed.

'Dirce's speciality,' said Thurza. 'Very good, isn't it?'

'M'm, superb.' Emily licked her spoon childishly, then flushed as she looked up to catch the amusement in her husband's eyes.

'You look like Jamie when you do that,' he said, grinning.

'A little difficult, wouldn't you say, when he's the image of you?'

'A fact that gives me great pride and pleasure, I assure you, *carinha*.'

'Let's hope that when you have a daughter she will resemble Emily a little more,' said Thurza genially. 'That nose of yours could be a handicap to a girl.'

There was a little silence, while Emily busied herself with meticulously folding her napkin, relieved when Maria brought in the coffee tray.

Thurza told the girl to take it outside on the verandah so that they could enjoy the starry evening as long as possible. Emily was grateful for the more muted light of the candles, though felt ill at ease when Luc led her to the bamboo settee and settled himself alongside her, capturing her hand. Thurza smiled indulgently as she handed them their coffee cups.

'You will need two hands, Luc, release her for just a moment.' She looked at Emily quizzically. 'I believe you've missed him today, haven't you, dear?' Luckily she went on without waiting for an answer. 'But Emily feels you don't care for her to speak of her life in Warwickshire, Luc. You can hardly expect her to erase the past twenty years like chalk from a blackboard, you know. Besides, I'm very keen to hear all about the old manor house where she lived, and what must be a fascinating historical background.'

Luc lit a cheroot and leaned back, his long, black-clad legs stretched out before him, his white shirt glimmering in the dim light. He recaptured one of Emily's unwilling hands and held it fast.

'Emily lived in the Dower House, not the Manor House, and it is her life there that I particularly desire forgotten. She may regale you with as much historic data of Compton Lacey as you wish.'

Emily was stung by the autocratic finality of his words.

'That particular period incorporates the first nine months of Jamie's life—*darling*,' she said, her tone patently saccharine. 'Am I to proceed as though he sprang into being at almost a year old?'

'I would prefer that Jamie is not informed of that time, yes,' said Luc heavily.

'Even though without Marcus Lacey we would both have been in a very unenviable situation!' Emily made no attempt to stem the bitterness in her voice, careless of any impression given to Thurza, who came unexpectedly to her support.

'Emily is right, Luc. It is only just that full credit is given to this man who married her for her protection.' Thurza sat, straight-backed, regarding her grandson with unwonted disapproval. 'After all, from what little I know, it sounds as though he was able to trace his lineage back a great deal further than the Fonsecas.'

Luc's mouth was rigid, his body tense, and he was obviously exerting considerable control over himself.

'A typical comment, Thurza,' he drawled finally, 'but totally irrelevant. My little wife has a stronger personality

than you imagine. She refused to *marry* Marcus Lacey, even
though she was fully aware that the poor devil had only a
limited time to live. Apparently that would have created
complications with the laws of inheritance, etc. She would
have let Jamie grow up with the slur of bastardy—did you
know?'

Emily felt stunned, cold with shock, unable to marshal any
defences, and was taken aback when the old lady spoke
sharply to Luc.

'That is naturally a surprise to me. I do not approve or
condone such a decision. But in the light of the alternative
readily available as Mr Lacey's wife, it took courage, I think.'
She looked searchingly at Emily. 'You have no other family?'

'Two old aunts in Scotland,' said Emily tonelessly. 'I felt it
hardly fair to confront them with my predicament. It was my
fault; my problem, after all. I had no idea what had happened
to Luc. If he were dead it was no use. If he were alive—well, I
had no taste for begging, even if I'd known where to contact
him. Besides, eventually the short time we had spent together
seemed ephemeral, unreal.'

'If it were so easily put aside,' said Luc harshly, 'it must
have been a great inconvenience to bear a son who looked so
much like me.'

'It didn't help,' agreed Emily bitterly.

'So this impression of connubial bliss you have been trying
to make on me has been a charade.' Thurza's shrewd old eyes
turned from one to the other. 'You must both have found it a
strain.'

'Emily has. I find it remarkably easy, and necessary. We
shall go on doing so,' said Luc with a warning note in his
voice. 'We have servants, remember, Thurza. Whatever we
feel in private our public attitude is one of newly wedded
harmony.' Emily moved away from him instinctively, but his
hard, immovable arm brought her back. 'I am tired and I
would like to go to bed. You will do so too, Emily. You may
read if you wish, the light will not disturb me. Goodnight,
Thurza.'

Luc rose and bent to kiss his obviously thoughtful
grandmother. Emily stood awkwardly.

'Goodnight, Mrs Fonseca.'

The latter regarded her wryly.

'You have avoided addressing me as anything in particular all day, my girl. I thought we'd agreed on "Thurza". Bend down and kiss me.'

Emily obliged, surprised.

'Goodnight—Thurza,' she said quietly.

'Goodnight, my dear. There are some paperbacks in the drawer of your bedside table.'

Luc stood with impatience, waiting for the little interchange to end, then took hold of Emily's elbow and bore her off in the direction of their bedroom. Any fears of his behaviour once there were soon dispelled, as he did exactly the same as the night before, apart from the shower. Emily averted her eyes while he stripped off his clothes, then she gathered up her nightgown and robe in silence and took herself off to the bathroom to undress before taking a final look at Jamie. When she got back to the bedroom, Luc was lying with his back towards her and was apparently fast asleep. Emily shrugged, quietly opened the drawer in the bedside table, and after a quick look through the handful of books it contained, decided to re-read *A Town Like Alice*.

CHAPTER TWELVE

IN some strange way the revelation of their true relationship to Thurza made life easier for Emily. There was no longer the need to pretend, something which had gone against the grain. Hypocrisy was one of Emily's least favourite human failings, and to have Thurza know the truth made dealings with her straightforward without having to watch every word she uttered.

The situation was by no means to Thurza's taste. She made no bones about the fact that Emily should try to effect a reconciliation with Luc.

'Whatever you say, my girl,' she said in her usual astringent manner, 'the fact remains that Luc was nearly demented when his memory finally returned, and you with it. He burned up the telephone lines to your friend—Mrs Crawford, if I remember correctly?'

Emily nodded. They were taking their after-breakfast stroll with Jamie in the pushchair, and had just passed out of earshot of the noisy macaws.

'Better than dogs as regards intruders, but ear-splitting at times,' said Thurza. 'Let's sit on the garden seat and put Jamie to crawl around on his blanket for a while. Did you speak to Luc this morning?'

Emily shook her head, dumping her son on the grass with a selection of toys, perching a floppy white sunhat on his head.

'I woke when he did, but decided to play dumb and pretend I was asleep. I'm a coward.'

'No, I wouldn't agree there. A coward would hardly take on a dying man to cope with during a pregnancy.'

'But Marcus wasn't a "dying man", as you put it, until well after Jamie's birth. He was the one who looked after me until then. I was sick all the time and constantly tired, not really the sort of burden to wish on a man with a death sentence.'

'No doubt it took his mind off it very effectively.' Thurza bent to retrieve a rattle. 'And now the poor man is dead and you and Luc are very much alive. Are you going to remain at loggerheads indefinitely? I'll be very honest and say that I would very much like to see a brother or sister or two for Jamie before I die.'

Emily laughed ruefully.

'You don't mince words, Thurza! Anyway, you look pretty fit to me; better than I do, so I don't think you can pull that one for a while.'

'Then tell me, Emily, why do you feel enmity towards Luc, when I know very well that his feelings for you never altered?' Thurza's voice lost its usual cadence of authority in her anxiety to clarify the situation.

'I was anguished when I heard nothing from Luc.' Emily looked down at her hands, flushing. 'He was the first—the only man to—to——'

'Yes, I understand. Go on.'

'I thought he was Lancelot and Galahad and the Black Prince all rolled into one. I suppose the hours I spent in that ancient old house made the past more real to me than the humdrum present I lived outside it, and Luc was everything I had ever dreamed of. We spent as much time together during those five days as we could. My life was transformed. What happened between us was entirely mutual; utterly natural and inevitable. So that when he had to leave so suddenly I felt as though half of me had gone with him. Then came the agony of that awful silence. Every day was an endurance test of time to be lived through somehow until the post arrived again. But nothing came, ever. And then I realised I was pregnant. There are no words to illustrate how I felt—I was utterly desperate. You know the rest.' She turned impulsively to the other woman. 'If only I could have been told what had happened to Luc, somehow, in some way, my life would have been easier. It was the not knowing that nearly destroyed me. And in some way half of me never recovered, and I just don't feel the same. Luc should have let Lydia tell me, even if he made no direct communication with me himself.'

Thurza was thoughtful and silent as she watched Emily replace the hat on Jamie's unwilling head.

'Luc was stunned when he learned you had apparently married so quickly,' she said slowly, her brow furrowed. 'Then the day he learned of Jamie's birth he shut himself up in his study for a day with a whisky bottle and refused to emerge. After that he went back to the mine and began to work an eighteen-hour day, driving himself mercilessly. Eventually he learned to live with himself—and me—again and I thought that would be the end of it, until your Mrs Crawford rang here to speak to Luc. By the greatest of ironies he had left for England only a day earlier to attend a conference and give some lectures.'

Both women were quiet for some time, watching the child as he made fruitless efforts to catch a brilliant blue butterfly.

'You're not what I wanted for Luc,' said Thurza, characteristically frank. 'I had my heart set on a Brazilian girl brought up to cope with a house like Casa d'Ouro.'

'I'm in full agreement. I had no wish to leave England,' said Emily sadly. 'But Luc made it utterly impossible for me to do anything else, so I shall just have to make the best of it. Although,' she slid a sly little look at Thurza, 'Luc's grandfather married an English girl a lot younger than me, and *she* seems to have coped remarkably well.'

Thurza laughed and patted Emily's hand.

'Well said, my dear! We'll just have to try to rub along together, won't we?'

Any further soul-searchings were cut short by a roar of frustration as Jamie fell on his back and both of them rushed to comfort him, pushing him back to the house for their *merenda*, the mid-morning snack.

Life fell into a fairly civilised pattern, helped greatly by preparations for the party. Luc came home to lunch each day, returned each evening in good time to play with Jamie for an hour, but refused adamantly to associate himself in any way with the approaching festivities. Emily and Luc occupied a sort of no-man's-land where each treated the other with civility and a wary, tense neutrality, while Thurza played a role very similar to that of a U.N. peace-keeping force, ready to step in whenever the truce looked likely to break down. Each night Emily and Luc retired to their bedroom together, for all the world like any normal married couple, except that behind the bedroom door not a word was exchanged beyond the obligatory 'goodnight'.

Despite this artificial situation Emily found herself beginning to unwind, her appetite better, her pallor changing to a faintly sunkissed glow by her strictly rationed sessions in the garden each day. After-dinner conversation became a pleasure rather than an ordeal, and Luc even told Emily a little about his working day, which interested her enormously and gave her a greater insight into what made this complex husband of hers tick.

'By the way, Thurza,' he said one evening, 'I haven't seen Chico since we arrived.'

'Chico?' asked Emily.

'Chico is a toucan,' said Thurza. 'At least that's his official description. To me he's a constant headache.'

'Doesn't he live in the aviary?'

Thurza looked at Luc significantly.

'No indeed. He has a perch out near the maids' room, and is supposed never to come inside the house.'

Luc grinned.

'Whereas in fact he enjoys tea and toast with me every morning before the rest of the household is up.'

'I thought you never drank tea!' Emily was highly amused.

'He doesn't,' said Thurza acidly. 'Luc drinks his usual coffee and he makes a pot of tea especially for that wretched bird—you may well laugh, Emily, but every now and then he decides to go what I believe the dear Queen does these days— walkabout, isn't it?'

'Is it difficult to get him back?'

'I hope every time that he *won't* come back,' said Thurza bitterly, 'but he does, after pecking holes in every *mamao* and tomato he can find ripening on anyone's window ledge. Then I shall have to despatch the maids with grovelling notes of apology and various fruit to make up the deficiencies. So lowering!'

Emily was enchanted. She lay laughing helplessly, her head near Luc's shoulder on the back of the settee in the morning room. Luc put a hand over hers and her laughter died away instantly. He stiffened, removed the offending hand and stood up.

'I have a little work I must do in the study for a while,' he said wearily, the lines at the corners of his eyes suddenly pronounced. 'Do not wait for me, Emily. I am sure you are tired. I will say goodnight to you now, Thurza.'

There was a lengthy silence after Luc had closed the door quietly behind him.

'For a moment there I saw things as they could be,' Thurza sighed.

'I know,' said Emily defensively, 'but I need time. I realise things can't go on for ever like this, but I just—need more time.' She rubbed her eyes like a tired child. 'I think I will go to bed. I'm very tired, though I can't imagine why when all I do is a lot of nothing.'

'You look a great deal better on it,' Thurza assured her, 'so get as much rest in as you can. You'll need it for Saturday.'

'Oh yes—Saturday.' Emily felt no enthusiasm at the prospect. 'Will it be very grand, Thurza?'

'Brazilian ladies like to dress up; silk, satin, that sort of thing.' Thurza looked at her in enquiry. 'Are you worried about what to wear? If it's any help, my dress is grey and violet printed chiffon, suitably high in neck and sleeve, as becomes my age.'

'Your age! I shall be delighted if I look half as good as you if I reach seventy.'

'A very nice turn of phrase, Emily.'

'I meant it!'

'I know. That's what made it such pleasant hearing. Now go to bed.'

Emily took herself off to see Jamie and prepared for bed obediently. She had read several chapters of a rather dull historical novel before the door opened and Luc came in.

'I thought you would be asleep.' He stood at the foot of the bed, staring down at her moodily.

'I sleep in the afternoons, you know,' said Emily reasonably. 'I find it difficult to get to sleep at night without reading for a while.'

Luc came towards her, sitting on the edge of her bed.

'There are other ways of wooing sleep.' His eyes stared hypnotically into hers, and very slowly his hand moved to touch her hair. Motionless, Emily lay looking up at him as his head came slowly down towards her. His mouth hovered above her own for what seemed like minutes, then he lightly kissed the tip of her nose and got up. She watched him strip his clothes from the powerful body that gleamed like copper in the light from the lamp, held motionless by some strange paralysis as, just the same as each preceding night, he slid into bed with his back to her and settled down to sleep.

'Goodnight, Emily.' His voice was barely audible.

'Goodnight, Luc,' she answered, her lips dry, then returned to her novel, the words on the printed page suddenly as meaningless as though they were in a foreign language.

Next morning Emily made no pretence of sleep when Luc got up, and she lay unashamedly watching him dress in the fresh set of khaki trousers and shirt he wore every day. A lot of laundry, she thought drowsily. Luc realised he was being watched and came over to the bed, smiling faintly.

'I woke you—I am sorry.'

'I wake every morning.' She pushed a hand through her tousled hair, flushing a little as he touched a long finger to her cheek.

'Go back to sleep.' Then he was gone, only to return a few minutes later.

'Come with me,' he whispered, handing her her robe. 'I want to introduce you to someone.'

'What! I haven't washed . . .' Emily was dragged protesting through the door.

'He won't mind.'

They tiptoed along the verandah in the near chill of the early morning, taking care not to disturb anyone in the slumbering household, and entered the kitchen. There, perched on her son's highchair, was a glossy black toucan, his long yellow bill and bright blue eye turned on her with such a look of impudence that Emily giggled helplessly.

'The famous Chico, I presume. But Luc, he doesn't look real!'

'He's real enough,' said Luc, grinning. 'I expect he'll spare you a cup of tea from his pot if you would care for one.'

'Isn't that big of him! Yes, please.'

She sipped her tea, watching in fascination as the bird consumed a piece of toast, enjoyed a small bowl of tea, then hopped on Luc's arm for a lift to his perch outside. Emily stood up as Luc came back in.

'Now I'm here can I cook you bacon and eggs or something, Luc?'

'Thank you, but no. I had some coffee. Usually I have nothing else in the morning. However,' he looked down at her, his black eyes gleaming from beneath half-closed lids, 'this morning there *is* something else I would like.'

Swiftly he pulled her into his arms and kissed her mouth even as it opened to protest. For a moment she resisted, then yielded abruptly. After a long moment he thrust her away, and they both stood staring at each other, breathing raggedly. He started to speak, then changed his mind, shrugged and turned on his heel, leaving without a word.

Emily sat at the table limply, staring blankly, then she got up and wrung out one of Dica's snowy dishcloths in hot soapy water and wiped down the highchair. Something would have to be done with the irresistible Chico; one could hardly allow a toucan to share a chair with Jamie. She refused to think about Luc, then sat down again and thought exclusively of nothing else until the maids came in and caught her at it.

Jamie had to be content with more of Dirce's company that

morning than his mother's, as Emily became caught up in the
preparations for the party. Thurza usually liked to serve
several hot dishes as well as cold at her buffet suppers, and
was anxious to provide something different to augment the
usual repertoire at Dica's command. When Emily hesitantly
tendered her mother's recipe for the beef casserole she had
once made for Luc Thurza was delighted, and Maria was sent
to take the necessary meat from the freezer after breakfast.
Immediately it had thawed sufficiently there was a strange,
three-cornered cooking session with Emily giving instructions
in English to Thurza, from whom they were transmitted in
Portuguese to Dica, who carried them out with a broad smile,
cries of rapture coming from all sides as the tantalising odours
of the mingled ingredients began to rise from the enormous
pot.

Any constraint Emily anticipated when Luc came home to
lunch was lost in the vociferous welcome given him by his son,
who seemed indignant at Emily's desertion, coupled with
Thurza's account of the new dish Emily had taught Dica.

'I believe I may have tasted it before,' he said, smiling at
Emily over Jamie's head. 'But in the meantime have you
anything to offer a hungry man for lunch? What I was
allowed at breakfast was meagre in the extreme.'

Thurza watched in fascination as a flood of colour rose in
Emily's cheeks, but made no comment, merely chivvying the
maids to put on some speed with the meal.

'Of course, you *will* organise the drinks for the party, Luc?'
she asked as the shrimp bisque was served. 'I always think
that should be left to a man.'

'How many are coming?' he asked with resignation.

'About forty.'

'That many?' Luc groaned. 'Poor Emily will never
remember names! I shall stay close by your side, never fear.'

Emily smiled nervously, then looked guilty as Luc asked
Thurza if she knew that Chico was back.

'No, I didn't.' Thurza obviously had no pleasure in the
information.

'Didn't you mention it, Emily?' Luc's eyes gleamed across
the table.

'Er—no, it slipped my mind.' To Emily's distress the hateful tide of colour engulfed her again, and Thurza looked across at her sharply.

'I hope you're not coming down with a fever, Emily. The party is entirely for your sake, after all.'

'She would hardly be so inconsiderate as to fall ill at such a grossly inconvenient time, I'm sure,' said Luc silkily, and Thurza had the grace to look a little ashamed. She leaned across and patted Emily's hand apologetically.

'You know I didn't mean it like that, Emily. That bird affects my blood pressure.'

'Which is excessively normal for your age, so do not be dramatic!' Luc winked at Emily, who felt immediately better. 'What are you going to wear, Emily?' he asked idly.

'If something formal is necessary I have only two dresses suitable for hot weather, one red, one blue.'

'Blue,' said Luc, instantly.

'Why?'

He shrugged.

'I like you in blue.'

'Did you buy it in London?' asked Thurza with interest.

'Yes. It's quite plain, really, but I—I liked it.' Emily glanced mischievously at Luc. 'It was sinfully expensive.'

'I fully expect my wife to be appropriately gowned, Emily. Whatever the cost I am sure it is worth it.'

When Luc had returned to the mine Emily decided to forgo her nap in favour of the swim she had longed for ever since seeing the pool. A new gate of trelliswork now closed off the gap in the hibiscus hedge, and she unbolted it with anticipation. She threw off the huge brown bath sheet which served as a wrap, and in the plain white bikini she had owned since she was sixteen she let herself into the inviting blue depths, gasping momentarily at the cool water, then she struck out and swam six lengths quite slowly with her modest school-taught breast-stroke. Tiring rapidly towards the end of the last length, she hauled herself up the white-painted steps and collapsed in a heap on the bath sheet, gasping for breath. The sun was very hot and she got up wearily, still breathing heavily, decided the garden chairs were too heavy to move, and spread the towel far into the shade of the eucalyptus trees at the far end of the garden. She fell into a deep sleep, only to

awaken grumpily moments later to the sounds of shouting
and hard hands grasping and shaking her.

'Stop it,' grumbled Emily irritably, peering up at Luc in
surprise. 'What are you doing home?'

'You may well ask,' he said hoarsely, wrapping her in the
towel and picking her up.

'What on earth are you doing?' Emily was rapidly coming
back to her senses and realised the garden was full of people;
Thurza, Jamie crying his eyes out in Dirce's arms, Dica and
Maria apparently in hysterics with their aprons over their
heads—even José the gardener.

'What's happened?' she asked frantically, struggling to get
down. 'What's the matter with Jamie?'

'Nothing,' said Luc tersely, striding swiftly towards the
house past the ear-blasting macaws, with Thurza and the rest
following only slightly less rapidly behind him.

'Luc——'

'Shut up,' he said through his teeth. Emily was too
astonished to be angry, and it suddenly struck her how grey
Luc's face looked, with great drops of sweat rolling down it.

'Are you sick?' she asked, as they reached the bedroom.

He dumped her unceremoniously down on the bed.

'Only with worry, you—idiot girl!'

To Emily's consternation she realised he was shaking.

Thurza came in, her face lined with worry.

'Is she all right, Luc?'

'Yes. Tell Maria to stop crying and run a hot bath. Dica can
make some tea—Dirce can bring Jamie in here so he can see
his mother. Oh, and tell José to make sure that gate's bolted.'

Thurza obeyed with unwonted docility and the next
moment came back with a sodden crying little boy who hurled
himself out of her arms to get to his mother. He clutched his
arms round Emily's neck, hiccuping and repeating 'Mamae'.

'Whatever happened to "Mum-mum"?' asked Emily,
holding him tight.

'Precisely. What *did* happen to you, Emily?' Luc was
completely in command of himself once more, and he stood
beside the bed, looking accusingly at her.

'We were very worried, Emily.' Thurza sat on the edge of
the bed, and patted Emily's arm.

'I'm very sorry. But I haven't been long. I just fancied a swim instead of a nap as I was so hot after lunch, and I took my towel into the shade for a few minutes' rest. . . .' Something in their faces stopped her.

Luc held out an arm, his wrist with its gold Longines watch thrust before her eyes. It was five o'clock. Emily stared at it incredulously.

'It can't be!'

'I went back after lunch at a little past one. It possibly took you until say, one-thirty before you went in the pool. That is well over three hours ago. You will never use the pool alone again. Do you understand?' Luc's face was grim.

Emily smiled weakly.

'Why? Sharks?'

Her joke died a little death, as Luc bent over her menacingly.

'Jamie's crying brought Dirce running and she told my grandmother your bed hadn't been slept in. There was a frenzied search. This is a big house, and it took quite a long time. No one thought to look near the pool, as the gate was bolted on this side. So Thurza called me.'

'I'm sorry, Luc,' said Thurza, obviously distressed, 'but I was at my wits' end to know what to do.'

'Please don't apologise, *querida*,' Luc smiled gently at her, 'you did the right thing.'

'I still don't see——' began Emily, who was rapidly beginning to feel like a criminal.

'I unbolted the gate as a last resort,' went on Luc, interrupting her. 'Even then I didn't see you. On that brown towel, right under the trees, you were almost invisible. But then José, the gardener, returned from an errand and said *he* had bolted the gate during the afternoon, so I began to search.' He let out a deep breath. 'And there was Sleeping Beauty.'

'But I felt as though I'd only dozed for a moment or two,' said Emily dazedly, smoothing Jamie's hair, then looked down to see he had dropped off to sleep, worn out with emotion.

'Give him to me,' said Thurza. 'I'll just sit on the verandah and nurse him while you have a hot bath, otherwise you may get chilled.'

Emily handed over the sleeping child reluctantly and sat up quickly, only to fall back against the pillows again as the room swam round and great black dots danced before her eyes.

'Heavens,' she said faintly, then gasped as Luc swung her up in his arms and carried her next door to the bathroom.

'I'll manage now,' she said firmly.

He ignored her, unwrapping the towel and stripping off her bikini as impersonally as if she were Jamie. He deposited her in the bath, and deaf to her protests sponged her vigorously all over, quickly scooping her out again to put her on the cane chair while he dried her thoroughly. Wrapping her in a dry towel, he took her back to the bedroom and laid her down on his bed.

'Where are your nightgowns kept?' he asked.

'But I want to get dressed——' Emily stopped short at the look on Luc's face. 'In the top drawer of the chest.'

He took one out and came over to the bed, motioning her to sit up.

'I can do it, thank you.' The hateful, ever-ready flush rose immediately.

'Having gone this far, *linda flor*, I hardly think now is the time to turn prudish!'

Without more ado he sat her gently upright, unwrapped the towel and dropped the white broderie anglaise garment over her head, then fetched her satin wrap and enveloped her in it.

'Are you warm enough?'

She nodded, eyes downcast, then looked up at him pleadingly.

'I don't have to go to bed, do I? I seem to have slept far too much today already. Please let me come on the verandah with Jamie and Thurza.'

He looked at her expressionlessly.

'Will you promise to lie on the sofa?'

'Faithfully. I won't move.'

'Very well. I will bring something to cover you in case you get cold. That is not a warm dressing gown.'

Emily smiled shyly. 'It's pretty, though, don't you think?'

Luc's eyes softened and he smiled back genuinely for the first time since he'd found her.

'It is beautiful. Now I think you should brush your hair, it is standing up on end.'

This was enough to bring Emily to her feet instantly, only to sit down again, feeling decidedly weird.

'What is it?' Luc knelt beside her, frowning blackly.

'Nothing much—sort of giddyish, that's all. Perhaps you would fetch me the hairbrush.'

'Better still, I will brush it for you.'

Luc drew the brush through the fair strands, already showing lighter streaks of colour where the sun had caught them. Slowly and methodically he restored her hair to shining order, then he laid the brush down and picked her up.

'You'll get tired of doing this.' Emily felt uncomfortable at his proximity.

'I think the habit could become addictive,' he said gravely, and walked slowly back with her to where Thurza sat holding a still sleeping Jamie in her arms.

Luc laid Emily carefully down on the settee, watched critically by Thurza.

'You look better now—fetch the light rug from the foot of my bed, Luc, in case she feels cold, that robe isn't much protection.'

'But very decorative,' murmured Luc, smiling wickedly at Emily as he went off to do Thurza's bidding.

'I'm very sorry,' began Emily apologetically. 'I can't imagine what made me sleep like that. Sleeping sickness isn't prevalent in Brazil, is it? I swam a bit too much and honestly only meant to have a few minutes' rest in the shade as I was tired.'

'I shall ask the doctor to come down tomorrow. He can check you over to make sure.'

'Good idea.' Luc returned with the rug and tucked it over Emily's knees. 'Now lie still and keep out of mischief for five minutes while I have a bath.'

'I was thinking it might be better to cancel the party,' said Thurza thoughtfully, looking at Emily with a worried frown.

Emily shot up in alarm, ignoring the egg-beater apparently whirring inside her head.

'Please, don't do that. There's another day before the party. I promise to sit still, do nothing, eat everything I'm given.'

She looked up at Luc in appeal. 'People will think I'm afraid to meet them. Besides——' she smiled at them both ingenuously, 'I've never been to a party like this.'

'How can we resist such a plea?' Luc looked down at her militantly. 'But one false step, one attempt at insurrection, even——'

'Yes, yes, all right,' said Emily hastily. 'I *have* given my word.'

'If you're sure, Emily,' said Thurza doubtfully. 'Ah—I think my little love is waking up.'

Jamie stirred in her arms and blinked up at her drowsily, muttering indistinctly.

'What did you say, my precious?' asked his great-grandmother adoringly.

'Vo-vo,' repeated Jamie plainly, then came fully awake as he heard the delighted laughter of his parents.

'You have to admire his timing,' said his mother proudly.

CHAPTER THIRTEEN

EMILY obeyed her orders to the letter next day, lying meekly on the verandah settee with Jamie in the playpen beside her. Thurza came at intervals to sit with her, but the greater part of her time was spent in overseeing the frenzy of preparations for the party. José's wife came in to help as the maids turned out the two main connecting reception rooms and brought them to gleaming, burnished perfection. José ensured that the patio was tidied, swept, washed—even the aviary had a turn-out, to the annoyance of the protesting occupants, and its brass bars polished for the occasion.

Emily was frustrated by her enforced inactivity, but Jamie, obviously pleased to have his mother to himself, entertained her by demonstrating how easily he could pull himself to his feet and sidle along the side of the playpen, carefully holding on to the rail, with a look of such intense gratification on his face that his mother laughed outright. He was rapidly learning to say several words in both languages, and had no trouble at all in making his desires known to anyone who would listen.

Jamie soon tired of so much physical exertion and sat down to play with his favourite engine, 'chuff-chuffing' endlessly to himself as he pushed it to and fro. Emily watched him dreamily, marvelling at how quickly her life had changed. Just a short time ago she had been, to all intents and purposes, a grieving widow with a lonely future, and now she was in a different house in a different country half a world away, leading a life completely foreign to anything she had ever known before, as another man's wife. Well, more or less. With Jamie looked after by maids, no cooking or housework of any kind to do, in fact waited on hand and foot, Emily was beginning to feel decidedly useless. Unable to venture anywhere at the moment without someone anxiously querying her whereabouts, she felt as much penned up as the macaws in their great shining brass cage. In fact, from one point of view this whole house was just one great gilded cage where she was held prisoner by the ties of love; love for her child, of course Whatever feelings she had for Luc could best be described as amorphous at present.

He had been very kind after his initial anger over yesterday's foolishness had cooled down. She was bound to admit that some inner chord had been stirred by his attitude towards her over the past day or two, almost erasing the memory of the hard, implacable man who had threatened to fight her in court for possession of his son. Emily's face hardened at the thought. What kind of man would threaten a woman with such treatment! She must never forget the basic granite of Luc's nature whenever the softer, kinder Luc took over to cozen her into thawing towards him.

'That's a strange expression on your face, Emily.' Thurza broke briskly into her reverie, instructing Dirce to put the coffee tray on the table beside her. 'I thought you were sleeping, until I saw the frown.'

'Mere guilt at lying here while all of you are so busy,' said Emily lightly. 'It's too bad to have to loll about when I could be contributing.'

'Nonsense! There are more than enough of us to see to everything.' Thurza poured a larger cup of coffee than usual and added plenty of hot milk. 'I think you ought to drink more milk, Emily.'

'Honestly, I'm fine; there's nothing at all the matter with me.'

'H'm, we'll see. Dr Ferreira is coming to have a look at you in half an hour or so. I had a word with him earlier.'

'But, Thurza, I feel such a fraud.' Emily frowned. 'Does he speak English?'

'Yes. Did most of his training in America, so no problems there.' Thurza turned to Jamie, who was clamouring for her attention. 'What is it, my lovely?'

'I rather think he's asking for his elevenses, too,' chuckled Emily.

Thurza threw up her hands in apology.

'Vo-vo's sorry, darling. Here, you can ring the little bell for Dirce.'

Jamie was so delighted to comply that eventually he had to be forcibly parted from the silver handbell before anyone could resume a conversation. In the heat of the disagreement that ensued between the little boy and Thurza, the slim, elegant man whom Maria had shown through the main door stood unnoticed, a smile on his long, intelligent face as he watched the family group.

'I trust I do not intrude,' he said finally, coming forward to greet Thurza, who smiled at him ruefully offering him her hand.

'Forgive me, Dr Ferreira, this young man has rather a forceful personality. We were indulging in a clash of wills.' She turned to Emily. 'May I present Dr Ferreira, my dear. Doctor, this is Luc's wife, Emily—and this is their son, Jamie.'

The doctor took Emily's hand for a moment, murmuring *'Muito prazer'* before looking at the small boy who was now silenced by the simple means of a mug of orange juice hastily fetched by Dirce. He laughed.

'At least it is evident that this young man is not the patient.' He sat down beside Emily and took her hand. 'Senhora Fonseca tells me you were not feeling well yesterday.'

Emily flushed with embarrassment.

'I was stupid and overdid some swimming, then I went to sleep for a long time in the garden where no one could find me. I upset everyone very thoroughly, but I don't feel ill. In fact I feel very well today, Dr Ferreira.'

He held her wrist silently for a moment, looking at his watch, then apparently satisfied with her pulse he asked a few routine questions about her general health and smiled reassuringly.

'Nothing to worry about, I would say, young lady. Possibly you have overtaxed yourself lately.' He turned to Thurza. 'Will you bring her up to the hospital on Monday and we shall run a few tests? She could be a little anaemic, which could account for the dizziness. We shall see.'

Thurza was relieved.

'Do you think she's well enough for this little party I'm giving tomorrow, Doctor?'

'As long as she does not exert herself then I see no reason why she shouldn't enjoy the party every bit as much as I—and all the guests—will. Until then.'

Dr Ferriera bowed to them both and bent to look at Jamie before leaving.

'Another Fonseca in every detail!' His eyes twinkled as he made his adieus.

'Well,' Thurza relaxed in her chair, 'that's a relief! I was very worried about you yesterday. And worried was scarcely the word for Luc, poor boy. He was frantic!'

Emily stirred restlessly.

'I'm sorry to have caused so much trouble. I'll try not to do it again.'

'Well, never mind, let's forget about it and concentrate on tomorrow evening. Maria Braga is coming at five to do my hair—would you like her to do yours?'

Emily was doubtful.

'I'd thought just to knot it up on top of my head.'

'Then let her do it for you. She's really very good, and she might just as well do both of us while she's here.'

At seven-thirty the following evening Emily had to admit that her hair looked much better than if she had struggled with it herself. Still in her robe, she looked at herself in the mirror, turning this way and that to see her head from all sides. The glossy fair hair had been swept up puffily in a seemingly careless pompadour, secured in a swirling knot at the crown of her head, leaving soft curling fronds on her forehead, at her ears and at the nape of her neck. She looked up expectantly as Luc came in in his dressing gown, his hair still damp.

'What do you think of my hair?' Emily demanded.

Luc studied her gravely.

'Very, very lovely,' he said at last. 'When are you putting on your dress, so that I may see the finished effect?'

'I'll just go and tuck Jamie up and then I'll add the final touches.'

Luc smiled mockingly.

'Are you afraid to stay in the same room while I dress?'

'Hardly!' Emily made a face at him as she passed. 'After all, it's hardly a novelty by now.'

She tiptoed in to Jamie's bedroom and straightened him out as usual, covering him up, lingering over the process as long as she could. When she returned to the bedroom Luc was at his impressive best in white dinner jacket and narrow black trousers, with a loosely tied black bow at the neck of his white silk shirt.

'I hate ties of any sort,' he groaned, loosening the bow a little more. 'Do you think Thurza's idea of what is proper will be satisfied?'

'Oh, I think so,' Emily put her head on one side consideringly. 'Very elegant.'

'H'm.' He sounded disbelieving. 'I need a drink. Come down to the patio as soon as you are ready and I shall have something cool for you.'

As soon as he was gone Emily stripped off her robe and reached into the wardrobe for her dress. It was a little awkward to do up the long zip unaided, but she managed it eventually, and then stood examining herself in the mirror that lined one of the wardrobe doors.

The dress was plain and unornamented, a sheath of pale aquamarine silk, strapless, cut straight across her breasts to fall uninterrupted to just above her ankle bones, the shimmering fabric hugging her narrow hips lovingly, the skirt slit to just below the knee in the front to allow for movement. High-heeled sandals, mere strips of kid in the same colour, gave Emily height, a touch of nerves and excitement adding a glow to the face she made up with extra care, darkening her brows and lashes and using a slightly more vibrant shade of lipstick than usual. When she was ready she added the final touch, a long, long scarf of matching aquamarine silk was thrown around her throat to hang down her back to the hem of the skirt, its edges finished with ostrich feathers dyed to match the dress.

Emily walked slowly along to the steps leading down to the courtyard. Lights had been strung to glow effectively among the palm fronds and gave an immediate air of festivity to the patio. Luc looked up as the macaws warned him of her arrival, standing very still as he gazed up at her in silence. Emily made her way carefully down the steps in the new sandals and he came to life, coming forward to meet her.

'This is my blue dress,' she said unnecessarily. 'I hope you approve.'

'How could I not?' His voice was husky as he took her hand. 'You look—breathtaking; very sophisticated and beautiful.'

'I'm glad you like it,' she said in a matter-of-fact voice that gave no inkling of the havoc he was causing by the unwavering burn of the black eyes that strayed over her from top to toe. 'It was a frightful price.'

'*Nao faz mal*—it is beautiful. Only one thing is lacking.' Luc brought out three small jewel boxes from his pocket and led Emily to the lights over the improvised bar. The first box held a magnificent oval aquamarine pendant from a fine gold chain, the second a ring, a matching aquamarine flanked by four small diamonds on either side.

'Luc!' Emily was at a loss. 'They're exquisite!'

'Allow me.'

He slid the ring on the third finger of her right hand and moved the silk stole a little to fasten the pendant round her neck. Then he opened the third box and slid the ring inside on her left hand to join her wedding ring. Emily looked silently at the large baguette sapphire between two rose-cut diamonds and stared up at Luc, overcome by the magnificence of the jewels. She was spared the struggle to find further words by the appearance of Thurza, magnificent in floor-length grey chiffon printed with violets, a silk-lined stole of violet chiffon around her shoulders, diamonds glittering in her ears to match her ring.

'Let me see you, Emily,' she commanded. 'Turn round. Yes—perfect. Striking without being vulgar.' She bent forward to examine the pendant lying on Emily's breast. 'So the jewellery arrived, Luc.'

'Today, after a great deal of telephoning.' Luc's mouth lifted at the corners. 'I had to use all my powers of persuasion.'

Emily was fascinated by the play of light on the rings.

'Were they being altered?'

'Bless you, child,' said Thurza indulgently. 'They were being *made*, not altered. Luc had the stones made up into the pendant and ring especially for you, though I believe the sapphire ring just needed altering in size.'

Emily felt disorientated by her sudden acquisition of so much costly magnificence.

'There was no need . . . I mean, I never expected——'

'My wife would naturally be expected to wear jewels as beautiful as her clothes,' said Luc carelessly, then signalled to José, who, transformed into a waiter for the evening, had unobtrusively appeared to await their order. A little of Emily's glow dimmed, but she pulled herself together firmly and smiled brightly as she accepted her drink, going on to compliment Thurza on her dress.

'No one will be looking at *me* tonight, my dear,' said the older woman with a smile. 'Thank you just the same. All eyes will be turned on the new Senhora Fonseca—and some of the eyes are likely to be just a tiny bit green!'

Before Emily had time to ask what she meant the first of the guests had begun to arrive, and she took her place with Luc and Thurza to receive them.

A bewildering list of names was murmured which she despaired of ever attaching to the right faces, but she smiled radiantly and said what she hoped were the right things as Luc presented the Estate Manager, the Commercial Manager, the Chief Engineer, the Head Chemist, her mind reeling as her hand was kissed by a succession of men of varying ages, all of them dark, few of them tall, each one accompanied by a wife who, regardless of age or figure, was coiffured and gowned with an elegance that bordered on the elaborate on occasion, but was always superb down to the last detail.

All of them looked at Emily with a curiosity politely veiled in courtesy, and she was fiercely glad that her dress, her hair, and above all her jewels, were rivalled by no one.

It was pleasant to see an even faintly familiar face as Dr Ferreira arrived alone, followed by the Prefeito—the Mayor, murmured Thurza discreetly.

Then two elderly men of medium height arrived to greet Luc in English, to Emily's delight.

'Emily,' Luc slid his arm round her shoulders, 'I would like you to meet John Trelaur, the Mine Captain, and Tom Enys, the drill doctor, both crusty bachelors—their description, not mine—and both countrymen of yours.'

Emily smiled warmly as each man shook her hand in turn, welcoming her to Campo d'Ouro before greeting Thurza.

'Never thought this grandson of yours would take the plunge, Mrs Fonseca,' said John Trelaur, blue eyes twinkling.

'Nor have the good sense to pick an English girl,' put in Tom Enys.

'I was set such a good example by my grandfather,' said Luc suavely, 'what else could I do but follow suit?'

Thurza laughed appreciatively, tapping her grandson playfully on the arm, while his other arm tightened round his wife's slender bare shoulders, Emily glanced up automatically to meet black eyes gazing down into hers with every appearance of devotion. She flushed and dropped her eyes as a husky voice interrupted them, feeling Luc stiffen.

The two Cornishmen moved away to mingle with the crowd at the bar, and make way for the trio who stood waiting to be presented. A handsome, rather portly middle-aged Brazilian stood flanked by two young women, each of them strikingly beautiful in different ways.

Rose Red and Snow White, thought Emily with interest as Luc presented Ildefonso Machado, the company lawyer, and his daughters Analha and Teresinha. The latter was the lady in red; vermilion chiffon in handkerchief points with a neckline slashed to a depth that riveted all male eyes in the vicinity, a fact Teresinha acknowledged with a flash of great dark eyes and a flick of tumbling black satin hair. Analha, in white cotton lace, was equally dark and vivid, but her face was as sweet and charming as her sister's was unashamedly, sexily alluring.

'*Que coisa!* To bring a bride back from Inglaterra, Luc!' Teresinha's heavily accented English came from pouting vermilion lips as she cast an all-encompassing look at Emily that took in every last detail and dismissed it as unworthy of her attention. Her father frowned and hastily intervened.

'Who could blame him? You are to be congratulated, Luc. Senhora, please accept our sincere wishes for your happiness.'

'Thank you, you're very kind.' Emily decided it was time to take a hand in the procceedings. 'Please allow us to offer you a drink.'

Even as she spoke, more guests arrived, who proved to be Luc's Carvalho relations, and once more she was engulfed in introductions, with much kissing of cheeks this time as they claimed the privilege of family.

'Well done,' said Thurza approvingly, when it appeared everyone was present, 'you bore all that well, my dear. How do you feel?'

'Dazed, but fine otherwise. Do you think I was a disappointment?'

'On the contrary, I can assure you. Now, Luc, is everyone here?'

'Not quite.' Luc waved a hand towards a sandy-haired young man of incredible height who was loping down the steps, the lights glinting on his gold-rimmed glasses as he came up to them breathless and smiling, his hand outstretched.

'Mrs Fonseca, Luc—forgive me, I'm late.' He stopped dead, blinking as he took Emily's hand. 'And you are Emily—I suppose I should say Mrs Fonseca Jr.'

'Emily will do very well.' She smiled at the newcome, with such warmth he was apparently rendered dumb.

'This is Bob McClure, Emily,' said Luc. 'We were in college together——'

'So he took pity on me and gave me a job,' put in the American, grinning.

'And you just happen to be the best geologist in the U.S. of A.,' retorted Luc.

'And you must be the luckiest guy under the sun,' asnwered the other with such sincerity in the gaze riveted on Emily's face that even the dim lighting failed to conceal

Emily's brilliant blush. 'Holy Moses, I didn't think anyone could still *do* that!'

'And if you carry on like that she'll never *stop* doing it,' said Thurza with asperity. 'Now then, Mr McClure, get yourself a drink and then I must herd my guests to the supper table.'

She moved off with the American, leaving Emily and Luc alone for a moment, apart from the voices and laughter.

'You are quite sure you feel well, Emily?' Luc lifted her chin with a peremptory finger.

She nodded, smiling.

'I feel fine, really. Now perhaps we should help Thurza marshal her troops.'

'*I* shall be pleased to help you Luc, *querido*,' a husky voice interrupted, and Emily turned a thoughtful blue gaze on Teresinha Machado, who smiled lazily up at Luc, a slender red-tipped hand stretched out to touch his white sleeve. 'Perhaps Luc has told you; I am accustomed to aiding Dona Teresa on these occasions.'

'It must have slipped his mind.' Emily smiled meltingly at the girl with all the forbearance she could muster. 'It's *so* kind of you, Miss Machado. Nevertheless this time you'll be able to enjoy yourself so much more just as a guest, I'm sure, now that I am here to take over.' Still smiling, she ignored the amused admiration on her husband's face and mounted the steps to the verandah, the feather-tipped ends of her scarf floating behind her as she almost collided with Thurza at the top in her fury. The other woman looked over Emily's shoulder at the couple at the foot of the steps, Luc's arm still held fast by the beautiful Brazilian girl.

'Having a chat with Teresinha?'

'It was more a slight skirmish. I presume that, despite her colouring, she is the one with the green eyes you mentioned so cryptically?' Emily kept her tone light, but inwardly she was in a rage.

They went to inspect the array of food on the long buffet table set up on the far verandah, Thurza inwardly very much tickled by Emily's badly concealed militance.

'I must confess I always thought she would do well for Luc. Well educated, beautiful, accustomed to running a large household; her mother's dead and she rules Ildefonso

Machado's home with a rod of iron. Analha is artistic—paints landscapes, she's a different kettle of fish, but a very nice girl. I must say I really thought Luc was about to take the plunge with Teresinha at one stage.'

Emily pretended to be absorbed in checking on the various dishes keeping warm on the hotplate.

'What prevented him?' she asked casually.

'He took a trip to England, my dear, and everything changed. By the time he came back my poor Antonio was dead and Luc was preoccupied with all the duties of the *patrão*—also in trying to forget a certain young woman.' Thurza cast her a significant look.

Emily's chin lifted in the way that was rapidly becoming familiar to the other woman.

'Miss Machado offered to help you, Thurza. I told her that now I'm here her help would no longer be necessary.'

'Very right and proper. *You* are Luc's wife, Emily. It is your duty to fulfil that position in all ways to the best of your ability.' There was something in the shrewd old eyes that made Emily turn away hastily. 'Now then, my girl, ring the little bell and let us feed the troops.'

All through the demanding evening Emily circulated amongst the guests, Luc sometimes at her elbow, sometimes not, as the pressures of host took him away from her. Bob McClure appeared like magic whenever she looked in need of support, and Emily was grateful to the lanky, charming American, especially when language difficulties arose, as only a sprinkling of the Brazilian guests spoke enough English to make conversation a practical proposition. One of the most fluent was Mario de Carvalho, Luc's cousin, a slim young man whose flowing dark hair and the red rose in the lapel of his white suit gave him a studiely romantic air, which he exploited to the full. He was lying in wait for Emily when she returned from a check-up on Jamie.

'Luc is very, very fortunate,' he said, cornering Emily at the end of the verandah. He stood too close for comfort, gazing soulfully down at her. She smiled at him uncertainly, wishing Luc would appear.

'How kind of you to say so, Senhor de Carvalho,' she said politely.

'So fair and cool, a creature of the moon,' he said extravagantly, capturing her hand. 'Is there fire beneath that calm, little cousin?'

Before Emily could reply a familiar husky voice interrupted.

'And you would like to be the one to ignite it, *amigo*?' Teresinha Machado brushed past them, smiling mockingly over her shoulder. 'Do not presume on your relationship *too* much, Mario—*caro*.'

Emily watched her go with an intense dislike she hoped was not too obvious, then smiled brightly at her companion.

'So nice to meet you, Senhor de Carvalho. . . .'

'Mario, *por favor*!' he said fervently, his eyes glowing.

'Ah, here comes Luc,' said Emily with relief at the sight of the tall figure approaching them with purpose.

'*Como vai*, Luc?' said the young man, suddenly full of propriety.

'*Bem, 'brigado*,' answered Luc briefly, something in his demeanour telling his cousin to depart with promptitude.

'What are you doing with Mario in this dark corner?' Luc's eyes were blazing, to Emily's indignation.

'Precisely nothing. He was impressing me with his romantic charm, I think—which I merely found embarrassing.'

'You should not have allowed it,' he said harshly, taking her wrist in a bone-cracking grip and forcing her to walk quickly at his side to rejoin the guests in the reception rooms. Emily was furious.

'What's the matter, Luc, lost your little playmate?'

He stopped dead, looking down at her with menace, his eyebrows in the black bar across his forehead that usually meant trouble. Emily stumbled against him and he held her captive with a hard arm.

'What does *that* mean? Tell me!'

Emily licked her lips, her mouth suddenly dry at the look of cold anger in the eyes glaring down at her.

'Teresinha—the lady in the vulgar red dress,' she snapped defiantly. 'You seemed happily occupied with her earlier on.'

The verandah was now deserted, and Luc jerked her face up to his to kiss her mouth so hard her lips ground against her teeth.

'There is an insolent phrase in Portuguese which you might learn,' he said tightly, his face raised a little from hers, 'just in case I am compelled to use it again. It is *"cala boca"*, or in English, shut up, little wife. Now come, some of our guests are ready to leave.'

It seemed a very long time before the last of the convivial crowd showed signs of departure, by which time Emily's smile began to feel pasted on her face.

'*Boa noite*, Senhora Fonseca such a pleasure to meet you.' Analha Machado smiled shyly and pressed Emily's hand. 'I hope you are very happy here in Campo d'Ouro. Perhaps one day I may come to visit you and meet your little son?'

Emily smiled warmly.

'Of course. Please. Whenever you wish.'

'*Eu tambem?* Does that include me also?' Teresinha's challenging glance stung Emily, as the girl stood close to Luc in a proprietorial attitude he was apparently doing nothing to discourage, merely smiling down at her indulgently.

'I shall be pleased to receive you at any time,' lied Emily.

'We are all very interested to meet your son,' said Teresinha. 'His existence was a great surprise; so romantic, the forgotten bride, *nao é?*'

Inwardly outraged, Emily kept her face in its polite social mask as Ildefonso Machado kissed her hand and shepherded his two daughters away. Only Bob McClure remained, and he soothed Emily's ruffled feelings by holding her hand in a mangling grasp and gazing down at her earnestly from behind his spectacles.

'It's a great pleasure to make your acquaintance, Emily. Perhaps you'll cheer up a lonely bachelor's existence and let Luc bring you to dinner at my place some time soon.'

'I'd be delighted,' said Emily warmly, glad to mean what she said this time.

'I'll look forward to that.' The tall American released her hand, said goodnight respectfully to Thurza, clapped Luc on the shoulder and left them finally alone.

'Well, I think that all functioned very successfully,' said Thurza cheerfully, looking triumphantly from Luc to Emily. 'Your wife made a very good impression on everyone, Luc.'

He raised an eyebrow at Emily.

'Greater on some than on others.'

She ignored him, moving to kiss Thurza goodnight.

'It was a wonderful party, Thurza, thank you.'

'Would you like something to drink before you go off to bed?' asked Thurza, well pleased. 'I noticed you drank and ate very little all evening.'

'I was too busy trying to remember names and make sure no one was neglected.' Emily yawned widely. 'What I'd love is a cup of tea.'

Luc turned her towards the door.

'You go to bed and I shall bring a tray to our room. May I do the same for you, Thurza?'

'No, dear, I'll see to it. I'd like some hot milk, I think, and I shall make Emily's tea at the same time. You can come with me to the kitchen. I sent the maids to bed once they'd cleared up.'

Luc waved Emily away.

'Off you go. I shall not be long.'

Emily wandered slowly into Jamie's room and inspected her sleeping son before reaching the haven of her own room. Suddenly she desperately wanted sleep, the hectic evening all at once catching up on her and making her stupid with fatigue. She trailed her feather scarf across the bed and drifted over to the dressing table, staring at her reflection dispassionately as her fingers fiddled behind her trying to find the hook at the top of the zip. Her eyes glittered in her flushed face, rivalling the brilliance of the aquamarine that hung between her breasts. Did Luc consider her fairness insipid beside the vivid, glowing beauty of Teresinha Machado? More than likely. In the straight blue sheath she no doubt appeared sexless in comparison with the Brazilian girl with her incredibly narrow waist and the lush curves both above and below it. The damned woman's probably even highly intelligent as well, she thought crossly. Funny no one had thought fit to mention her before. She'd been just a shade too obvious in her take-over bid, though, and Emily was fairly sure that she wouldn't try that little ploy again. Grinning at her own smug expression, she turned her attention again to her zip as Luc came in carrying a tea-tray.

'I thought you'd be in bed by now,' he said, frowning.

'I can't undo the hook on my dress.'

Luc put the tray down on the dressing table and turned her round, his fingers cool against her skin as he examined the fastening.

'It is caught in the silk. Hold still, or it will tear.'

He gave a final tug and the hook was free, her back suddenly chill as without warning the dress dropped to the floor before Emily could clutch at it. She dived instinctively to retrieve it, but Luc was too swift for her and jerked her up against him, her feet clear of the restraining folds, his arms crushing her ribs and his lips bruising hers in an onslaught whose very suddenness made Emily unable to resist. Helpless before the spate of passion all the more frightening for its sheer silent intensity, Emily submitted to an embrace whose only aim was subjugation. The temperate, considerate man of the past few days was gone, succeeded by a merciless, frightening stranger who ignored her feeble attempts to free herself, his hands and mouth overcoming her with an effortless strength that ignored any futile denials. His mouth holding hers, he pushed her flat on the bed, one hand indolently restraining her as he shrugged himself out of his clothes and removed the one remaining fragile scrap of covering left to her.

Their panting, ragged breath mingled together as he raised his head a little to look down at her flushed, mutinous face, his eyes gleaming like jet through half-closed lids as he laid a finger on her mouth to stop her furious protest.

'Say nothing.' A chill ran down her spine at his whisper. 'I will wait no longer.'

A great wave of indignation surged through Emily, and she made one last violent effort to free herself. Luc merely laughed softly, deep in his throat, and controlled her efforts with insulting ease, demonstrating his dominance with his mouth, his tongue, his questing, inflammatory hands and, at long, long last, struggle as she might, with the thrusting mastery of his body.

When it was over Luc lay still, keeping her captive, while Emily lay beneath him, too exhausted to attempt escape, hating him for his superior strength, hating herself for her idiotic weakness, appalled at her stupidity in putting herself in a position where all this had been made possible. But above all she hated her despicable body. It had fought, up to a point, but it had lost. And, worst of all, it had enjoyed the process of its defeat to a degree which made her squirm to think of it. Tears of mortification rolled from the corners of her eyes, and Luc, immediately responsive to the movement of her body beneath his, opened his eyes to see the tears sliding from beneath the closed lids. Instinctively he kissed away the tears, sliding his mouth down her nose to her rebellious mouth—and then, to Emily's disbelief, it was all happening all over again, except that this time there was far too little fighting and regrettably more submission. And deep, deep down in the far recesses of her scarcely functioning mind was the knowledge that this time there was a response it was utterly useless to ignore.

CHAPTER FOURTEEN

EMILY'S eyes opened unwillingly as the early morning sunlight poured through the thin white curtains. She moved a little and found that an unaccustomed feeling of restriction was caused by a hard encircling arm around her waist, and a long bare leg thrown over hers. She lay perfectly still, flatly refusing to think of the events of last night; no use in crying over spilt milk. Thinking of milk reminded her of Jamie. There was no sound from next door, but it must be well past time for her to investigate. Cautiously she freed herself from Luc's unconscious embrace, looking at his face with an impersonal scrutiny as she slid out of bed. He lay relaxed, his sleeping face younger, less marked with care and responsibility than when awake. The blue silk dress still lay on the floor in a heap, accompanied by Luc's clothes, tangled wildly with her feathered stole, which looked unlikely to recover from the experience.

She bent wearily to pick up the dress, only to find herself scooped up and restored summarily to her former place, with her husband propped on his elbow looking down lazily at her embarrassed, indignant face. She struggled upright determinedly, avoiding his eyes.

'I must go to Jamie.'

Luc glanced at his watch.

'It is past ten, *carinha*,' he said, amused at the sudden horror on her face. 'He will be in the garden with Dirce by now, so you may as well stay where you are.'

Emily flung out of bed, diving for her dressing gown.

'Thurza will wonder what's become of me,' she muttered, wrapping it round her. 'I must——'

'My dearest wife,' drawled Luc, reclining against the headboard, his hands behind his head, 'no one will think it strange if I wish my wife to remain in bed a little late with me on the only morning of the week I am free to enjoy her company. After all, it was exceedingly late before we finally got to sleep.'

Emily turned on him hotly.

'Look here, Luc Fonseca, last night you—well, you took me by surprise. You needn't imagine it was an experience to be repeated. I meant what I said about not sleeping with you. . . .'

'Ah, but you did—eventually.'

'I know, but only, but only because——'

'But only because you were so exhausted with my lovemaking that you couldn't help but do so.' Luc's eyes gleamed maliciously. 'And now you are going to tell me you detested the experience so much you never wish to repeat it. *Que vergonha!* For shame.'

Emily stared at him mutely. The hateful knowledge in his eyes precluded all possibility of denial. He knew all too well, and so, unfortunately, did she, that what had passed between them last night had been no unbearable experience. Far from it. After the first instinctive resistance there had been nothing she could do to prevent the surge of response that had risen to make their lovemaking a very mutual satisfaction.

'It was just sex,' she said flatly.

'A very natural process, but you do not wish it to happen again?'

'No, thank you.' Emily moved to the door. 'Without love it's just animal.'

'And you do not love me, Emily.' Luc lay watching her broodingly.

'No—no, I don't,' she choked, and fled to the bathroom away from his disturbing black gaze that seemed to see right into the secret places of her mind.

For the next few days life went tranquilly on at the Casa d'Ouro. Emily's visit to the doctor was postponed when he was called away on an emergency, and another appointment made for the following week. She spent her time almost exclusively with Thurza and Jamie, as Luc took to arriving home later and later, and on the plea of mounting paperwork, spent his evenings after dinner in the study, coming to bed long after Emily. Jamie thrived in his new environment, causing great excitement one morning by taking his first steps unaided, to the adulation of his great-grandmother and the maids, all of whom behaved as though no child had ever achieved such a feat before.

'You must admit that ten months is very early,' said Thurza. 'I remember Luc was just as forward, though.'

Emily smiled fondly at her excited, triumphant little son, prey to a lethargy which had increased since the party.

'I feel quite guilty at how little I do here,' she said idly. 'I'm less use than those macaws. We both inhabit a gilded cage of sorts, but at least they have *some* function as warning signals. I'm quite useless. At home—I mean at the Dower House there was always so much to get through in a day, but at least Jamie was in a playpen. How I would have managed once he started walking I can't imagine.'

'Don't try. Enjoy your present leisure and concentrate on getting yourself more robust. Perhaps giving a party so soon was a bad idea.'

'Nonsense! I enjoyed it very much. Besides, I'm fully aware of your reason for doing so.'

Thurza smiled at her smugly.

'Now everyone knows that I fully endorse your presence here. They were able to see Luc's wife as a member of the family, not a little outsider we were obliged to take in merely to gain possession of Jamie.'

Emily grinned at the old lady's candour.

'Yes. And I appreciate it. I realise you must have been very reluctant to have Luc marry some little nobody who had—to be blunt—produced an illegitimate child. Jamie was the sugar on the pill I represented.'

'True,' admitted Thurza. 'But after one look at him it was only too obvious that you weren't passing off another man's child as Luc's.' She held up a restraining hand at Emily's involuntary protest. 'Besides, Emily, you obviously came here to Brazil under protest. I'm not so geriatric yet that I can't see that your marriage is causing you both a great deal of turbulence. Sometimes I think you're on the point of harmony, and then suddenly you are both formal and distant again, but, somehow, never indifferent.'

Emily laughed ruefully.

'Nothing gets past you, does it? Nevertheless, we are trying to make a go of things, if only for Jamie's sake.'

Thurza snorted.

'For Jamie's sake! Emily, when are you——'

Whatever else she intended to say was lost as Maria came out to announce something to Thurza. Apparently the Machado sisters had come to call.

Emily inspected her son quickly and deposited him in the playpen, glad that she was wearing a favourite dress that morning, a thin coffee-coloured lawn with a trail of yellow-centred white daisies wandering down the full skirt. Thurza greeted the two girls in local style with kisses on both cheeks, and sent for coffee as they turned to greet Emily. Analha Machado, in a demure yellow cotton dress, smiled warmly at Emily, taking her hand and wishing her a shy good morning. Teresinha, dressed in skin-tight pink trousers and much unbuttoned silk shirt, acknowledged Emily briefly, her attention immediately fixed on Jamie, who smiled at the visitors with an expression so like his father Emily felt regrettably smug at the look on Teresinha's face.

'Very like Luc, is he not?' Thurza smiled indulgently as Analha went on her knees alongside the playpen and touched Jamie's hair, making the type of baby noises that are universal. Teresinha stood still, looking at the child with something almost akin to hunger in her vivid face.

'Nossa Senhora!' she muttered. 'He is the—image, I think

you say—of Luc, Senhora Fonseca.'

Unsure which Senhora Fonseca was being addressed, Emily remained silent until the other girl looked towards her.

'You are to be congratulated.' Teresinha subsided gracefully on the sofa beside Emily, accepting the cup of coffee Thurza handed to her. 'You have a beautiful son. How very fortunate that he resembles Luc so closely.'

Emily took a cup from Thurza and handed it to Analha before replying.

'It certainly pleases Luc very much,' she answered quietly.

'May I pick him up, Emily?' entreated Analha. 'I may call you Emily?'

'Of course. Do take him out of the pen if you like. Perhaps he will demonstrate his new accomplishment.'

With a little coaxing from Thurza, and a great deal of encouragement from his mother, the little boy took three unsteady steps unaided before plopping down on his bottom with crows of triumph, his face alight as he saw a tall figure coming towards him.

'Da-da!' he said joyfully, and Luc came forward swiftly to pick up his son and greet the visitors, his free arm held out to Emily. She went to him with unusual alacrity, lifting her face for a kiss that proved more lingering than the occasion warranted. Luc kept her close as he chatted with Teresinha and Analha, and Jamie once again proudly showed his walking ability to his father, provoking laughter from Luc as he tossed his son high in the air to screams of delight.

Such unbridled domestic felicity proved too much for Teresinha, and firmly refusing pressing offers of lunch, she shepherded a disappointed Analha away from the sight of Lucas Fonseca in the role of proud father.

The visit left Emily much more happily disposed towards her husband and their relationship, if not completely to Luc's liking, was a great improvement on the barely concealed hostility that had prevailed since the night of the party.

One evening they dined with Bob McClure, as promised, with John Trelaur and Tom Enys as the other guests, and despite being outnumbered four to one, Emily felt no constraint in the all-male company. She was happy and relaxed in the convivial atmosphere, able to contribute to the conversation herself owing to Bob McClure's fascination with antiquity. Under Luc's encouraging gaze she talked at some length of Compton Lacey, her listeners genuinely interested in her account of its history. When they returned to Casa d'Ouro afterwards Emily lingered companionably with Luc over a nightcap, and for once prepared for bed minus the feeling of constraint that was usual when she and Luc retired at the same time.

Emily found her visit to the hospital to see Dr Ferreira less trying than expected. Thurza accompanied her and went round the pleasant little building with her before settling herself in a waiting room while the doctor subjected Emily to a thorough examination, took samples of blood and urine, and asked a variety of questions.

When Emily was dressed and sitting in front of his desk once more he raised an eyebrow and smiled at her across his clasped hands.

'I'm sure you realise there is every probability that you are once more pregnant, Senhora Fonseca.'

Emily nodded, smiling back ruefully.

'I've been telling myself for some time that it was merely the different way of life, but of course I'd accepted the possibility. With Jamie I was very sick, but this time I merely feel a bit languid, with an overwhelming desire to sleep all the time.'

'You are probably a little anaemic; we shall see. And, of course, until the report on your urine sample is confirmed it is not official. However, other signs all indicate that you will present your husband with a playmate for your son in, I should say, seven months or so. You agree?'

'Oh yes.' Emily gave a funny little smile. 'A small Christmas present, I expect.'

She rejoined Thurza thoughtfully, deciding it was only just to inform Luc of her news before telling his grandmother. After lunch, or perhaps after dinner would be better. She listened abasently to Thurza extolling the virtues of Dr Ferreira, wondering how Luc would react.

Luc failed to appear for lunch. He had left a message with the maids to the effect that he was going down the mine to investigate the possibility of a new lode.

'A vein of ore,' explained Thurza.

'Bob McClure said something about it at dinner the other evening,' said Emily. 'I must ask Luc to explain it all to me properly, so that I know exactly what happens. I can't help feeling a bit apprehensive at the thought of men working so far beneath the ground.'

'I used to be at first,' admitted Thurza, a faraway look in her eye, 'but it is an experience you will never be able to share with Luc. Our miners are a superstitious breed, they won't allow a woman down the mine; even a priest is tabu because of his cassock. Yes, Maria?' She broke off as the maid came along the verandah with Bob McClure hard on her heels.

'Forgive the lack of ceremony, ladies,' he said, his kind face full of distress. 'I'm sorry to be the one to have to break this, but——'

Thurza rose to her feet automatically, her back as straight as a lance.

'What has happened?'

All the blood drained from Emily's face and her heart missed a beat, then resumed, pounding heavily in her breast like a drum.

'Now there's no need to get uptight,' began Bob miserably.

'Get on with it, man!' rapped Thurza.

'My findings have confirmed a lode present at a deeper level, and Luc went in to inspect the tunnel we're mining to meet up with it.'

'Please, Bob!' implored Emily.

'Luc went in with Zé Villela, the assistant to John Trelaur, plus the shift boss and about half a dozen men. There was a rock burst, and I'm afraid they're trapped behind an extensive rockfall.'

Thurza sat abruptly, looking for once every minute of her age, and Emily swiftly sat beside her, taking a cold hand in her own, chafing it gently, her eyes fixed on Bob McClure's.

'Was anyone injured?' Her voice seemed to be coming from a long way off.

'We don't know. But there has been some communication by means of hammering on the steel-compressed air mains.' He went down on one knee in front of them, his face urgent. 'Please try not to worry too much, they should be able to bleed off compressed air for oxygen if they need it, and they have their cap lamps for light. If they use them sparingly they'll have light until we get them out.'

Emily stared at him in dismay.

'How long will you take to get them out—hours? Days? What's being done to get them out—aren't you pulling the rocks away?'

'It isn't that simple, honey,' said Bob gently, and Thurza straightened, squeezing Emily's hand tightly. Bob swallowed, and went on unhappily, 'It will depend on the extent of the fall. They can't go at the clearance like a bull at a gate, you know, they have to clear the fall slowly, shoring with steel arches and timber as they go. This has to be done with great care. I'm sure neither of you, and certainly not Luc, would want further injuries in a reckless dash to get them out. It could take anything up to a day or two, maybe longer.'

'Thank you for letting us know personally,' said Thurza, pulling herself together. 'I'm sure you must be needed, so we'll let you get back.'

'Don't worry yourself sick now, Emily.' Bob was obviously at a loss to know how to comfort the white, still girl.

Emily smiled faintly.

'Don't ask the impossible, Bob, but thank you again.' She walked to the door with him, then returned to sink down on a chair, staring unseeingly in front of her.

'I had a piece of news to give him today, Thurza,' she whispered, dry-eyed. 'The doctor confirmed my suspicions this morning. I'm pregnant.'

'Oh, my dear!' Getting up resolutely, Thurza gave Emily her hand. 'In that case, I'll ring for lunch. You need feeding up more than ever now. I might have known that was why you were so peaky-looking. We'll eat in peace while Jamie's still asleep.'

The thought of food made Emily's gorge rise, but she sat at table obediently and drank some clear soup, then gave up.

'It's no use, Thurza,' she said after a while, laying down her knife and fork. 'I just can't swallow. The stuff won't go down. I keep thinking—imagining——'

'Well, stop it,' said Thurza roundly, pushing her own plate aside impatiently. 'We won't help matters by getting morbid.'

'No,' agreed Emily, then, unable to keep back the thought obsessing her, 'What if he's injured!'

Thurza's breath drew in sharply.

'We have no way of knowing, of course, but remember they wear protective helmets and have enough sense to get out of the way at the first sign of trouble. And don't forget, they *have* been in communication.'

'I'm sorry,' said Emily in remorse. 'I'm no help at all, am I, and you must be more worried than I am.'

'I believe you are a great deal more attached to Luc than you allow yourself to admit,' said Thurza, her old eyes shrewd. 'Isn't it time you let him know?'

Emily swallowed hard.

'If I'm given the chance I'll do my utmost to put things right between us,' she said huskily, her mouth dry at the possibility that the opportunity might never arise.

They got through the day somehow. Feverishly Emily played with Jamie, pushed him round the garden in his chair, and insisted on giving him his bath and his supper herself in the kitchen. The maids were so stricken about their master that they were no company for the little boy. Jamie, blissfully unaware of the cloud hovering over Casa d'Ouro, insisted on feeding himself, and the ensuing mess took everyone out of themselves for a while in helping to clear up.

Twice the phone rang. Thurza had stationed herself in the morning room alongside one extension, and Emily left Jamie to Dirce, flying to the old lady's side. The first time it was John Trelaur, the Mine Captain, assuring them that rescue operations were well under way, and that they were in regular communication by means of knocking on the air mains. The second time it was Bob McClure, reporting on the further progress of the clearance operation, which to Emily seemed to be proceeding at a snail's pace.

'It's the only way, Emily,' said Thurza sternly. 'Any faster and it could result in a further fall.'

Emily flinched.

'Luc must be hungry,' she said, changing the subject hurriedly.

'Thirst is more of a problem, I expect. But eventually they may be able to pass canteens of water through before the fall is cleared completely.' Thurza's eyes softened as they rested on Emily's white face. 'Now go and bring Jamie in here to play for a while before he goes to bed.'

Emily obeyed like an automaton. She felt cold right through to her bones. Ever since Bob had arrived with the news a chill seemed to have permeated through her entire body, and even hugging Jamie to her fiercely did nothing to alleviate it. She took Jamie along to where Thurza was stationed in the morning room, and both women derived a little comfort from watching him crawl around the room, pulling himself upright on the furniture and reminding them forcibly that, whatever their inner torment, life must go on outwardly normally, for Jamie's sake.

It was after the baby was settled down for the night that the waiting became agony. Neither made any attempt at dinner and settled for incessant cups of coffee and tea brought in unasked by a wan, subdued Maria. To pass the time Thurza began to reminisce about days gone by at Casa d'Ouro, telling Emily of receptions given that far outshone the modest affair of the previous week.

'At one time,' related Thurza, a faraway look in her eye, 'we had many more British people here in key positions, and it was possible to make up a cricket eleven. One of the social events of the year was a visit from Rio Cricket Club for a weekend. We'd put up the visitors here and, apart from the match, there were lunches and dinners and a fancy dress dance. . . .' She smiled naughtily. 'I enjoyed myself enormously at those affairs. Comes from having a basically frivolous nature, I suppose.'

'You—frivolous?' Despite her anxiety Emily couldn't help laughing.

'Oh yes.' Thurza's eyes twinkled. 'I haven't always been a wayward old tartar, you know. At one time I was a gay, giddy girl just like everyone else. It used to cause trouble with Jaime on occasion. He used to say I liked nothing better than chattering away at cocktail parties, a glass of wine in my hand, flitting from group to group like a butterfly.'

Emily felt wistful.

'I don't think I've ever been a gay and giddy girl,' she said quietly.

Both women were abruptly quiet. They gave up any

pretence of being cheerful and sat, tense, their whole energies given over to the sheer torture of waiting.

'Couldn't we have gone down to the mine?' burst out Emily at one stage.

'No.' Thurza shook her head decisively. 'We'd be no use, only in the way, and someone would feel they had to look after us.'

'Yes. Yes, of course you're right.' Emily subsided into silence again, uttering a silent, fervent prayer that God would allow her to see Luc again, unharmed and able to listen to her.

I hope he'll want to listen, she thought bleakly. I want him to know that I love him, if he's still interested. He had to be interested, surely, to make love to her like that the other night. But then it was he who had told her it wasn't necessary to love in order to make love. She stared blindly at her tightly clasped hands. She knew now that she had never stopped loving him, though until today she had been too stupid, or was it stubborn, to realise it. Her love for him hadn't died at all, it had merely been shut up in some sort of mental deep freeze waiting for the key to unlock it and set it free again, very much alive. Alive! At the thought Emily was gripped with despair. Please let him be alive, let him know that she loved him, had never stopped, only she was too hurt, too stiff-necked to admit it, even to herself.

'What is it, Emily, do you have a pain?' Thurza was watching her with anxious eyes.

'Nothing I can take a pill for,' said Emily apologetically, 'it's just this interminable waiting. How long have they been down there, Thurza?'

'Since nine this morning, according to John Trelaur. Twelve hours.' Thurza rose to her feet. 'Come, Emily, let's have a look at Jamie, move around a little. We shall easily hear the telephone if—when it rings.'

Emily obeyed, and for a while they paced along the verandah, looking up at the brilliance of the stars. It was a terrible thought that they were up here in the balmy, perfumed night, breathing in the soft air, watching the glittering pinpoints of light in the velvet sky, when somewhere far below them Luc and the other men were shut away in a dusty tomb.

The maids were huddled together in the kitchen instead of in their own quarters when Emily volunteered to make more tea. Glad of something to do, they hastily provided a tea-tray, Dirce insisting on making some dainty little crustless sandwiches filled with cucumber and prawns. Listlessly both women managed a couple of these, washed down with several cups of tea. As Emily was pouring out the second cups the telephone rang. The teapot slid out of her nerveless fingers on to the tray, splashing them with scalding tea as Thurza seized the instrument and listened intently to the voice on the other end of the line.

'Thank you, John, thank you very much for letting us know so quickly,' she said after a couple of interminable minutes. 'Please convey my grateful thanks to all those who are working so hard.'

'What is it, Thurza—tell me!' implored Emily.

'They've very nearly completed the rescue operation.' Thurza was suddenly white and limp. 'Another hour or so and the men should be out. Luc is perfectly all right.'

Emily dropped on her knees beside Thurza, buried her head in the older woman's lap and burst into tears. Thurza let her cry, smoothing the pale hair with a comforting hand for a while before reverting to her usual bracing self.

'Come along, Emily,' she said briskly, patting the bowed head. 'Up you get and go and wash your face. Luc won't want to come home to a wife covered in red blotches.'

Emily scrambled to her feet, sniffing loudly.

'No, you're right. Sorry. I'll go and do some repair work.' She looked back at the open doorway. 'Did Mr Trelaur say Luc was completely unhurt?'

'He just said he was all right. Now go along and do something to yourself, you look a sight. By the way, perhaps you'd better call Dirce in here. I feel suddenly too old and weary to totter to the kitchen.'

Emily's Portuguese was progressing, and a couple of halting phrases and a lot of arm-waving soon sped Dirce off to her mistress, while Emily went off to try to repair the ravages of her crying bout. When she returned Thurza was sipping brandy from a large balloon glass and waved to a similar glass on the small table beside Emily's chair. Emily made a face.

'Go on, drink it,' commanded Thurza. 'Do you good after the day we've spent. Unwind those tense nerves.'

Despite her dislike of the taste the fiery warmth of the brandy helped Emily considerably, permeating through her body and dispelling the frozen feeling that had chilled her since the news of the accident. The two women were able to chat quite normally, though neither troubled to disguise the fact that one ear was cocked, listening for the sound of Luc's jeep. Dirce and the others were happily engaged in preparing a meal for the *patrão*, and the whole atmosphere of the big house was perceptibly different. Emily marvelled silently. All because of one man. It was gone two in the morning before the sound of tyres skidding to a halt on the gravelled drive outside the open window heralded Luc's return. They both hurried out on the verandah to welcome the tall, dusty figure coming wearily towards them. Luc's face was colourless with fatigue beneath the grime, his eyes glittering in a tired, triumphant smile. His grandmother reached him first, Emily, suddenly shy, hanging back as he embraced Thurza wordlessly. His head lifted and his eyes met hers, and Emily instinctively responded to the unmistakable appeal that drew her towards him like a magnet. He moved towards her simultaneously, and Thurza tactfully took herself off kitchenwards as Emily threw herself into Luc's arms, rubbing her face blindly against his, reaching up to touch his hair, his face, the tears flooding unchecked as his arms closed round her fiercely and his mouth met hers. For a long time they said nothing, each holding the other as though afraid to loosen their grip for an instant, a fraction, lest the other disappear.

When it was possible for her to speak Emily said unsteadily,

'I imagined you crushed, dead, suffocated—all sorts of horrors——'

He pressed her head against his chest protectively.

'It was nothing like that, *querida*. I'll tell you all about it tomorrow, but right now I need a drink, a meal and then bed.' He lifted her face to his. 'Though not necessarily in that order,' he muttered against her lips.

Suddenly Emily was euphoric.

'You didn't mention a bath in your requirements, Senhor

Fonseca,' she said gaily, 'otherwise I think your order of priorities was perfectly correct!'

'*Deus,* Emily,' he groaned, crushing her to him again, 'all I could think about these past hours was that smile!'

'Darling, darling,' Emily felt tears threaten again. 'Come. Let's go to Thurza. She's been wonderful. I don't think I'd have kept in one piece without her.'

They walked slowly along the verandah, arms round each other.

'Were you truly that worried, Emily?' There was no mistaking the undisguised longing in Luc's simple question.

'I nearly went out of my mind—Oh, Luc!' Anything further she might have said was stifled in an embrace that threatened to cut off her air supply altogether, succour arriving by means of a dry little cough from Thurza, who stood by the candlelit table on the verandah, watching them with a smile.

'Put your wife down for a moment, Lucas Fonseca,' she said dryly, 'and apply yourself to this steak. We'll join you; for some reason neither of us has had much appetite today.'

'Splendid idea, Thurza; that glass of beer looks like the answer to a prayer!' Luc seated himself with alacrity and allowed both women to wait on him hand and foot, anticipating his every wish, while managing to tuck into quite a substantial meal themselves. He told them a little about the accident, glad to report that beyond one broken arm and a fair amount of bruises and scratches, no one was hurt. Emily jumped up to pour coffee, as Luc consumed the final morsel of cheese, and leaned back in contentment to light a cheroot, running a caressing finger down her arm as she filled his cup.

'You needn't think this handmaiden bit is a permanent arrangement,' warned Emily, her smile incandescent. 'It's only because you gave us such a fright.'

'It almost makes it all worthwhile!' The glint in his eye made her toss her head.

'I'm sure it was all a ruse to attract sympathy, just like Jamie!'

'And how is Jamie today—any new accomplishments?' All the time he was talking Luc's eyes never left Emily's face, and she had difficulty in concentrating on her replies.

'No,' she said breathlessly. 'It's still three steps and down down on his bottom.'

Thurza watched them fondly, drank the last of her coffee and rose to her feet. Luc instantly followed suit, bending his head for her goodnight kiss.

'Goodnight, Luc,' she said, patting his cheek fondly. 'Thank God you're safe. After all this excitement I'm ready for my bed—and I should think both of you are, too.' With what looked suspiciously like a wink she bent to kiss Emily's cheek and left them alone.

'Was Thurza right, Emily?' asked Luc huskily, pulling her to her feet. 'Are you ready for bed? The same bed as your husband, *carinha*? I want very much to lie all night with you in my arms, to hold you and know that I'm not going to have nightmares about that black hole down there.'

Emily trembled.

'After you've had your bath,' she said, deliberately prosaic, refusing to look at him.

He took her hand and made off at great speed towards their bedroom.

'I will have the swiftest bath on record,' he promised, sweeping her along with him.

Emily giggled helplessly as he began to strip off his clothes before they had even left the verandah.

'What are you doing? What will the maids think?'

He turned on her fiercely, picking her up to hold her against his bare chest, that smelt unashamedly of sweat and dust.

'They will think I am a man impatient to make love to my wife—and they will be right.' He set her roughly on her feet inside their room. 'Two minutes.'

Luc was back in what seemed even less, a bath towel wound round his hips, his hair dripping.

'You're not even partially dry,' scolded Emily, frowning in mock disapproval.

'Do you mind?'

'No.'

'Why did you bother to put this robe on?'

'Instinct.'

'Have you any other instincts?'

'I—I think so.'

'Then show me, *querida*, show me!'

At the touch of Luc's skin against hers Emily discovered she had instincts hitherto undiscovered. The release from the tension of the day resulted in a euphoric outpouring of all the love and warmth in her nature Luc had demanded, so that the night was a wonder of revelation that left them shaken and unbelieving in each other's arms when finally the storm had passed and left them in a tangle of arms and legs that held each other fast, reluctant to let each other go even into the escape of sleep.

'Did I tell you I love you, Luc?' she murmured sleepily into his throat.

A tremor ran through his body.

'Repeatedly, *carinha*. Did you truly mean it, or was it just— the heat of the moment?'

His breath caught at the wickedness of her throaty chuckle.

'I had no idea I was capable of behaving like that, Luc! But I did mean it—I *do* mean it. I've never really stopped loving you really, but—well, I think I locked all the feelings for you away subconsciously when you left me alone, abandoned me, as I thought.' She laid a finger on his lips to stem his protest. 'Yes, I know it wasn't really like that, but I *thought* it was, which did the damage. Knowing you might have been killed today was the key that unlocked the door on my emotions. I didn't know how I could bear it if I—if you—if I never had the chance to tell you.' She pushed herself frantically against him, murmuring deep down in her throat as he kissed her and cuddled her close with comforting noises, as though she were Jamie. Jamie!

Emily pulled sharply away from Luc.

'What is it?' he asked instantly.

'I didn't go in to see Jamie before——'

'Before I chased you to bed.'

'I never gave him a thought,' she said, full of guilt.

Luc laughed delightedly and slid out from beneath the sheet. 'I will go and look at him. Don't go away.'

In a moment or two he was back, his naked body silvered by the moonlight through the window for an instant before he came in beside her and held her close once more.

'I was so absorbed in being a wife I forgot to be a good mother,' Emily said remorsefully. 'Is he all right?'

'Sleeping like an angel. And do not be so self-critical. You are a perfect mother.'

Emily was silent for a moment as she suddenly remembered her news.

'Just as well, really,' she said, wriggling closer to him.

'What do you mean?'

'Well, shall we say I've solved the problem about what to give you for Christmas.'

Luc propped himself on an elbow to look down at her, switching on the bedside lamp.

'It is April, Emily. Why are you thinking about Christmas?'

Emily gave him a smile of such pure happiness Luc's breath caught in his throat.

'That's when we shall have our next child, God willing.'

A blaze of delight flared in his eyes and he came down beside her again, holding her painfully tight. Then suddenly he held her away again slightly.

'But that is in only eight months' time . . .?'

Emily began to giggle.

'Precisely. Either we are more than ordinarily compatible, my darling husband, or those Fonseca genes of yours are frighteningly ruthless!'

Luc grinned at his tousled, flushed wife.

'Do you mind, *carinha*?'

'Not a bit. Besides, Thurza will be pleased. She wants to fill the place up again, she says. You can't deny we're off to a good start!'

He pounced, crushing her to him, frantically kissing her in every place he could reach, heedless of smothered, laughing protests.

'Hey!' she gasped with difficulty. 'You're supposed to treat me like a piece of Dresden china now I'm in a delicate condition—like they do in books.'

Black eyes glinted down wickedly into blue ones.

'I'll start tomorrow!'

Forthcoming Titles

DUET
Available in June

The Catherine George Duet — **DEVIL WITHIN**
GILDED CAGE

The Sally Wentworth Duet — **DARK AWAKENING**
THE HAWK OF VENICE

BEST SELLER ROMANCE
Available in July

GLASS SLIPPERS AND UNICORNS Carole Mortimer
SWEET VIXEN Susan Napier

MEDICAL ROMANCE
Available in July

THE CALL OF LOVE Jenny Ashe
A HEART UNTAMED Judith Worthy
WAITING GAME Laura MacDonald
THE WESSEX SUMMER Sarah Franklin

Available from Boots, Martins, John Menzies, W.H. Smith, most supermarkets and other paperback stockists.

Also available from Mills & Boon Reader Service, P.O. Box 236, Thornton Road, Croydon, Surrey CR9 3RU.

Readers in South Africa - write to:
Book Services International Ltd, P.O. Box 41654, Craighall, Transvaal 2024.